ABOUT THE AUTHOR

Lexie Winston has been an astronaut, rock star, princess and time traveller. In her dreams. But none of the dreams have lived up to what becoming an author has been like. She gets to live in a world of pure imagination, and her heroines get to do the things she's always wished she could.

When not writing books, Lexie is a mother of two gorgeous teenagers and the wife to a patient and understanding man. They live in Western Australia and are lorded over by a black toy poodle. She loves camping, reading and if her iPad was stolen, her world would explode. (It has the kindle app on it.)

And you can find all links at

www.lexiewinston.com

SPIES LIKE US

MITHOS
BOOK TWO

LEXIE WINSTON

ALSO BY LEXIE WINSTON

The Collectors Division

(Paranormal Reverse Harem Series)

Guardian

Guardian's Blood

Guardian Ascending

Collector's Division Omnibus

Neighpalm Industries Collective

(Enemies to Lovers Reverse Harem)

Abandoned Girl

Broken Girl

Tormented Girl

Wanted Girl

Cherished Girl

Loved Girl

Superficial Girl - Jacinta's Story Part 1

Superficial Girl - Jacinta's Story Part 2

Neighpalm Industries Collective 1-3

Neighpalm Industries Collective 4-6

Seductive Sins Collection

(Reverse Harem Series)

Glorious Gluttony

Gangs, Guns, and Glory

Glory Glory Hellelujah

Crowning Glory

What's the Story, Morning Glory?

(Seductive Sins Omnibus)

Galaxy Circus

(Sci-Fi Reverse Harem Series)

Apprentice

Stagehand

Whisperer

Mama - Galaxy Circus Novella

Performer

Ringmaster

Interlude

A Night Most Wicked - Galaxy Circus Novella

Broken Promises

(Dark Poly Romance Series)

Secrets Kept

Lies Untold

Trust Broken

M.I.T.H.O.S

(Contemporary RH)

Spies Like Me

Spies Like Us

Coming March 2024

Storm View Stories

(Contemporary Standalone RH)

Ice Me Out

First published by Neighpalm Publishing in 2024

Spies Like Us - MITHOS 2

Mobi format: 978-0-6459663-4-3
Print: 978-0-6459663-5-0

Cover design by Dazed Designs
Editing by Elemental Editing

This one is for Jessica. Without her my words would be a bunch of rubbish and unreadable. She forgives me for my regular failure to meet deadlines when my muse is being an asshole. Bless her flexible self.

AUTHOR'S NOTE/TRIGGER WARNINGS

Hi before you go any further I just wanted to warn you I made a mistake and I am aware of it but it was too late to change it. I called the priest in book 1 Father Sweeny. This was before I thought too much about it and I gave him a wife and son. Later I realized catholic priests don't have either but I wanted the church to have a confessional. So I made them Lutheran because they do have a form of confession. But it was too late to change his name to Reverend Sweeny. So he is called a pastor and goes by the name Father Sweeny which I know is incorrect. Just go with me on this please, and I apologize to anyone I offend, it's for the sake of continuity between the books.

Also there are a few lines of Arabic in this book. I did try and find someone who spoke it to check it for me but was unable to, so I am relying on google translate and two other sites I used to double check, to be correct. Again if I got these wrong I apologize.

This book contains drug use, human trafficking, and dub con.

CHAPTER I

L athan bends down and closes Bishop's eyes, avoiding the bullet hole in the middle of his forehead. "How did someone get a jump on a highly trained agent like Bishop?" He stands back up and looks around before gesturing to the body. "He's still warm, and the blood is only just now clotting, but we didn't see anyone walk past us. Where did they go?" He peers into the dark tunnels leading away from the cell area like he wants to keep following them.

"Unless there is another entrance to the tunnel that we missed back there, then they must have gone the other way. Billy and the rest of the football team are still at the party, right?" I add. "Were they there when you guys entered the bedroom?" I ask Miller and Ryland.

Ry nods as Miller steps over Bishop and looks around the rest of the area. "Yeah, he was standing by the bedroom door, practically with his ear against it. I had to tell him that we were triple teaming the new girl before he moved away from the door." He grimaces apologetically.

"That's weird, because he seemed concerned about my drunk act. If it wasn't for that video, I would have guessed he was one of the good guys."

"Pfft, he just gave us a slow wink and walked away. I'm almost certain he doesn't suspect anything, or he didn't. What the fuck did Bishop do to get himself killed? Did he rat us out? Are our covers blown?" Ryland has this cute little wrinkle between his eyebrows as his gaze follows Miller around the room.

"Well, even if they weren't before, they are now," Miller says, pointing up at something toward the top of the room.

"Fuck," Lathan exclaims as he catches sight of the blinking red light. "Hopefully they aren't monitored twenty-four seven." He pulls out his phone and starts doing something with it. "I'm going to hack the signal, delete the last bit of footage, and loop it so we can explore a little longer, but on the upside, when we get back to the house, I can go through it and see if it shows who killed Bishop."

"You can do all that with a phone?" I ask, nodding at the cellphone in his hand.

He looks up and nods absently before looking down again. "Of course I can." Hearing how calm and confident he is gives me a sense of relief. I'd be fucked if I were on my own, but this seems like it's all in a day's work for him.

I move over to one of the cells. They are surprisingly modern. They have glass fronts, kind of like a zoo. The doors are open to all of them, so I carefully step inside and have a look around. They smell sanitized, and there is a comfortable-looking bed. Off to one side is a door that leads into a bathroom. "These aren't short-term holding cells," I call to the guys, my words echoing slightly. I spy another flashing red light in the cell, and again in the bathroom. "These all have cameras too," I tell Lathan as I step back out. He nods his acknowledgment, and I assume he takes care of their feeds as well.

Miller is doing the same on the other side of the room. "These were also specially built. Someone is responsible for them. Maybe we need to look at construction companies in town, because the plumbing in the bathrooms required a professional."

"We really need an invite to the sex club. I have a feeling it's the answer to all of this. Sex makes great blackmail material, or even an effective incentive." Ryland gazes around the area, his eyes settling on the tunnel leading away. "We don't have time to follow that, but we need to come back and check it out at another time."

"Alright, I managed to clear all the footage, but let's get out of here. We've been gone a while, and we don't want anyone to get suspicious." Lathan stuffs his phone back into his pocket, but then he looks at Bishop. "What are we going to do about him?"

"We're going to have to leave him. We don't want anyone to know we were down here. We can call Percy and tell him what happened, but until he either turns up dead somewhere or we report him missing to the police, we have to pretend life is normal." Ry shrugs. "We don't want to tip anyone off that we know about his death."

"Did he have family?" I ask. Unlike Ryland, Max, Dayton, and myself, most agents recruited by MITHOS don't actually have much, if any, family. It makes it easier because they don't have to explain where they are disappearing to or where they work. I wonder what Dayton's cover story is for his family. I know Max and Ry's dad is one of the few people who knows about MITHOS.

"No, he was a foster kid recruited right out of high school. One of the MITHOS foster families recommended him for the position," Ry tells me, and Miller just grunts.

"Better check any other recommendations from that family, because he sucked."

Some of our agents, when they want to move away from active duty, will become foster parents. They keep an eye out for potential agents, and foster kids get a good home. The smaller teams of two and sometimes three agents are perfect for this, because you don't have to explain a poly group to anyone.

We start heading back the way we came. "Now

that I hacked the feed, we can keep an eye on what happens down here. I'll be able to see when they move Bishop's body and if anyone else uses this tunnel or the cells," Lathan explains as the four of us start to jog.

"How much time passed between him giving me that drink and us finding him down here? I kind of lost track of time while we were dancing," I ask after a long silence, the sounds of our breaths echoing through the tunnels. "Was there time for Billy and the boys to bring him down here? And if they did, then what did he do to score a bullet in the brain? When we watched that video, it looked like Billy wanted him on his side, so why is he dead?"

"It was about forty minutes. Plenty of time for them to come down here. We only walked for about fifteen before we found the body, so that still leaves at least half an hour for them to find him, kill him, and get back to the party. I'll scan through the footage and see if I can find any answers." Lathan's hand on my shoulder is a comforting reassurance, because I have completely started to spiral about us all being made.

"This is bullshit. See? This is why I don't like to work with a team!" I lash out at the three of them, my worry making me bitchy. "When I work on my own, I only have to worry about me."

I hate this nervous feeling that comes from wondering if we've blown the case, if they are going to pack up their operation and leave, and if we're going to miss out on stopping this end of the operation and rescuing countless trafficked people.

"And this is why we don't like rogue operatives who think they can do whatever they want without running it by the team," Miller sneers. "You're just as bad as Bishop, doing your own thing. You easily could have been the one with the bullet in your brain."

I squeeze my hands into fists and barely resist the urge to punch his face.

"Hey, whoa, stop! No, this shit is what's going to blow our cover. Until we know something concrete, we are going to continue business as usual, you understand?" Ryland glares at Miller and me. I mime zipping my mouth shut, and he just rolls his eyes like a child.

I slow down and let the two of them get in front of me.

"Hey, are you okay?" Lathan slips his hand into mine and gives it a squeeze as he comes along side me. He leaves it there as we keep walking down the damp tunnel, and I'm not going to lie, it feels good.

"Yeah, shit, sorry. I didn't like him, and I know we talked about eliminating him, but it's all the not knowing why and how and who that's bothering me. I don't care that he's dead. I know that sounds callous, but he's one less problem to worry about, and it also gives us a whole heap of new issues."

"Hey, it's going to be okay. I'm very good at my job. I'm positive I wiped us from those cameras. I know working as a team is different for you, but it will all work out. Bishop was a loose cannon, so things will run much more smoothly now that he isn't causing problems. You'll see." The other two are farther ahead of us now, their heads bent together as they talk quietly.

"What's their deal?" I ask, unable to hide my curiosity anymore.

He looks at them, and a smile spreads across his face.

"I'm sure you've realized by now that Ry and Miller are a couple. They have been together since halfway through their first year of MITHOS training."

"Is this case going to be a problem for them? Miller may have to do things that will make Ryland jealous."

Lathan smirks. "See, that's the thing, nothing makes Ry jealous. He is so confident and secure in his relationship with Miller that whatever happens at work is just that—work. In fact, Ry is a bit of a perv, so I bet you he gets off on hearing what Miller has to do for the job, but the two of them are solid. Ry keeps Miller grounded. Without him, Miller would probably be as much of a loose cannon as Bishop was. He definitely has trauma in his childhood, so this job is probably a little too close to home, and it's bringing that all back. I would say that's one of the reasons he's lashing out at you. He doesn't like change. Bishop was the last major change we've had, and you saw how well that went—not to mention there's your mom."

I stop and put my hands on my hips. "Yeah, what the fuck is that? The two of them seem to have a fairly close relationship, and I thought I knew everything there was to know about my mom."

"You know what your mom is like. She's a sucker

for a wounded soul, and that's exactly what Miller is. He didn't realize that you and her are close. You paint a really good public persona. We thought you were nothing but a rich airhead socialite, flitting around the world on your parents' money. He hated you because you have such a wonderful mom and were wasting it... or that's the impression we got. I guess she was protecting your ghost status as well, and she has a natural mothering instinct. She looks after all of us as much as she can, but they have a special bond. You know we had a mission in Jordan last year. She came over, and we visited the royal family and were introduced to your grandfather. He also took a liking to Miller. We sat in the royal box at one of the world cup qualifiers. Miller and Ry are as mad about soccer as they are about each other."

I gasp and hold my hand up to my chest. "You better not have let my grandfather hear you calling it soccer. It's football. The only proper football in the world. Actually, you don't want my dad to hear you call it soccer either. The damn Englishman would fire you on the spot."

Lathan chuckles. "Yup, we hear about it every time we slip up from Miller too."

I shake my head, and my laughter stops. "Wow, I had no idea. My grandfather has never said anything to me either. Gosh, I'm a horrible person. I'm so self-involved, I have no idea what my parents are doing outside of my little bubble. Some secret agent I am."

"I wouldn't be too hard on yourself, Kenzie. Being

a ghost operative is a whole different ball game. I don't doubt it's easy to get lost in your persona without having a team to pull you out, and on your downtime, you probably spend all your time trying to recover yourself."

"Maybe." I'm not entirely sure he's wrong. I do feel like I'm three people sometimes. There's the airheaded socialite, the ghost agent, and the real me—the me who just wants to sit at home, eat her mom's cooking, and laugh at her dad's jokes. I also possibly wouldn't mind having a boyfriend or some regular girlfriends to do girl shit with, but my girlfriends live the same kind of life I do. Maybe Dad was right. Maybe it is time to come in out of the cold, so to speak.

We make it back to the secret entrance. Ry and Miller have already gone through, so I follow Lathan, get back on the bed, and twist the antlers back the other way, closing the door.

"Now what?" I ask, bouncing to my knees on the bed. I know what I'd like to do, but I'm trying to be a team player.

"I'm sure Billy has made it no secret that the four of us are in here. People will be watching closely to see us exit. It will be gossip for the next week. We need to be convincing, and right now, no one's lips are swollen enough. Although your lipstick is on Lathan's mouth from when you were making out before, it's not on either of us," Ry says seriously, though I can see the twinkle in his eye, and I don't doubt that he's excited about this.

Lathan lifts a hand to his lips, like he's going to wipe it off, but Ryland jumps forward and slaps his hand. "No, dude, leave it, and we need to mess everyone's hair up and wrinkle our clothes. We're supposed to look like we've all been fucking."

I arch an eyebrow at him, and he smirks. I pull my lipstick out of my pocket and give my lips another quick coat before returning it, and then I move toward the shit stirrer. He grins, but just as I approach him, I turn and grab Miller, yanking him toward me. The girlie shriek of surprise that leaves his mouth would make me laugh if I wasn't plastering my lips to his and threading my fingers through his hair.

I think he's going to reject me for a moment, and I can't even begin to examine how much that hurts, as I run my tongue across his lip for entrance. His body shudders, his arms wrap around me, and then he grabs my ass, grinding into me as he opens his mouth and kisses me back. Our tongues tangle as we fight for dominance. My hand tightens in his hair, and I tug. He groans into my mouth and grinds his hard cock into me, and this time, a little sigh leaves my mouth, and his lips kick up into a smirk. Fuck, it's always such a fucking tug-of-war with this man.

I pull away, both of us breathing heavily. My lipstick is smeared across his mouth, and his eyes are hooded, but his pupils are blown. I'm sure I look much the same. I can't say his kiss didn't affect me—it was freaking awesome—but there's no way I'm telling him that.

"That was hot," Ryland says, and we both turn to look at him. He's so close, he probably could have joined the kiss if he leaned in.

"Don't touch me again without my permission," Miller snarls at me before stumbling backward.

Oh fuck, did I just violate him? Horror shoots through me. Holy crap, I'm no better than the people we're trying to stop.

I'm about to apologize when Ryland scoffs, "Fuck, man, don't even pretend that you're upset. You've had a lot worse done to you on missions and never said a word. Stop trying to be an ass." Ry sounds pissed, and he's glaring at Miller now. "That's not fair to Mac. She's trying to maintain our cover, and you're being difficult to spite her. Should I start calling you Bishop Two?"

My temper rises. "Seriously? That's fucked up. Screw you, Miller." My need to get even takes over. One thing Miller is going to learn about me is that I won't hesitate to fight back. I turn to Ryland. If Miller wants to play stupid games, then I can give as good as I get. I wonder how he's going to feel about me kissing his boyfriend.

I step up to Ryland and wrap my arms around his waist, and he looks down at me. He knows what I'm doing, and he is very much a willing participant in getting even with Miller. He doesn't wait for me to kiss him, instead swooping down and sliding his hands into my hair. He pulls my head to the side, angling it for maximum access to my mouth. Slowly, he leans in, and out of the corner of my eye, I see Miller's fists clench and feel a lurch of pleasure. Take that, asshole.

Ryland nips my lip, feathering tiny kisses from one corner of my mouth to the other. My knees weaken a little, and I lean into him. His arms tighten around me, and my body presses against his, my breasts pillowing against his hard chest. He nips and sucks my lips before pulling away, and I chase him with my mouth, whimpering with need. He doesn't make me wait any longer, and this time, he doesn't tease me. He takes my mouth with a breath-stealing passion, his tongue stroking mine, and I can't help but wonder what that tongue would feel like against my pussy. I shudder and melt into him, trusting him with my pleasure. His fingers brush my hair out of the way, and one hand closes around my neck, collaring it and squeezing ever so gently. A bolt of pleasure shoots straight to my pussy, and this time, I groan into his mouth. His lips curve, and when he pulls away, his eyes are filled with desire, and he has a pleased smirk on his face. My lipstick is also smudged across his lips.

I can't stop myself from pressing a finger against my own lips, as if I can prolong the feeling.

Banging on the door brings me back to my senses. "Hurry up in there, other people have needs too," some asshole yells, and I blink away the lusty fog and turn to look at Lathan.

"Well, does it look like we've been getting down and dirty in here?" I ask him. He'd been watching from the bed, and he has a dazed look on his face as well. I can't say that doesn't make me happy. Obviously we're doing something right. He adjusts himself and nods quickly.

"Yeah, I think we're good." The banging happens again, the person on the other side is getting impatient, and the glaze in Lathan's eyes clears. "If you pretend you're incoherent, I'll say I'm taking you home."

"We'll stay. Maybe Billy will approach us once he sees you leave," Ryland agrees, and when I finally look at Miller for his thoughts, I find him staring at me with death in his eyes. Huh, I guess Ryland is the only one in the relationship that doesn't get jealous. I don't have time for his insecurities though. He can continue to hate me, but I also don't want to insert myself into an obviously solid relationship. I'll be keeping Ryland at arm's length from now on.

"We'll head back to our place, fill the others in on Bishop, and call Percy and let him know. We'll have to discuss our game plan."

Miller and I stay silent. I am happy with Ryland's and Lathan's decisions, so I don't feel like I need to add anything.

I mess up my hair and rub my eyes a little, smudging my eyeliner and mascara, then I pull off my long-sleeved top and wrap it around my waist, leaving me in just my bra and skinny jeans. Lastly, I lean down and pull on the laces of my boots so they are undone, then I look at the guys critically. I reach out and unfasten Ryland's button-up shirt, leaving it hanging open.

"Pull off your belt and throw it over your shoulder," I tell Miller. "We can't do anything about your T-shirt unless you're willing to rip it a little." It's a vintage band shirt, and I know he's not going to want to do that.

"No," he snaps but unbuckles his belt before pulling it out.

Turning my back on him, I look at Lathan. I reach out and shift his glasses slightly so they look crooked, then I undo a few buttons and fasten them the wrong way. He looks freaking adorable, and I just want to forget the rest of the mission and spend the night making out with him.

"Perfect," I declare, and he blushes. See? Adorable.

"Let's do this." I go to the door and yank it open, staggering slightly. Lathan jumps forward and catches me.

The couple waiting to use the room just gapes in shock as four of us walk out, then I hear the girl mutter, "Lucky bitch," as we pass by.

CHAPTER 2

"Hey, miss? Can we get another pitcher?" A man at one of the booths waves an empty pitcher at me as I deliver a couple of bourbons to the table two down from him. I give him a nod of acknowledgement while smiling at the customers I'm serving.

"There you go, boys." I slide their drinks onto the table before putting the tray under my arm and winking at them. "Can I get you anything else?" One of the men grins before taking a sip of his drink.

"How about your number, sweetheart?" the other one asks, reaching out and caressing my leg. These two have been drinking steadily for a while and have gotten bolder and more handsy as the night wore on.

It's my first shift at the Life Lounge, and so far, it's been fairly normal. I started around five, and there was a steady stream of patrons for after-work drinks. Then the dinner rush happened, and after those people cleared out, it became packed with men and women looking to hang out and hook up.

It has a surprising amount of men in suits who look like they aren't locals. I asked one of the other servers about it, and she just told me to shut up and keep my head down. Apparently asking questions will get me into trouble. They all seem to have conversations with Matthew as he does rounds, schmoozing with the patrons and shouting drinks like there's no tomorrow.

Anders gave me the staff rundown earlier today. There are three other girls serving apart from me, and all seem to be around their early to mid-twenties. One of them, Carla, has that wide-eyed look of someone who is traumatized, and she flinches when someone touches her or a patron shouts too loudly. The other two, Meredith and Samantha, or Meri and Sam as they told me to call them, both look as high as kites, and they are working the room like pros. Anders said they are roommates, and both of them have drug problems. All their money goes to supporting their habits.

I find it interesting that all four of us are "troubled" and have problems. Matthew certainly has a type of employee he likes to hire. Is that because no one is surprised when they end up missing?

The other bartender's name is Keith, and he's probably in his early thirties. He has oily, slicked back hair and wears his shirt with a few too many buttons open. He also wears a gold medallion that glints in the bar lights. Thank fuck he wasn't on duty when I applied for a job. He's not unattractive, but he gives me the creeps. Giving him a blow job would have required hazard pay.

"Maybe, if you play your cards right." I wink at the guy and deftly avoid his hand as he tries to slip it farther up my leg. The bar uniform is very much like the ones Hooters waitresses wear—short shorts that barely cover my butt cheeks and a tight, little black top that dips low and leaves nothing to the imagination.

I head back to the bar for the requested pitcher of beer, and my mind drifts back to last night.

Lathan drove me back to the governor's mansion where we told Max, Dayton, and Anders about Bishop. To say they were shocked would be putting it mildly. Lathan immediately grabbed his laptop and started searching through the camera files, looking to see what happened to Bishop.

"It wouldn't surprise me if he pushed too hard for information instead of just letting it happen organically. He was always in such a rush, impatient to get things done," Dayton suggested. The three of them had been watching TV when we arrived. I got the feeling they were waiting for the guys to get home safely, which was kind of sweet.

"Yeah, and if he asked the wrong question to the wrong person, then it would seem suspicious. I've been very careful not to ask questions. I just let Matthew overhear me talking to Max on the phone or catch me watching dubious porn. When he asks questions, I pretend to be a little reluctant to share but do in the end." Anders swiped a hand through his hair, his agitation at the news of Bishop's death evident.

"That's right, you have to make it seem like it's their idea. If you rush in like a bull in a china shop, then they are going to get suspicious," I said, flopping down on the sofa next to Lathan, who muttered under his breath as his fingers flew across the keyboard.

"What's with the outfits?" Max smirked as he pointed to me and then Lathan's shirt all buttoned up wrong. I still had my long-sleeved shirt tied around my waist. I was overheated even on the walk back to the car, because I had to pretend to be intoxicated all the way in case anyone followed or was watching. My adrenaline was high too. I was only starting to cool down now.

"Well, we had to pretend that the boys triple-teamed me when we found the secret door. Ryland and Miller weren't prepared to let Lathan and I explore on our own." I rolled my eyes, and Lathan snorted. "Seriously, this town is fucked up. The amount of devious shit I saw tonight was amazing."

"Wait until Sunday. All of them will be at church, dressed completely differently and acting piously," Anders drawled and shook his head.

"They were lucky we didn't get caught," I grumbled.

"Okay, I managed to clear out all the footage of us and loop it so it didn't show anything after Bishop was shot. I traced it back, and it's being recorded on a server with no live feed. I guess there's really no need for it to be watched twenty-four seven. They weren't expecting anyone to be down there, so that's something." Lathan's head flopped backward, and he looked up at the ceiling, sighing before meeting our eyes. "There are no cameras leading from the ranger's cabin to the cells, so I don't know how he got there, or whether Billy was with him or not, but I can see him talking to someone down in the cells, and he is on his own. Whoever it is, they are just off camera, and I can't find another angle that shows them. They obviously know the right spot to stand in. Unfortunately, there is no sound on the cameras either, so we can't hear who it is or what they are talking about. Bishop looks shocked then worried, and then there's a flash, and he falls down with the bullet in his head."

"We will just have to wait then. If his body hasn't turned up in twenty-four hours, I'll go to the police and report it. His cover was one of Dad's staffer's kids. It requires a bit of effort on our behalf to maintain our cover." Max shook his head and leaned forward, putting his elbow on his knees. "Do you want to let your dad know or should I?" he asked me, and I shook my head.

"You do it. I have to get home. If one of you wouldn't mind, can you drop me off at the end of the driveway? I don't trust Miller not to lock the attic window if he gets home before me."

"Is he giving you trouble?" Dayton asked, his voice soft and rumbly, making a shiver run down my spine.

"Nothing I can't handle." I waved off his concern,

even though I was a bit bummed. Although I was dead set against joining this team, I came around a little bit. I guessed my attraction to them all helped, but if Miller wasn't okay with it, then it would never work.

Lathan went to put his laptop down, but Max stood up and stretched, his shirt rising with the motion, and I was momentarily distracted by a set of washboard abs. "I'll take you home," he offered, and I looked up.

Lathan frowned. "You shouldn't be seen driving her around at night. She left the party with me, so in case someone is watching her, I should be dropping her off at home."

I stood up and slapped Max on the shoulder. "He's got a point."

Max sat back down and nodded, though I could see the disappointment in his eyes, and my own feelings echoed it. "I'll give your father a call then."

"Say hi to him for me, and tell him I'll call him with an update after my first shift ends." I turned to Anders. "I'll see you for my first shift tomorrow?"

"Yes, be there a little early for your uniform and so I can give you a rundown of what you will need to do."

"Okay, boss." I saluted him and gave the other two a wave as I followed Lathan back out to his car.

When I returned home, the attic window was still open, and Miller hadn't returned. I considered staying so we could talk about what happened, but then I remembered that Jessica would be with him, so I went to bed. She probably came in an hour later.

"Mac." The voice jolts me out of my memories. I'm leaning against the bar, and Anders is on the other side of me, wear a quizzical look on his face.

"Sorry, I zoned out for a moment," I tell him, placing my tray on the bar. "Can I get another pitcher of whatever booth seven is drinking?"

He grabs a clean pitcher, holds it under a tap, and starts filling it. "How's the night going?" he asks over the noise of the crowd. There's a football game playing on all the TVs, and the commentators can be heard over the loud din of the patrons. I'm not paying attention to what is going on, but by the sounds the crowd has been making, I assume the home team is losing.

My eyes shift to the side where Keith is, and although he's serving someone and looks to be distracted, he could quite easily be listening, so I put on a bright smile. "It's really good. Everyone is so nice and friendly, and I've made some good tips."

"Good to hear. Let me know if anyone gives you a hard time, okay?" he replies as he turns the tap off and hands me the pitcher with two more clean glasses.

"Sure will, thank you. I'm so grateful for this job," I gush, laying it on thick. I turn and see that Matthew is sitting at the end of the bar, a glass of whiskey in hand as he chats to a couple of men. I deliberately walk in his direction with an exaggerated sway to my hips. We are almost certain he is part of the ring, and I need an invite into the sex club, so I want his attention on me. The two men he's with leer at me, and I smile shyly at them before dropping my eyes.

I deliver the pitcher to the table, and when I turn back, they are deep in conversation with Matthew again.

I take my time cleaning up a table that was just vacated. The police haven't advised Max of Bishop's death yet, so if nothing happens this evening while I'm at work, they are going to report him missing in the morning. Apparently, all the main players attend the church in town, including the police chief, who is Billy's father. It will be good to get everyone in the same room so I can put faces to names. Lathan checked the camera footage this morning, and Bishop's body is still where we left it.

With my tray piled high with empty glasses and plates, I head back to the bar. Conveniently, Matthew and the two men he is talking to are standing at the end where all the dirties get unloaded. The plates head into the kitchen to get washed, but it's part of my job to stack the glasses and put them into the washer before removing them and putting them where they belong.

Again, I smile as I pass them, but this time they don't look away from their conversation. I gather the plates and return them to the kitchen before returning to wash all the glasses. As I pass behind them, I hear one of the men ask about the next shipment. I keep going, not even pausing when I hear this. My back is to them as I wash the glasses, but there is a mirror behind the bar so I can actually see everything that's going on. The man who asked about the shipment is tall, with dark skin and eyes, and a hooked nose. Maybe he's of Middle Eastern descent. He has an abundance of gold jewelry on his hands, and his suit looks designer and custom made. The other man is slightly shorter and Asian, and his suit is also custom made and designer. He has no jewelry on, but he does have tattoos on his hands.

"The shipment will arrive next week. We'll keep it in storage until after the auction and then ship it out as required," Matthew replies as I bend down and slide the tray of glasses into the washer.

I hear a small whistle, and when I stand back up and peek over my shoulder, I see the two men's eyes are locked onto my ass.

"That's a nice new waitress you have there," I hear the Asian man mutter while I keep my head down and continue to stack the next tray of dirty glasses.

"She's obedient too," Matthew replies. "Got down and sucked Anders's dick like a pro to get the job. Brock over at the high school tells me she used to be one too. The Standishes have taken her in."

"I might be interested in sampling the goods myself," the Middle Eastern man says as I bend down again and pull out the tray of glasses, the steam from the machine coating my face in a fine layer of mist.

"I think we have someone interested in her already," Matthew tells them, and I struggle to keep my body from reacting. I don't even think they realize I can hear them.

"You do?"

"Yes, the governor has two sons who just returned to town. By chance, we found out that the older one is into domination. He is keen on ownership and has taken a liking to that one. She's in his class at school. The boss would like to have something to hold over the governor, especially since he rejected the offer to join the fraternity years ago. The boss plans on using her to get what they need. The son will be getting an invite to our next open night... possibly the younger brother too. It won't hurt to have both of them in our pocket."

I turn around and walk down the bar a little to slide the tray of glasses into a slot, then I push my damp hair back out of my face, hiding my excitement that Max and Ryland might be in with the traffickers.

"What a shame," he mutters, but Matthew slaps him on the back as I head toward them, none of them noticing that I have been listening to the conversation. Idiots. I slide the other tray into the washer.

"Don't worry, we'll have something to keep you happy. Your favorite will be there too."

"Hey, Mac," Anders calls, and I turn around to face him. "You can take a break."

I wave and head back out to the break room. It's perfect timing. I need to send Lathan a message. I know he and Dayton are hiding in an office across from the bar, taking photos of all the patrons as they come and go. I want to make sure he took a photo of these two so we can use facial recognition to ID them. I only hope they came in the front and not the back with Matthew. I was too busy to see which way they came in.

I grab my phone, a pack of smokes, and a can of soda out of my locker and head out the back door. I quickly send Lathan a message, asking him to keep an eye out for the two businessmen. I light up the smoke but just hold it in my hand. It's only there in case anyone comes looking for me.

LATHAN

Will do, how's it going?

KENZIE

I overheard an interesting conversation. I'll fill Anders in, and he can tell you all.

LATHAN

Have you been able to explore the club yet?

I snort out loud as I respond.

KENZIE:

Hardly, it's been busy since I walked in. I'm closing with Anders, so he can show me what to do. Maybe we will get a chance then.

LATHAN

I'll hack the security tapes and cause a glitch so you can poke around. Just let me know when.

It's so handy having a techy on the same team. If I'd been on my own, I would have had to plant a device, which would have given my tech operator a way in, then call them to let them know it was done and wait for them to get back to me. This is so much easier and time saving.

"How's your night going?" The question startles me, and I want to kick myself for not paying attention to my surroundings. I shove my phone into the tiny back pocket of my ridiculous shorts and turn to face Matthew.

"It's been good. I didn't expect it to be so busy. Your club is really popular," I gush, bringing the cigarette up to my lips and taking a drag.

He frowns. "I'm not sure Martha is going to be happy if she smells that on you." He nods to the offending cigarette.

"Yeah, you may be right. It's a nasty habit. I only do it when I'm nervous, and I was super nervous tonight. I really want to make a good impression."

His eyes slide down my body and back again, and he loses the frown. "I wouldn't worry too much about that. I'm heading out for the night. Anders said he's going to walk you through closing, and then he's going to give you a lift home. I promised Martha that I would get you home after your shift."

"Oh, okay, thanks. That's really nice of you." I smile at him.

He chuckles. "She would have my head if I let any of her kids get lost. One of the others that's living with you is starting tomorrow too, a Michael or a..." He trails off.

"Miller," I supply, and he snaps his fingers.

"Yeah, that's it. Well, I guess I'll see you at church tomorrow." He wanders down the alley and disappears around the corner.

I heave out a sigh of relief and throw the burning cigarette on the ground, stubbing it out with my toe. Thank goodness I texted Lathan instead of calling him.

I grab my phone again.

KENZIE

Matthew is leaving. Can one of you follow him?

LATHAN

Dayton will.

I heave out a sigh of relief. Having backup isn't horrible. I don't have to worry about where Matthew goes, and I can concentrate on exploring the club.

LATHAN

The two men you described haven't left yet, but I'll keep an eye out.

I blow out another heavy sigh and head back inside, wondering if we will get a chance to poke around tonight after work.

CHAPTER 3

When I get back to the bar, the two men who had been with Matthew are nowhere to be seen, but then I really don't have any time to worry about it because after the football game finishes, the tables and chairs are cleared away, the music is turned up, and the empty space becomes a dance floor. If I thought we were busy before, then it's nothing compared to what it's like once this happens.

Meri and Sam move behind the bar to help Anders and Keith serve drinks, leaving Carla and me to wait on the booths around the outside of the dance floor. Thank goodness I'm fit, because we are slammed all night. I see Miller and Ryland come in with the group of people they hang out with. I get glares from the girls in the group, but Carla has their table, so I'm able to avoid any kind of confrontation about the previous night.

Jessica and I didn't speak to one another at all

today. We were woken up early to help Martha with the chores, and from the moment she woke up, she gave me death glares. I vacuumed our room while she dusted the furniture downstairs. The other kids all had set jobs too, as well as about ten loads of laundry from all of us. Martha must not do any housework throughout the week, leaving it all for us. It wasn't until I was about to leave the house in the afternoon to go to my first shift that Jessica stopped me.

"You better stay away from Ryland Turner and his friends. Sophie has plans for them, and you really don't want to get in the way of Sophie's plan," she hissed, digging her nails into my arm. "That would not be healthy for you." Either she didn't know about Bishop or she's a damn good actress.

I was glad when they weren't placed in my section.

"Hi, what can I get you?" I'm looking at the tablet I use to send orders to Anders as I approach a table. When I look up, I almost trip over my own feet. It takes all of my acting skills not to react when I see the two people sitting together on one side of the booth.

"Ms. Walsh, aren't you a little young to be working here?" Max's eyes sparkle with amusement, but he has a frown on his face.

"Matthew is a friend of the family, and he's happy to give Aunt Martha's kids jobs. Let's face it, no one else will," Stella Standish sneers as she snuggles into Max's side. "A low-class job for low-class people."

"Stella," Max scolds, brushing a hand over her side. I don't know why, but my eyes zero in on that hand just for a moment, and I feel an irrational wave of anger before I remember what that hand had done to me recently, then I want to kick myself because jealousy does not belong on the job, especially ours. "Not everyone is as lucky as you and me to have loving, caring parents."

She smirks and presses a kiss to his cheek. "You are so kind and right, but I think this time my words are pretty fitting." She looks me up and down. "Could you not find a smaller uniform?"

I want to snort with amusement. The dress she's wearing is almost as indecent as the outfit I have on, but I just paste a tight smile on my face. "Mr. Turner, Ms. Standish, lovely to see you. What can I get you?" I try my hardest to be polite, since I don't want to get fired on my first day, and I know Stella is the type of person who would complain to Matthew.

"What would you like, Stella?" Max asks her, and she looks up at him and flutters her eyelashes. I want to gag, but I don't.

"Why don't you surprise me?" she purrs as Max grabs the drinks menu from the table and looks it over.

"I'll have a bottle of Sam Adams, and Stella will have a dirty swingers," he tells me, and I watch with amusement as she loses her simpering smile and frowns. All the cocktail names are dirty. Hell, there's one called the malibukaki daiquiri, and it's super popular. It comes in a shaker, and you pour it into shot glasses. It can be shared amongst a bunch of people or one person can drink the lot. "We'll also get two three-dollar hooker shots."

This time she turns and smirks at me. "That should be easy enough for you, right, Mackenzie?"

I hate women like Stella. Women should be cheering each other on, not trying to climb all over each other to get to the top. She's the worst kind who enjoys other people's misfortunes.

"Are you sure you don't want a blow job? They are my—I mean *our* special tonight." I smile brightly, winking at Max, and Stella's lips purse tightly.

Max chuckles quietly, pressing a kiss to her head. "Sure, why not? I love a good blow job." He smirks, bless his dirty little heart.

Stella glares at me as I add the extra shot to the order.

"I'll be right back." I give Max a flirty smile, ignoring Stella altogether. She's going to have to try a lot harder than that to upset me. I wonder what Stella would say if she knew her boyfriend was balls deep in me earlier in the week.

I head back to the bar, and by the time I get there, Anders should have my drinks made. He's responsible for making everything that Carla and I put into the system, while the other three service the people who come up to the bar.

I go around to his side of the bar, grab a tray from the shelf, and lean against the bar while he finishes making the drinks for Carla's order.

She smiles wanly at me. "How's your night going?" I ask, and she shrugs.

"It's been okay. Tips have been pretty good. I've almost saved enough to buy a bus ticket."

"Oh, where are you going?" I ask her.

"Anywhere that isn't here. This town isn't right." Her eyes cloud, and she shudders visibly. "Be careful who you get close to. My advice is to keep your head down, study hard, and get the fuck out of here the minute you turn eighteen. Don't hang around, hoping things will get better. Get into a college far away from here."

We chatted as we set up the tables before opening, and I told her that I was hoping to get into college.

My mouth drops open in shock as she picks up the tray once Anders places the last drink on it and disappears.

"Whoa. What the hell?" I watch her walk away, her shoulders hunched. She is giving off *stay away from me* vibes.

"Carla was roommates with the girl who was found dead in the field or ditch. The official report was an overdose, but Carla insisted that her roommate never touched drugs. Lathan hacked the coroner's files and discovered pictures of the body. She had a bullet hole in the middle of her head, but the police report was falsified, and the 'official photos' had the bullet hole puttied over and masked," Anders says quietly as he quickly makes the three shots and Stella's cocktail.

I pull a bottle of Sam Adams out of the fridge, pop

the top, and place it on the tray. "Sounds familiar. I wonder if that's what they'll do with Bishop?" I say dryly. "That's going to be a little tricky for them, since his cover is supposed to be the governor's staffer's kid."

"Yeah, your dad is going to send an agent to pose as his family to collect his body. I think it's going to be trickier to hide it with him than the girl. She had no family to claim her body, so she was cremated, and her remains are in storage in case anyone else comes forward."

A wave of sadness washes through me. It would be horrible to have no one claim you or care enough to take care of your remains.

"Did you see Max come in?" I ask him, changing the subject.

"No, but he did say he had a dinner date with Stella tonight. Are they here?"

"Yeah, that's their order." I nod to the tray he just finished, and his eyebrows jump.

"Did Stella or Max order?" he asks, and I snort.

"Who do you think?"

"It would have to be Max. Stella wouldn't order anything like this. She always had a glass of prosecco whenever she was here previously. I've heard her complain to Matthew about how dirty the names of the drinks are."

"So do you think the women have no idea about the sex trafficking? Granted, I haven't met many of them, but Martha and her older niece seem fairly freaking uptight."

"Who knows? Sophie is too, apparently, but the two girls she hangs out with are not stingy with their affections, or that's what the guys told me is the gossip around the school."

"They are here too. Carla has their table."

"Are Ry and Miller with them?" Anders asks, and I nod. "They talked about going back to the ranger's cabin tonight and retracing their steps to see where the tunnel led to, but I guess they changed their minds."

"Why? Max obviously has an in with Stella, not to mention I overheard Matthew talking about the governor's sons possibly getting an invite to a special occasion. Surely they could be focusing on something else now instead of trying to keep those girls happy?"

Anders shrugs. "Their cover is still in the high school. It was the easiest place to stick so many agents without suspicion, so they have to continue to maintain it. Come on, Mac, sometimes we have to do things for the good of the mission."

I lift the tray and huff out a breath. "I know, but they are fucking annoying. I have no idea why I was so excited to attend high school. It blows."

He chuckles as I walk away. I make my way through the crowd, dodging writhing bodies, and arrive back at their table. I place the tray on the surface and pass out the drinks.

"Can I get you anything else?" I ask suggestively,

looking at Max and ignoring Stella. He reaches for the blow job, and with his eyes locked on mine, he throws it back.

Stella's gaze flits between us, and her eyes narrow. She sits up and drags her cocktail in front of her, taking a sip. "Max, how about we drink these and get out of here? We can go back to my place where we can be alone. It's so noisy and crowded here." She wraps her lips around the straw suggestively and takes a sip, but as she pulls away, she knocks the drink over, and it splashes violently across the table, splattering the front of my uniform with liquid.

"Oops, I'm so clumsy," she says unapologetically, wearing a fucking smirk on her face. What I wouldn't give to wipe it off permanently. I hate this bitch. She better not come back in again, because I can guarantee I can be just as clumsy as she is, and a cocktail on that white dress is going to be hard to hide. I look down at my front. Thankfully the uniform is black, but it's sticky, and I smell like a fruity distillery now.

I feign an uncomfortable smile. "If you don't need anything else, I'll just go clean up."

"We'll have a bowl of peanuts please," Stella says, and I grimace.

I whirl around and stalk back to the bar, the liquid soaking into my tight uniform. Anders frowns as I grab a packet of peanuts and tip it into one of the small bowls for serving.

"What happened?" he asks, looking at my damp clothes, and I grab a napkin and try to dab some of the liquid out, but all it does is smear damp napkin across my shorts.

"Ugh." I toss the napkin into a bin. "Stella had an 'accident' with her drink," I tell him, grabbing a cloth to wipe up the mess. "Can you make another dirty swingers?"

He chuckles and quickly makes another drink, pouring the ingredients into a metal shaker before giving it a quick shake with both hands, then he pours it into a glass with a flourish. "Hopefully this one stays in the glass. Why don't you go clean up in the bathroom? Otherwise, you're going to be uncomfortable for the rest of the night."

"Thanks, I will. Sticky underwear isn't fun." I return to the table with the drinks and peanuts and clean up the mess. I don't say anything this time. They both ignore me, talking quietly to one another.

Once I'm done cleaning the table, I return the cloth to the bar and head toward the bathroom. They are in the back of the club, so I have to wind my way through the crowd. I pass by Ryland's table, and I feel eyes on me, but I don't stop to see who's looking at me. I don't want to end up with another drink in my face, and those girls are vicious. I don't doubt one of them would try, especially if they knew that I was in that room with the boys last night, and from what Jessica said, I don't doubt they know.

The toilets are all individual and not gender specific. I'm almost certain they aren't just for relieving one's bodily functions. Throughout the night, I've seen couples disappear into them. I pick an empty one. They are clean, and there is a large bench the sink is recessed into, leaving enough room for someone to sit comfortably while being railed. I pull the door closed behind me and look at myself in the mirror. The liquid is starting to dry, and there's a residue staining the black fabric, not to mention the bits of napkin. I'm a mess. I bet it lit up under the black lights as I walked across the dance floor.

Sighing, I pull off the top and shorts and set them both on the sink. Standing in just my panties, I debate whether or not I want to pull those off too. Before I can make a decision, though, the door opens behind me, and someone slips into the little room. I squeak and whirl around to face whoever came in. Fuck, I forgot to lock the door, and I'm nearly naked. Someone's about to get the surprise of their life, but when I meet familiar eyes, I relax. The corner of Ryland's lips curls up in a smile, and his eyes heat as he scans my body.

"When I decided to follow you to the bathroom to find out how your night was going, this was not what I was expecting. Can't say I'm disappointed though."

CHAPTER 4

I put my hands on my hips and raise an eyebrow. "Did you consider knocking? I could have been peeing," I ask blandly, and his smile turns into a smirk.

"Nope, I figure we're going to be a team, so we can watch each other pee." I can't believe this guy.

"Dude, there is such a thing as boundaries," I retort, slightly exasperated. Ryland Turner is nothing like I expected. I turn my back to him, grab my top, then turn on the tap. I run it under the water, using my finger to get all the white napkin off.

I hear him groan behind me, and when I look into the mirror, his eyes are locked onto my ass.

"God, I love thongs," he mutters, and it's my turn to smirk. His eyes meet mine in the mirror, and he stares at my bare breasts, adjusting himself before frowning.

"Where's your bra?" He looks at the countertop before narrowing his eyes suspiciously.

"Relax," I tell him. "I didn't need one in this top. It's tight enough to hold the girls in." I wring out the fabric, happy with how it looks, before doing the same thing to my hot pants.

"What happened?" he asks, leaning against the door.

"Stella wanted to make a statement," I tell him, and he groans.

"God, that woman is awful. I don't envy my brother at all."

"Yet you guys are hanging out with her sister and friends. It's no wonder none of you had gotten further on the case if you've spent your time here partying and socializing instead of running leads."

Ryland frowns. "We got leads."

"Hardly. Has anyone asked where Bishop is?"

"Yeah, Michelle did. She seemed genuinely disappointed and surprised when we told her he didn't come home from the party last night. Lathan told her we thought he might have been with her, and she denied it, and then she got pissed because she thought maybe he'd gone home with someone else."

"So it isn't likely any of them know the truth?"

"It doesn't seem like it," he replies as I turn to the air dryer and activate it, sticking my shorts underneath. It shouldn't take long for them to dry.

"Anders said he thought you were going back to the tunnels to see where they lead to. Are you still doing that?"

"We were going to, but Jessica caught Miller as he

was sneaking out."

"Jessica went up to his room?" I ask, spinning around. "We're not supposed to be up there. She's getting bold."

His eyes drift down to my breasts, and his lips kick up again before his eyes come back to mine. "I get the feeling Sophie is putting on the pressure. I think Billy may have been saying something to her at the party last night when we were supposedly in that room. He's planting seeds that Miller and I are closer than just friends. She keeps saying things like, 'Wouldn't it be amazing if brothers were both dating sisters?' I've tried my hardest not to encourage her, but it's getting harder and harder."

It's my turn to smirk as I turn to keep drying my shorts. He sounds pained, and I can't say I'm disappointed about that. We all have to do things we don't want to.

I change the subject. "Matthew left for the night. Anders and I will have a chance to poke around. So far, the entrance to the club is nothing obvious. It's either not in this club or it's hidden. I haven't seen an elevator or a set of stairs that lead anywhere. Heck, it might not even be under this club. We've been going on assumptions, but with the tunnel system, it could be anywhere under town, or even in a private house."

"No, Anders said the same, but tonight will be the first time he hasn't been supervised while cleaning up. I'm pretty sure you helped secure his cover when you got down on your knees and blew him. He said

Matthew wants to have a meeting with him tomorrow after church to discuss a new role he may be interested in. We're hoping they are going to ask him to serve at the next sex party. From what we can work out, it's on the third Friday of every month."

The dryer switches off, and my shorts are dry enough, so I pull them back on before grabbing the top. I switch the dryer on again to do that next.

"That means we have two weeks before the next one. Do you think the sex parties are held as previews for the auctions? A try before you buy kind of deal?" I ask over my shoulder.

"Probably," Ryland replies. My top dries quicker, but it's still damp. I've been in here long enough, though, so when the dryer switches off again, I decide it's good enough. I spin around and squeak. Ryland is so close, my breasts brush against his chest. He reaches out and plucks my shirt out of my hand, and then he backs me up, moving me carefully so I'm not pushed up against the dryer. His hand collars my throat with enough pressure to hold me in place. I could get out, but I really don't want to. A shiver runs down my spine as his fingers flex around my throat.

"Now that business is out of the way, you're not going to send me back to my table without letting me have a taste of what you've been teasing me with, are you?"

I gasp as he leans in and wraps his lips around my nipple, sucking it into his mouth. I groan, and my core throbs as he suckles it before releasing it with a pop.

He pulls back and smirks. "Delicious, just like I thought it would be. See you around, princess." He winks, handing me my top before opening the door. He comes to a sudden stop, and I see Miller over his shoulder.

"I was just looking for you," he says, grinding his teeth together as his eyes scan the length of my half naked body.

"I was just helping Mac clean up," he tells him and pulls the door closed so I don't hear what's said next.

Great, now Miller's going to hate me even more. My mind goes back to Ry's mouth on my nipple and his hand on my throat, and my core throbs. Holy fuck. He is potent. I can kind of understand how Miller becomes a ball of mush under his hands.

Shaking off my lust, I dress and head back out into the club. The noise is an assault on my senses after the quiet bathroom, and I feel a headache start to build behind my eyes. As I make my way through the club, Stella waves me down, so I detour past their table.

"We'd like the bill please," she tells me curtly. "This club is too noisy and not intimate enough for us." She isn't even looking at me, she's looking at Max, her eyes filled with lust.

"Yes, the bill please. I can't wait to get you alone." He nods but doesn't turn his attention to me, fully focused on the girl next to him.

"Okay, I'll just grab it for you." I head back to the bar, that annoying feeling of jealousy itching inside my chest. What the fuck is wrong with me? I like Max, and fucking him was fun, but this feels like it might be more than that, and I don't like that feeling. This is all becoming very complicated, and I need to simplify it.

No feelings, Kenzie. That's your mantra, and you need to remember it.

It doesn't take long to shove their bill into a leather wallet and return it to the table. Neither of them pays attention to me, and my mind is back in the game, so I don't care. I'm busy after that, running drinks back and forth for more booths, and I don't even notice when they leave. When I get back to the table, there is already another group in it, but I grab the bill wallet. Inside is the correct money, as well as a twenty-dollar tip and a note.

I enjoyed your blow job immensely. Can't wait to have another.

I roll my eyes and stuff the twenty into my apron before returning to the register and cashing out the bill. I wonder if Stella will be giving him a blow job tonight, or will he get down on his knees and lick her pussy?

"Are you okay?" Anders asks, bumping my hip, and I force a smile.

"Yup, fine. Max and Stella left."

Anders's brow creases, and he looks closer than I would like him to. "You know he's just maintaining his cover."

"Pfft." I wave him off. "Of course I do. Anything to break the case, right? I'll probably have to fuck some randos, too, if I end up working down in the sex club."

This makes his frown a little deeper, but he doesn't disagree. He knows it's true.

"We only have two hours until we close, and then you and I can poke around. I haven't been left alone long enough to search for the entry to the club, and we decided breaking and entering wasn't necessary yet. If it had taken him much longer to trust me, though, we might have had to."

"What's up the set of stairs?" I ask him. There's a locked door that leads to the level above the club.

"Depending on how big the crowd is, we open those doors, and then there's a large dance floor and another bar up there, as well as some dance cages. How do you feel about dancing? You may be asked to," he replies, working on another order for Carla.

"Yeah, I don't care," I say distractedly as my eyes catch on Sam and Meri. They have a quiet conversation, and then I watch as Sam says something to Keith before leaving in the direction of the bathroom. "I wonder where she's going." I nod in Meri's direction, and Anders scoffs as he notices Sam missing.

"I don't think we'll open the top level tonight. Matthew didn't say anything before he left, and the crowd isn't huge. Go find Sam. I guarantee she's snorting some coke or popping some pills. That's the only reason they disappear. She should be easy to manipulate. They've been working here nearly a year, and if anyone knows about the sex club and will talk about it, it's them. Carla just clams up."

"Okay, will do." I leave him and hurry after the girl.

I find her heading down the corridor of the toilets, but instead of going into one, I find her in the staff area out back. Her locker is open, and she's scratching around in her handbag.

"Phew, it's been so busy. Is it always like this?" I lean against the locker next to her, startling her.

"Oh, Mac, I didn't see you there," she says, shaking her head and then continuing to dig around in her bag. "Yeah, sometimes it's even busier." She pulls out what I'm assuming is a joint and smiles sheepishly.

"Just going to head out and have a smoke."

"Mind if I come?" I ask, and she shrugs.

"Be my guest. Smoking is always better with friends."

We head out the back door after she shoves her bag in the locker. She quickly lights up and takes a long drag, holding it in before blowing out the pungent smoke. I struggle not to wrinkle my nose. Weed always smells so gross.

She takes another drag before holding it out for me. "Here, take a hit. It's always easier when you're a little high."

"Yeah, my feet are killing me, but the tips have totally been worth it. I've made bank."

She chuckles. "You have to give Anders his cut, since he's been pouring your drinks all night, but yeah, they do tip well here."

"I'm saving for college, and every bit helps," I tell her, holding my lungful of smoke before blowing it out.

She eyes me carefully as I take another drag, running her eyes up and down my body.

"You know if you want to make some extra cash, you may be able to. How do you feel about topless waitressing?"

"They do that here?" I ask, going for wide-eyed but interested.

She shakes her head. "No, not here, but I can make a suggestion to Matthew next time he needs one."

"Yeah, that would be great. Like I said, I'll take every extra bit of cash I can."

Sam nods. "Yeah, Meri and I feel that way too, and we're not particularly fussy about how we earn it. There's a chance to make a lot if you really want, but it means doing things that society says is wrong." She tries to sound mysterious, not giving me too much information.

"Oh?" I ask, trying to sound interested but not too fascinated, but this is the first conversation or hint at the sex club so far.

She smiles brightly and takes the joint back from me. "Yeah, you know what? I talk too much. See how you do, and if Matthew likes you, he might tell you more."

"Is it illegal?" I ask quietly, looking around like I'm trying to be sneaky. "Because I've done illegal. I've had to do some things I'm not proud of to get by."

She smiles gently. "Haven't we all? Hey, can you run back in and swap with Meri? She needs a hit of this too."

"Yeah, okay, no probs. I'll send Meri out." I wave goodbye and head back in, the mellow feeling of the marijuana hitting me as I return to the bar.

"Meri, Sam needs you for a moment. I'll cover you," I tell her sliding into her spot behind the bar with Keith.

"Are you sure?" She looks from me to Keith, biting her lip, but I wave her off.

"Yeah, sure, how hard can it be? I can pop tops on bottles and mix spirits. I'll ask Keith or Anders for any of the fancy things."

"That would be great, thanks." She smiles gratefully and hurries in the direction I came from.

"Hey there, girlie. How's your night been?" Keith smiles at me, his eyes locked onto my tits as he rings up someone's order. "It's nice to have a new pretty face to look at."

"Not sure it's my face you're looking at, Keith," I joke, and he chuckles as he hands the change to his customer.

"Well, can you blame me? You've got a mighty perky pair of tits." He sidles close to me and leans in to whisper in my ear. "I wish I'd been on the day you came in to apply. I bet you looked pretty on your knees, and I bet you suck cock like a pro."

I force myself to blush and look away from him like I'm embarrassed. "I really needed this job," I mutter, and he pats me on the ass, copping a handful of cheek to squeeze. He backs me up against the bar and presses his body against mine so I can feel how hard my tits have made him.

"It's alright, darling. None of us think any worse of you. In fact, it turns me the fuck on." He winks, rubbing his erection against me before returning to serving as I hide a shudder of revulsion. I don't know what it is about Keith, but he really creeps me out, and I've had to fuck some creeps before.

I serve a few customers while I wait for Sam and Meri to return. It's easy and mind-numbing, and I smile and flirt, but there's this edge of apathy. Despite the weed in my system, I feel kind of hollow. What is this feeling? I'm exhausted all of a sudden. Was Dad right? Am I ready to have a team to back me up and give me support? Am I ready to give up spreading my legs to get the job done? I feel like I need to scrub my body to remove Keith's touch from me, and hell, that isn't my usual MO. Normally, that would be par for the course, but now I just feel dirty.

What I really want to do is go home, have my mom wrap her arms around me, and give me a hug. I want my comfort pj's and my mac and cheese, and I want to pretend I'm normal. Maybe I really do need a break. It's time to reassess what I want from life. I just need to get through this case. Maybe it's the actual case that's fucking with my head. The trafficking of unwanted teenagers is making me sad. Why can't everyone be lucky enough to have a family that loves them like mine does?

CHAPTER 5

A fistfight breaks out on the dance floor, knocking me out of my depressing thoughts. Anders and Keith both leave the bar to help the bouncers, leaving Carla and me to manage the bar. Most of the people waiting turn to watch the fight, so we get a moment of reprieve before people lose interest, and then we get slammed again. Sam and Meri return at the same time as Keith and Anders, and we finish off the night in our assigned positions. By the time the doors close at two, it takes a good half hour for us to push all the customers out. The girls help me gather the glasses and wipe down the booths.

"The cleaning crew will be in later in the morning to do the bathrooms and dance floor," Keith explains as he pulls on a leather jacket. "Anders will give you the rundown on cleaning the bar and mopping the floor. He'll also show you how to change the kegs if any are needed." He turns to Anders. "Make sure the empty kegs are stacked in the alcove to be picked up by the distributor in the morning. We have that wine thing next week, and we got a hookup with a distributor, so they are sending us some cases of wine. They'll drop them in the alcove, so make sure there's space."

"Sure thing," Anders agrees, and Keith winks and looks between the two of us.

"Don't have too much fun. Matthew said you have to run Mac home, otherwise Martha will get her panties in a twist. She has church in the morning." Keith shakes his head and chuckles as he walks out, followed by the three other girls. Sam and Meri wave cheery goodbyes, but Carla keeps her head down and ignores both of us. It doesn't take long for the rest of security to clear out either, leaving Anders and me all alone.

He tosses me a cloth. "Start wiping down all the bottles at Keith's station," he tells me as he pulls out his phone and sends a text. I'm assuming it's to Lathan. Once he puts his phone back in his pocket, he walks over to me and bends over, looking like he's showing me something. "We have half an hour to clean up, and then Lathan is going to fix the video feed to make it look like we left so we can poke around a little."

"Sounds good," I mutter, keeping my head down so my lips can't be read. Anders and I work quickly and quietly. There really isn't a lot to do, just the main bar area. We wipe down all three pouring stations and the bar and all the shiny metal surfaces. I pour some half bottles together and replace the empty ones with full bottles, then I gather up the two trash bags and run them out to the bins in the alleyway. When I return, Anders nods his head toward the cool room. "Come on, I'll show you how to change a keg, and then we'll roll the empties out to be picked up."

He leads me past the staff area and through a door and down a hallway. We pass an ice maker and a dry stock storage room before we reach a large cold door.

"That leads out to the back of the club." He points to a door off to the side. "The whole club takes up the block, so that's the street that runs behind the club."

He grabs the handle of the walk-in refrigerator and pulls down, dragging the large door backwards. A rush of cold air flows out, and I shiver. He snorts as I rub my arms and legs.

"Let's make this quick, otherwise you're going to turn into a Macsicle." He leads the way in and shows me how to change a keg, just in case.

"So are there any random doors or possible places that could be hiding an entrance to a sex club?" I ask him as we roll the four empty ones out the back door.

"Nothing that sticks out. We need to check the coat room, and I'd like to look in dry storage with the racks of alcohol to see if they slide to the side. I haven't been left alone to do that yet." He rolls his two kegs against the wall, and I push mine next to it before looking around.

There's quite a large alcove. Sure enough, there's another door that I'm assuming is the door to the upper floor, but there is also a service elevator. I point to it.

"Does that only go up, or does it go down?" I ask him, and his eyes widen.

"It goes up to the other level, but it doesn't really get used. That would require more security, so Matthew tends to only use the inside stairs. I think I remember Keith saying it went down to an old cellar, but I didn't think anything of it at the time. Do you think people would use it to get into the club? Surely lots of people would be seen coming and going. Someone would have noticed something." He sounds dubious, and I bite my lip while I'm thinking.

"We kind of need to see where it goes. I'm assuming it's locked." I point to a card reader off to the side of the elevator. "Do you think Lathan can hack it?"

"Probably, but not in time for us to check it out tonight. I'll see if he can organize something for tomorrow after work. Miller starts tomorrow as well, so I don't doubt that you two will be on cleanup duties together. I'll probably have to drive him home too."

"You know, I was thinking about those tunnels," I say as we make our way back into the club. "They looked old. They have to be some old prohibition tunnels or part of the Underground Railroad. Maybe we should go to the local library and see if there is anything there about the town's history. There might be a map that will give us more of an idea on where the entrance to the club could be."

"We really need to go back and explore those

tunnels. We were waiting for Bishop's body to be moved, which I'm guessing will happen when Max reports him missing tomorrow after church, but that's not a bad idea in the meantime. If you say you're going to study for school or something, no one will be suspicious." Anders leads the way back into the club.

"Martha would probably have an orgasm if I told her I was going to spend the afternoon at the library studying after church." I chuckle as the two of us check out the shelves in the storage room. None of them are hiding an entrance or even move away from the wall. We head back into the walk-in refrigerator to do another check, but there are no secret passages in there either.

"How about the bathrooms? It wouldn't be suspicious because people naturally go into one, and nobody is paying attention if they come back out until later," I suggest.

"Let's look," he agrees, but it's another dead end. We finally check the coat room, but there is nothing but some lost property.

"I'm going to go out on a limb and say the entrance to the sex club isn't here," I say to Anders as he growls in frustration. "The club may not even be under this one. The girls may have been confused. Their foster sister was terrified, so they may have gotten mixed up."

"Damn it. Back to square one. I thought for sure it would be." He turns all the lights off, plunging the main room of the club into darkness as we retreat to the staff area.

I grab my things from my locker as Anders grabs his phone and car keys from his.

"I have Monday, Tuesday, and Wednesday off work. Maybe we can explore the tunnels on one of those nights."

"Why don't you come over to our place on Monday, and we can have a team meeting and come up with a game plan? You can share what you learned at the library. I don't think we can risk being overheard talking about it tomorrow night."

"No, you're probably right. You never know who is involved. Meri and Sam obviously have some knowledge of the sex club. She implied that if I worked hard and made a good impression, I could make some extra cash on the side. She specifically said topless waitressing, but she also implied that there were more opportunities." We walk out the side door and into the alley, locking the club behind us.

We walk to the parking lot in front, where Anders parked his truck. I know that Lathan is around somewhere, but as I gaze around the parking lot, nothing stands out, which I guess is the point. There are still a few cars parked in it because there's a twenty-four hour diner across the road that has quite a few people in it. I'm assuming they are making a last-ditch effort to sober up before driving home.

Anders reaches out and clicks the button on his key fob to unlock his truck. The truck beeps, and its lights shine briefly. I grumble as I take in the monstrous behemoth in front of me. I'm not a short girl, but I may need a boost to get up into the truck.

He chuckles and goes to the passenger door and opens it. A running board drops down, and he offers me a hand. "Princess, your chariot awaits." His eyes twinkle with amusement as I take his hand and use the step to get into the vehicle. When I'm settled inside, he closes the door behind me and hurries around to the other side.

I take a moment to breathe in the scent of the interior. It smells new but not new enough that it doesn't smell like him as well. It has this woodsy, smoky scent that I noticed on him when he leaned in to talk to me tonight. It smells amazing, but I don't want to make it obvious that I'm trying to breathe it all in, so I turn my head to face the window as he puts his key in the ignition and starts it.

It roars to life and settles to a quiet rumble as we make our way out of the parking lot. "I'll drop you at the end of the driveway. Martha gave Matthew instructions not to wake them when I drop you off, and you have a key, right?" he asks, and I nod.

"Yes, she told me where the key is on the back porch, which is handy for future sneaking in and out."

"Well, just be careful you aren't caught," he warns. "Do you have the drugs for your roommate?"

"Yeah, I stashed them underneath my dresser drawer. It should be easy enough to inject her if I need to, but she also kind of sleeps like the dead once she starts snoring."

"Yeah, but you don't want her waking up to pee and discover you're gone," he cautions, and I guess he has a point. I haven't heard her get up and pee in the middle of the night, but there is always a first time for everything.

We make our way through town and out the other side before he opens it up a little. I tell him about the conversation I overheard between Matthew and the two unknown men. He says he will let Max and Ryland know they are both going to get tapped for an invite. It doesn't take long before we arrive at the end of the driveway, and he pulls into the bus stop. I unstrap and open the door. Thankfully the step drops down, otherwise it would have been a long drop to the ground, and I'm tired.

"See you at church tomorrow, and thanks for the lift," I say before jumping out.

"Mac, be on alert at church. All the major players should be there. Get Miller to tell you who is who."

I scoff. "Yeah, if he's talking to me. Ry cornered me in the bathroom while I was cleaning up after Stella spilled her drink all over me," I explain.

"So what was the problem?" There are no street-lights out here, but the interior light shows me Anders's frown.

I grimace. "I might have taken off my top and shorts so I could wash them in the sink, and I might have been mostly naked when he cornered me. Miller saw, and it wouldn't be hard for him to make assumptions. Good thing I don't have to climb back through the attic window. I'm sure he and Jessica are both back now and closed it behind them."

"Pfft, don't worry about Miller. He's mostly all show. You two have to work together more than the rest of us, so he's going to have to get over it."

"Are you guys still hoping he's going to be asked to work in the sex club as well? Did he have to do an audition like I did?" I ask Anders.

"Nah, James called and asked him to give him a job. I overheard the conversation. Matthew grumbled a bit but gave him a job. James must have said something that convinced him. I heard him say something along the lines of, 'He better perform. Both of them better perform.'"

"I wonder what they could have been talking about," I muse. "Sex acts?"

Anders shrugs. "Maybe. I guess time will tell."

"Will Miller be okay with that?" I ask. "I always get the feeling he's judging me for using my body."

Anders chuckles. "Nah, that has to do with your mom more than anything. Miller will do whatever he has to in order to get the job done. Trust me, and the fact that he's bi makes him a huge asset."

"That's actually a relief to hear. I didn't think he'd be unprofessional, but he doesn't go out of his way to be particularly friendly either." I nod my head in the direction of the house. "Let's hope he gets over it quickly. I don't think he and Ryland are on the same page about me, and it might cause issues."

"Look, that's their problem to sort out. You do your job, and I will make sure their shit isn't going to leak into this situation," he assures me.

"Okay, I'll see you tomorrow then." I lean in to give him a kiss on the cheek, but he turns his head, and it's his plush mouth I end up meeting. His big hand comes up to hold my head, and he kisses me hard. I'm shocked and a little pleased, his tongue licking over mine seductively before he pulls away, leaving me blinking with surprise.

The small smile on his mouth is cute as he says, "Goodnight."

Shaking off my surprised daze, I mumble, "Good-bye," and climb down from the truck. I stumble back a little, still shocked from the surprise kiss, but I manage to get the door closed, and he pulls away slowly so he doesn't kick up dust in my face. Turning, I hurry down the driveway. There's a cold breeze, and I'm not wearing enough to keep myself warm. I have to remember to throw a sweatshirt in for tomorrow night.

I find the key exactly where Martha said it would be, and I quietly unlock the door before returning it. Then, I creep inside, trying hard not to make any noise. I head upstairs and down the hallway to our room. Just as I pass the doorway to the attic, a hand reaches out and drags me in. I clamp my mouth shut, not wanting to wake anyone. I was kind of expecting this, but it still made me jump.

Miller pins me against the stairway wall, his naked chest flush against mine. I can't really see him in this light, but I can feel and smell his peppermint-scented breath against my face. His chest is rising and falling faster than normal, like he's angry, and I brace myself for his tirade.

I'm waiting for him to tell me to stay away from Ryland or something, but his fingers drift up my side, drawing softly across the exposed skin between my top and shorts. It drifts higher, brushing over my nipple before he hooks it into the collar of my top. To my complete shock, he drags my neckline down, exposing the same nipple Ryland wrapped his lips around. My breathing picks up to match his as he leans in and takes it into his mouth, running his tongue around it. His other hand comes up to smother the yelp that escapes me as he uses his teeth to bite it hard. I struggle, but then he releases it and licks over his bite mark quickly before leaning into my ear.

"I get to do the same things to you Ryland does, but I'm not going to make it pleasurable, so I suggest you stay away from my boyfriend," he rasps before pushing away from me and heading back upstairs.

I allow my head to hang as I get my breathing under control and tuck my boob back into my top. Joke's on him, because I don't mind a little bit of pain, but now I'm going to have to get myself off before bed if I want to sleep. God, he's so confusing. I don't have the energy to deal with his mixed signals crap. I'll worry about it once I've had a few hours of sleep.

I continue to our room and quickly undress, exchanging my work uniform for Miller's big T-shirt I stole. Climbing into bed, I use the image of Ry kissing Miller to get myself off in no time before rolling over and going to sleep.

CHAPTER 6

Not going to lie, it's super hard to get up for church the next morning, but Martha won't let me miss it.

"If you're going to work in a den of iniquity like that, then you're going to have to pray to the good lord for forgiveness," she lectures me as I climb into her car with the three young girls. The boys and Jessica went with James in his car.

I rest my head against the window in the back seat and close my eyes for the trip, the sun shining through the tinted window making me drowsy. Martha has already nagged me about what I was wearing. Apparently black is not acceptable at church, and she made Jessica give me one of her summer dresses to wear with strict instructions to go back to the thrift store for more appropriate church attire this week. Of course Jessica glared as she threw a dress at me. It's a pastel yellow skater dress, which is short, but apparently, it's more appropriate than a tartan skirt and band shirt with black tights, despite it being too small around the boob area for me, making my cleavage kind of obscene. It has pockets, though, so that's a win. I love a dress with pockets.

I only had my boots to wear, and by then, Martha had given up the fight. She just shook her head and muttered to herself.

"What was it like?" Cassie whispers to me, her eyes wide with interest. "Did you see the sex club?"

Next to her, I can see Sally trying not to be too obvious about listening, but she is.

"Nah, nothing like that. It was just a bar—families drinking and having dinner and watching the game before the younger crowd came in for more drinking and dancing," I mutter out of the side of my mouth quietly without moving my head. I'm going to have to find myself an energy drink at some point today, because coffee alone is not going to cut it.

"They say it's easy to get served beer, and that no one checks for IDs."

I shrug. "I don't know, but Miller and Jessica were there, so I'm going to guess that's true. I don't have anything to do with what security does or doesn't do."

"So there weren't people fucking on the dance floor?" Sally presses, and I crack my eyes open to look at her.

"I mean, there could have been, but I didn't see anything like that."

She wrinkles her nose in disappointment, and I

smother a smile before closing my eyes again. The rest of the trip is quiet, with Cassie and Sally murmuring to each other. Stephanie is listening to Martha drone on about her hopes for today's service and the fact that she and James are going out for lunch after church, so we're to find our own way home.

"I'm going to spend the afternoon at the library," I tell her when she pauses for a breath. "I want to get ahead with all my reading so I don't get behind," I tell her, and she turns and beams at me before looking back at the road. I'd thrown my school bag in the trunk before we left the house.

"That's the right attitude, Mackenzie. You'll be getting a scholarship before you know it."

"Here's hoping, Martha," I reply enthusiastically. Sally and Cassie roll their eyes, and I smile.

The parking lot is super busy when we pull in. I asked Cassie what denomination the Standishes were, and she told me it was some weird Lutheran hybrid that had confession and communion just like a catholic church, as well as actual confessional booths. They also call their pastor Father Sweeny which is weird. She told me Martha will expect me to confess my sins to the pastor so that I can start my new life on the right path.

Considering the guys think the pastor may be part of the trafficking ring, it really won't hurt for me to go along with that.

We get out of the car and are joined by James, Jessica, and the guys. Jessica has her hand tucked through Miller's arm, and she's monopolizing his attention. Damn it. I need him to sit next to me so he can point out all the key players.

"Cassie," I hiss pulling her aside. "I need you to run interference for me."

"Huh?" Her brow wrinkles, and she looks adorably confused.

"I need to talk to Miller. Can you distract Jessica?" I ask her, and her eyes widen before they narrow suspiciously.

"Sally said she heard you got it on with Miller and Ryland and their friend Lathan at the party on Friday night," she probes. There's no judgment in her tone, only morbid curiosity.

"How did Sally hear that?" I ask, and she shrugs.

"Sally knows all the good gossip. So is that why you need to speak with him?"

I guess it's as good as any excuse, so I nod.

She grins and quickly agrees. "Sure, anything that will get him out of Jessica's clutches. Though watch out, because here comes Sophie and Stella with their parents, and both of them are glaring at you." She nods behind me, and I whirl around to find both girls on the Turner brothers' arms. I see Lathan, Anders, and Dayton trailing a little bit behind them. Stella looks smug as fuck as she snuggles closely into Max's body. Ry and Sophie look a little less cozy. In fact, she just looks annoyed, and she's glaring at Miller, not me. Jessica quickly extracts her hand from his arm and moves away from him. Well, that's one way to get him on his own. I guess she doesn't want to get caught in the crossfire of Sophie's wrath. She's a smart girl. I won't need Cassie after all. She glances around at all the tension and scurries off with Sally and Stephanie.

I start to wonder if Max spent the night with Stella, but I stop the minute I start to feel a little hurt. I need to focus on getting the job done, and not stupid feelings that are messing with my head. I can look more closely at them when I don't have a case to solve.

Martha greets their parents with enthusiasm, giving them both kisses and hugs. Their mother is just as enthusiastic, with the two men shaking hands and exchanging quiet whispers.

"Oh, Martha, your generosity knows no bounds," the woman gushes, catching sight of me. "You got a new face since last week."

"Mackenzie, come and meet June and Ted. Ted and James are brothers. Mackenzie had a rather nasty last home, so we're hoping that being with us will bring some clarity and purpose to her life she didn't have previously," Martha tells June, who purses her lips. I don't doubt she knows my fake backstory, and I can see her judging me already, but I expected that. June, like her daughters, is slim and blonde, with the same cold and calculating look in her eyes. It looks like the apple didn't fall far from the tree with those two. June's eyes scan me from head to toe, like she's cataloging all my flaws. Her lips purse when her gaze pauses at my cleavage before she nods like she's decided something in her head.

"I'm sure she will flourish under this town's guidance," she says to Martha, who titters her agreement.

Ted is also watching me, but his gaze is predatory. He also heard my fake backstory, and instead of being judgmental, he's intrigued. I feel the need to shiver in disgust but control it.

"It's lovely to meet you." I drop my eyes demurely and smile gently at the other two Standishes.

"You're so lucky to be taken in by Martha and James. They'll see you on the straight and narrow soon enough." June nods. "And confessing your sins to God will wipe your soul clean as well," she encourages me, and Martha claps her hands in agreement.

"What a marvelous idea. I will ask Father Sweeny to take your confession after the service. I'm sure you will sleep better at night once you are given penance."

Penance? I have no idea what they are talking about. Do they mean words of forgiveness from some dude who's probably getting off on hearing the sins of his parishioners? I'm pretty sure that's not going to make me sleep better, but I guess I can pretend.

"If you think it would help." I gnaw on my lip with my teeth, and both James's and Ted's eyes lock onto it —not that June or Martha are paying any attention. They are congratulating each other on such a wonderful idea. Max has been pulled into a conversation with Ted and James, and Stella is still hanging off him like a rash.

The younger kids have moved farther ahead, and it's just Jessica, Sophie, Ryland, Miller, and me remaining in a small circle off to the side of our guardians.

"I'm not sure there's enough forgiveness in the world for you, you whore," Sophie sneers quietly and tries to hang on tighter to Ryland, but he extracts his arm.

"Sophie, that's not okay," he scolds, and her face falls. "I'm going to sit with Miller, okay?" he tells her, and her nose wrinkles in disgust and her eyes turn cold.

"I think maybe you need to confess your sins to the pastor too, Ryland. What would your father say if he knew you had impure thoughts about another man?"

Ryland shakes his head and looks disappointed. "My father is a lot of things, but homophobic isn't one of them. It seems I may have misjudged you, Sophie. You talk about tolerance and acceptance in your little morality club, but you don't actually mean it."

"Having sexual relations with a man is a sin," she hisses, and I see red. I hate this small-minded bigotry.

"Does it only count as half a sin if he's just fucking men half the time and women for the rest?" I ask, putting a finger against my cheek and cocking my head.

"You're disgusting. You should keep your cheap whore mouth shut. God will strike you down with an STI for your sins. What did you do, take them at the same time? Or did they take turns?"

"Hey, don't knock it until you try it. Oh, and don't forget Lathan too. After all, I have three holes for them to fill." Sophie's face turns red with anger while Jessica looks between me, Ryland, and Miller. I think she's wondering if I'm telling the truth or not. Seems like the girl may be a little smarter than her friend.

Before she can spew any more hatred toward me, the crowd starts to head into the church. Sophie spins and flounces off, with Jessica hurrying after her. I see them meet Michelle and Lucy on the stairs, and the four of them follow the older Standishes, Max, and Stella into the church.

Lathan, Anders, and Dayton join us as we mount the steps. "Good morning, princess. How are you feeling?" Anders asks quietly. He and the other two have takeaway coffee mugs in their hands.

"Please, please, please tell me you will grab me one of those next week as well," I plead, groaning. "I'm so freaking tired, and I've had to listen to Martha complain all morning about my clothes. Not even my own mother made such a big deal about what I was wearing at seventeen."

Lathan passes me his with a smile, and I take it. I don't care if it's black as sin, I need the caffeine, but to my surprise, it's as milky and sweet as I like it. I take a sip and hand it back. "Thank you." He just winks.

"I'm guessing she had more important things to worry about, considering what you do for a living," Dayton points out dryly, and he's not wrong.

"Touché." I have to give him that.

"Come on, let's sit at the back, and we can tell you who everyone is." Ry takes my hand and drags me inside. I can feel the rest of them follow behind me. When Ry slides into the pew at the back, Miller puts his hand out and stops him from dragging me next to him.

"We have to sit up front with Martha," Miller grits out from between clenched teeth. Ryland blinks, and I can see how shocked he is that Miller stopped him. He frowns, but Miller ignores him and drags me farther down the front before pulling me into an empty space two rows behind Martha and James.

The other foster kids are sitting between us and them, while Jessica is sitting with Sophie, Michelle, and Lucy, so I suspect maybe Miller isn't telling the truth, and this has more to do with me not getting too close to Ryland.

"What the hell?" I growl as he shoves me in and then sits down, effectively blocking me.

"Ryland would have been too distracted by your pretty tits. Now shut it and let me point out the players," he mutters out of the side of his mouth without looking at me.

Huh, okay, a compliment! I feel like I should take his temperature or something, or maybe he's decided to at least be professional so we can solve this case. He probably wants to get me as far away from his team as he possibly can.

"Okay." My eyes follow his, and he's looking at a pew across from where the Standishes sit. There is a man and a woman. The man is balding but broad shouldered. He's sitting next to a petite, dark-haired woman. "That's David Thompson and his wife, Lisa—Billy's mom and dad."

"So that's the chief of police?"

"Yeah, we definitely think they are involved because of the falsified police reports."

"The younger girls basically confirmed that. They were told that he was a regular at the sex club, which is why their foster sister was too scared to say anything. They didn't say anything about his wife."

Miller shakes his head, still not looking at me. "So far, we don't suspect any of the wives... or at least there's no reason for us to suspect them. Did they mention whether their foster sister had seen Ted or James?"

I shake my head. "No, and I'm pretty sure they would have told me if she mentioned it."

"Hmm, I wonder if they never showed their faces when she was there, or if she was threatened to keep her mouth shut."

"I bet they wore masks. There's no way she would have left those girls there with a sexual predator if she knew. Foster kids are pretty big on protecting one another from what I understand."

He grunts. "Yeah, some of them are, and some of them become predators." He sounds bitter, and I can tell he's speaking from experience, but I won't push him. He will tell me if he wants me to know.

A woman walks up to the front. She's wearing a lovely pale blue fitted dress with matching heels, hat, and clutch. She looks like the quintessential Stepford wife, with perfectly curled hair and artfully applied makeup. She could give my mother a run for poise and style. She greets Martha and June with a kiss on each cheek before greeting their husbands and sitting down in the remaining space.

"That's Melissa Sweeny, the pastor's wife." I look closer and recognize her from the photo I saw of the original group.

My gaze goes back to Billy's parents, and I find them talking to Brock Marshall, the slimeball guidance counselor.

"Okay, who else?" I ask, but before he can answer, the pastor steps up on the dais, and a hush falls over the church as the remaining stragglers find their seats.

CHAPTER 7

"Welcome!" The pastor spreads his hands in a welcoming gesture. He's tall and seems slender under his robes, with perfectly parted blond hair that's combed to the side. His white teeth are practically blinding as he smiles down at us. He's the perfect Ken to Barbie it seems. "It's lovely to see so many faces on this Sabbath. Let's bow our heads and pray."

Everyone does as he says, and he starts droning on. I don't pay attention, but Miller nudges me and nods at a man in the pews across from us. "That's Isaac Palmer. He's the coast guard captain, and rumors say he and Matthew are lovers, but it's only that, rumors. They don't live together and are very rarely seen in public together, so I'm not sure how those rumors started."

I snort quietly under my breath. "After Sophie's little rant, I can't imagine why," I say sarcastically, and

I reach out to give Miller's hand a squeeze. It can't be fun to have that kind of vitriol spewed at you. He allows me to give it a squeeze but removes it without any words. I guess that's progress. "Isn't he Charity's ex? I'm sure someone told me that, and he used to be abusive. That screams trouble."

"Yes, but now he's married to the woman next to him, Lucinda." There's a slim, red-haired woman sitting next to him. Her hair is cut in a short bob just under her chin, but I can't really see any facial features from here except for a flash of red lips. She's wearing a tight black jumpsuit and high heels, and she sticks out like a sore thumb amongst all the other pastel wearing churchgoers. She's also the only other one in the church who doesn't have her head bowed like us. She's studying her fingernails and looks bored as shit.

Movement in front of me has me turning away from the Palmers and to the pews in front of us. I can see Kevin and Charity sitting in the same pew as Max and Stella. They have a little boy with a cast on his arm sitting between them. That must be Charity's son, Deacon. There is another couple sitting next to them, but I can only see their backs, so I'm not sure who they are or if I'd even recognize them.

"Who are those two next to Kevin and Charity?" I ask, nodding in that direction, but before he can answer, the prayer ends, and the congregation mutters their amens. The pastor starts his sermon, and Miller is silent while he drones on about morals and the path of righteousness, his gaze searching the room like he's looking for something. He keeps talking, but when his eyes reach me, he stops looking around and focuses, like he's directing the sermon straight at me. I tune in to what he's saying, and he's preaching about abstinence and purity and ridding ourselves of sins so we may go forward in life with God on our side. I have a feeling today's sermon was specifically prepared to make the new member of the congregation feel so small and pathetic that any words of forgiveness from the pastor will be welcome and cherished. It feels prepared and rehearsed. I drop my head, like I feel shame, even though I can still feel his gaze on me.

Miller turns to look at me and chuckles quietly to himself. The pastor's gaze goes from me to him, his eyes narrowing slightly before he moves past us.

"Wow, that was intense," I comment.

"I would guess it's safe to say you are on his radar."

"Do we think he's the ringleader?"

Miller shrugs his shoulders. "Not sure. Martha didn't require me to confess my sins to him, but that might change if Sophie says anything to her mom about my and Ryland's proclivities." Miller is actually putting aside whatever animosity he holds toward me and being professional, and you could just about knock me over with a feather.

"You two aren't hiding that anymore? Sophie sure seems to know all about it."

Miller shrugs again. "Anders told us about the conversation you overheard last night. We decided that Ry and I didn't need to be quite so discreet, especially after Friday night's rumors. We were playing a stupid drinking game last night at the club, and Lucy said she heard we had a foursome on Friday night. She asked if you had enough holes for all of us, and Ry was annoyed and made some snarky remark about you not needing to have all the holes."

"Holy crap," I whisper, and he smothers a grin.

"Yeah, it takes a lot to get him riled, but when he does, he has a temper. Lucy and Michelle thought it was interesting, but I'm not sure they believed him, so they suggested a drinking game and dared Ryland to kiss me. He did. She and Michelle thought it was fun, Sophie not so much, which is why she was clingy. The decision was made, though, that Max is going to make it clear that he and his brother are interested in some fun and they want you and me. They are hoping the ring will jump at the chance to have leverage over both of them and, in turn, their father."

"The conversation I overheard between Matthew and the two men last night seemed to imply that was what they were hoping for. Well, I guess that's going to give us more chances at bringing the ring down." I nod my agreement, but I knew we were heading this way.

"Yeah, I'm not sure it's going to be that easy. They'll probably expect them to prove their loyalty somehow, but I may get asked to speak to the pastor as well if Martha hears about my homosexual tendencies. I'm sure that won't stay quiet for long."

In fact, Miller and I aren't the only two with their

heads together, whispering during the service. In front of us, Martha and June are doing the same thing.

"And we think the therapist is judging whether we are damaged enough or not?"

"Yes. Brock gives recommendations, and then Daniel says yes or no."

"So he must be fairly high up."

"At this stage, it could still be any of them or none at all. We don't know enough." Miller sounds as frustrated as I feel.

"Well, I doubt it's none of them. You don't have cells like that hidden underground unless you have nefarious shit planned," I whisper dryly.

"Yeah, you're right. We need to get back in and check out those cells."

"I'm going to the library after the service so I can see if we can find any other way to access them, or if there is a map showing how far under the town they are."

"And Max is going to speak to Chief Thompson about Bishop being missing, so hopefully that means they will move his body so we can get back into them. We haven't wanted to risk going back in until his body is moved."

"That's probably smart. Lathan couldn't even see who killed him or where they came from, which is weird. You would think that the security cameras would lead farther away from the cells, but he said there weren't any in either direction, just of the actual cells."

The congregation starts singing, and Miller and I can't talk anymore, so we open our hymnals and pretend to sing along as well.

While we are singing, my eyes drift to Max and Stella. Because there is a gap between the base of the pew and the back, I can actually see Stella's hand drift up Max's thigh. They are sharing a hymnal between them, and it's covering what she's doing from Kevin and Charity's view. Her hand drifts across the front of his pants, and I can see her start to rub circles over his dick. I grit my teeth, and a small growl escapes before I can stop it. Miller's gaze follows mine, and he smothers a snicker as Max pushes her hand away and we see him scold her quietly. She pouts but keeps her hands to herself.

"Poor Max, I don't envy him one bit. Stella won't be happy until she gets her hooks in him."

I keep my mouth shut. I don't need Miller knowing that I'm jealous. Heck, it makes me as bad as him. Nope, going to keep my feelings on lockdown.

The hymn comes to an end, and the pastor drones on again. My attention shifts back to the couple I asked about earlier and never got an answer for. "Who are those two?" I ask him and nod at them.

"Oh yeah, that's Tim and Rebecca. They are old family friends of the Turners. Kevin and Tim are in the same MC, but Tim doesn't have a lot to do with it anymore now that he's married. They run the Mug Shot Diner."

"Oh, I think I walked past there the other day. Tim

was having a tattoo done by Kevin when I went to see Dayton the last time. He seemed a little judgmental. Do we think they are involved?"

Miller shakes his head. "Nah, we're pretty sure they are squeaky clean. Tim worships the ground Rebecca walks on, and they just announced they are having a baby. If they are involved, we haven't seen any proof."

"Well, that's two less to worry about." My eyes scan the rest of the congregation as I wonder who else may be involved with this plot.

"Lathan did some digging into contractors, and it turns out that Ted has a son from an affair he had prior to his marriage with June," Miller announces casually, and my head whips around so I can stare at the side of his face.

"What? I thought they were childhood sweethearts?" I exclaim. "They were in that photo I saw in the cabinet at school."

Miller nods. "They were, but it turns out Ted wasn't very faithful. The son's a little older than Stella, and he owns a contracting company in the next town over. He goes by his mother's name, and the only reason we found him was because his company keeps cropping up on town council records. His company won every single tender or bid for the council for the last five years. It seemed a little strange, so he dug further. He and his dad have a relationship, but it doesn't seem to extend to June and the girls."

"Do you guys think he installed the cells?"

Miller shrugs. "It fits."

We fall silent, and I try to put everything we've learned into order. We know there is a network trafficking young Americans out of the country to be used as sex slaves. This seems to be the epicenter of the missing teens. There appears to be some dark underbelly that exists in this town, but is it a part of the trafficking operation, or is it just an underground sex club?

From everything I've managed to overhear, it sure sounds like it's the hub of operations, and the deaths and missing teens all from the area are definitely suspicious. We could do something about it and eliminate those we suspect are involved, but without knowing for sure, we would just be grasping at straws. We need proof. We also need to find where their records are stored. There must be some record of transactions and where these kids were sold to. MITHOS would like to recover as many of them as possible. They have teams on standby to go in and extract them from their own private hells. Dad and Uncle Theseus are in the process of setting up a rehabilitation center for them. Some people will never get over that kind of trauma, but they want to ensure they have as much help as possible.

The service drags out for about two hours. It's close to midday when we all give our final amen and the pastor excuses us to enjoy the remainder of our Sabbath.

Miller and I stand up, and I groan as I stretch out my back before making for the exit. As we shuffle out of our pew to join the masses leaving the church, I hear Martha call our names. Miller visibly slumps.

"Damn it," he grumbles as we both turn to face the woman who is waving us toward the front of the church instead of going with the flow and leaving.

"I guess we're about to confess our sins." I tuck my arm into his and drag him forward. "Come on, it will be fun. I bet I can make his dick stand up quicker than you can," I tease Miller, and he gives me a reluctant smile but doesn't push my arm away. Progress.

"I bet you can indeed. Just looking down your top has made the whole service very uncomfortable for me," he admits, and my mouth drops open in shock. He chuckles and takes over leading me toward our pretend foster mother.

"Aww, I'm so happy to see the two of you getting along better," she says, clapping her hands together as we approach. "See, I knew the good lord would be great for your spirit."

I have to force myself to smile and not roll my eyes. Miller just grunts. A man approaches us. He's probably in his late twenties, and he's wearing what looks like a guard's uniform. He's quite attractive, with sandy blond hair and dark brown eyes, but they kind of look dead inside. Martha beams at him.

"Hi, Martha, I just wanted to say a quick hello before I have to run off to work." He gives her a kiss on the cheek, and she grabs him before he walks away.

"Oh, Simon, this is Miller and Mackenzie, two of our current foster children. This is Simon. He is one of our success stories. He works as a guard down on the docks. We're so proud of how far he's come since he used to be with us."

"Hi." I smile shyly at him, and Miller just nods his head.

"Hey there. If you work hard and follow Martha's and James's suggestions, I'm sure you'll go as far as I have. Maybe even further." He winks. "Sorry I have to run. I'll catch up with you next week."

He leaves with a wave, and Martha turns her attention back to us. She reaches out and puts her hand on my arm. It's surprisingly cool. "Mackenzie, I'd like you to make use of the confessional before you leave. Rid yourself of all those negative emotions and thoughts so you can really start yourself on a new and enlightened path."

She doesn't say anything to Miller, so I guess he's safe for another day. I sigh and look from her to the confessional over in the corner.

"Father Sweeny always takes confession for about half an hour after service. I'm sure your study will go so much better if the weight on your soul has been lifted," she continues, and I know she's not going to stop until I give in.

Joke's on her, there is no forgiving my soul after all the people I've killed, but she doesn't know that. I wonder if she knows that when I step in there, I'll be gaining audience with someone much more depraved than anything my pretend backstory has committed. I look at her closely, and I can't see any deceit in her eyes, only concern.

"Okay, Martha. If it will make you feel better, then I'll talk to the pastor."

"Dear, it's not about me feeling better, it's about you," she responds, but she gives me a small push toward the confessional. Miller starts to follow me, but Martha swaps her hand from my arm to his. "Let her go alone, Miller. She won't want witnesses to her confession." Miller winces, and I can see she has dug her nails into his arm. Whoa, that seems a little like overkill.

"Hey, Miller." Lathan approaches. "We're just going to grab some lunch at the Mug Shot. Do you want to join us?" I look around, and Ry is being dragged out the double doors by Sophie. I guess she's still trying to put some distance between the two guys.

"What a wonderful idea," Martha gushes. "Mackenzie can catch up after her confession."

"Actually, I'm going to go study at the library. Are you leaving yet? I need my bag out of the car," I ask her, and she shakes her head.

"No, dear. We're having lunch with the Sweenys and a few others, so we have to wait until Daniel is done. How about I go and get it for you while you're in confession?" she suggests.

I didn't put my laptop and gun in it, so I don't have to worry about her snooping. "Thank you, I'd appreciate it."

I can't put it off any longer. It's time to enter the

proverbial lion's den. I walk over to the booth. It's a weirdly elaborate setup, something you'd see in an old catholic church. The door is open a crack, so I swing it toward myself and enter, pulling it closed behind me. As I look around, a little window opens in the wall.

CHAPTER 8

"Ah, hi," I say, pretending to feel awkward. "I guess I'm here to confess my sins."

"Sit down, child, and tell me what plagues you," the same voice from the sermon instructs, so I sit on the hard little chair and gnaw on my lip with feigned nerves, just in case he has a camera feed or something.

"Like what?" I hedge, sounding unsure.

"Well, have you done anything you are ashamed of recently? Something that God may frown upon?" the pastor prompts without being too blatant about it.

"Um, yeah, I guess."

"Why don't you tell me about the last thing you did you were ashamed of?" I kind of want to gag about how creepy this is, but I don't know if he can see me. I start to chew on one of my nails instead.

"Well, um, I kind of let my history teacher bend me over his desk and fuck me. I also got down on my knees and sucked the bartender's dick at the Life Lounge so I could get a job."

There's an awkward silence. "Anything else?" the pastor presses, and I fidget a little before sticking my hands under my thighs and sitting on them, kicking my feet back and forth.

"Um, I had a foursome with three of the guys from my school at a party that I went to. I snuck out from my foster home." I hope this doesn't blow up in my face and he tells Martha I've been sneaking out.

"Oh, and what kind of things did you do during the foursome?" The pastor is breathing a little harder, and I can see movement through the mesh of the confessional. Although I can't make out features, I can see the shadow of his actions, and it looks like he's stroking his cock. Gross.

"Well, I let them fuck my pussy and my ass while I sucked the last one's cock," I tell him in a fake whisper.

"And did you let them fill you with their seed?" he asks, and I nod.

"Yes, I was dripping at the end." If there's something I know how to do, it's getting dirty old men riled up.

"And how did it make you feel?" he asks, and I shrug.

"I liked it. I like sex if I get orgasms, and they made sure I had them. Is that a sin, Father?" I ask, and I hear an exhalation of air.

"Well, I should probably ask a couple more questions so I can establish this correctly." Fuck me, he must have some idiot parishioners. I can't believe he thinks I'm that dumb, but I am a foster kid, so maybe he thinks we're all dumb and needy. "Do you touch yourself?"

"Yeah, I do. It feels good, so why shouldn't I?"

"Well, you should be saving yourself for your future husband. Maybe if you showed me how you touch yourself, I could tell you if it's a sin or not."

Fucking hell, it's all I can do not to screw up my nose. What a fucking creep. I really don't want to touch myself in here. I bet there's a camera. "Can you see me?" I ask, looking around the booth for a camera, and sure enough, up in the corner, a red light flashes. I'll have to get Lathan to erase all the footage once we break this ring.

"God can see you, and he will be judging," is his response.

Fuck! I reach my hand under my dress and pretend like I'm touching myself, sliding my other hand up to caress my breast.

"God can't see through material," the pastor says huskily, his breathing heavier.

Ugh. I drop my hand from my breast and lift the hem of my dress, drawing it back, and at the same time, I shove my hand into my panties, and continue miming touching myself.

"Remove your panties so God can fully see your sins."

I shake my head and start to remove my hand. "I

don't know about this," I start, but the pastor interrupts me.

"Do you want to go to hell, Mackenzie?" So much for anonymous confession. "Shall I tell Martha about everything you've been doing so she can ensure you can't leave the house to commit more sins?" he snaps.

"No, please don't, I need the money from my job," I beg, forcing tears into my voice when all I want to do is choke the life out of this pervert.

"Well then, I suggest you show God how you touch yourself. Take your panties off, pull that dress up, and make sure your legs are fully spread."

If this pastor isn't involved in the sex trafficking ring, I will retire from MITHOS altogether. Shaking with fury, which I hope he thinks is fright, I slide my panties down my thighs and calves, kicking them off when they get to my boots. I spread my legs and lick my finger before running it over my clit, playing with the little ring in the hood a bit. I am not turned on in the least, so the spit is going to have to give me a bit of lube while I fake my way through this.

I close my eyes and rest my head back, and I can hear the pastor's breathing increase. I'm almost positive he's jacking himself off in there.

Before I can start to ramp up my act, I hear a little knock. It's on the pastor's side of the confessional. "Daniel, honey. The Turner boys have just reported one of their friends missing. They could probably use some divine support right now."

"Fucking interfering bitch," I hear him curse

quietly under his breath. Louder, he calls, "I'll be there in a moment, honey."

"I'll wait for you," I hear her say, and I smother the smile that wants to cross my lips. I have a feeling maybe Melissa isn't as naïve about what happens in these confessionals as Daniel thinks.

There's a rustling sound like he just stuffed himself back into his pants before he says,

"Ah, um, we will have to continue this at next week's church meeting. In the meantime, you should pray hard to God and ask him for his divine forgiveness for your wicked thoughts and deeds. You are a sinner, child, and I am not sure that there's anything good to come of your life. I believe you belong to the devil now, but maybe if you pray, God will hear your prayers and send you guidance." I hear him exit the booth.

I drop my hand and pull my dress down.

That all seemed so weird and random. I'm not sure how they are getting away with testing the foster kids and anyone they deem suitable like that. Maybe it's just me, because they already knew of my reputation, or maybe they are actually blackmailing kids. If they are forced to do those sorts of things in front of the camera, then it's no small leap to think they are being forced to do more to keep that footage quiet.

I'll have to tell the guys my theory, but it wouldn't hurt to suggest that Miller should confess during the week and see if he's asked to perform lewd acts as well. Sighing, I bend down and stuff my panties in the pocket of my dress and leave the booth. I can't be bothered with wrestling them back on over my combat boots, and it's not like I'll be flashing anyone at the library.

No one is in sight. The church is completely empty of people, so I head out front, hoping Martha will be there with my school bag. I don't actually need it because I'm not actually going to do schoolwork, but it has my phone in it.

Out on the steps, I find a crowd of people. On one side is Martha, June, Ted, and James. Martha smiles and waves me over when she sees me.

"How did it go?" she asks, and I shrug, not meeting her eyes.

"It was okay, I guess," I tell her, and she reaches out and places a hand on my arm.

"It's the first step to a new life, just remember that," she says gently, and I nod as she passes me my school bag.

My gaze goes to the other group of people at the top of the steps. It's Max, Ryland, and the chief of police with Father and Melissa Sweeny.

"Oh dear." Martha sees where my gaze went. "The Turner boys just told Chief Thompson that one of their roommates is missing," she says, wringing her hands together.

I allow my eyes to widen with shock. "Missing?" I ask, and James nods, pursing his lips.

"Hmm, this is a quiet, friendly town, and we never have any trouble, so I can't imagine what happened to him." Pfft, what crack is he smoking? He even admitted his former foster kids had gone missing.

"Probably fell in with the wrong group of people," June agrees.

"Well, hopefully they find him soon," I say, and I catch sight of Miller, Lathan, Dayton, and Anders waiting at the bottom of the steps. Stella, Sophie, Jessica, Michele, and Lucy are with them.

"Why don't you go and join your friends, dear? There's nothing we can do, and we're still waiting on Melissa and Daniel to go to lunch," Martha suggests.

"Um, we're not friends. I'm just going to head to the library and get some work done. I have to work again tonight, so I don't have a lot of time," I tell her. It's almost one, and I need to be back at the Life Lounge at seven. I'm hoping I can ask one of the guys to run me back to the Standishes' so I can get changed. I head in their direction after waving to Martha and James. Thankfully, Dayton and Anders see me coming, and together with Lathan, they move a little bit further away from the girls so they can't overhear our conversation.

As I go to pass Sophie, she reaches out and grabs my arm. "Where do you think you're going?" she demands, and I snatch my arm out of her grasp.

"Fucking hell, Sophie, what are you, the gatekeeper of all guys in this town? I want to say hello to Lathan and his friends." I nod in their direction.

"How do you know them?" She puts her hands on her hips.

"What's it to you? For someone who is supposed to be the president of some chastity club, you're awfully damn possessive of a lot of men. If you must know, I met Dayton when I had a piercing done the other day, and I work with Anders at the Life Lounge, but you know that, you were there last night," I point out, showing her how ridiculous she's being.

"Keep your loose legs away from them. My sister is dating Max, who is their best friend, and she will not stand for them hooking up with trash like you. I'm sure the governor's aides wouldn't like their sons doing the same thing. It wouldn't reflect well on them."

Fuck my life. What was I thinking, being excited about working a case as a high school student? Fuck this shit. If it wasn't so important, I'd ask Dad to replace me. No more high school assignments for me, but then again, I've known some women and men in their twenties who act like they never left high school at all. That's only in Princess Kensington's superficial social circle, though, not any of the low-life scum I've had to dispose of.

"Sophie, leave her be. Don't waste your breath on trash like her." Lucy pulls her friend away, and I can hear them hissing to one another as I make my way over to the guys.

"Trouble?" Dayton asks, his gaze on the girls behind me, and I roll my eyes.

"Amateur high school shit. Nothing that's going to make me cry." I smile at them. "Would it be okay if one of you gave me a lift back to the Standishes' place so I can get changed before work, and then run me back into town?" I ask.

"Sure, no problem. What time?" Dayton asks before either of the other two can answer. Lathan smirks as Anders pouts.

"You get to run her home, so I don't know why you're upset. I'm going to have to sit in the car and run facial recognition on people coming and going all night again," Lathan grumbles.

"Did you get any hits last night?" I ask him, and he nods, his eyes moving to where Miller and the girls are. Max and Ryland have joined them, and we watch as Martha and her friends start to walk in the direction of Main Street. I guess they are off to have lunch.

"I did. How about I meet you at the library in a little while, and I can fill you in on what we learned?"

"Why don't you come now?" I ask, and Lathan grimaces.

"Max arranged for us to have lunch with Stella, Sophie, and their friends."

I force a smile despite feeling slightly annoyed inside. I'm doing all the freaking work, and they are going around town, lunching. It's no wonder they haven't gotten anywhere.

"Okay, sure. I'm just going to grab a coffee and something to eat, and then I'm heading over there. If Dayton can pick me up about half past three, then that should give me plenty of time to change and get back to the Life Lounge before my shift starts."

Dayton agrees as Max calls his name. The three guys give me a wave, and I leave them be, ignoring the piercing looks both Ryland and Max are giving me.

I follow in the same direction Martha and her group went. I figured they are going for lunch, and I'm sure wherever they go will have coffee. As I walk, I pull my banged up foster kid burner phone out of my backpack and send my dad a message. It doesn't take long for it to ring, and I answer, stopping to sit down on a park bench so I can talk to my dad. I don't want Martha to turn around and demand to know who I'm talking to.

"Hey, Dad." I lean back on the bench and put my backpack next to me.

"Kenzie, honey, is everything okay?" It's his first question every time.

"Yeah, I just needed to hear the sound of your voice," I tell him, trying to wash away the ick I feel from the pastor with the loving sounds of my dad's voice.

"How's the case going?" he asks breathlessly. He sounds like he's walking somewhere.

"It's going," I hedge, and he grunts.

"Talk to me," he demands, and I sigh.

"We have lots of theories, but no proof, and we have to be careful where we stick our noses. It seems like it's a widespread conspiracy... like a lot of the town's major players have a hat in the ring."

"Can I do anything for you?" I shake my head even though he can't see it.

"No. Hopefully now that Max has officially reported Bishop missing, they'll drag him out of the tunnels, and we can explore them. I'm heading to the library. The tunnels are old, even if the cells aren't. They must have been part of the Underground Railroad or prohibition tunnels, and I'm going to see if I can find the entrance to them."

"Well that sounds like a plan. What else?"

"We still haven't found the entrance to the sex club, but there is a service elevator next to the club I'm working at, which Lathan is going to hack, and we're going to see if that leads anywhere, but I think if it did, people would be seen coming and going."

"Have you made any more progress in being asked to work in the sex club?" my father asks, and I screw up my nose.

"Without going into any detail, I have been thoroughly auditioned, and I don't think it will be long before I'm offered a chance to make some more money."

My father clears his throat, and there's an uncomfortable silence. That's been the worst thing about having him as my handler. Neither of us are happy discussing some of the lengths I go through to trap a mark.

"Well, good. I have a chip arriving at the Turners' tonight for the team. Make sure they get it implanted."

"I'm a little surprised they didn't have one. I thought it was standard protocol for all agents nowadays."

"It is, but Team Basilisk is basically the last to have it done. They've blown off all summons every time they've been to the Lighthouse," my dad growls, sounding annoyed, and I chuckle. "They are almost as infuriating as you sometimes."

"Hey, that's a little mean," I whine, and he snorts.

"Truth hurts. How are you all getting along?" His voice softens.

I think for a moment about how I want to answer this.

"Kenzie?" he prompts.

"Now that Bishop is gone, it's mostly smooth sailing. Although it's only been, what, twenty-four hours? Only time will tell," I reply, and hear him huff out a sigh.

"And the part that's not?"

"Miller." I decide to be honest, and again, I hear a long suffering sigh. "Though to be honest, he was better today, so maybe he's coming around." I think back to how he was mostly civil during church.

"Get it sorted, Kenz. Your mom will be very sad if you two aren't at least pretending to be civil. Hell, even the king likes him."

My dad refers to his father-in-law as "the king," even to his face. My grandfather gets a kick out of how irreverent my dad is since he's used to everyone kissing his ass. Mind you, it's because he loves his daughter and she very, very much loves my dad. If it were anyone else, he'd probably have them beheaded.

"Yeah, I'm trying, Dad, I promise," I assure him.

"Oh, and call Katie. She said you have a thing, and you haven't spoken to her since you hit Georgia," he tells me.

"I'll call her as soon as I get a chance. I may need you to send the jet so I can make a quick appearance as Princess Kensington. I promised Katie I'd go with her," I tell him.

"Just tell me when," he replies, and we say our goodbyes. It was nice hearing his voice, and I feel a lot more settled now, the ick factor from church gone.

I shove the phone into my bag and lean back, closing my eyes and soaking up the midday sun for a moment. Hopefully Bishop's body will turn up in a day or two, and we can make some more progress. I'm done with small-town USA and ready to be back into international intrigue, because despite all the drug dealers, crooked politicians, and criminals I've had to take down, I'm not sure I've ever felt as icky as I did in that confessional. I'm not religious, but there is something very wrong with what that pastor is doing. It's sacrilegious as well as criminal.

If I get a chance to arrest that asshole, I swear I'm going to enjoy it.

CHAPTER 9

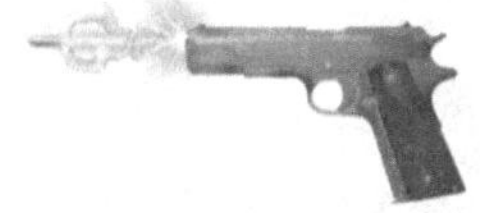

I lost track of where Martha and her group of friends went for lunch, but when I hit Main Street, the Mug Shot diner that I saw the guys in the other day is full of people. I can see both Dayton's and Ryland's cars parked in front. I guess they got there quicker by driving while I was on the phone with Dad.

I desperately need to pee, and I'm starving and need coffee, so I head inside. I'm greeted by a teenager who offers to show me to a seat, but I just want to grab some food and go. It's super noisy with laughter and voices, so I'm assuming the church crowd has filled it to capacity. I see Stella, Max, Dayton, and Anders at one booth and Ryland, Lathan, Miller, and the girls at another. I don't want to sit at either of those tables and be subjected to snide, catty remarks while I'm eating. I ask the girl for a menu and place an order to go—grilled cheese, a cup of tomato soup, and a caramel macchiato. While it's being made, I head in the direction of the bathroom. I don't take long, but when I walk back, I pass a private dining room. The door is mostly closed, but it looks like whoever entered last didn't shut the door properly.

"We have to move that body from the tunnels and plant it somewhere now that he's been reported missing. How did he get there in the first place? And which one of you idiots shot him?" I hear someone say. I stop and look at the decorations on the wall next to the private dining room. Luckily for me, there are photos of famous celebrities who have all eaten at the Mug Shot over the years.

"It wasn't me, but I sent Billy to deal with it while we're at lunch." I'm assuming that's the chief of police.

"Yes, that's a complication we didn't need. It's all well and good getting rid of dead weight with no family or friends, but that kid was the son of Governor Turner's aide. There are going to be questions," I hear someone else grumble.

"And we will make those questions go away. Don't worry, we've got this. It's not our first rodeo," someone else reassures the grumbler.

"I think we need to have another club night sooner rather than later. We need to lock the Turner brothers down. We need some more blackmail material. We have Max Turner fucking that street kid in his office, but I want something on the younger brother too. He's a fag, so it should be easy enough if we offer him that other foster kid of yours, James, that he seems to have taken a liking to." Just like we suspected, they are going to use that footage to keep him under their thumb. We really need to find out where they keep all that blackmail material. Once we take down this crew, we don't want it to fall into the wrong hands.

I hear some muttering but can't make out what's said.

"There's also a shipment coming in next week. We will store it below until we get a buyer." That sounds like Ted, but I didn't hear him talk enough to know for sure.

"Our patrons are getting impatient. They want to see the merchandise up for sale." I don't recognize that voice, but it's definitely a male. I wonder if the women are in the room and listening intently.

"I'll put up a sign saying that the Life Lounge will be closed for a private function on Friday. We'll arrange a viewing of the products soon." That's definitely Matthew.

A commotion in the dining room has me spinning around, and I see Martha, June, Melissa, and Lisa walking toward me.

"Ah, Mackenzie, there you are." Martha smiles, and her gaze goes to the photos in front of me. "Isn't it exciting? All of those famous people have eaten here! The girls and I were just next door in the dress shop. It has some lovely things in it. Maybe you could ask Matthew for an advance on your wages so you can buy more clothes."

"Yes, my Stella and Sophie got a lot of their

wardrobe from there. It's classy and sophisticated." I can hear what June is saying. *Unlike you!*

"Maybe, but for now, I have food to collect and a history assignment to research for. Have a good lunch." I tell them all goodbye and hurry past them, thankful they thought I was starstruck and not actually listening at the door.

I know the men are definitely involved. I look up and see a security camera in the hallway. I'll get Lathan to hack it so we can get an accurate count of who is in the ring. Does that mean the women aren't? They weren't in the room. It's looking like they may be completely innocent in all this and victims of their circumstance like the trafficked teens.

When I get back to the counter, my order is ready, so I thank the server and head back outside. The library isn't far, so I walk in that direction. It's a two-story brick building with arched windows, eight big columns in front, and large double glass doors at the entry. I push them open, and a cool breeze with the scent of books hits me in the face. I smile. I love libraries. They remind me of my dad's office, both at home and at the Lighthouse. My grandfathers also have impressive libraries in the palace and estate.

I look around, but I can't find a librarian or anyone to help me, so I wander until I find a cluster of chairs and a table, and then I make myself at home. I pull a pen and notepad out of my backpack as well as my phone before pushing them to the side and focusing on my food. I unwrap the foil-covered sandwich and take the lid off my soup. The smells that hit my nose are divine, and my stomach rumbles with encouragement. There's probably a sign somewhere that says I can't eat in here, but there's no one around to tell me no, and I haven't seen said sign. If I get caught, I'm going to plead ignorance.

Taking a bite of my grilled cheese is like a religious experience. The bread has the right amount of crunch while the cheese is hot, stringy, and tasty. After my first bite, I break it in half so I can dip a small portion into my soup. That doesn't disappoint either. It's creamy, tangy, and flavorful. I would love the recipe, because this is most definitely not from a can. I could live on this kind of comfort food when I'm home from assignment. It's why my mom's mac and cheese is one if my favorite things in the world.

It doesn't take me long to devour my lunch, and once done, I get up and throw my garbage in a nearby trashcan. Sitting back down, I take a sip of my coffee and look around the area I'm sitting in. There are plenty of book-filled shelves, but I also see a bank of computers, as well as an old-fashioned card filing system from pre-computer days.

I decide my best bet will probably be searching the catalog. I consider using the old card filing system, but that will take a lot longer, and I need the time to explore, so I head for one of the computers and sit down. I grab the nearby mouse, and when I move it, the screen brightens with a welcome message.

Damn, it looks like I need a current Summerville

library card to access their catalog. Now I'm going to have to find someone who works here.

I look around, and there still isn't any sign of anyone on the ground floor, so I head in the direction of the big, sweeping staircase behind the circulation desk at the front of the library. I climb the stairs to the second level and search the rows of shelves for someone to help me. It's not until I get to the very back of the library where the shelves end that I find someone. There is another bank of computers with a seating area for studying, but also a small area dedicated to the history of Summerville. There are photos and knickknacks, manuscripts and plaques. It's also where I find the librarian—a wizened old man, with thinning hair wearing a beige cardigan and slacks. He has a duster in one hand, and I can hear him humming as he works. He's shaking his money maker along with the song in his head, and it's so freaking adorable, I can't help but smile.

"Excuse me?" I call out, but he doesn't hear me. I step a little closer and raise my voice. "Excuse me?"

The poor old thing jumps and whirls around, gasping as he clasps his feather duster against his chest. I feel guilty as fuck. Jesus, I hope he doesn't keel over and die. "Oh my goodness gracious. I didn't hear you at all," he drawls with the slightly raised voice of someone who is going deaf. He has the cutest little round, wire-rimmed glasses perched on the end of his nose, and he's wearing a plaid button-up shirt with a bow tie with frogs on it. He's not as old as I first guessed—maybe mid-seventies.

"Well, a youngin' in my library. I didn't think I'd ever live to see the day again." He looks me up and down, narrowing his eyes slightly before smiling. "What can I do for you, honey?"

"I'd like to access the computer system to do some research, but I need a library card. Can you help me with that?"

You would think I offered him a million dollars with the way his eyes light up and he nods. "Oh my goodness, yes! Right this way. We need to go back down to the circulation desk, but let's take the staff elevator." He puts his duster down and bustles toward the back of the library, gesturing for me to follow.

Smiling, I trail along behind him. My eyes scan over the information regarding the town in the hopes it might mention something about the underground tunnels. Unfortunately, I don't see anything out in the open.

"It's been a long time since I've seen someone your age in my library. I'm afraid with the advent of the internet, the little ones don't venture into her hallowed halls anymore," he laments as we go down in the lift. It's big enough to squeeze a cart of books and a person inside and not much else.

"I'm doing some specific research on the history of Summerville, and I thought what better place to find it," I explain, and he nods before exiting the elevator when we get to the ground floor. He doesn't stop walking until he reaches the circulation desk. He sits down on the chair as I walk around to the front.

"Yes indeed. We have some wonderful history books on Summerville in the library. Now, let's issue you a card so you can get right to the good stuff." He pushes his glasses up his nose and peers at the computer in front of him. He mutters under his breath as he waves the mouse around violently until he looks satisfied and releases it, putting his hands on the keyboard.

"Name?" he asks.

"Mackenzie Walsh. Mac."

"And your address, dear?" he asks after tapping away at the keyboard with one finger.

"Oh, um, I'm not sure, actually. I've only been there a few days and, well, no one has ever told me," I tell him, feeling a little embarrassed. I didn't bother to learn it because I'm not staying, but it fits with the profile of a foster kid, so I'm not too worried.

"Oh!" He sounds slightly perturbed.

"I just moved in with Martha and James Standish," I tell him, and his eyes widen, and the confusion clears as he starts typing.

"Oh yes, okay. I'll just put Serenity House in the address box. Don't worry, dear, everyone knows where that is." I think he's trying to be reassuring, but I'm not sure that it is.

He hits enter, and a machine to the side of the computer hums and squawks and spits out a card. He picks it up and hands it to me, beaming with pride. Fuck, he's cute.

"There you are, dear. Now would you like me to show you where all the town history is kept?" he asks, getting to his feet again. "What exactly are you looking for?" He leads me back to the elevator. "All the Summerville information is back where I was."

"Actually, I'm looking for information on the Underground Railroad or if they had prohibition tunnels in Summerville."

He stops and turns to look at me, his lips pursed. "Oh? Why are you looking for that?"

"History assignment for school. We have to come up with something interesting about the town that maybe people haven't heard of. I know the South's history is tangled up with both of those things, so I thought it would be cool to see if Summerville was involved in either of those."

His expression smooths out, and he nods. "Yes, you're not wrong, the South's history is rich and varied. You don't sound very Southern yourself," he says as we start moving again, the elevator taking us back to where I first found him.

"No, I'm not, but there aren't a lot of options for teenagers about to age out of the system. I was sent down from Maryland, as this was the only opening available for me." We step out, and his eyes go to the faded bruise on my face.

"Bad home?" he asks, and I shudder.

"You have no idea." Again, those pursed lips come out.

"Hmm. Well, you just be careful. What looks sunny and rosy on the outside often hides a rotten core, but you look like a smart girl. Be careful whom you trust and put your faith in."

This guy seems like he's on the up-and-up, and I go with my gut. "Yes. After my experiences at church this morning, I plan on being super careful."

He looks around like he's worried someone is listening. "Keep your head down, work hard, and get out. Despite its appearance, this town is not safe for people in your circumstances." The old man repeats the same warning that Carla had given me the other night. I guess it's not as much of a secret as the ring hopes it is.

"What do you mean? I'm sorry, I didn't catch your name," I ask as my heart rate increases.

"I'm Benjamin Butterworth, but you can just call me Ben, and what I mean is that there is an underbelly in this town that chews people like you up and spits them out. I am not talking about the Raging Scorpions."

"What do you know?" I ask him as we stop in front of a bookcase.

"That to be young and pretty and alone in this town can be dangerous. You shouldn't go anywhere by yourself. If you're talking about the tunnels running under the town, what I know is that someone came and removed everything that mentioned the old tunnel system a few years back."

Just like that, my hopes sink, and I'm back to square one. Of course they would have done what they could to erase any evidence of their wrongdoings.

CHAPTER 10

ANDERS

As I sit across the booth from Stella and Max, it's all I can do to keep my face neutral. Stella was so sympathetic to the fact that our friend was missing. She assured us that Chief Thompson would find him well and safe.

"He probably just drank too much and ended up in some silly girl's bed, or he's sleeping off a hangover. Those parties can get pretty wild, you know," she says indulgently. "I remember them from my high school years. The things that would happen used to make me blush." She giggles.

"How was work last night?" Dayton asks me, changing the subject.

"Good. We had a new girl start, and she did well—not a drug addict like Meri and Sam and not timid like

Carla. I think she's going to be an asset. Matthew certainly seemed pleased with her."

Stella practically hisses at me, and I blink in surprise. "That girl is nothing but a cheap whore. Did you see how slutty she looked? She propositioned Max, you know. I've been considering asking Matthew to let her go. She's going to ruin the club's reputation if she propositions the patrons. What if she uses it to solicit clients here in Summerville?"

"She propositioned you?" I ask, sounding surprised. Mac never said anything to me about that.

Max shakes his head and rolls his eyes. "No, she offered me a blow job shot, not an actual blow job. She said it was the drink special."

I smother a chuckle, and I can see Dayton doing the same. They weren't the drink special last night, but it's fucking funny that she did it to piss Stella off.

"I bet she would have gotten down on her knees right there in front of everyone and sucked your dick if you had even shown an ounce of interest," Stella sneers.

The waitress comes over to take our order, and it puts a stop to her tirade for the moment. Max asks Dayton how work is going, but Stella hisses and narrows her eyes, and we follow her gaze. Mac just walked in the door of the diner. Just when I thought we'd distracted Stella from the topic, she appears.

"I'm not sure how my aunt does it," she mutters, her eyes narrowing as Mac walks up to the counter and places an order before slipping out the back, I'm assuming to use the bathrooms.

"What do you mean?" Dayton asks politely. He's at least putting in an effort to keep up the charade. I can't be bothered.

"Well, she keeps trying to make an effort to make those kids of hers into something, and we all know that's never going to happen. Trash will always be trash, even with an education. I'm sure she will end up on the street, hooked on drugs and selling her body for her next fix. You see it happen all the time."

"I don't know about that. Mac seems like she has a good head on her shoulders," Max says. "She's certainly bright. Ry said she's fluent in French."

"I have no idea how. Didn't you see the bruises on her face and hear the rumors going around the school? Brock told me they are all true, she has a record for solicitation. I bet her pimp beat her up."

The server returns with our drinks, placing them in front of us. All of us but Stella use our manners and thank her. She seems frazzled, but it's busy in here, so it's understandable. Stella just ignores her. I already knew this woman was the kind of trash she keeps calling Mac, but that just adds one more mark against her. It hurts no one to be polite.

Mac returns, grabs her food, and leaves out the front. I'm assuming she's heading to the library like she told us earlier.

"People are able to better themselves," Dayton says

gently, and Stella turns her attention back to us now that Mac is out of sight.

She smiles brilliantly. "Of course they can." She reaches over and pats his hand. "Look at the two of you." She gestures between me and Dayton, and I'm pretty sure the look of confusion on his face matches the one on mine.

"What do you mean?" I ask her, not sure where she's going with this.

"Well, neither of you let the color of your skin or nationality hinder you in any way. Both of you have jobs, albeit neither of them are particularly secure, but you are actively working to better your circumstances," she says condescendingly, and I just stare at her in shock.

The table is dead silent as the three of us try to process the racist drivel that just came from her mouth.

"Nope, I'm out of here." I shake my head, sliding out of the booth to stand next to the table. "I can't sit here any longer and listen to the shit that comes out of your mouth. I'll see you later, Max. I have a meeting with Matthew. Please don't bring her home to our house." I say all of this calmly as Dayton also slides out of the booth.

"Yeah, I've got some work to catch up on at the parlor. See you later." The two of us don't wait for Max to respond. I feel a little guilty leaving him there with that woman, but that's his cover to bear. He looks resigned but mutters, "Goodbye," as I hear Stella whine, "What did I say?"

I don't hear his response. It's swallowed up in the chaos of the diner as we leave. Mac is nowhere in sight. I was hoping we could catch her before she went to the library, but I guess we weren't quick enough.

"Can you believe that girl?" Dayton asks, pushing his fringe, which is longer than the rest of his hair, back off his face.

"What kind of white supremist shit was that? Did Ry or Max ever mention that this town had a problem with that sort of thing?" I ask him, and he shakes his head.

"No, and you would think they would have mentioned it, but now that I think about everyone we've met since we've been here, they are predominantly white."

"Lucy and Michelle aren't," I point out, nodding through the window at the group of people the other half of our team is with.

"No, but they also don't live with their families. They are obviously here for a specific reason, now that Lathan has discovered who their fathers are, but what?"

"I guess we'll find out eventually. I have to go meet Matthew over at the club. I'll see you at home after?" I ask him, and he nods.

We go our separate ways. Our cars are parked on opposite ends of the street, since we were too late to grab ones right in front like Ry and Max did. I park my truck in the club parking lot and go into the alley, knocking on the side entrance. Matthew said he'd be here checking inventory.

It doesn't take long before he sticks his head out. "Anders, good, just in time. That shipment of wine was delivered earlier, and we need to move it to the basement to store it. The senior chapter of the morality group has booked the club on a weeknight for some paint and sip thing... or maybe it's a book club thing. I don't know, but the wine was a deal Melissa Sweeny arranged. I need help moving the barrels. They are freaking huge." He holds the door open, and I enter, letting it close behind me.

"You weren't expecting barrels?" I ask him, and he snorts, shaking his head. "No, I was expecting a few cases of bottles. This is enough wine for fifty book groups." He leads the way into the back, past the dry storage, and to the door that's next to the walk-in refrigerator. "There's no way I can fit them up here, so we are going to put them in the basement storage until I can speak to Melissa about what she wants to do with them. It's not like they can dip wine glasses into the barrel. She'll need to decant the wine somehow."

He opens the door that leads to the alcove that Mac and I put the empty kegs in last night. They are gone, and in their place are some fresh ones, but there are also three large wooden wine barrels taking up the rest of the space. They are as high as my waist and probably three feet across.

"Wow, they are huge. How are we going to get

them into the lift?" I ask him, and he grimaces. "I think we're going to have to roll them on their ends. Between the two of us, we should be able to handle it." He pulls out a card and swipes it across the reader. The elevator doors open, and he reaches in and presses a button that I assume is going to keep the door open while we transfer the wine.

"We'll do it one at a time. I have a dolly in the basement, which should make things easier to move once we get down there."

Together, the two of us move a barrel onto the elevator. It isn't easy. The round shape of the barrels makes them difficult to grip, but we finally figure out a system that works, and we get the first one into the elevator. He presses a button, and the doors close, then I feel us move down. When the doors open, he presses a button again to hold them in place. He steps out and gets a hydraulic pallet lift and wheels it back.

"Okay, if you tip the barrel on the edge, I'll slide this underneath, then you can walk next to it to make sure it doesn't tip either way."

I chuckle. "Hundreds of liters of wine would make a mess."

We do that, and once the lift is under it, it's a breeze to move. I just walk next to it to support it. We stack them in a spare space in the back of the room. There are all sorts of things down here—poker tables, slot machines, even one of the cages from the dance floor at the top of the club. I know the hinge is broken, and we're waiting for it to be repaired. I didn't realize this was where he stored it.

By the time we get the third one down here, we've both worked up a sweat and are breathing a little harder.

"Come on, let's grab a drink." Matthew slaps my shoulder, and we head back into the club. He leads the way out to the dark bar, only turning on the lights behind it. He grabs a couple of beers then slides one across to me. He holds it up, and we clink them together.

"Cheers to good help. Thanks, man. Keith messed up his back last time we did that, so he can't help anymore."

"You've done that before?" I ask, not hiding my surprise as Matthew takes a long drink of his beer.

"Yeah, those women are always having wine nights. I think they sell the rest on the side, or maybe they have amazing wine cellars at home, who knows, but it's at least every six months or so."

"Huh?" I take a sip of my own beer, the cold liquid soothing my parched throat. Despite how fit I am, that wasn't easy. Those barrels were heavy.

"Listen, speaking of good help, we're closing down on Friday night. I have a private party that we cater, and I was wondering if you wanted to earn some extra cash. The money is good, and the perks are off the charts. The clients like looking at hot young bartenders."

I let my eyebrows jump with interest and nod

eagerly. "Yeah, man, that would be good. I'm always up for a bit of extra money, but what's the catch?" I ask, sounding a little suspicious. "Sounds too good to be true."

"Good, well then, I have a task for you. That new waitress, Mac? I need a video of you fucking her in the dry storage. I want some blackmail material to hold over her. I want her to serve at this private party too, and she has to be topless. A video of her having sex with you that I can show her foster mom if she doesn't cooperate is exactly what I need."

"Oh, ah…" I hedge, not wanting to seem too eager, and he waves a hand at me.

"The girl was a pro back in Maryland, so I'm sure you won't have any problems. I'll make it clear to her that it would be beneficial if you feel relaxed on your break. She's not stupid, I'm sure she will jump at the chance, but just in case, I want the video footage."

"Don't you have any of the blow job she gave me?" I ask, and he grimaces.

"No, it couldn't see below the counter. All those cameras are focused on the registers, so I know if someone is stealing from me. The dry storage is perfect."

"Yeah, okay, she's a hottie. I'll happily bend her over if that's what you need."

"Thanks, and I'll be happy to give you the extra work." He holds out a hand, and I shake it, sealing the arrangement. I hope I get a chance to let Mac know what's happening before tonight.

We finish off our beers, and Matthew asks me questions about Bishop. I have to pretend like I have no knowledge of his whereabouts and feign sadness, but before long, I take my leave and head home. I'm hungry, and Stella ruined lunch for me. I might grab a sub on the way home and then try to catch a few minutes of rest before this evening. I can't deny that I'm excited to get my hands on Mac. I didn't get to return the favor last time, so I'm hoping to return it tenfold tonight. I can't wait to see how her pussy feels wrapped around my dick. Fuck, I'm hard just from thinking about it, and it's uncomfortable behind the slacks I wore to church. Maybe I'll have a quick shower and rub one out. That way, I won't embarrass myself when I finally get my hands on her lush ass.

CHAPTER 11

"So there *are* maps and information on the tunnels somewhere, but you're not sure who has it?" I cross my fingers metaphorically, but when he shrugs, my hope fades.

"There was, but if I could hazard a guess, they are probably all destroyed by now. I'm pretty sure there's some kind of illegal trade going on in this town and those tunnels are the key to it."

"What makes you think that? And can you tell me who checked everything out?" I ask him, and he shakes his head.

"No, I wasn't here, and I didn't notice until a few months after it must have happened. By then, Jean, whom I shared this job with, had passed on. Rest her soul."

My stomach sinks, and my excitement fades away. "So there was information about it, but now it's all gone?"

"Yes. It was from the Underground Railroad that ran from the coast here up to Savannah. They used to smuggle them in here because it wasn't as well patrolled as the port there. Later on, it was used to smuggle liquor down from Savannah and distribute it to surrounding counties during prohibition. Whoever took it was thorough, but they missed a book." He reaches into the bookcase and pulls out a large, hardback book. *Life in Summerville. A Photo Display by CJ Smith.* He flips it open, and there, across the two middle pages, is the layout of the town, and over the top of it is a vellum map of the underground tunnel network, and it shows the entrances. "Is this what you had in mind? It goes on to give you the history of the tunnels and more details about the families who ran them. It's fascinating. Actually, the people you live with now, the Standishes, go way back to the time of slave trading, which is kind of ironic." He mutters that last little bit.

"So what else do you know about the underbelly of this town?" I ask, deciding to push my luck. Ben seems to know a lot about things others may not talk about.

Ben closes the book and hands it to me before crossing his arms and leaning against the shelf he just pulled the book from.

"We get a lot of out-of-towners a couple of times a month. They blow in, spend a lot of money, and leave just as quickly. I'm not sure if it's drugs or what, but I did overhear them talking about a sex club."

"A sex club here in town?"

"Yes. As a homosexual in this town during a time when it wasn't accepted, you learn to keep your ears and eyes out for the subtext in conversations. This sex club isn't one of those ones you might find in big cities, ones with paid exclusive memberships but are out and proud for the world to see—no, this one is a dark and dirty secret hidden where only people with the right 'friends' are invited in. This is not a legit thing with rules and regulations that a patron needs to follow for the safety of all involved. This one is dark and disturbed, and not everything is consensual. Like I said, you need to be very careful, my dear, that you don't end up on the wrong end of it."

"Thank you for sharing that with me." I reach out and give his arm a squeeze. I can see his concern for me in his eyes, and I don't want this kind old man worrying about anything. "I'm more than I might seem. I know how to handle myself." That's all I can say unless I want to give myself away. "And I have a circle of people who will look after me when the time comes. You never know. This underbelly may have just tried to cash their last check."

He doesn't look so sure, so I change the subject.

"Can I check this book out?" I lift it into his line of sight.

"I'm afraid I can't let that one leave the building. It's the only remaining record of those tunnels, and I really want to preserve it."

"Damn." I can't hide my disappointment.

"Tell you what. How about we photocopy the main

page showing the layout of the town and the old entrances to the tunnels, and then we can do the same thing for the overlay? You won't get the same effect because it will be on paper, but it will still show you everything."

"Yeah, okay, that works," I tell him, and he grins.

"Follow me." He leads the way to the other side of the first floor to a photocopier that's sitting there. "It will just take a moment to switch on. I don't bother anymore because no one ever comes in to use it."

He flicks the switch and then leans against it while it makes a humming sound that says it's waking up. "You know, there used to be an entry in the library in the basement. It's all boarded up now, but we are one of the oldest buildings in town," he tells me proudly.

I open up the book and peer at the map. Sure enough, the library has an entrance. It shows at least seven or eight more entrances throughout the town. Funnily enough, the basement of the Life Lounge, which used to be a printer many years ago, shows an entrance, but there hasn't been enough traffic coming and going for it to be the regular entrance on open nights.

Ben leans over me. "This is the church, although it's not the same building that used to be there during that time, so I'm assuming that entrance was closed when the new church was built ten years ago. And that entrance there is on the grounds of June and Ted Standish's place. It's listed with the historical society, so their entrance may very well still be intact."

I can see the forest where the ranger's shack is. It doesn't show an entrance on it, but the tunnels run underneath. I'm assuming it's a new one.

"What's this section?" I ask, noticing an anomaly on the map. It looks like one large, central space, but then one side of it looks like its cordoned off into rooms, kind of like the cells but on the opposite side of town from the ranger's shack.

"I'm not sure." He shakes his head. It's a very large area, and I'm wondering if maybe that's where the sex club is. When I look at the corresponding building above it on the map, it is a large building, but it isn't marked.

"What's this building?" I ask him, pointing it out.

He leans in and looks. "That's the movie theater, roller skating rink, and arcade now, but back then, it was the hotel." His eyes widen with excitement, and he pokes at the empty space I inquired about. "Oh wow, rumor has it, the woman who ran the hotel also ran a brothel and a speakeasy on the side. What if that's where it was, underground? That would explain that big area with small rooms." He beams like he solved world hunger, and I can't deny my own excitement.

That makes sense. Lots of foot traffic, and no one noticing extra people coming and going if it's an entertainment precinct with a large amount of patronage.

Ben quickly makes me copies of both the town map and the tunnel overlay.

"Would it be alright if I had a look in the basement?" I ask him as we finish up. I want to see if the boarded up entrance has been disturbed.

"Go ahead, dear. I'll put this back on your table if you want." He takes the map from me. "Take the elevator down. We store all our mistreated books and old, outdated things down there. One day, I'll find time to rebind or fix them, but until then, that's where they live. I won't join you though. I can't leave the library unattended, you understand, and the dust gets up my nose. My poor old bones can't handle the cold either. I'll hang on to these things until you're done," he tells me as we head back to the little elevator. At the ground floor, he steps out but leans in and presses the button again, swiping a card over a security thing much like the one outside the Life Lounge.

"Hey, our elevator to our basement at the Life Lounge has one of those too." I point to it before looking at his swipe card. There's a logo on the side, but I can't make it out.

"Yeah, it was a city-wide mandate. All city buildings, businesses, and homes with basements had to have them installed so that random people couldn't just wander into basements by accident. They were worried about lawsuits."

"And the same company installed them all?" I ask, and he nods.

"Yes, a company in the next town over won the bid, and the city paid for everyone who had basements with elevator or stair access to install them. Pain in the ass if you ask me. Nobody just wanders into a basement by mistake, but it is what it is."

My mind is whirling as the little wrought iron gates close on me, leaving Ben on the outside. He waves, and I wave back absently as I descend.

"The light switch is—" I don't hear the location because he disappears from sight.

The elevator goes dark as I sink into the basement, and I pull my phone out of my pocket and turn the flashlight on. As the doors open and I step out, the room lights up. Oh, that must have been what Ben was trying to tell me. It's motion activated.

I wrinkle my nose as the odor of dust and mold hits me. There are tables with books piled high on them, but as I get a little closer, I decide that they've been down here a long time. Ben's going to have his work cut out for him if he plans to restore them. I accidentally bump one table, and a pile of books tumbles to the side, and a mouse runs out. "Way more work."

I was expecting it to be a little basement, but as I look around, the size of the room is a lot bigger than I expected. Moving away from the elevator, I walk through shelves that have all sorts of crap stacked on them. Of course there are more books, but there are also knickknacks galore as well as a very old photocopier, a couple of old TVs, some computers circa the late eighties, and some VCR players. Farther down is a whole library of VCR tapes. The next shelf has some double-stacked boom boxes, and next to them are audio books on tape.

I guess this is where they store all their outdated stuff instead of getting rid of it. Farther down, I find a whole floor to ceiling shelf of vinyl records. There's everything from movie soundtracks to classical to hits of the seventies. I'd love to be able to flick through them, but that's not going to be possible.

I've reached a wall, but there's another door. I turn the handle and push through to find another storage room. This one smells even dustier. The light turns on as I step into the room. They've obviously had those features updated, even if they haven't touched all the crap stored in here.

The books in this room are much older, all hard-bound with leather and foil accented covers or stamped leather. There are a couple of ancient type-writers, and a really cool old cash register that wouldn't look out of place in an old-fashioned malt or candy store.

I bypass all the cool stuff, even though I desper-ately want to fiddle with things and make my way around the walls. No one has been down here in years. There's a fine layer of dust across everything, even the floor, and I leave footprints behind me. Finally, I get to the old tunnel entrance. It's tucked away behind another set of shelves, and I never would have seen it unless I walked the perimeter like I did.

Although, it's not boarded up like Ben said it was. The door has a plank across it, but it's easy enough to lift out of the way. I go to turn the handle when I hear something. I pause and listen, my heartbeat increasing as I try to breathe quietly.

I hear something again, and as I go to turn around, a hand wraps around my mouth, and I find myself pressed up against a hard body. I start to struggle, but a low chuckle has me stilling.

"I thought you were supposed to be a super spy, but you were so distracted you weren't keeping an ear out for anyone else," Lathan scolds right next to my ear before releasing me, and I spin around.

I smack his chest. "You scared the crap out of me. You're right, I wasn't paying attention. I didn't even hear the elevator leave and come back."

"I couldn't find you when I arrived, but I saw your backpack. The nice old man at the circulation desk told me you were down here and swiped the elevator to send me down. I think he thought we were having some kind of secret rendezvous, because he winked at me." Lathan scratches his head, and I smother a smile.

"That, or he thought you were cute," I tease him, and he blushes. So freaking adorable.

"What have you found?" he asks, peering over my shoulder.

"This is one of the entrances to the tunnel system under the town," I reply, then I tell him what Ben told me about most of the records being destroyed. "But luckily, he has one that was missed. I have a photocopy, and we can explore the entrances." I wrinkle my nose. "Actually, I can do Monday, Tuesday, or Wednesday, but I have to work the rest of the week."

"It's risky for you to sneak out. Maybe we could do it during the day. Max would cover for us at school. We'll have to talk about it. It really depends on when they move Bishop's body."

"Oh! I overheard some of them talking. I couldn't see everyone in the room, but Chief Thompson said he was having Billy move him today."

Lathan's eyes widen at my news. "That's good. We'll be able to get in there, maybe tonight while you're at work."

I'm annoyed that I can't go with them, but I get it, we need to explore the tunnels. "Fine, but there's nothing stopping us from looking at what's behind that door now," I suggest, and he nods and pulls out his phone to use the flashlight.

"We can't go too far. If we take too long, the old guy will come looking for us," Lathan warns as I reach for the handle.

"That's okay, we'll just make it look like we're making out down here. I'm sure he will be thrilled." I chuckle and turn the handle, pulling it toward us.

To be honest, I expected it to be boarded up behind the actual door, but instead, to my surprise, it's open, and a rush of cold air hits me in the face. "Huh?"

"Not what you thought?" Lathan asks, and I shake my head.

"No, Ben was sure it was boarded up, so that's what I was expecting. We know no one's come through this way in a long time. It would have shown in the dust."

"Not necessarily," Lathan argues. "New dust could have covered old footprints."

"Yeah, I guess. Come on, let's have a little look." Before we step into the tunnel, he gets the plank of wood that was barring the door and sticks it in the gap so the door doesn't close fully.

The tunnel is dark, and the small spot of light from Lathan's phone is enough to illuminate the floor in front of us. This tunnel is skinnier than the one from the ranger's shack. There's barely enough room for us to walk side by side. It also doesn't go in a straight line.

The two of us are quiet as we make our way down it. Although I'm dying to ask him questions, I'm not sure if the noise will carry, and I don't want anyone to hear us in case somebody else is down here.

I'm not certain how far we've gone when the tunnel opens up and splits, branching off in two directions.

"Crap, I'm not sure which direction we went in, so I have no clue where any of these lead to," I whisper to Lathan.

"We need a compass. I think I have an app on my phone," he whispers back, but before he can look, a sound down one of the tunnels has us freezing.

I strain my ears to listen. It's voices, and sure enough, they are floating down the tunnel like I suspected they might.

Lathan grabs me by the hand and pulls me back into our tunnel. There's a small alcove not far back, and we squish into that. Lathan's body is pushed flush against mine, covering me completely, and his dark clothing hides my light-colored dress. He puts a hand over my mouth, and I roll my eyes. Like I'm going to talk? He flicks the light off on his phone, and we're plunged into darkness.

CHAPTER 12

We wait, my heart pounding with adrenaline as the voices come closer to us. It sounds like two male voices. I shift slightly, trying to move Lathan off me so I can hear better, but he keeps me pressed against his body, his arms braced against the wall next to my head. The rustle of his clothes as he breathes makes it difficult for me to make out the conversation. I wriggle a little more, and he pins me harder as he presses his mouth against my ear.

"Stop moving. They are going to pass us any moment, and you're making it tricky for me to concentrate," he whispers, his voice husky and deep, sending a shiver of desire through my veins. I wriggle a little more, but the feeling of his hard cock against my ass has me pausing and inhaling sharply. "Exactly," he hisses, but we fall silent as the voices get even closer.

"You're lucky the boss didn't kill you too. You jumped the gun, showing that asshole the tunnels."

The voices become clearer as they pass through where we were just standing. I don't recognize it, but I do know the one who replies.

"Nah, he was cool. I'm pretty sure he would have been perfect, and if not, he would have had plenty of money to spend at the club. As a bored, rich child of a politician, he practically oozed corruption." I can hear the sneer in Billy's voice. I try to push Lathan out of the way so I can see who the other person is, but he keeps me trapped. He spins his body, still holding me in place, and reaches his hand around the corner and snaps a couple of photos on his phone.

"Where are we going to dump this asshole?" the other voice asks.

"We'll take him out to the hot springs and weigh his body down. We can tell people he drowned after drinking too much. He disappeared after the party, after all," Billy replies, his voice fading as they get farther away.

"And the bullet hole in his head?" the voice asks dryly, but the response is lost with the distance.

I push Lathan, hoping he will move, but he turns around to face me at the same time, and I end up knocking his phone out of his hand. It clatters to the floor. "Shit, sorry," I whisper, hoping I didn't smash his screen or anything.

"It's okay, I have a cover on it, but stay still so you don't step on it." He crouches down and feels around in the dark. There isn't a single bit of light to be seen, so I know he's going to have trouble finding it. I hold my breath as I wait for him to locate it, but my impatience grows, and I start to step forward to help just as he goes to stand up.

"Found it," he starts, but his head gets caught on the skirt of my dress, and his upward movement is impeded. A woosh of breath leaves my mouth as my bare pubic mound makes contact with his face, his hands coming up to steady himself on my calves so he doesn't fall over with the impact.

"Mac," he mumbles, and I bite my lip to stop myself from giggling. "Why aren't you wearing any underwear?" Lathan's voice is muffled, and his warm breath drifts across my pussy, making me shudder with anticipation, but I hold still.

"The pastor made me take them off?" I whisper as he breathes out another large breath that makes me want to moan, and he's not even touching me.

He mutters a curse. "That bastard. I have a bullet with his name on it for that alone." His hands caress my calves, and I can practically feel him warring with himself.

I pull my skirt back so he's not suffocating under there and slide my hands into his hair, not wanting to force him to make a choice. He needs to do that himself, but I want to let him know I'm not opposed to anything that may be going through his mind at the moment. Hell, the same thing is running through mine. I'm dying for him to stick his tongue out and have a taste. Using my nails, I run my hands through his hair, and he shudders and takes a large inhale.

"God, you smell incredible," he mutters, and I run my nails over the back of his head as he tentatively swipes his tongue through my folds. I don't let him get away with that hesitant crap though. I want this, and I want it now, and I am fully on board with what he has in mind.

"Harder," I beg breathlessly, and I guess he takes that as permission, so the next swipe of his tongue is firm and confident, and I feel my eyes roll back in my head as Lathan feasts on my pussy. He doesn't fuck around. He uses his mouth, lips, and tongue and eats my cunt like he's a condemned prisoner and I am his last meal on Earth. It's almost too much. I feel tears leak out of the corners of my eyes as he keeps me on the precipice of pleasure, riding that crest perfectly without sending me over.

"Please, God, please, more," I plead, my hands clenching his hair.

He chuckles darkly as he pulls away just as I was about to come.

"No," I sob out, but he takes pity on me. Running two fingers through the mess he made, he slides them home. I cry out with relief as my channel flutters around them. He curves his fingers slightly and pulls them out before slamming them home again. My knees buckle, and it's all I can do to stay standing as he wraps his lips around my clit and sucks hard. That, combined with his fingers inside me, sends me flying over the edge, my orgasm rolling through my body, making me moan loudly. He eases off on my clit but continues to finger fuck me, drawing out my pleasure.

I'm impatient now, so I tug on his hair and drag him up my body. He smiles and wipes his mouth on my thigh before removing his fingers, giving into my demands. He stands up and takes my mouth with his, the taste of me on his tongue musky and heady.

While our tongues tangle, fighting for dominance, I reach down and undo his belt, then the button and zipper on his pants before shoving them lower. One of his hands hooks the neckline of my dress and drags it lower so my breasts tumble free. He takes one into his mouth, sucking and laving his tongue over the nipple, and the roughness of my lace bra creates an exquisite friction with his wet mouth. Reaching into his boxers, I stroke my hand up and down his length a couple of times, a smile stretching across my lips at the sound of his moan. Hearing him come undone is intoxicating. He reaches under my thigh and lifts my leg, wrapping it around one of his hips before pushing his boxers down and notching his hard, smooth length at my entrance. There's no light, but I can feel his eyes on mine as he slowly sinks into me. My head bangs back against the wall, and I moan at the sensation. He's hot and hard and long, and he feels amazing.

"God, you feel good." He leans in and kisses me as he rolls his hips, hiking my leg higher so he can get a better angle. Lathan thrusts into me over and over. Our mouths don't part as I have one of the most sensual experiences of my life. Never before have I kissed this much during sex, and I have to say, I don't hate it. In fact, I'm a fan, and he soon has me back on the edge of an orgasm. This time, he doesn't draw it out. Instead, he keeps fucking me through it, and my whole body shudders as I come hard. My own pulsing channel drags him over the edge as well. Our guttural moans of enjoyment echo loudly through the tunnel, and I can only hope and pray that Billy and his companion are far enough away that they don't hear us.

CHAPTER 13

Despite the cool air in the tunnel, both Lathan and I have worked up a sweat with our little team bonding exercise. He still tastes like me when he leans in and gives me a quick kiss. I dig my panties out of the pocket of my dress and use them to clean up the mess Lathan left behind. Grimacing, I throw them in the corner of the alcove as Lathan bends down to retrieve his phone once more. This time, I don't thrust my pussy into his face by accident.

"Come on. The old guy has to be wondering where we are by now." He grabs hold of my hand while switching the flashlight back on so he can guide us back the way we came.

I chuckle, but I am secretly pleased that he's holding my hand. I'm slightly embarrassed about how ridiculously girlie I feel, but it's kind of nice not to fuck, kill, and escape before the cops arrive. It kind of makes me long for a bed so we can snuggle. I bet

Lathan is killer at snuggling, and I'd really like to try it out. God, I'm turning into such a sap.

When we arrive back in the room, he releases my hand while I close the door and bar it again. He is scrolling through the images to see what he managed to capture, if anything, in the tunnel.

"Well, we recognized one voice, and that was Billy. The other guy is Ashley. That's Daniel and Melissa Sweeny's son," he explains as he looks through the photos.

"The pastor's son?" I ask as he holds out the images he caught. Right there, in full color, are two obvious guys—one with Bishop's body draped over his shoulder.

"Yeah, he and Billy are tight, so it's really no surprise." The photo only shows the back of the two men, but there is no missing Billy's hulking form or Bishop's limp body.

"You'll have to point him out to me at school on Monday," I tell him as the two of us make our way back through the room to the elevator. We press the button, and the doors slide open. I hit the G for ground, and the doors close behind us. "Oh, hey, Ben was telling me that the town council had all the card scanners installed by the same company. He practically suggested that they all operate the various lifts throughout town. We just need to get our hands on one of those cards, and Anders and I can use it to explore under the club."

The elevator comes to a stop, the cage doors open,

and the two of us step out. Before Lathan can respond, we notice a very pissed-looking librarian. Ben's standing there with his arms crossed and his toe tapping, looking at his watch, but then his eyes run the length of us, and although he is still pursing his lips with annoyance, I can see his eyes sparkling with mirth.

"If I'd known it was going to take that long for the two of you to have a quickie, I wouldn't have sent him down to find you." His gaze stops on Lathan, and his eyes run the length of him. "I have to say I am impressed. High school boys never looked like you when I was there. More's the shame."

I giggle as Lathan blushes, and Ben shoos us away. We head back to where I left my bag. Lathan left his laptop there as well, and as we both sit down, he pulls it out. I sit down next to him, showing him the map Ben printed for me. He taps his keyboard a few times and brings a digital map of the town up on his screen identical to the one I photocopied. I show him the larger area under the movie theater and tell him what Ben told me. His eyes widen with excitement.

"That's great, Mac. We never would have found that without this map." I preen a little under his compliment. I'm confident in my skills, but it's nice to get a little praise. It's also not particularly true, since I'm sure once we searched the tunnels, we would have found it, but it could have taken a while. "I'll let Max and the guys know when I get home. I have a card duplicator at the house, so if we can get our hands on one of those, then we are good to go."

"Promise you won't go and explore without me?" I ask him, and he wrinkles his nose.

"I can't promise that. You aren't as flexible as we are, and we want to finish this."

I pout, but he has a point. "Fine. Before we leave, if you distract Ben, I'll try to get his card. I noticed he keeps it next to his computer on the circulation desk." Lathan quickly agrees to the plan. "Okay, so we have a possible location for the sex club, and we have the possible location of where the merchandise is kept. What else do we know?"

"I got a hit on those two men you asked me to run facial recognition on." He taps his keyboard, the map disappears, and two profiles pop up on the screen. I recognize both men as the ones talking to Matthew last night. He points to the Asian one.

"That is Hinata Adachi. He's the head of a prominent yakuza gang in Japan and Lucy's father. The other one is Amir Habib, and he fronts a Lebanese mafia style group and is Michelle's father. Both groups are suspected to be heavily involved in gun and drug smuggling and human trafficking."

"Really? Huh, I never would have guessed Michelle's nationality as Lebanese. She looks African American, but maybe her mother is. And their daughters live with Sophie Standish as exchange students? That seems convenient. Why?" I ask Lathan, and he shrugs.

"Not sure why that would be the case. Maybe it's an everyday reminder that someone else is pulling the strings."

"And we're sure this part of the ring is not the head of the snake so to speak?" I ask him, and he shakes his head.

"No. Most of the missing kids I've managed to find have shown up in Europe. We think the ring leaders are located over there somewhere. Both Hinata and Amir have ties to a Swiss bank and homes in Zürich." He pulls up the images of all the missing teens Miller had shown me on my first day. "These ones that are highlighted have appeared in porn produced by a Russian production company located in Berlin."

I lean back on my chair and think about what we know. "Okay, so how do they get the kids from here to Europe then?"

Before he can answer, there is a commotion at the front of the library. Ben leads Ryland, Miller, and the girls they are always hanging with back to our table. Lathan slams the screen of his lap top closed as they approach, and Ben looks annoyed about something.

"There you are." Sophie smiles insincerely, ignoring me and focusing on Lathan. "When Lucy asked where you went, and Ryland explained you were doing homework at the library, I thought it would be a good idea if we all joined you."

They spread out around the large table.

"We didn't realize you were keeping questionable

company though," Lucy sneers, and Michelle and Jessica giggle, but it's kind of half-hearted.

"If you want to check out books, you're going to have to sign up for a library card," Ben announces, glaring at me like it's my fault they are interrupting his quiet, serene sanctuary.

"We won't need to check them out," Sophie says, dismissing him without even looking at him. Ben huffs and storms off back to his desk, muttering about how he's glad he never had asshole teenagers.

"Annoying old fag," Michelle mutters under her breath. I feel my eyes widen before I look at Miller and Ryland, who pretend they didn't hear her, though I can tell by the clench of his jaw that Miller is not so blasé.

They ignore me and start talking amongst themselves about homework and gossiping about irrelevant stuff at school. None of them give any indication that they know what their parents are up to. Jessica gets up and walks into the stacks. She seems to be making more of an effort to study. I didn't even see her grab her bag when we left the house, or maybe Ry or Sophie drove her home to retrieve it. I guess being a foster kid, you have to work that much harder to prove yourself. I really do feel sorry for her despite her bitchiness. She's just doing whatever she needs to fit in and feel needed, and I can respect that.

Lucy, Michelle, and Sophie put their heads together and start to whisper. I ignore it and pretend to keep doing homework. I get a highlighter and make notes on the map where the entrances to the tunnels are from the overlay section. It gives me a better idea of how many there are. Thankfully Sophie isn't paying attention. I wouldn't want her to ask me why I highlighted her house. I wonder if Max has been there, and if he has seen it and asked about it. I make a note to ask him.

Miller, Ryland, and Lathan have their heads together as they talk about something I can't hear. This feels awkward as fuck, and I'm pretty sure I'm ready to leave. I start to pack my things as Sophie gets up and disappears in the direction Jessica went in. I catch Lathan's eye and nod in the direction of the circulation desk. We still need to grab that card so he can copy it.

He returns the subtle nod, and I wave a half-hearted goodbye, but no one is paying attention, so I start to slink away.

"Mac?" Shit, I guess someone was paying attention. I turn to face Miller.

"Yes?" I smile but brace myself for whatever is up his ass now.

"Ry's going to drive us to work this evening. Be ready by half past six, okay?" Wow, that was so not what I was expecting. I'm kind of shocked, but I quickly nod.

"Yeah, okay, that would be great, thanks."

I take my leave, but on the way past the stacks, I hear some aggressive whispering, so I slow down to eavesdrop.

"What the fuck are you doing? I told you to drive a

wedge between Ryland and Miller." I peek around the corner. Sophie has Jessica pinned up against a bookcase, her nails digging into her arm. Poor Jessica looks terrified.

"Sophie, I tried," she whimpers, "but he's just not into me. Maybe you have to face the fact that they are into each other and whatever you are trying to do is failing." Jessica stands her ground despite her obvious terror, and my opinion of her goes up.

"You're useless. Why don't you offer to suck his cock? That should help." Sophie has lost all kindness and only sounds nasty. "Or spread your legs and let him have a go at that tight cunt."

My eyebrows jump as Jessica shakes her head. "You know I'm a virgin and waiting for the right person." My eyes flit to the little diamond ring on her hand that is the same as Sophie's—the ring that announces her purity.

Sophie scoffs. "Please, like any of us are honest about that. You're foster kid trash, just like that new slut at your home. If you don't distract Miller, I'll destroy your name in town. There's no way you'll get a scholarship once I'm done with you."

I see tears well in Jessica's eyes and decide I can't let this go on any longer. I bump my backpack into the corner of the aisle and trip like I'm clumsy. Out of the corner of my eye, I see Sophie release Jessica and step back. When I right myself, I look up and smile.

"Sorry, I'm such a klutz." I pull my backpack up over my shoulder. "Everything okay here?"

"Mind your own business, tramp." Sophie pushes past me and returns to the table. My eyes drift to Jessica's arm. I can see four perfect half-moon prints with small droplets of blood welling on her skin.

"Are you okay?" I ask again, and Jessica bites her lip and shakes her head. "Threw your lot in with the wrong crowd, huh?"

Jessica nods, wiping away her tears. "She's going to ruin me. I need a scholarship. I want to do forensics, and there's no way I can afford to do that."

My mind starts to whirl. I'm almost certain Dad would love to add another forensics specialist to MITHOS, and what's better than one who doesn't have any preconceived ideas? I can almost guarantee he'd pay for her to go to school.

"Shit, Jessica, you don't need that kind of trouble. I have somewhere to be, otherwise I'd take you with me. Ask Lathan to run you home. You can sit with me in class and the other foster kids at lunch." She frowns, and she looks over my shoulder. "Come on, do you really enjoy being mean all the time?" I'm actually genuinely curious if that's her default mode. Foster kids are tough and standoffish, but I saw a different side of her.

"I hate it," she snarls. "All the posturing and pretentiousness. I wanted friends, and when Sophie deigned to give me the time of day, I was shocked. I guess I let her manipulate me. I'm not even into Miller. I mean, he's pretty, don't get me wrong, but he's kind of an asshole, also..." She trails off and looks around to make sure no one else is nearby. "You're much more my type." She winks, and my mouth drops open in surprise. "But the Standishes would freak if they knew I was bisexual, so Miller is convenient."

I chuckle. "He really is, isn't he? And I'm sorry you have to hide your real self. I'm flattered."

"Please, bitch, you know you're hot. I don't suppose you're into girls too?" I'm pretty sure she's joking as I grimace slightly.

"I've experimented, and it was fun, but I'm definitely more of a fan of the sausage than the taco," I say lightly. I'm not lying, I've had sex with women before for the job, but it's not what I lean toward.

"Shame." She smiles and pushes a stray hair back from her face. "Do you really think Lathan would take me home? Sophie is going to make my life hell, and I just want to get out of here."

I pull my phone out of my pocket and send him a message. It doesn't take him long to reply in the affirmative, and a few moments later, he appears, his backpack over his shoulder and keys in hand.

"Come on, Jess. Mac said you needed a ride. I can't stand it over there any longer. I'm not getting anything done anyway."

Her face brightens with relief. "Just a second." She hurries past us to grab her stuff.

"Make a commotion on the way out so I can slip the card off Ben's desk?" I ask him, and he nods, his eyes narrowing as he looks around. He pulls a few books off a shelf.

"Grab a couple as well. I'll drop mine, and hopefully that will keep his attention. You can slip yours on the desk and grab the card at the same time," he suggests and passes me a couple of books.

"Good thinking," I say as Jessica returns, looking a little shaky.

"Okay, let's go." She walks ahead, and I understand the hint. She doesn't want to talk about it.

We wind our way through the library and find Ben sitting behind the circulation desk. He looks up as we approach and smiles. "All done?" he asks, and I nod, sliding my books onto the table.

"We sure are," I say as Lathan fumbles his pile and they tip, dropping a couple onto the floor.

"Shoot," he exclaims as Ben jumps to his feet and hurries around to help him. I quickly glance around the table and find the card sitting next to the keyboard. I lean forward and slide it across the desk and into my pocket. Ben and Lathan stand up, holding the books.

"Hmm, if you're reading these kinds of books, maybe you should see a doctor," Ben says skeptically, looking between Lathan and me. When we look to see what the title is, I chuckle, but Lathan blanches. *Common Causes of Erectile Dysfunction in Men.*

"Human biology homework," he says blandly, and Ben nods, smiling widely.

"I'm sure it is. Mac looked very satisfied, so I'm guessing it wasn't for personal reference."

Lathan blushes as I giggle again, but Jessica is

looking at where I shoved the key in my pocket. Damn it, did she see what I did? I'm going to have to come up with an excuse fast in case she asks.

"Well, okay, bye then, and thanks for your help, Ben." I grab Lathan by the arm and drag him out, Jessica following behind. I snatch the keys out of his hand.

"Here, why don't you go to the car? I just want to talk to Lathan about his erectile disfunction," I joke.

Jessica chuckles. "Thanks for your help with Sophie. I was horrible to you and don't deserve it, but I appreciate it," she says as she takes the keys, waving goodbye and heading toward Ryland's sports car parked directly in front of the library.

"Whoa." Lathan's eyes widen as we follow her path to the car.

"Right? Anyway, I was thinking that they must have dumped Bishop's body by now. I'm assuming they were talking about the hot springs that Dayton took me swimming in the other day. How about I suggest he takes me swimming again, and we accidentally stumble across his body?" I slide the card out of my pocket and slip it into his hand. He then puts it in the pocket of his jeans, the movements barely noticeable.

"That's good thinking. Otherwise, we could be waiting a long time for his body to show up. He was headed to the tattoo studio last I saw him. He hates Stella. I don't even think he ate."

We walk down the library steps together. At the

car, I go to part ways, but he grabs my arm and leans in, his nose brushing against my ear, making me shiver.

"I can't wait to get my mouth on you again. You were fucking delicious." With that fucking announcement, he releases me, winks, and goes to the driver's side. I'm kind of gobsmacked, and I can see Jessica laughing at me. Who would have thought Nerdy Sexy has a dirty mouth?

Feeling flushed and off balance, I give a half-hearted wave as they drive away. Once the car disappears down the street, I shake off my surprise and start walking toward the tattoo studio.

CHAPTER 14

The bell over the door tinkles as I walk into the tattoo studio. The smell of antiseptic is strong, but it's not unpleasant, just reassuring. No one but Dayton is in the shop, and he seems to be filling a gumball machine. Frowning, I walk over to see exactly what he's doing. He smiles when he sees my confused expression.

"We're trying something new. This town isn't exactly the kind of place where people regularly get tattoos. Luckily for us, we have clients come from all around, but we're hoping this might bring in some new local clients. It's a lucky dip tattoo. Basically, you stick the coin in and turn the handle, and out pops a ball with some flash art in it." He holds up one of the little plastic balls, and I see a slip of paper inside. "That's the tattoo that you get." He cracks it open, and there's a little skateboarding ghost on the piece of paper.

I grin. It's kind of cute.

He pops it back in and keeps loading the balls into the machine. "You weren't at the library as long as I thought you would be," he comments as I place my bag on the ground and jump up onto the tattoo bed and watch as he works.

"Ry and Miller showed up with those girls in tow," I explain, leaning back on the tattoo bed. "It wasn't pleasant."

He chuckles. "I don't blame you. Why do you think I'm here? I couldn't stand sitting at the table with Max and that harpy, Stella, any longer. She has issues. She kept making sly racist comments to both Anders and me, so we bailed. Max will be pissed, but we have better things to do with our time."

"God, what a vapid bitch. Her and her sister are two peas in a pod. I caught Sophie threatening Jessica with violence if she doesn't distract Miller from Ryland. Are we sure the women have nothing to do with the trafficking? Sophie certainly shows some aggressive tendencies."

He stops loading the balls and purses his lips. "There's no evidence of it at this stage, but it's something to consider. Did you find what you were looking for at the library?" he asks.

"Yeah, I did. I shared everything with Lathan. He can bring you all up to speed when you're together again, but we also discovered that the tunnel under the library isn't boarded up like the librarian thought.

We saw Billy and Ashley carrying Bishop to dump his body."

Dayton's eyes narrow, and he's suddenly laser focused on me. "Oh? Did you happen to hear where?"

"Yeah. Want to take another swim in the hot springs?" I suggest, and he quickly puts the rest of the balls in the machine and jams the lid on before carrying it off to the side. He returns to his drawing desk and grabs the set of keys that are sitting there.

"Let's go. We will pick Anders up on the way. He had a meeting with Matthew after lunch, so he can fill us in on what he said. It won't hurt for them to think the three of us are going out there to fuck, since it will help sell yours and Anders's cover."

I jump down and grab my bag as he ushers me out the back to his gorgeous car. We climb in, and then we head in the direction of the mansion.

"Speaking of our cover, why are you located in the tattoo studio? Surely that's not going to wield too much information on the case."

"Well, you know I already had an established relationship with Kevin and this town, so I wouldn't have been able to go anywhere else, and it frees me up to poke around. While you are all working your angles elsewhere, Lathan and I can follow people like I followed Matthew last night when he left the club."

"Where did he go?" I turn my body to face him as he makes his way through the town center and heads toward the governor's mansion.

"I followed him to the shipping docks where Ted Standish has offices. I couldn't get close enough to hear what they were saying, but he stayed about an hour and then I followed him to a motel on the outskirts of town. He went into a room there and stayed for a couple of hours."

"Did you see who he was meeting?" I ask, and he wrinkles his nose adorably.

"Yeah, when he left, I caught a glimpse of the person behind him. It was the coast guard captain, Isaac Palmer."

"Okay, this is good. So he visits Ted first, the shipping magnate, and then the coast guard captain. Surely that points to them possibly transporting the merchandise via ships."

"I mean, sure, but does a business meeting usually involve being naked? Because I saw a lot more of Isaac than I was hoping to."

"Oh! So not a business meeting?"

He shakes his head.

"Well crap," I mutter as he pulls into the mansion's driveway before stopping in front of the house.

"Wait here. I'll grab Anders, and we'll be on our way." He puts the car in park and runs into the house. I unstrap and climb into the back seat so that Anders can have the bigger leg room.

Just as I get myself situated, my phone beeps. It's a message from my dad, reminding me to call Katie. Now seems as good a time as any. I tap in my cousin's number, which I have memorized. It barely rings before she answers.

"Hello?" She sounds cautious. She wouldn't recognize the number of my burner phone.

"Hey, Dad said you needed to speak to me."

"Kenz, how's the South? Is high school all it's cracked up to be?" She sounds like she's laughing at me, and I mentally flip her off.

"Ugh, be glad we never attended one," I grumble, resting my head against the seat and closing my eyes. "It's fucking awful. I can't wait to be done."

"And how's the new team?" she probes, not hiding her curiosity. "What's it like to work with backup? Are they all up in your business constantly?"

"Surprisingly no. They kind of let me do my thing, and they do theirs. It's working well so far, but it's only the first week, so we will see how this week goes."

"Keep me updated. I can't wait to hear all about them. Listen, that art gallery opening we committed to in New York is next week. Are you going to be able to make it? Both our parents are going to be there."

"Yeah, I can wing it. I'm not sure what kind of excuse I can give the Standishes for not being at the house. Get Dad to send the jet. I'll need a blonde wig. Can you arrange that and an outfit for me? I'll literally be able to appear and then leave as soon as possible."

The house door opens, and Anders and Dayton come out. Anders has a travel coffee mug in each hand, and Dayton also has one. He's carrying some towels too. They climb in, and Anders passes one of the cups back to me.

"Yeah, that shouldn't be a problem. We'll check

out the closest private strip to Summerville. We wouldn't want poor little foster girl Mackenzie seen getting onto a private jet."

"I'll come up with some excuse as to why I won't be home that night. Hell, I haven't made any female friends, so I can't even use a sleepover excuse, and there's no way the Standishes will let me sleep over at a boy's house, so I can't use Lathan as a cover either."

"What about a college visit? You could get an early admission with a tour of the campus as an incentive."

I sit up. "Hey, that's a great idea, and they are both so pro college that they will be enthusiastic. Can you get someone working on it? I need to receive it this week."

"We'll send it through the guidance counselor at school so there's no question," she assures me before we hang up.

"Thanks for this, I really needed it. Operating on little sleep is not fun," I say to Anders as I take a sip of the coffee he passed me.

"No problem." He turns slightly so he can see me as Dayton gets us back on the road. "Dayton told me you and Lathan saw them with Bishop's body."

"Yeah. They are going to weigh him down and dump him in the springs," I confirm before taking another sip of my coffee, the warmth and sweetness perking me right up.

"You're leaving town?" Dayton asks, his eyes meeting mine in the rearview mirror.

"Just for twenty-four hours. I committed to a

gallery opening before I got this assignment. Sometimes people pay for wealthy patrons and socialites to come so they get more media coverage. It's a great cover for Katie and me. How can we be killing people when we've been seen at these events by hundreds? But this one is a friend of my mother's, and the funds raised are going to a battered women's shelter that my mother is a patron of, so we volunteered."

"When is it?" he asks, and I look at the information Katie just sent me on the phone.

"Next Wednesday in New York. I'll leave first thing in the morning and be back Thursday in time for my shift at the bar."

"Matthew had me meet him at the bar earlier. He had three wine barrels we needed to move into the cellar downstairs. I can confirm that the elevator does go down there. I didn't get a chance to poke around because he was with me," he tells us.

"Lathan and I managed to steal a card that should allow us to use the elevator. He's making a copy of it so we can poke around after work if you want," I offer, and he nods.

"He told me about a private party that he was throwing and that they require a hot young bartender to serve at it. He thought I would be perfect for the job and that I would earn three times as much as I would in one night at the Life Lounge."

"And you jumped at it, right?" I ask, and he shakes his head.

"Nah, I didn't want to seem too enthusiastic. I told

him I thought it sounded too good to be true and asked what the catch was."

"And?" Dayton asks, not taking his eyes off the road.

"I have to lure you into the storeroom and fuck you. They want to catch you in the act so they can hold it over you. They want to blackmail you into serving topless and possibly doing more. He wasn't blatant, but I think they want to pimp you out."

"He told you that?" I ask, sounding skeptical. "What if you hadn't agreed?"

"I probably would have wound up floating face down in the hot springs too, but with the work I've put in, I'm pretty sure they knew I'd be a sure thing."

"Well, okay then," I agree, and he narrows his eyes.

"Are you okay with that?"

"Please, it won't be the first time I've been walked in on. It will be fine, and it will get us both where we need to be," I reassure him, but then I have a moment of doubt. "As long as you're okay with it. I'm not sure we'll be able to get away with faking it like Max and I did. I think you're actually going to have to fuck me." Jesus, here I am waving off any concern because it's standard practice for me, but I'm almost certain it's not standard practice for these guys. Lathan all but confirmed Miller was fine with it, but what about the rest of the team?

The concern in his eyes disappears, and they sparkle with excitement and no small amount of desire. "Trust me, sweetie, it will be no hardship giving you an orgasm or two to secure our cover." His lips curve up on one side, showing me a dimple I hadn't realized was there.

"Well, that's ah... good." I feel awkward all of a sudden, and I want to slap myself. I know this is for a mission, and I feel like this should just be standard protocol, but I kind of feel like it's more.

We've all been dancing around what's between us, and this is just one more step toward something. What it is, I'm not sure, but after my afternoon delight with Lathan, my previous swim date with Dayton, and the incredible sex with Max, I'm going to be four out of six with Team Basilisk. Then there's whatever is going on between me and Ryland, but that's a whole other problem. I am wary about our interactions because of what he has with Miller. Lathan told me they are definitely a couple and they are solid. He also implied they would like to have a girlfriend but haven't found one to fit their dynamic. Ryland seems to be looking to me to fill that role, but Miller? Miller is so wishy-washy. One moment, he's aggressive, and I think he wants to slit my throat and shove me into one of the tunnels below the town where I'll never be found, and then other times, he's professional and job oriented. Then there's what he did to me last night after I got home from the club. I'm discombobulated by him, and that's so disorienting.

We fall into a comfortable silence as the car accelerates, heading toward the hot springs. Dayton has the radio tuned into some local station that's playing old country music. I close my eyes and let the soft sounds sooth me.

"How was the confession with the pastor?" Dayton asks after a few miles. I wrinkle my nose and open my eyes. Both of them are looking at me.

"Gross. He's definitely a part of the ring. He was trying to see how far he could push me, but we were interrupted before too much could happen."

Anders leans over the seat and puts his hand on my knee, giving it a squeeze. "Are you okay?" he asks, and I have to take a moment to think about it.

It's weird. In the past, I just did whatever was required of me to get the job done. There's a slight disconnect between the role I'm playing and who I am, and I've just kind of gone by the Nike motto of just do it. Having someone not only show interest but also willing to talk about it is kind of refreshing. Previously, I would have just bottled it all up, got the job done, and then unloaded on my therapist as soon as I returned from a mission. I have no idea what's causing the issues, but my mind keeps returning to my relationship with Team Basilisk.

"Yeah, I'm okay. The sex part of it doesn't bother me, I'm used to it. Not being able to put a bullet in the villain's brain is really annoying me. In most of my missions in the past, I already knew my targets were guilty, and I was just carrying out their sentencing. Having to wait until we have all these ducks in a row is kind of frustrating."

He chuckles but leaves his hand on my knee. It

feels nice, comforting, and warm. "I imagine that would be difficult. This is normal for us. Our team has always had to gather solid evidence for MITHOS. Although there have been kills during the process, usually we are just putting criminals behind bars and not actually assassinating them. Any that require kill orders are always given to someone else."

"Yeah, that would be me or one of my fellow ghosts. I'm finding it difficult to be patient." I sigh heavily, and he gives my knee another squeeze.

"How are you finding working with our team?" Dayton takes his eyes off the road and glances my way.

"To be honest, it's not as bad as I thought it would be. I thought you or Max would micromanage me, but you seem to be okay with me doing my own thing. I am a little disappointed in how slow this is all going though. I was hoping we could wrap it up within a week." I'm not unloading my feelings for them or whatever this is.

He chuckles again, and Anders removes his hand, facing the front again. "Unfortunately our assignments are never that quick. You and I have it lucky. Imagine being Max and having to pander to Stella."

I don't hide the shudder that rolls through my body. "Seriously, I think I'd shoot her myself."

"He comes home and spends at least half an hour in the shower after being with her. He says he feels dirty, and they haven't even really done anything."

I feel a huge amount of relief at hearing this. Hypocritical, I know, considering I have not only fucked him, but also Lathan, and I have done things with both Dayton and Anders. I have no leg to stand on when it comes to being jealous, but I admit I am. I hate that fucking woman.

"God, I can't wait to see her face when we arrest her father." Petty, I know, but so fucking worth all the aggravation.

"I don't know about you, but I can't wait to have a few months off." Anders stretches his arms above his head as high as the car will allow. "I just want to eat, drink, sleep in, and play some golf with the guys. I wonder if the king will let us visit and use his private golf course again." He looks at Dayton who shrugs.

"I don't know. What do you think, Mac?"

I feel my eyebrows jump. "You played golf with my grandfather? On his private course? Heck, he won't even let me play on that, says I dig up all the greens with my atrocious swings. I can hit a target at almost impossible distances, but I can't coordinate hitting a small, round white ball."

"Yes, he likes playing with us. All his other stooges lose on purpose, so he likes how we don't let him win."

"How does my uncle feel when you win?" I'm curious. My mom's older brother is the heir to the crown and is a little bit of a spoiled man child. He's not a bad person, simply indulged.

"I think the fact that he knows we could assassinate him in his sleep keeps him from losing his temper. He treats us like family," Anders explains, and I can't help the surprised gasp that leaves my mouth.

"You threatened him?" I almost can't believe what I'm hearing. That's practically a death sentence.

"No, your grandpa made it a topic of conversation at dinner the first night. He asked us how many ways we killed people in the past and wanted details. I think it was his roundabout way of getting Prince Kahled to respect us. He's never caused any problems and asked us to teach his son self-defense. He thought it would be good if he didn't have to rely on his security detail alone."

"Ugh, my cousin Kamel is a pain in the ass. He is the quintessential spoiled playboy. He makes our act look tame. He hangs out in a lot of the same crowds as Katie and me. Does he know you're spies? Because he has the loosest lips when he's been indulging with the latest recreational drugs."

"Nope, just friends of the family through Sadie."

"And he would have believed that because my mom is known for picking up strays."

The car decelerates as we pull onto the dirt road the hot springs are on. Before we get around the corner, Dayton barks out, "Fuck," before yanking the steering wheel to the side, causing the car to fishtail on the loose surface, but he manages to avoid the other car that took the corner wide and fast.

The back end slides back and forth a couple of times before he gets it under control. Thankfully I was wearing my seat belt, or I would have tumbled around in the back, possibly giving myself new bruises.

"Are you okay?" he asks as we pull to a stop, turning around to look at me.

"Yeah, I'm fine," I tell him, pushing my hair back out of my face. "Did either of you see who was driving?"

"No, but I got a plate number," Anders says, pulling out his phone and typing in a message. "I'll send it off to Lathan, but I'm going to guess that was Billy and Ashley fleeing the scene."

"Shit, that's not good. We can place them here. That's going to make us a target." Dayton smacks a fist against the steering wheel, and I reach out and give his shoulder a squeeze.

"We can just tell the cops we didn't get a look at the plate, and we were too busy trying to survive so we didn't even get a description of the car."

"Not to mention all the dust," Anders says, pointing out the window. He's right, it's thick in the air and makes picking out details tricky.

"We stick to our story when the police ask. We were coming out to go skinny dipping and have some 'fun.'" I use air quotes. "They are going to make their own assumptions about the three of us fucking. It will help sell my backstory of being loose. I don't think you should say you paid me to be out here. You want to be able to come back and work with Kevin again, and if people think you pay for sex, that might damage your career."

Dayton shakes his head. "Nah. Let's just go with

you're young and cute, and you work with Anders who wanted to get to know you better."

"Yeah, they'll know I was tasked with auditioning you by Matthew, so it all fits."

"Okay, let's go then," I agree as Dayton gets us moving again. It's time to discover Bishop's body and finally put him to rest. As much as I disliked him, I haven't liked pretending we don't know he's dead. Nobody deserves to be treated like trash, especially once they've passed on.

CHAPTER 15

We decide to act as if we are going on a date. We're not sure if they put a camera out here to see if anyone discovers the body, so we are going to have to make it look real. The three of us laugh and make jokes as we arrive at the hot spring. We drop our towels, and the boys sandwich me between them. Dayton brushes my hair to the side and places kisses along my neck. I allow my head to fall back, enjoying the sensations, and take the opportunity to look around for any hidden cameras. Anders, who is in front of me, slides his hands up my inner thighs, under my dress.

"How about we get you out of these clothes, and we have some fun in the water?" he says loudly.

"I can't see any cameras," I whisper before replying, "Sounds fun."

He gathers my dress and starts to peel it over my head. He isn't expecting me to be without panties, so when he pulls it over my head and discards it, leaving me in just my bra, he stops and stares for a moment. He hisses a quiet, "Fuck," before he unbuckles his belt.

"Just because we can't see it doesn't mean there's nothing there," Dayton warns quietly, reaching up to undo my bra and letting it fall down my arms. Anders pulls his shirt over his head, and I pull away from them and step back toward the water.

"First one in gets my ass!" I call and spin around to hurry to the water's edge, not waiting for their reactions.

I can hear them pushing and shoving each other, but then I see Bishop's body floating on the surface. They didn't bother weighing it down, they just tossed it into the water. He's face down, so I can't see what they did about the bullet hole.

I scream and back away. "Oh my god! There's a body floating in the pool!" I run back to the guys, who are both in their boxers, and they stop what they are doing and look toward where I point. I grab Dayton's arm, and he pulls me into his body. It's warm and smooth, and I love how it feels against my naked skin, but I can't get distracted by it. Anders bends down and pulls his phone out of his jeans pocket, then he walks toward the pool, lifting it to his ear. I'm assuming he's calling 911.

"Yeah, I found a dead body. I'm in Summerville, Georgia at the hot springs just out of town. It's floating in the water."

He listens for a moment and answers a couple of

questions before hanging up. I pretend to be terrified in Dayton's arms, and he rubs a soothing hand over my back before helping me into my dress and wrapping one of the towels around my shoulders.

"They said not to go near it, and they'll be here soon. Fuck, I can't believe it. I thought he'd be found holed up with some chick," Anders says flatly without turning around to face us.

"Hey, man, what's wrong? What do you mean?" Dayton calls, keeping up the act.

"I recognize the tattoo on the body's back. It's Bishop, man."

"Fuck." Dayton helps me sit down on the other towels while I keep up my distraught act, and then he hurries down to the edge of the pool. He swears loudly again and goes to step into the water, but Anders puts his hand on him.

"They said not to disturb the body or crime scene. They told us to go back to our car and they will send the police and paramedics."

Dayton runs a frustrated hand through his hair but nods and turns around and walks back to me. Tears run down my face as the two of them get dressed.

"You really think it's Bishop?" I ask, and they nod.

"Yeah, I was the one who gave him that tattoo," Dayton tells me as he pulls his shirt over his head before slipping his feet into his socks and shoes.

They help me back to my feet, and the three of us walk somberly to the car and hop in it to wait for the police. I don't wipe the tears from my eyes because I want to put on a good show for the authorities.

"Well, if there were any cameras, I think that was fairly believable," I comment. "I really am sorry about what happened to Bishop. Even though you didn't see eye to eye, I know he was part of your team for six months. I'm sorry I didn't say anything earlier." I feel a little guilty. This whole time, we've been business as usual, and here they are, mourning their teammate—even if he was a dick.

Both guys shake their heads. "Don't be, the guy seriously had it coming. Even Lathan didn't like him, and he's the most laid back person in the group," Dayton explains.

"Yeah, that's because Bishop was always calling him a nerd and telling him girls like big dicks, not big brains." Anders shakes his head, and I wince.

"Note to self, stop calling him Nerdy Sexy."

"No, you do it affectionately. He loves that. Bishop was jealous of Lathan's intelligence—about everyone's skills, actually—and could be nasty about it."

"We really were going to talk to your dad about him once the mission was finished. None of us liked him, and Miller downright hated him," Dayton confirms.

I chuckle darkly. "Sounds familiar."

"Pfft, hang in there. Miller will come around. We saw the two of you with your heads together at church today, and you saw how strongly he reacted to Bishop when he said nasty things to you. Miller just needs to get out of his own way," Anders assures me.

We fall into an awkward silence, and after a while, we finally hear sirens in the distance. "Remember, we came out here for a swim. We saw the other car but didn't recognize anyone or even get a plate number," Dayton instructs us.

"What color and make are we going to say it was?" I ask. "I think we should all say something different, then they will think we definitely don't know who it was."

We agree to the plan and wait for the police to arrive.

It's at least another hour before we are allowed to leave. The chief of police himself shows up. I stay in the car while he talks to Anders and Dayton, playing the good, terrified schoolgirl. The deputy asks me a few questions but quickly dismisses me as unimportant, just a piece of ass the guys brought out to the pools for some fun.

They walk back down the track—I'm guessing they asked them to identify the body. It doesn't take them too long to return, the paramedics carrying a stretcher with the sheet-covered corpse on it.

The guys shake hands with the chief of police

before climbing into the car. We're quiet while Dayton starts it and turns around, avoiding all the emergency vehicles before we head back into town.

"We identified him and told Chief Thompson we would inform his family. They will decide what they want to do with the body. I'll call Percy as soon as we are home so he can make arrangements. They puttied over the bullet hole, so the ME said they are going to have to do an autopsy. He suggested drowning while intoxicated as a possible cause of death," Anders says, turning slightly to face me.

"Yeah, but how are they going to claim he got out there?" I point out.

He shrugs. "Who knows, but Percy or whoever goes for him will pretend to be a grieving family member and accept their rulings. We don't want to tip them off to anything. The truth will be placed in his file."

"Dad will have him buried on MITHOS grounds, with the other agents who lost their lives in the field —not that he deserves it," I say, muttering the last part. "Well, at least the tunnels are clear for us to search now. I think I have a pretty good idea where the club is. The map showed a large section under the movie theater. Maybe while we're working tonight, you and the others can check it all out. You could always break into the library and use the tunnel in the basement to gain entry. I doubt it will even have a night guard," I suggest to Dayton. "Just watch out for people down there. I overheard them saying they are going to have a club night this Friday. It will be interesting to see if they bring in auction merchandise or if they have regular whores who attend as well as their members."

"That means sometime between now and then, those cells downstairs are going to fill up. Maybe while we are down there, Lathan can put our own cameras throughout the tunnels to see if we can figure out how they are coming and going," Dayton muses.

"Ugh, I wish I could come too. I want to see what's down there." I pout like a toddler, and Anders chuckles.

"Yeah, but you and I also have a job to do." He winks, and I perk up.

"Oh, that's right. So how do you want to play this? Do you want me to fight you? Do you want me to be, 'Oh yes, Daddy, please spank me?'" I ask, and Anders's eyes light up with desire.

"I think you need to be an enthusiastic participant with Anders, but when it comes to the sex club, you need to be a little more reluctant. We need them to auction you to Max. We trust that you know how to play this. We're just here for backup."

"Also, the tracker for Miller arrived. I need to insert that, but I won't have time before work tonight. We wrap up at twelve on Sundays, so we can go back to ours and do it before I take you both to the Standishes," Anders tells me as we arrive at the end of the dirt road to Serenity House.

"Okay. Thanks, guys. I wish I could say this was

fun, but it would have been more interesting without a dead body."

"We need a do-over," Anders declares.

"And I still need to collect my winnings," Dayton reminds me.

"You're on, but let's find a spring that hasn't had a dead body floating in it, yeah? See you tonight, Anders." I wave goodbye as I climb out, holding my dress down because I'm still not wearing underwear. Throwing my backpack over my shoulder, I hurry down the driveway as they pull away. It's only three thirty, so I might take a quick nap before I have to get ready for work. We don't need to be there until seven, and Miller organized for Ryland to drive us both, which was nice and surprising of him.

When I walk through the back door, I find Cassie in the kitchen, making a cup of tea. She looks up and smiles at me, but then she looks closer and notices I've been crying.

"Hi, how was your afternoon? Did you get plenty of work done? Is everything okay?" She bombards me with questions, and I smother the smile that wants to break free.

I groan, shaking my head and leaning against the wall. "Not really. I did a bit, but then Sophie and her crew showed up. They were awful, so I went to the hot springs with some friends, and we found Bishop's body floating in the water."

"Oh my god! He was dead?" she asks, and I nod.

"Wow." She seems kind of stunned, but then she

shakes her head. "Yeah, Jessica came back a couple of hours ago. She looked like she was crying. This tea is for her." She nods at the cup she just made. "I was just going to check on her."

"I think it's safe to say that Jessica has come to her senses about the people she hangs out with. Don't be surprised if she's nicer and wants to hang out at lunch now," I warn her, and she shrugs.

"I don't care, I knew it was bound to happen. Steph and Sally may not be as accepting, since they tend to hold grudges."

I chuckle. "That doesn't surprise me. Would you like me to take that up to her?" I ask.

"Yeah, that would be great. Martha called earlier and said she and James weren't going to be home this evening—dinner at his brother's place—so I'm just going to make some grilled cheese for us for dinner."

"Okay, I'm going to take a nap. I have to work tonight, but I'll set my alarm to come help. What time are you going to do it?" I ask her, but she waves me off.

"The boys can help me. I'll wake you half an hour before they are ready so you have time to shower and dress for work," she offers, and I don't bother arguing.

"Thanks, that would be great. Ryland is picking Miller and me up at six thirty, so maybe five thirty."

She agrees, and I take the tea upstairs. When I get to our room, Jessica is asleep, so I put the mug on the nightstand next to her bed and dump my backpack next to my own. I strip off the dress and throw on my oversize shirt, and then I dig out a fresh pair of underwear, sliding them up my legs, before climbing into my bed. I pull my phone out of my bag and set the alarm before rolling over and closing my eyes. I hope it doesn't take too long to fall asleep.

The house is loud and hectic when I finally make it downstairs after showering and putting on my uniform. Thankfully, Matthew gave me two yesterday, otherwise I'd have to wear the dirty one from last night. I need to do some laundry before my next shift on Thursday.

A piercing whistle sounds across the kitchen, and the rowdy teens fall into silence as they all turn to look at me. "Holy smoking hot pants," Ty mutters and grins wolfishly at me.

I roll my eyes and join them at the table. "Settle, tiger. It's hardly my fault their uniform makes me look like this."

"And you've seen it before, asshole. Sybil used to wear one just like it." Stephanie slaps him on the back of the head as my eyes meet Miller's and hold for a moment. I'm not stupid, I know I look good, but the sheer desire I see in his gaze is kind of staggering, and I'm speechless for a moment before he quickly blanks his expression and takes a bite of his grilled cheese.

"You look good, Mac," Jessica says kindly, and they

all turn and stare at her like she had a personality transplant. She looks around and shrugs sheepishly. "Yeah, sorry I was an asshole," she apologizes, and just like that, all is forgiven.

"Trust me, Sybil never looked like that," Will argues. "She was all long limbs and little titties. It looks so much better on Mac."

"How about you all shush and eat?" Cassie instructs. "Mac doesn't have long before she has to go." She slides a plate in front of me.

"Did you all help her?" I ask, picking up my sandwich. "You didn't make her wait on everyone, did you?"

Stephanie shakes her head. "No. Jessica, Sally, and I helped make them, and the boys are going to clean up."

"Good. I'm sorry I wasn't here to help. I promise I'll do better next time."

"Don't worry about it. It will all even out eventually." Cassie waves me off, and I decide I definitely want Dad to see if these kids are interested in being recruited by MITHOS. They are such a great bunch of kids, and I don't want to see them get bounced around if the Standishes end up being crooks.

CHAPTER 16

The club is a lot quieter this evening. There is still a big dinner crowd, but the dance floor isn't so packed with people. Anders is busy teaching Miller how to make drinks, so we haven't had a chance to get caught fucking yet, but I know it's coming. Matthew has been a solid presence at the end of the bar the whole night, so I guess he doesn't want to miss out on his chance to catch us.

None of the rest of Team Basilisk come in. Ryland said they were planning on using the tunnel in the library to access the network. It would be easier than going out to the ranger's cabin and going from there. Lathan managed to clone the card, and they were going to slip Ben's back on his desk on their way past. Hopefully he didn't notice it missing yet.

Ryland and Miller said they spent the rest of the afternoon in the library, and it was closing when Anders called to tell them about finding Bishop's body.

They followed along with the act and told the girls. Miller said they looked shocked and upset upon hearing of his death, so either they were Academy Award winning actresses, or they really knew nothing about it.

I approach a new table of patrons who just arrived. It's a group of men, and when I look up, I'm surprised to find James, his brother Ted, Father Sweeny, and Brock Marshall, the guidance counselor. A wave of goosebumps washes across my skin as the four of them leer at me.

"Hi, welcome to the Life Lounge. The kitchen is closed, but can I get you something to drink?" I give them my spiel, smiling politely.

"Good evening, Mac. Can you get us a pitcher of beer and let Matthew know we're here?" James replies.

"Miss Walsh, I see you didn't need my help getting a job." Mr. Marshall sounds annoyed.

"Oh no, thanks anyway, but I stopped in after school and had an interview, and they gave me the job on the spot."

"Must have been a good interview to hire you on the spot," he mutters, and Ted elbows him.

"Oh, it was." I wink at him, and he blinks with surprise before he recovers quickly.

"I bet." He leers at me, and I feel dirty.

"It's good to see the young generation working hard to better themselves," the pastor announces piously.

"I'm trying to earn as much money as I can for

college," I tell him as I put their order into my tablet. "So was it just the one pitcher of beer?" I ask, looking around at the four men.

"I'll have a scotch, neat," Ted says, his eyes cold as he answers me. I thought James's stare was cold, but his is practically warm compared to his brother's serial killer countenance.

"Okay, great, they won't be long," I tell them and head back to the bar, passing Matthew on the way.

"James, Ted, Mr. Marshall, and Father Sweeny are in booth ten, and they asked for you to join them," I tell him, but before I can continue, he grabs my arm.

"Once you finish their order, why don't you take a break?" He's looking at me intently, and I know what's about to happen.

"Oh, yeah, that would be great." I smile brightly, and he releases me.

"Take Anders with you. He looks like he could use a little break too. He seems a little uptight, if you know what I mean," he suggests, nodding to my teammate. "The new kid and Keith will be fine on their own."

I hear what he's saying, and my smile drops before I nod. "Yeah, okay, um... sure." I make myself sound a little reluctant.

"Come on, Mac. Sam told me you are interested in making some extra money. I may have an opening for Friday night's private party, but I have to know how badly you want it. Looking after your fellow staff members is part of being a team player."

"Yeah, okay, Matthew. I'll make sure Anders is

taken care of." I paste the smile back on my face and continue to pick up my drinks. Anders is busy pouring Ted's scotch, so I sidle close and lean in, pressing my breasts against his arm.

"Matthew is watching us," I warn him before saying, "Meet me in the storeroom?" A slow, sleazy smile crosses his lips.

"Sure can," he replies, putting the scotch on my tray. Miller, who is standing next to him and pouring the beer for my order, looks between us, but he doesn't say anything. He knows what Anders has been asked to do. I wonder how long it will be until he's tasked with doing something to prove his loyalty.

Miller places the pitcher on the tray and adds four glasses to it. Without another word, I lift it up and head in the direction of their booth. I weave around the outside of the dance floor. There's less people compared to last night, so I'm not too worried about getting bumped and spilling things.

When I arrive at the booth, Matthew has joined them. I hadn't even noticed he wasn't at the end of the bar anymore. I slide their drinks onto the table, putting the pitcher and glasses in the middle and setting Ted's scotch in front of him.

"Can I get you anything else?" I ask, but they all shake their heads.

"Take that break, Mac," Matthew says, a hint of steel in his voice. "Carla can serve us if we need anything."

"Carla's here?" Mr. Marshall's eyebrows jump, and

he looks around the room enthusiastically. Now that they mention it, I realize Carla disappeared ten minutes ago and hasn't reappeared yet. Maybe she's on a break.

"Yes, but I think she's taking a break."

"I'd like to see her. She's my favorite server, apart from you of course, Mac." Mr. Marshall winks, and I internally think about putting a bullet in his head. His brain matter would look so pretty splattered across the leather booth behind him.

"Tell her to get her ass on the floor if you see her," Matthew snaps. Gone is the affable bar owner, and in his place is a predator. "I don't pay her to slack off."

"Ah, okay, yeah. She's probably just in the bathroom. She wasn't looking so great before." I make up an excuse on the spot. "You wouldn't want a town-wide case of the stomach flu if she gives it to our customers. That wouldn't be good for the club. We might get investigated by the health department," I say, intentionally sounding like an airhead.

Matthew blanches. "Ah, no, that wouldn't be good. Fine, tell her to go home. I don't need her making all our customers sick."

"Nobody wants the health department poking around," Father Sweeny chimes in, nodding sagely. Asshole.

I wave goodbye and pass the bar, dropping my tray before heading out back. I pass the bathrooms and get to the staff room, where I find Carla huddled on the ratty sofa. She's shaking like a leaf and has tears running down her face.

"Hey, are you okay?" I ask her, and she shakes her head, unable to pretend that she's fine.

"No. There's someone out there I don't want to see." She looks at me, her eyes imploring me not to make her go back out there.

"It's okay. I told Matthew you had the stomach flu. He said to go home. If you slip out the side door and into the alley, you won't even have to cross the club."

"Oh God." She slaps a hand over her mouth. "Thank you."

"We've all been there." I point at my face. Despite the small amount of makeup I applied, you can still see a hint of the bruises.

Anders arrives in a rush and stops dead, looking at the two of us. "Oh!" I want to giggle at his confusion, but I don't want to upset Carla further.

"Can you walk Carla out to her car? She was just leaving," I tell him, and he nods.

"Yeah, okay." She gathers her stuff, and the two of them slip out the side door without another word. I heave out a huge sigh and head toward the storeroom. I'm sure Anders will find me when he returns. I need to withdraw some cash and sneak it into Carla's bag—a large enough sum for her to leave town immediately. I have a feeling she may be the next dead body if we're not careful.

In the storeroom, I lean against the wall next to one of the shelves and wonder how long it will be until someone is going to come and "catch" us in the act.

I don't have to wait long before Anders returns. He finds me with my eyes closed and my head back against the wall. This town is getting to me. I'm primarily an assassin. I go in after the case has been investigated and execute the kill order. Although I get close to the target, I never have to be involved in what they've been doing. This time is different. This time I'm assisting with the investigation, and all the dirty details are nauseating. I can't remain detached. I'm becoming invested, and I really don't like how that feels. I'm not sure I can do this case after case without losing myself to the tragedy of it all. At least with being an assassin, I had satisfaction in knowing the bad guys were dead. I have no idea what will happen to this ring. They'll probably go to jail, but I doubt they will get punished permanently.

I feel him crowd in close to me, one of his hands on my hips and the other against the wall. "There are cameras in here, so we have to make it look good," he tells me as his lips descend, and he kisses me.

I slide my hands around and up his back, pulling him closer. One of my legs comes up to wrap around his hip as our tongues slide deliciously against one another. He tastes minty, like he's been chewing gum, and his lips are pillowy soft. He nips and sucks my own lips, grinding his pelvis into me. I groan at the contact, and his hand creeps up to cup my breast. It's dark in the storeroom. Neither of us turned the lights on when we came in, so only the light in the hallway is illuminating anything.

"Open your eyes, Mac," Anders whispers as his mouth leaves mine and he presses kisses across my face to my neck.

I hadn't realized I allowed them to drift closed, so I open them and find him staring at me. "Are you okay?" I see the worry in his eyes despite his hands roaming for the camera. I give him a quick little nod before pushing him away slightly. I'm supposed to be the aggressor, and I have no doubt the tapes will be watched later.

I peel my top off and toss it to the side before grabbing his hands and putting them on my naked breasts. He takes my cue and massages them before leaning down and wrapping his lips around a nipple. His mouth is warm and hot, and he has the perfect amount of suction, sending a bolt of lightning straight to my core. I reach for his pants and open his belt buckle before unzipping them and sliding them down. He bites down as I reach into his underwear and wrap my hand around his dick. Fuck, I'd forgotten how thick it was, and my fingers only just touch as I stroke up and down a couple of times.

"As much as I would like to see your pretty mouth wrapped around my dick again, we probably don't have a lot of time," Anders says, glancing at the doorway like he's nervous.

I nod and release his cock. Stepping back, I slide

my hands into my hot pants and peel them down my legs, underwear and all, leaving me naked.

"Fuck," he hisses and scrubs his hand across his jaw, reaching for his cock with the other. His gaze runs the length of my body before he holds out his free hand. "Come here and let me feel it," he demands, and I slide my hand into his and allow him to pull me back into him. His hands, which are rough and calloused, run all over my body like he can't decide which part to touch first. One stops on my ass cheek and gives it a rough squeeze, and he groans. "Jesus, you could bounce a quarter off this. I just want to get my teeth into it." He snaps them at me, and I giggle, surprising both of us.

Getting my head back into the game, I reach for his shirt and tug it up his body. He caves to my demands and releases me, lifting his arms up and allowing me to strip it off him. Next, I press my breasts to his chest and rub my body against his. He's hot and hard, and I feel my need coating my thighs as one of his hands slips down to play with my clit and the ring in it.

"I want to get my teeth on this too," he tells me quietly so the camera can't hear him "Next time I get you naked, it won't be for the camera or for the sake of this case. I'll take my time and taste you, wanting to feel you come on my tongue before I sink balls deep into you."

I shiver, and my slutty pussy weeps for him. "I could be down with that," I tell him as he spins us and pins me against the wall, his fingers circling my clit before dipping down and spearing into my needy cunt. I groan and bang my head against the wall at the sudden intrusion. Anders isn't playing around and starting slowly. He forced two in before pulling out and adding another. My mouth drops open, and I start to pant as I roll my hips against the onslaught of his fingers.

"Fuck, you're tight. I need to stretch you to get my cock in," he says, speaking louder this time so the cameras pick it up. "I never would have guessed you were so tight. Fuck, your ass must feel incredible. Maybe next time you'll let me fuck you there."

"Not unless you do plenty of prep work. Your weapon would wreck me," I tell him between pants, and he chuckles darkly.

"We'll see," he promises vaguely and then removes his hand before grabbing me under my thighs and lifting me. He pins me to the wall as I wrap my legs around him to steady us.

"Reach down and line me up," he tells me, his eyes on mine, and in those dark depths, I see how much he wants this. It's almost as much as I do.

Do I wish we weren't doing this for the mission? Sure, but to be honest, if we weren't on this mission, I think we all would have spent weeks dancing around all the sexual tension before we did something about it. Being thrown in at the deep end and forced to act like this has made us drop all those ridiculous societal niceties and allowed us to just enjoy how it feels—or that's how I feel anyway. Despite not knowing each other well, we seemed to have just clicked, and the sexual chemistry with all of them is off the fucking charts. No, I'm not sad or ashamed about how I feel at all.

I do as he instructed, and our moans as he slowly slides forward are embarrassingly loud. He doesn't get all the way in, having to pull back and thrust harder a couple of times, but when he's finally seated, I feel full and fucking incredible. My hands come up to play with my tits as he kisses me hard.

"Fuck, you feel like heaven," he mutters, pulling away and resting his forehead against mine. "Give me a moment, or this will all be over before Matthew can even bust us."

I snort and tease him by clenching my pussy muscles. He grunts and releases one hand from my ass cheek, giving it a slap. He pulls out and thrusts hard, and my eyes roll back in my head and drift closed as I enjoy the sensations of him fucking me while we are all alone and pretending a camera isn't recording every move. It doesn't take long until I feel my orgasm building, the tingling sensations pulsing through my nerve endings.

"God, yes, right there," I exclaim when he rolls his hips a certain way that practically punches his cock against my G-spot, causing me to gasp out loud.

CHAPTER 17

"Well, when I said Anders needed a break at the same time as you, this wasn't quite what I had in mind," a dry voice says from the doorway.

I roll my eyes behind my eyelids before gasping and snapping them open, pretending to be shocked we've been caught. Matthew is standing there with raised eyebrows. Fuck, I was so close to an orgasm too, and seeing him has made all of that go away.

Anders doesn't stop rolling his hips. "Hey, man, stop cockblocking, I'm almost done," he calls over his shoulder. "Stay and watch if you have to, but let me nut."

I start to struggle and push him away, but he just pins me tighter against the wall, his hand coming up to collar my throat. I can't help but moan loudly. It feels fucking incredible. I had no idea, but there is a serious submissive side to me, one that really likes being dominated. I'm almost certain it has everything to do with these men. I have never enjoyed being dominated like this before. I try to play the aggressor as much as possible with my missions. It gives me control. Who would have guessed I would like giving all that up?

"Don't bruise the merchandise," Matthew says conversationally, leaning against the wall and cocking his head to the side. His eyes drift down to Anders's ass, and I realize he has no interest in me at all. I feel a sudden flicker of worry for Miller. I wonder if he will be asked to service Matthew or be serviced by him.

"The little slut likes it. You should feel how her pussy just tightened." Anders is working hard, holding me up while fucking me, so his words come out in a rush. I should be completely turned off with Matthew watching us, but it kind of does it for me. I wish it was one of the other guys, but it doesn't take long before I dig my heels into him and beg him to thrust harder. My orgasm is just out of reach, and I need something to tip me over.

"Hey, Matthew, have you seen Anders and Mac? Keith asked me to find them. Now that Carla has gone home, we could use the help." My eyes widen as Miller's voice comes from behind Matthew.

"I'd say I've seen them. Why don't you have a look yourself?" Matthew chuckles and steps out of the way, allowing Miller to step into the storeroom. He slaps him on the shoulder. "See the perks of working here? You get to rail the staff if you work hard and are loyal.

Why don't you get over there and have a turn as well. You always look so miserable, you'll scare off the ladies, though they do like the silent broody type. You won't care, will you, Mac?"

My eyes are on Miller, who is staring, blank-faced, at Anders, but when Matthew says my name, I turn to look at him. His eyes are narrowed, and his lips are pursed.

"You want to make sure Miller is relaxed on his first night too, don't you, Mac? Do this, and I guarantee I'll give you a job at the private gig we're holding on Friday. You'll make bank."

Miller stays where he is. Fuck, I'm about to take away his consent so I can secure my cover. I hope he forgives me. "Sure, why not?" I pant my response. "As long as you promise to give me the job, I'll relax whoever you want me to."

Anders slows and turns around, piercing Miller with a look. "Get over here and let her suck your cock. She has a mouth like a hoover."

He pulls out and drops my legs from his waist. My pussy practically weeps its disappointment as he swaps places with me. He leans against the wall and has me face the other two, my naked front exposed to them both. Matthew shows no interest, but I see Miller's jaw tighten ever so slightly as his gaze rakes over my naked body. Pushing not so gently on my back, Anders bends me over before he thrusts deep again. I don't fake the grunt of shock that leaves my mouth as his cock breaches my entrance. Anders is not a small dude, and this angle is tighter.

Matthew chuckles. "Go on then, or are you a fag like the rumors say? Just close your eyes and think of that Turner boy you hang out with if that's the case. I heard that works. A wet hole is a wet hole if your eyes are closed," Matthew tells Miller.

I wonder if that's his go-to move with women. There was no mention of previous female partners for him, so maybe he's never had to fake it before.

I see the moment Miller realizes there's no choice but to join in. Fuck, I wonder if he's wishing he never came back here now. His hands go to his belt as he moves toward us.

"Nah, I've been wondering how that mouth feels since her pretty, battered face arrived at the house. Seeing those marks on her face made me hard. I had to rub one out after sitting across the table from her at dinner."

My eyes widen as he approaches me with a smirk. He knows he's shocked me and is happy about it. Matthew can't see his face now, so it doesn't matter.

"So you like both cock and pussy?" Matthew asks, sounding overly interested in Miller's response as he stops right in front of me and shoves his pants down, palming his cock. The silver line of piercings is right in front of my eyes, and now I'll know the kinds of noises he makes when I tug on them with my teeth.

"Yeah, I'm not fussy. Like you said, a wet hole is a wet hole. I have a feeling this wet hole will be exceptional." Miller grabs my hair tightly, and I cry out as he yanks me toward his cock.

"Try not to bruise her again please. Some people don't like seeing their meat battered," Matthew says.

"Go on, baby, show Miller how good you can suck his dick," Anders encourages me and gives me a slap on the ass. My mouth drops open, and Miller takes advantage, sliding his dick home. I gag as he pushes it straight into my throat, and my eyes water. He pulls back, allowing me to breathe a little.

"Be a good girl and make me come," he says, his eyes locked on mine. His amusement is gone, and now there is only straight desire. I'm so caught up in our stare down that Anders has to slap my ass again to knock me out of it. I reach up with my hands to grab his dick, but Anders leans forward and tugs my hands behind my back.

"Uh-uh. Mouth only," he orders, so I start to lick around Miller's cock head, running my tongue around the groove before dipping into the eye. I look up, and he's still watching me, the grip on my hair not loosening at all. I move to the shaft and tickle the rings with the tip of my tongue before gripping one and giving it a tug. This gets a slight intake of breath in response, but it still isn't what I'm looking for. I want to see him come undone.

Anders renews his efforts. Up until that moment, he was still letting the two of us get situated, but now he starts thrusting again. His hands sneak around to play with the ring in my clit while Miller guides his cock into my mouth. I bob up and down in time with Anders's thrusts, hollowing my cheeks and sucking. He keeps pushing deeper and deeper until he passes my gag reflex and slides down my throat. I breathe through my nose as the two of them work me between them. He stays there a moment too long, and I feel myself start to panic, but then just as I'm about to struggle, he retreats. I glare up at him through teary eyes, but he just smirks. He's getting off on pushing my limits, and I may have enjoyed it if I didn't see Matthew behind him, his eyes on Miller's ass and his cock in his hand.

"God, man, you should feel this pussy. I thought with the rumors of her being a pro, it would be wrecked, but it grips my cock like a glove, and she loves what you're doing to her. It pulses every time you thrust. How does she feel, man?" Anders babbles behind me, and I almost smile, but Miller thrusts again, and I can't. I renew my efforts, although I'm struggling to focus on his dick with my arms locked behind my back while Anders pounds my cunt and plays with my clit ring. It flutters madly, and I can feel my orgasm barreling toward me. Miller thrusts in time with Anders, and I feel his cock jerk in my mouth. He kindly taps one finger on my head, letting me know he's getting close.

"Feels like fucking heaven," Miller finally replies. "I want to see my cum on her skin." He pulls out and uses his hand to lift my body so I rest with my back against Anders's chest. The whole of my body is exposed to his view. He moves slightly so he's actually blocking me from Matthew's sight, and I feel a wave of gratitude—not that he's looking at it anyway. Matthew shuffles so he has a clear view of Miller's hand wrapped around his own length as he pumps it with hard, quick strokes.

I'm mesmerized as he leans in and pinches one of my nipples with his other hand. It's enough to send me over the edge I was perched on, and I gasp, throwing my head back and closing my eyes as my pussy clamps down hard on Anders's dick. My orgasm rolls through my body, sending my nerve endings haywire. Anders grunts and thrusts, but he leans his head on my shoulder, and his whole body shudders as he can't hold out any longer. At the same time, I feel a splash of hot liquid against my lower belly and pussy, and I open my eyes and watch as Miller, his neck muscles corded and his jaw tight, paints my body with his cum. That sight, combined with Anders's continued little thrusts, is enough to tip me over the edge again, and I come for a second time.

"Holy fuck. God, this is grade A pussy. She came just from that," Anders mumbles to Miller as I hear a grunt and turn to see Matthew coming into a napkin he has pressed against his cock. I should feel dirty and gross that he just got off watching us, or I'm guessing watching Miller, but I just feel boneless and amazing.

Miller moves again, blocking Matthew's view, as he runs his hands through the mess he made. A smile unlike any I've ever seen before is on his face.

He rubs his cum into my skin and leans in, muttering, "Now you're going to go to bed tonight smelling like me and feeling me all over you. Don't wash it off," he demands before bending down and pulling his jeans up. It's like a switch is flipped, and the passionate man is gone. In his place is the cold, cruel person I've come to know. He fastens his pants, turns around, and pushes past Matthew, returning to the bar. Matthew chuckles as he cleans himself up.

"I think we broke him. Never mind. He'll do what we want him to now. I have that all on camera. You too, Mac, and if either of you say anything to anyone, I'll tell your foster parents what you did here. How long do you think it will be before you're both on the streets then?"

My eyes widen, and I struggle away from Anders, whose dick is still in my pussy. I feel his cum leak down my legs as I pick up my clothes. "Please don't. I need this home. I don't have long before I graduate, and I need to get into a good college." The desperation in my voice is clear, and Matthew just smirks as he tosses his napkins to the side and does up his pants.

"Well, I guess you better do as I say then. Now clean up and get back out there. Anders, you don't get to fuck her unless I say you can, alright? When you clean up when we close, make sure you keep that dick away from her. I have plans for her, and that doesn't include any of you indulging in a little fun," Matthew orders as he tosses more napkins at me, which I grab.

"Sure, boss, thank you for the treat," Anders agrees

affably, plucking one of the napkins out of my hand and wiping his dick before redressing. How he managed to keep his jeans and underwear mostly on while I was completely naked, I have no idea. I got a little caught up in the fun.

"But... But..." I start to argue with Matthew, but he just steps forward and slaps me, my head jolting to the side from the impact. Tears well in my eyes from the pain, and I gape at him, holding my cheek.

"I own you now, and you better not think about running off to tell anyone. This town is not as nice as it looks, and there is no one who is going to help a desperate little slut like you, especially one with a solicitation record. Hell, I'm an upstanding business-man, you'll get laughed at. Keep your mouth shut if you want to keep breathing and living freely," he threatens before winking and leaving without another word.

Conscious of the camera filming us, Anders bends down, picks up my uniform, and tosses it at me. I drop the napkins I was holding to grab my clothes out of the air. "Get dressed, break's over," he tells me and goes to leave. As he walks past me, he leans in. I'm worried he's going to blow his cover by checking to make sure I'm alright, but all he does is whisper, "Remember what Miller said. Leave his cum where it is. Let's keep the emotional man child happy." Then loudly, he says, "Hurry up."

My mouth drops open, and I gape at him as he leaves me naked, alone, and well fucked.

CHAPTER 18

LATHAN

We had a short team meeting, minus Mac, after we all returned in the afternoon. Ry made us coffee, and we sat in the conservatory again. It seems to be our go-to meeting place, as there is enough room for all of us. I brought everyone up to speed on what Mac and I found under the library.

"So you saw Billy and Ashley carrying Bishop's body? But that doesn't explain why Mac wasn't wearing panties when Dayton and I took her to the hot springs." Anders has a smirk on his face, and the others all look at me with surprise. Asshole!

I glare at him, but he just keeps smirking at me.

"What does Anders mean, Lath?" Ry is the first to break, just like always.

Max chuckles. "Poor Mackenzie, she's really struggling to keep her underwear on during this mission."

I feel my cheeks heat as I think about how Mac and I had sex in the tunnels under the library. I've never been so attracted to a woman before. She's smart, funny, and freaking ballsy as shit. She makes all of the other female agents we've had look like amateurs. I also think there's something a little fragile about her. I know she and her parents have an amazing relationship and she's close to them, but in her line of work, she really has to distance herself emotionally, and I think it can wear on someone after a while. All I wanted to do was find a bed and hold her. I'm not sure if Mac is the snuggling type though.

"Um, well, it wasn't my fault she wasn't wearing panties... or not completely," I argue, and I tell them about her session with the pastor. Anders and Dayton already knew, but the others didn't.

"We knew that was the case. I'm surprised he risked that in the confessional though." Max rubs the stubble on his chin. He doesn't shave because Stella hates it and keeps asking him to shave it off. She says it gives her a rash, so he refuses to. I call it his forcefield.

I feel so sorry for him. He came through the door about an hour after I arrived home from dropping Jessica off. Anders and Dayton had already gone for a swim with Mac. He didn't say anything, and he went directly to the shower and didn't emerge for another half an hour. Ryland and Miller were home by then. Ry quizzed him, but he's tight-lipped on what occurs between him and Stella. He did say he hasn't slept with her, using the excuse that he respects her purity vow. Apparently, Stella was head of her morality group in her senior year as well. She can't argue with him, since she still wears the purity ring, but we can see she's wearing him down. He says he feels dirty even just kissing her.

Although we haven't talked about it as a team yet, I can see Max is smitten with Mac. Everyone is, and it's a subject we need to broach.

"So you're saying nothing happened in the tunnels between you and Mac?" Dayton's eyes are narrowed on me, and I look from him to Anders.

"Did she tell you something did?" I hedge, and I know I said the wrong thing when Dayton grins.

"No, but we know all your tells, and avoiding answering a question is one of them. Spill."

Without going into detail, I tell them what happened. Ry laughs like it's the funniest thing he's heard, but the rest are quiet for a moment as they contemplate what I told them. I forge on, knowing our team will dance around the subject until the mission's over and we end up going our separate ways. She will return to her ghost status, and we will miss out on someone who would suit our team perfectly.

"I really like her. I'm sick of being alone. I want someone to come home to at night, but none of the agents we've trialed before suited us. None of them were as skilled and talented as she is, not to mention she's kind of awesome, and all of them picked favorites amongst us. That was never going to work.

Mackenzie won't pick favorites, I can already tell. She likes all of us and respects us, even Miller, who has been downright hostile to her. She also isn't going to get annoyed when I'm lost in my work and can't focus all of my attention on her, or when Ryland and Miller need alone time. Hell, she even stands up to Max when he's being all daddy dom." Dayton and Anders chuckle at that.

I can hear the desperation in my voice, and I'm shocked at it. All of this was just sitting below the surface, and I hadn't realized. I guess I've been bottling up more than I thought I was. "I'm sick of living out of a suitcase and can't wait to put down roots in our new house. I don't want to look at another mission for at least a couple of months once this one is done." I really am tired, and I hadn't realized how dysfunctional our team had become with Bishop in it. We've all kind of avoided hanging out together because he always did something to wind someone up. I miss my friends, the men who have become my brothers.

Again, there's silence for a moment. My heart is racing, and I'm worried I've spoken too soon, but Max slowly raises his hands in a defensive gesture. "You aren't going to get an argument from me. I fell for her the minute she dropped her towel in defiance. I agree with you completely, but it has to be unanimous. This team has come too far to let it fall apart. Unlike the Bishop issue, this has the potential to break us if we are not in agreement."

"I like her. I'm certainly willing to give it a try, but

we all need to agree," Anders adds, looking at Miller and Ryland. Before either of them can give their input, Dayton speaks up.

"Guys, is there any point in talking about this? Mac might not even want it. She seemed pretty adamant about keeping her ghost status when her dad sprung this on us."

"Yes, she did, but that might have changed too. We certainly changed our opinions," I argue.

Miller and Ryland are whispering to each other, and I'm not sure how it's going. Both of them have excellent poker faces, but Miller hasn't stormed off, so that's something.

"Well, until we know how she feels, there's no point in continuing this conversation." Dayton is always practical.

"No, but it won't hurt for us to know where we stand," Anders reasons.

"If we're all not in agreement, then there's no point in even broaching the subject with Percy or her," Max agrees as we wait for Ryland and Miller to give us their opinion.

"Don't be such a stubborn asshole," Ryland snaps, standing up and glaring down at his partner. "You know this will work, but you're being a fucking dick."

My eyes widen as I stare at my teammate in shock. He's so freaking easygoing that when he does explode, it's surprising.

"Calm down," Miller says, waving a hand at his

partner, and we all know he said the wrong thing as Ry sneers at him.

"You're so busy trying to prove you're better than anyone else and resenting her for the relationship she has with her parents that if you got out of your own way, you would see how this is the perfect solution. Hell, if this worked, we could marry her, and they would actually be your parents, you fucking dumbass!" Ryland is shouting by the end.

"Whoa, who said anything about marriage? I thought you wanted to fuck her," Miller deflects, which is definitely the wrong move.

Ryland growls. "Stop it. This is serious. You're so hot and cold all the time. You're the one who is causing problems now, not Bishop, and definitely not Mac. Pull your head out of your ass."

Ryland storms out of the room as Miller gets up and chases after him with a small glimmer of panic in his eyes. He has to be careful. It takes a lot to upset Ryland, so he must feel pretty strongly about this. Hopefully they can sort it out without it becoming a bigger issue. The rest of us just look at each other. I get up to follow them, but Max waves me back down.

"They need to sort this out between themselves. Ry will be okay. Miller wants this, he's just too stubborn to admit it. You know what he's like. Seeing Percy get shot was devastating for him, even if it was fake. He doesn't trust very easily, and when you make it into his inner circle, he will protect you with his life. He feels like he failed Percy and Sadie."

"But it wasn't real," I argue, and Max sighs.

"For a few moments, it was, and he lost the man he considers a father and hero worships. You know how bad his life was until Percy rescued him from the horror show of foster homes he experienced. He's having trouble forgiving Kensington, and realizing how close she is to both Sadie and Percy is also a slap in the face. I think he feels like they hid it from him."

"Well, they kind of did, always keeping us apart," Anders points out, and Max shrugs.

"I guess they feel like they had a reason. Let's table this conversation until Miller comes to a decision. It's too important to force this on him."

Anders and Dayton fill us in on finding the body and the subsequent response from the authorities.

"Chief Thompson is a good actor. He said all the right things and went through the right motions. You never would have guessed he was in the know," Dayton says.

"Yeah, him and the medical examiner. I'm not sure about the rest of the police force, but I guess only time will tell," Anders says before telling us that Matthew expected him to fuck Mac in front of cameras tonight. "They want blackmail material."

"But they already have that," I argue, but Max shakes his head.

"No, Mac doesn't know about that. They need something to hold over her head. The other one is to hold over mine."

"Tonight would be as good a time as any to check

out the tunnels." Dayton has been quiet this whole time, listening and planning. "Bishop's body has been removed, and they are going to be distracted while dealing with that. We may not have many more days if they are having a club night on Friday. The auction will certainly be soon after."

"It seems like it, considering what Mac overheard. Those two guys Lathan identified as Lucy's and Michelle's fathers have ties to trafficking in Europe. I think it would be safe to assume they are here to make sure everything goes smoothly. Are you still monitoring the auction page, Lathan?" Anders asks, and I nod.

"Yes, it's still inactive. I have it set to alert me the minute it comes back online."

"Okay, I'd also like to poke around the docks again. With Isaac Palmer in the mix, I bet they are using Ted's shipping containers to smuggle them out of the country. We need to look into the customs inspectors at the port. They must have one of them in their pocket, or at least some blackmail material on them." Max gets up and stretches before gathering the empty coffee mugs.

"We need to find where they keep all their blackmail material. We've theorized that's what they use the sex club for, but they must keep those cameras on an internal server or something. I was able to hack into the ones in the tunnel, cells, and the school, but I haven't been able to find any that show signs of this sex club," I tell the guys, annoyed and frustrated at my lack of success.

"Okay. If we find the club, we'll poke around and see if we can find their security area. They have to have one. I'm guessing we will find all the tapes there. Let's plan to leave around ten. The Life Lounge is only open until twelve tonight, so that gives us a couple of hours while you guys are at work," Dayton tells Anders.

"Matthew will be at the club, we already know that, so we only have to worry about where the rest of the suspects are." I stand and pick up my laptop. I need to scan the card, and the rest of my equipment is in my room.

"Actually, we don't have to worry about that. Stella told me that her mom has book club with her female friends, and her dad was going to the club for a drink with the partners. She was trying to get me to come over to her place." Max wrinkles his nose, and I can guess what she wanted from him. "I told her I was expecting a phone call from Dad, and I would see how long that took. I can now call her and use the discovery of Bishop's body as an excuse not to go."

With that, Max takes the dirty mugs to the kitchen, and I return to my bedroom to clone the card. On my way past Ryland's bedroom, I hear a low moan, and I smother my chuckle. I guess the two of them sorted out their issues. That, or Miller distracted Ryland with sex. Hopefully it was the former. I really want to know where we stand with Mac.

Breaking into the library is a piece of cake. The alarm system is old and easy to hack, and Ryland picks the back door lock like it was nothing. There are no cameras in the library except one, which points at the circulation desk, and it was easy enough to hack the feed and loop it so it doesn't show us moving through the library.

The four of us are dressed in black as we creep across the library to the elevator. There's no one in the library, but we stick close to the shadows in case anyone driving past just so happens to look in the big front windows.

I lead the guys down to the basement, and the key card works perfectly. When we get to the tunnels, we all flip our infrared goggles down. We decided we didn't want to risk flashlights in case someone is down here.

"Billy and Ashley came from that direction and went that way," I tell them quietly when we get to the fork in the tunnel. "I had a look at Mac's map while we were in the library, and we need to follow the path they took. It leads in the direction of the big space under the movie theater and then branches off in different directions. The exit in the movie theater would be the closest to a parking lot. I'm assuming they shoved his body in the back of the car you saw to transport him."

"Okay. Guns out just in case. I'll lead. Dayton, you're on my six, and you two, watch our backs," Max tells us and pushes through to go first.

I do as he says and pull my weapon, waiting for Dayton to move before I go, and Ry is last. We don't get very far before Dayton stops and cocks his head.

"Did you hear that?" he asks and looks back in the opposite direction. We all wait. The sound of my breathing seems loud in the silence, but I hear nothing.

Dayton shakes his head. "Never mind. I must have been mistaken."

"We're all a little jumpy right now," Ryland reassures him, and we start walking again.

"How did things go with Miller?" I whisper to my friend. "Did you sort anything out?"

I turn back to look at him, the green glow of my goggles destroying his features, but I see him shake his head.

"Yes and no. He said he would try. He drives me crazy. I know he's attracted to her. Heck, I know he respects her too, he's just all up in his head. You know Miller. Apart from us, Percy, and Sadie, he trusts no one, and it took forever for him to trust that they wouldn't betray him."

I turn forward, feeling slightly disappointed. "Yeah, Miller has some issues. Let's just hope he can get out of his own way long enough to realize how right this is."

Ryland puts his hand on my shoulder and gives it a squeeze. "Don't worry, Lathan. This will work out, you'll see."

We don't talk any more as we follow Dayton and Max. I can hear the two of them murmur to each other occasionally, but mostly, we're just quiet. I've been keeping an eye out for more cameras, but there doesn't seem to be any in this tunnel either. Only in the space with the cells.

I'm not sure how long we've been walking, but it isn't too long before Max stops again just before another alcove. He peers around the doorframe before moving backward.

"Lath, there's a camera. Can you hack it?" he asks, and I shove my gun into the waistband of my pants, pull my backpack off, and take out my mini laptop. MITHOS has tech guys who designed powerful computers in small devices, making it easier for missions.

They move out of the way, allowing me to move forward. I crouch down and brace my back against the wall as my fingers fly across the keys, searching for networks. The camera has to be operating on a system, I just need to find the right one. It doesn't take me long before I am able to hack it, and the picture from the camera comes up on my screen, as do nineteen other dark images. The first one must have infrared capabilities, because it shows an open alcove with two tunnels, and the camera is also facing a large steel door. One of the tunnels is where we are hiding, and the other one leads off in a different direction. The door has a card reader on it. If I think about the town above us, there are probably a few hundred yards between the library and the movie theater/arcade. I'm almost certain we must be under it, and if so, then this is where Mac and I decided the club could possibly be.

The other screens are dark, with no lights on anywhere, so I can't get a good idea of what we are looking at, but I'm going to assume these are all inside the club.

I loop the cameras to continue showing nothing before closing the laptop and shoving it back into the bag. Pulling the key card out of my pocket again, I tell them, "Okay, done. I looped all the ones on the same network. They were dark, but I'm assuming it's inside the club. I'm also assuming this key will open that door as well."

"We might as well try it. I doubt it will have an alarm. They wouldn't expect anyone else to be running around in these tunnels," Max agrees.

"What about that tunnel?" Dayton asks, nodding toward the one leading away.

"You and Ry can check it out quickly. Lath and I will go through the door. Turn on your comms so we can keep in contact." We all have earpieces in but haven't needed them up until now because we stayed together.

Dayton nods, and he and Ryland peel away, picking up the pace and hurrying down the tunnel.

"Ready?" Max asks me, and I nod, passing him the key. "Cover me."

"I didn't see anyone inside, but there could be rooms without cameras that are occupied. Go carefully." I pull my gun back out and follow my team leader, my adrenaline kicking in as we go through the door.

CHAPTER 19

DAYTON

Ry and I hurry along the tunnel to see where it leads to. It only goes another hundred yards or so and stops at another elevator. I pull out my card and swipe it. Stepping in, we ride it to the top, and it exits out of a building and into a parking area. I flip up my infrared goggles so I don't get blinded by the light that illuminates the area. This side is shadowed by the building and a wall that blocks off a loading dock. It must be the back of the movie theater and arcade. It probably doesn't get a lot of foot traffic and would make a good spot to load a body into a car. I wonder if this is how they bring people into the cells. At night, it would be easy.

"Let's head back to Max and Lathan. There's nothing to see here," I say to Ry. He swipes his card and presses the button to go down. "But they could have easily brought Bishop's body out this way and stuffed him into the trunk of the car."

"No cameras?" he asks, and I shake my head as we exit and walk back down the tunnel. I drop my goggles again so I can see in the murky darkness.

"No, it seems they only have them focused around major points."

"I guess they probably don't have the manpower to have them watched around the clock. It makes sense to have them focused on the cells and inside the club, if that's what that space is." He falls silent as we arrive back at the place where we left Lathan and Max. Neither of them are around, but the door is cracked. Ry slides his hand into it and goes to pull the door open when I hear something. I hold my hand up in a fist, and he freezes. We stand there, and I strain my ears to listen, but I hear nothing again.

"Must be the wind in the tunnels." I wave for my teammate to head through the door. We enter into what looks like a long hallway. Max and Lath are nowhere to be seen, so we follow the passage. On either side are doors. Ry stops and turns the handle on one, pushing it open. It's hard to make out what's inside with the goggles on, so I pull them off as Ry takes a flashlight out of his vest pocket. He turns it on and flashes it around. I wrinkle my nose at the smell. It's definitely been disinfected. The room shows a hospital grade bed with plastic coating on the mattress. On a side wall, there are a number of BDSM tools, including floggers, whips, and hand and foot restraints ranging from zip ties to leather and metal cuffs. The floors are cement, and there is a drain in the middle of it.

"Fuck," Ry hisses as his light catches on the drain. "That's not good." We pull the door closed and move on to the next one. "I wonder if they are all that clinical."

I open the door to the next room, and this one is even worse. There's no bed, just chains hanging from the ceiling with sharp hooks on them, and another drain in the floor directly below the suspension apparatus. "God, I'm going to be sick." Ry gags.

I look at the room, trying to get a handle on my emotions. I have to look at this objectively for now. I can get angry and grossed out later. I enjoy tying my partner up as much as anyone, but this takes it to a whole new sadistic level. "We need to check the hospitals in town and the surrounding areas. People must require medical attention after this kind of thing. Where are they being treated? There have to be records."

Ry pulls the door closed. "We'll get Lath to do a search when we get back. I don't know if I can handle looking at the other rooms."

"We need to. If they are all like this, then they are going to expect something different from Max when he joins. Domination is not going to be enough. They may expect blood to be drawn. Mac and Miller could be in danger. We may have to change tactics." I am more than a little worried for my teammates now. This is becoming way darker than I expected.

The flashlight is illuminating Ry's face, and I see him blanch at the idea of his boyfriend and the girl we are all growing to care for being subjected to any of this.

"Fuck!" He turns and heads along the corridor, opening and shutting doors. He gets two more down and stops, and then he turns to look at me, and I see his horrified expression. "I found how they are being treated."

I move over to him and peer over his shoulder. The powerful flashlight is illuminating a hospital room with shelves full of bandages, gauze, medicine, and vials of drugs.

"They must have a medical practitioner in their pockets, maybe a disgraced doctor or nurse, because no one with a valid medical license would be happy treating wounds caused by this kind of abuse." He sounds completely freaked out.

"You have to remember though, Ry, that some people actually get off on pain and degradation. Hopefully most of what goes on down here is consensual." I try to reassure him, but I don't think it's working.

"Not if they are making their sex slaves perform. Those kids being auctioned off don't have a choice," he argues.

"Yeah, I don't know, man. I have a feeling that what happens in this club and the auction may be completely separate enterprises." I'm starting to feel doubtful about what we know about the club. "There's no way they could keep everyone's mouths shut about this. Look at how many rooms there are, and we haven't gotten to the main club section. That's a lot of people to blackmail. This club may be an underground sex club, but I don't think it and the auction operate together. They have to be separate things, even if they are run by the same people."

"Well, I guess we'll know a lot more after Friday night. Try not to worry about it. Miller and Mac can handle themselves, and you and Max are going to get an invite. Between the four of you, I'm sure you can work something out," I reason, but I can see his mind is running wild.

He closes the door and opens the next one down from it. He heaves out a huge sigh of relief and steps aside. This one is more like a mainstream sex club. It has a normal bed with just a protector sheet, a set of blankets, and things to make it. There's a St. Andrew's Cross in the corner of the room and an adult-sized cage, as well as a weirdly shaped chair. I can see the potential to its shape and how it may be used. More bondage equipment is sitting on shelves, but there is no drain in the middle of this floor. There is, however, a big picture window showing the room next door, which is similar to this one. I'm sure it's for voyeurism.

"Come on, let's go find Lathan and Max. They have to be here somewhere," I tell him. We could use the comms, but they wouldn't have left without us, so they must be farther ahead.

He pulls the door closed, and we keep moving. There are three more sets of doors before we get to the end of the corridor. Another door bars the exit, so I push it open, and we both blink at the sudden onslaught of brightness. Thankfully we had both removed our infrared goggles, otherwise we would have been temporarily blinded.

This room is large, with overstuffed cushions and a lush, carpeted floor. There is a bar on one side of the room, and various fixtures to perform sexual acts on are scattered throughout the space—another St. Andrew's cross, a set of stocks, some spanking benches, and a main stage with a sex swing currently hanging above it. Another small stage in one corner contains a stripper pole, and there's also another large birdcage suspended in the middle of the club.

It's lush and luxuriously appointed, with stylish wall sconces to allow lower mood lighting when the main ones have been turned off. I can hear voices in a room beyond this one, so Ry and I head in that direction. Through a double set of doors, we find Max and Lathan in a small room off what looks like a main foyer. There's a reception desk with a coat room behind it. Through the open doors, I see that there is a changing room off to the side and a set of elevator doors directly on the far side of the foyer. That must be where everyone enters from. Max's and Lathan's voices come from another small room past the coat check.

"Hey, we found an exit. I'm guessing it's where

they took Bishop's body out. It was a loading dock with low traffic," I tell them as they look up when we enter.

"Did you check out those rooms?" Ry asks, and Max and Lathan shake their heads.

"No, we were going to look at them on the way out. We found all their security tapes and where they store their blackmail material." Max nods at a large storage section at the far end of the room, while Lathan continues to look through a video on the screen in front of him. "We were right about blackmail material. Each thumb drive is labeled with a name. This one has Brock Marshall's name on it. I wanted to see what the little creep was into."

Lathan hits a button, and the video on the screen starts to play. It shows the guidance counselor at the school, and he's dressed in a pair of boxers, his fat belly hanging over the waistband. He's on his knees, his hands are bound behind his back, and he has clamps on each of his nipples. A woman wearing black stilettos and a see-through black bodysuit walks around him with a flogger in her hand.

"God, you are a useless piece of crap. Sniveling and worthless. You can't do anything right," she sneers at him before lashing his naked back with the flogger. He cries out, and tears stream down his face. She's wearing a mask across her eyes, but I recognize her short red hair. It's Isaac Palmer's wife. She stops right in front of him and holds out one of her stiletto-clad feet. "Kiss my foot, you ungrateful wretch."

We watch as he leans forward and does as instructed.

"I guess he must be into degradation," I muse.

"Maybe, but then there's this." Lathan speeds the film up until it changes, and instead of him kneeling on the floor, he's on the bed, and he's fucking someone underneath him. He's grunting and panting out dirty words.

"That's right, you dirty bitch, take my cock like the whore you are." We can hear the girl sobbing, even though she's not struggling or fighting him or saying no. She's kind of just lying there and taking it.

Lathan shudders and fast-forwards it so we don't have to listen, but he must come, and when he gets up, we can see the girl. Her makeup streaked face looks familiar.

"Do we know who that is?" I ask.

"Yeah, she works at the Life Lounge with Anders. Her name is Carla," Ryland answers. "He said she is always timid and withdrawn, and flinches at the slightest sound."

"Well, that would explain why," Max says dryly, pointing at the screen as we watch her gather a robe and head through a door in the room, which I'm assuming is a bathroom. We didn't actually check those out.

"And there are hundreds of these in that cupboard. I even found the one labeled with my name."

"Did you grab it?" his brother asks him, and he shakes his head.

"Not yet. If they notice it's missing, it's going to be a problem. Now that we know how to get in and we have access cards, it won't be a problem to retrieve it."

"Shall we check the elevator?" Ry suggests as Lathan turns everything off again and places the thumb drives back where they were.

"Nah, it's not too late, and people might still be around. We don't want anyone seeing us use that elevator. I think it's safe to say that it's in the movie theater or arcade somewhere, if the one you guys used was in the back of it. Did you go far?" Max asks me, and I shake my head.

"A hundred yards or so."

"Maybe tomorrow night, we can pretend to go to the movies and sneak out and snoop around topside. Monday should be a slow night at the cinemas."

"Maybe we can ask Mac to join us. None of them work on Monday nights," Lathan suggests, and I smother a smirk. He's smitten with our temporary team member. I can't say I'm not. I'd be all for making it more permanent, but we need to wait and see what Miller decides. He's going to make it painful for all of us while he pulls his head out of his ass.

"Do we want to poke around some more?" Ryland asks as we leave the office, Lathan flicking all the light switches and plunging us into darkness again. Ry switches the flashlight on and leads us back the way we came.

"I don't think so. We found what we came for. I poked around while Lathan was scanning through the computers. There is nothing else to see here, except maybe the rooms we passed on the way in," Max says behind me.

"No need. Ry and I already did. Individual rooms for sex, some that are little disturbing, and a medical center."

"A medical center?" Lathan sounds surprised. "Why would they need that?"

We get to the door that leads to the hallway and file through, Ry closing it behind him. "For the same reason there are drains in some of the rooms. Dark and depraved shit happens in some of them." Ry's words are flat, but you can hear his disgust.

"Fuck, that's not good. Maybe we should rethink Mac's and Miller's involvement." Lathan sounds worried. Before I can tell him what I told Ry, Max chimes in.

"Don't worry. Hopefully I'll get an invite this week, and I can keep an eye on the two of them. If I don't, we will rethink the plan. I won't risk either of them."

We pass through the storeroom and out into the tunnel system again, walking back in the direction of the library. The only sounds are our quiet footsteps and my own breathing. We get to where it branches off to the library, but I stop when I hear noise again. It's louder this time, and I can tell it's definitely not wind in the tunnel.

"I hear something. Someone is down here." I point in the opposite direction we just came from.

"The cells should be in that direction," Lathan

says. "That's the direction Billy and Ashley came from with Bishop's body."

"Let's check it out, but go slowly," Max says, pulling his gun from his holster.

The four of us creep along the tunnel. It's actually quite a distance, but we must be moving across the other side of town toward the forest where the ranger station is. The sound gets louder the farther we go.

It sounds like voices murmuring, but then it stops. We continue to creep forward, and we arrive at the section of tunnels where the cells are. Staying back, away from the cameras, the four of us stop and stare at what we find. Three of the ten cells are occupied. There are people lying on the beds in each of the cells. I can't make out their sex or features because I'm not close enough, but I can clearly see the IV line going into each of their arms, rendering them unconscious.

"It couldn't have been them that we heard," I whisper to Max, and he shakes his head.

"No, we'll get Lathan to check the footage when we get back to the house."

"Should we rescue them?" Lathan asks, but Ry shakes his head.

"If we do, we'll tip off the ring to our involvement. We need to leave them for now, unfortunately." I can't see Lathan's face, but I can feel the tightness in his body at the idea of leaving them.

"They are well looked after. It looks like they have a catheter in as well. That takes some medical knowl-edge. We need to do a deeper dive into each of their backgrounds to see who has those skills," Max says thoughtfully.

"Yeah, Ry and I were discussing that earlier too. If they are as brutal as we think they are, then someone is patching people up," I reply.

"Unless they are just putting them in shallow graves," Lathan says flatly.

"Come on. It won't be for long. We're going to bust this ring wide open, and those kids there will be able to return to their lives." I nudge him back the way we came.

"Not sure that's any better if they were able to be taken," Ryland grumbles.

"Percy will see that they have a good place to go, you know that. Sadie won't leave him any other choice," I remind him, and he grunts noncommittally.

We move back the way we came. Whoever was here must have left through one of the other tunnels. We know one leads back to the ranger's cottage, but I'm not sure where the other one goes.

"Should we explore that one?" Ry nods in the direction we haven't been yet.

"No, not today. It's late, and Anders will be bringing the others back to the house to install Miller's tracker. I'd like for us to be there so we can tell them what we found. We also don't know which way whoever we heard went. I don't want to risk running into anyone," Max replies, vetoing the idea, and we follow his lead.

We stay silent as we hurry back the way we came,

leaving the library basement how we found it and walking single file across the dusty ground in case someone comes down here.

I'm anxious to get home and see how the others' night went. If it went as planned, then Anders and Mac will have secured her blackmail material. I'm not going to deny I'm curious about how it was. I'm dying to get some alone time with Mac, but I'm not sure it's on the cards for us at the moment. The hot springs will be out now that Bishop's body was found in it. I'll have to see if there is somewhere else close by. Maybe one day after school, I can convince Mac to go for a drive with me. I'd like to claim that last kiss she owes me. I wonder if there is a drive-in cinema close by, because that would be fun. My parents used to take me and my sisters when we were younger. We'd all pile into the van and drive an hour to the one a couple of towns over from where I grew up. It was always a blast, and one of my fondest memories of growing up.

I bet she missed out on a lot of essential teenage stuff like making out in the back of a car. After all, she said our picnic was the first real date she'd ever been on, and I'm determined to change that.

CHAPTER 20

My stomach is sticky with Miller's cum, and I'm sure people will be able to see it under the blue lights of the club, but when I pull my hot pants up, I find it sits below the waistline of the shorts. I quickly finger comb my hair the best I can before returning to the club. When I get to the bar, Anders and Miller have returned to serving, and both of them ignore me.

"Hey, Mac, take that to Matthew, will you?" Keith points to a tray of shots. "Sam and Meri are both busy." I look around the club and can't see either of them working any of the tables. Maybe they are getting high again like the other night. I pick up the tray and head toward the booth with most of our suspects. When I get there, Matthew, Brock, and Father Sweeny are the only people still at the table. Ted and James are missing.

I place the tray on the table before putting each of

the shots in front of the men. "What about these two?" I point to the two remaining ones, looking at Matthew.

"Oh, they will be back. They are just taking care of something." Brock giggles drunkenly at Father Sweeny's words, so I shrug and place them on the table as well. "I was sorry that you didn't get a chance to finish your confession today, Mackenzie. We will have to try again next week."

"Yeah, maybe," I hedge, shuffling like I'm uncomfortable.

"I'm sure that's not necessary. Since she's been working with me, I've found that she follows orders and directions perfectly. With the gentle guidance of James and Martha, I'm certain Mac is on the path to greatness." Matthew pats my hand in a fatherly way, like he didn't just watch two of his staff members spit roast me. All of us can hear the subtext, even though I'm not supposed to know what he's talking about.

"I really like this job," I tell him as he looks at something over my shoulder. I turn and see James and Ted. They are with Meri and Sam, and it looks like they are handing them something. I can't see what, unfortunately, but they look up and see me watching, then they say something and head toward us. The girls walk back to the bar and out to the staff area.

James and Ted slide into the booth and grab their shots, throwing them back. "Mac, could you get us another pitcher of beer? I'm thirsty," James asks, smiling at me and sliding over the empty pitchers with his empty shot glass.

"Absolutely," I reply as I gather the rest of the empties, trying not to notice the smudge of lipstick on James's mouth that perfectly matches the color on Sam's lips.

"You've got a little something," Brock says to James, pointing to his own lip. James's eyes widen, and he quickly rubs it off. I pretend not to notice, but as I lean across Ted to get a couple of extra glasses, I catch a whiff of sex that's not coming from me.

I guess I know what these two were doing. I wonder if they were paying Meri and Sam. Matthew didn't seem surprised at all. Do they prostitute on the side to feed their habits?

"I'll be back soon," I tell them and head back to the bar, placing their order with Keith and cleaning the empty glasses before moving out back. Sam and Meri are both on the couch. There's a line of coke in front of Sam as she leans over with a rolled dollar bill to snort it. She looks up at me but doesn't stop what she's doing. In front of Meri is just a rolled up note and some sprinkles of leftover powder. Her head is back, and she's looking up at the ceiling while the coke floats through her system.

"Do you want a hit?" Sam asks, wiping her nose with the back of her hand. "It makes the night go quicker."

I look at the clock on the wall. It's already half past eleven, so there's only a little bit of the night left to go.

"Nah, I'll be okay," I tell her, and she grins as the coke hits her bloodstream.

"Okay, cool, but if you want something, let me know. We have the best hookups. Our guys really take care of us and make sure we're looked after. They are so sweet. Sundays are my favorite day of the week. Their bitch wives have book club, and they come here to hang out," she rambles, her gaze not really focusing on anything as she leans back like Meri.

"You guys like Ted and James?" I push, knowing their tongues are loose from the coke. I'm sort of confused. I assumed they were being coerced or pressured, but that's not what this sounds like.

"Yeah, for sure. I just wish they could visit us at our place more often, but..." She trails off and looks around like she's checking that nobody is listening. "They are married, so they have to keep up pretenses at home, and we only get to see them on Friday night after poker and Sunday nights." The two of them must not realize that I live with James, otherwise I don't think they would be so forthcoming with all this information.

"They promised us they are going to leave their wives." Meri's head rolls to the side, and she looks at me through bloodshot eyes. Holy crap, how many lines did she snort before I came in here? "They said they have one big shipment that needs to go out in two weeks, and they will have enough set aside for us to move to Mexico together."

Whoa. That's interesting.

"Shipment?" I press, and both of them seem to

realize they said too much. Sam's mouth slams shut, and she stands up, yanking Meri to her feet.

"Come on, it's almost closing time, and James and Ted said they'd come back to our place for a while. Let's hurry so they aren't waiting."

I stand there, gaping, as the two of them head back to the bar. Holy crap, the shipment they are talking about must be the next auction.

I turn around and head back out to the club, my mind churning with everything I learned. I thought for sure Ted and James were happy participants and members of the sex club, and they might be, but it also sounded like they have a long-term relationship with those two girls. Are they just drug-fueled delusions, or could there actually be something more to this? Maybe we should be looking at the motivation behind all of this. Are their marriages not everything they appear to be? I've never seen Martha and James be affectionate with one another. Meri and Sam made it sound like Ted and James had ready access to drugs. Is that part of the deal? Drugs in exchange for young adults who can be sold at auction? James's part is letting them know which foster children who go through his house would be suitable, and Ted's role is providing the shipping containers. Maybe neither of them is the head of the ring. It's pointing more toward Father Sweeny or one of the others. I'm ruling out Brock because he's just gross, but Matthew is starting to look good as well. I guess Friday night will help shed some light on things.

When I get back to the bar, Sam has taken the pitcher of beer to the booth. The crowd has really thinned out, so I can see her laughing and smiling with the men. She doesn't seem scared or hesitant or worried at all.

I shake my head and turn to speak to Anders about what I just learned, but he and Keith are already cleaning their bar sections, filling up liquor bottles and dumping empties. My eyes catch on Miller, who has a cloth and is wiping down some booths in the back corner. Now's my chance to talk to him alone. I grab a cloth and tell Meri I'm going to help clean up. She just smiles and waves, off in her own world, singing along to the last couple of tracks for the night.

I come up behind Miller, so he doesn't see me and bolt. Placing the tray on the table, I put my hand on his arm. He startles but quickly recovers and stares down at me with that blank gaze. "What do you want, Mac?" he asks, continuing to wipe the table.

"Are you okay?" I ask him, and he finally stops what he's doing.

"Okay?" He sounds confused. He crosses his arms, but then he actually looks at me.

"Yeah, I'm sorry about what happened. It's not fair when you didn't have a choice." I kind of stumble awkwardly over the words. I've never had to apologize for giving someone a blow job before.

He's silent for a moment before a slow grin creeps across his lips, and he chuckles darkly. "Are you apologizing for sucking my dick? I can assure you it was no hardship on my behalf."

"Ugh, why do you always have to be an asshole? I'm trying here," I hiss at him. "I know it wasn't something you would have chosen if Matthew hadn't insisted, alright? It felt wrong because he was forcing you. Anders and I both knew what was going to happen and were on board with it. You weren't."

He's quiet for a moment, but then he slowly shakes his head and steps toward me, caging me between himself and the table. He leans forward, putting his hands on the table behind me, his mouth inches from mine.

"If you think that I didn't know there would be a chance I would be forced to participate when I came to look for you, you're wrong. I also enjoyed every single moment of it. I loved seeing tears in your eyes and my cock in your mouth. It would have been even better if it had been Ry destroying your pussy instead of Anders." He pulls away quickly, snatches up his cloth and tray, and returns to the bar, leaving me reeling.

Fuck. He always keeps me so off balance. He's really messing with my head. My eyes follow him across the club, but they stop when they meet Matthew's cold gaze. He's looking at me and smirking as he glances between Miller and me. I wonder how this looked to him. Did we look a little too cozy with one another, or did it look like we were arguing? He doesn't seem upset at all, only pleased. Who knows what that could mean?

I move on to the next booth to clear. I'm not close enough to Matthew and the rest of the men to hear what they are talking about. Miller and I go back and forth a couple of times as security starts to herd people out of the club and the music turns off. Finally, only Matthew and his group are left. We're busy cleaning when they all get up to leave. None of them acknowledge anyone as they walk out the door, and I head over to their table and start clearing it.

On the table is a fifty dollar note, a bag with a couple of pills, and a napkin with writing on it.

Mac, club is closed next Friday for a private event. You will be working. Don't expect to be home before morning. I let James know. Good work tonight. Enjoy the party favors. There's more of that if you're a good girl.

I take a closer look at the pills. I'm guessing it's ecstasy. I shove it all in the tiny pocket of my hot pants and clear off the table. We want to check out where the tunnels below us lead, and then we have to insert Miller's tracker. It seems like James is going to be distracted for a while, so I don't have to worry too much about getting home. Martha is bound to be asleep.

When I return to the bar, Keith, Meri, and Sam are putting on jackets and grabbing their stuff. Meri and Sam seem to be coming down from their coke high. All three of them wave goodbye, leaving Anders, Miller, and me to finish the job. It doesn't take us long, since most of it was done. Miller disappears into the staff room, and when I go out to grab my own jacket, he has a little laptop in his hands similar to Lathan's, his fingers flying across the keyboard as fast as our resident techy.

My mouth drops open in shock, and Anders chuckles as he joins us. "Miller is quite the tech savant as well. He's our backup in case Lathan is busy like he is tonight. He's looping the cameras for us so we can use the card to check out the basement."

Miller looks up and smirks. "Didn't you say you weren't very good at tech stuff? Maybe I am the better agent after all." He slaps it shut and stands up. "Done, let's go. Mac and I don't have a huge amount of time, and we still need to go back to the governor's mansion for you to insert the tracker."

We grab our things and make our way to the door next to the walk-in refrigerator. We lock it behind us, not needing to go back into the club again. There were no empty kegs to take out today, so the little alcove is empty. Anders pulls a card out of his back pocket and swipes it across the keypad.

"Lathan made us all a copy just in case. He has one for you too, Mac," he tells me as the keypad lights up green before the doors open in front of us. We hurry in, and he swipes the card again and hits the bottom button. The top one has a plaque with "Life Lounge" scrolled on it, but they said it isn't used to access the club, only the stairs on the inside.

The elevator descends, and the doors open to a dark room. Miller turns on a flashlight and shines it around, looking for a light switch. It doesn't take him long to find one, and soon, the room is lit up. It's full of old or broken furniture, and there are even a couple of poker tables and slot machines. They look a little newer, so I'm guessing the club has casino theme nights occasionally. There's also what looks like a large birdcage.

"What's this?" I ask, going over to it and opening the door, which swings wildly back and forth. One of the hinges is broken. I steady it and step in. The base of the cage is solid, and the bars are fairly sturdy.

"It's a dance cage from the club upstairs. It needs some repairs, so it was removed. It hasn't been fixed yet, which is why it's here for now," Anders says distractedly as he looks around, frowning.

"That's weird," he says, scratching his head. "Matthew and I brought some big wine barrels down here after church. He didn't want to leave them out in the alcove, they would have taken up too much space, but now they are gone. I can't see them anywhere."

He's right, there are no big wine barrels anywhere in the room, but I do spy large double doors down at the far end. There's a card scanner there too. "Shall we see where that goes?" I ask them, nodding at the doors. "Maybe it will solve where the wine barrels went."

Anders frowns. "I guess it couldn't hurt." He pulls a card from his pocket and holds it over the reader. Sure enough, the two doors click open. Miller pulls a gun and a flashlight out of his backpack and goes through them first. I feel so naked without my own weapon, but I trust that they know what they are doing. Heck, from what I understand, Miller's skills are on par with mine. I just itch to have security in my palm.

I follow behind them, goosebumps breaking out over my skin. Although I have my jacket on, it's cold down here, and I'm really not wearing much.

Anders and I follow behind Miller. All is quiet down here, but it gives me a creepy feeling. We travel quite a distance. One thing I notice about this tunnel is it's a little wider than the one from the library. They definitely could have fit large wine barrels down here.

Miller stops suddenly, and Anders and I struggle not to run into his back. I hear him curse quietly. We both step to either side of him so we can see what he's looking at. It's another small alcove, similar to the one Lathan and I hid in, with the missing wine barrels inside. Anders takes Miller's flashlight from him and walks over to look at them. The lids are resting against the side of the barrels. He points the light inside them, and this time, he's the one who curses quietly. "They are empty. Where could all the wine have gone?" He keeps moving a little farther down the tunnel, but he doesn't get very far. "Fuck, come here."

His voice sounds urgent, and Miller and I don't hesitate. He's standing at the end, peering into the room with the cells. I guess he remembered the cameras are there and doesn't want to get caught. It's no longer shrouded in darkness. This room has lights set between each of the cells, and they are dimly lit, providing enough light so we can see three of the cells are now occupied.

"Holy crap," I mutter, taking in the three occupants of the cells. They have IVs running into their arms, and catheter bags hanging off the beds at the end. "They are drugged. I wonder if they will stay like that until the auction, or if it was just while they were transported.

Miller, who has been quiet this whole time, chimes in. "Are we guessing that wine wasn't what was in those barrels, and that they are actually transporting them like that?"

"I think it's a pretty safe guess," Anders mutters angrily. "I can't believe they were below my nose, and I didn't even notice. Matthew was yapping the whole time, and I was too busy listening to him to notice anything was off about the barrels."

We back up, knowing we can't do anything about the prisoners for now. If we do, it will tip off the ring that someone is on to them.

I trip over something and almost fall, but Miller catches my arm and steadies me. A feeling of dread washes over me. The last time I tripped over something in a tunnel, it was Bishop's body. Anders shines the light at the ground, and I heave out a sigh of relief when it's just a big cushion. There's a large pile of them between two of the barrels.

"I guess that's why you didn't notice anything off. They were well padded to stop them from rolling around in there," I say, hoping it will reassure Anders a little. He must be kicking himself—not that he could have done anything without blowing our cover.

"Come on, let's get out of here. We need to insert your tracker and get home. We don't want to arrive at the same time as James. That would be awkward as fuck." Miller, who is still holding my arm, gives it a little tug before releasing it and letting Anders lead the way now that he has the light. He tucked his gun into the waistband of his pants and is walking next to me. Our hands brush occasionally, but he doesn't seem perturbed by it, so I don't move.

We make sure the double doors are secured behind us before we quickly move through the storeroom and back to the street. Anders's car is the only one left in the lot, and we jump in and head back to the governor's mansion without any more words. This case is weighing on all of us, and leaving those teens there doesn't help. We just have to make sure we do everything we can to stop them from going any further.

CHAPTER 21

RYLAND

We've only been home about half an hour when Anders's truck pulls around the back of the house. I feel the rush of excitement I always feel when I haven't seen Miller for a few hours. It's more intense now because he'll have Mac with him. I wonder what kind of mood he'll be in. He always gets so riled up anytime he has to spend time with her. He becomes wonderfully bratty, and I have to take him to task in such decadent ways. My body is practically humming with anticipation.

A chuckle has me turning my attention from the door to my brother. "Settle down. They will be here momentarily."

I flip him off, and we fall into silence, only the sound of Lathan's fingers on his keyboard breaking the quiet.

"I set up Anders's things in the kitchen. Percy sent trackers for everyone with instructions that we can't avoid it anymore." Dayton appears from the direction of the kitchen and takes a seat on the couch next to my brother.

"Isn't it going to look a little suspicious if we're all wearing bandages?" Lathan mutters absently.

"No, we can say we all got new tattoos. It would be good to put one over the scar to hide it anyway. I'll take care of it when the incision heals up," Dayton offers as Anders opens the back door and steps inside, followed by my boyfriend and Mac. They look tense, and I can tell by the set of Miller's jaw that something is wrong. This isn't a fight between Mac and Miller, though, because Anders looks upset as well. He's usually so even-keeled that it takes a lot to rile him up.

"What's wrong?" I ask, looking between them as Miller drops his backpack on the coffee table. It's one he keeps here at our place. He said he doesn't feel comfortable leaving his gun at Serenity House for anyone to discover. I wonder if Mac has one hidden there.

"We poked around downstairs. The storeroom does lead into the tunnels. We followed it and discovered some of the cells are now occupied," Anders tells us before heading to the kitchen and returning with some beers. He holds one out to Mac, who shakes her head.

"And we worked out how they got them down there," she adds as Miller also shakes his head for the proffered beer. Anders puts the two spare ones on the coffee table.

"Yeah, we know," Max tells them, grabbing Mac as she passes him and pulling her onto his lap. She struggles for a moment, but with a whispered word from him, she relaxes back into his body. I know they are both struggling with his involvement with Stella. They should really talk about it, but they are dancing around their feelings.

I have to admit, I was surprised by Lathan's balls when he brought up the subject this afternoon. He's usually not so open with how he feels, but he wasn't wrong. We have all reacted to Mac, and throwing our cards on the table and clearing the air between us was definitely needed. Miller is the only one who is being stubborn. I think I fucked some sense into him after his little tantrum. He admitted he's attracted to her and that he would at least try. He also admitted he was being stubborn because she's nothing like he expected and everything he could want in a woman—everything we both want—and that's intimidating to him. He thought he had her pegged due to her Princess Kensington persona, and he doesn't want to let his heart get involved only for her to destroy it. He might not survive it.

Miller has had a long struggle with self-worth and confidence. His mental health could be better, but Sadie helped him admit he needed support. If a relationship between Mac and Miller doesn't work out, he's worried he would lose the woman who has become a mother to him. Once he was pliant and well fucked, lying in my arms, I helpfully pointed out that Sadie was not the kind of person to pick sides. She would still love him, even if things between us and Mac didn't work out.

"We found the sex club today. All the blackmail material is kept in an office down there. We also saw the prisoners, but you know we can't do anything about them without blowing our mission," Max says.

"We know," Miller replies flatly. "Doesn't mean we didn't want to. Can we do this tracker thing so Mac and I can go please?" I can tell leaving the prisoners there bothered him. Hell, it bothered all of us, but timing is everything.

"It's all set up in the kitchen," Dayton tells Anders, who places his beer on the coffee table and waves for Miller to join him. I stand up. I want to hold my boyfriend's hand while Anders inserts the chip. I'm hoping we might get a quiet moment to talk before they leave.

"I'll take you home when you're ready," I tell Mac. "I'll use Anders's truck. No one will notice the difference since it's dark. That way, he can put everyone else's trackers in too."

"Thanks, that would be great," Mac says absently. I can tell she's distracted by the circles my brother is running over her thigh with his thumb and whatever he is saying in her ear. She doesn't look thrilled by whatever it is. I leave them be. If we're going to be in a multiple person relationship, then we need to let everyone worry about their own connection.

When I get to the kitchen, Anders is already jabbing the numbing agent into Miller's neck. He doesn't have a lot of tattoo free space, and his neck is one place where Anders doesn't have to cut through inked skin. I grab his hand and give it a squeeze. He looks up at me from his seat on the chair, and I can tell he has something he needs to talk to me about.

"How did tonight go?" I ask conversationally, looking between them. Anders tosses the numbing agent back into the tray on the table and picks up the scalpel.

"Good. Matthew got the footage he wanted," Anders says without looking away as he cuts carefully into Miller's skin. "Put those gloves on and dab at the blood for me so I can see what I'm doing," he tells me, nodding at the box of gloves. Miller releases my hand, and I do as asked. He doesn't have to cut too deeply, but it's still a little messy.

"So he has blackmail material to make Mac do what he wants? That's good," I reply as I watch Anders open a sterile package and drop the small, square microchip onto the tray. He uses a pair of tweezers to pick it up and slide the chip into the incision in Miller's neck. We don't talk while he does it, because none of us want him to mess this up. This is a new technology that MITHOS developed in the last eighteen months, and we haven't had a chance to have them inserted yet. The chip runs off the electrical impulses in the body or something. I have no clue how it works, but I bet Lathan does.

Anders puts in two stitches to close up the incision before taping some white gauze over it. "The stitches can come out in ten days, and Dayton can tattoo over it once they come out. I expect it's going to hurt worse than normal, though, over the fresh scar tissue. I have more numbing agent if we need it." He wraps up the mess in the surgical cloth before taking it over to the bin and pulling off his gloves. After, he returns to the table and sets out a fresh tray of equipment.

"Okay, you next." He gestures for Miller to move from the chair, but I shake my head.

"I'm going to run Miller and Mac home in your truck. Do the others first, and then you can do me when I get back."

"Okay, sure. I'll catch you later," he replies as he heads out to the conservatory to grab one of the others.

"I need to talk to you." Miller grabs my hand and drags me up to my bedroom. I stumble a little on the stairs from surprise but allow him to lead me.

When we get there, I sit down on the bed while he paces back and forth, running his hands through his hair. What the hell has him so worked up?

"Anders and I spit roasted Mac while Matthew watched," he blurts, and I feel my eyebrows jump in surprise. Well, this is surprising. I smother the smirk that wants to cross my lips as I feel blood start to fill my dick.

"Oh? Which end did you get?" I ask before adding, "Did you enjoy it?"

Miller stops pacing and turns to gape at me. "Which end did I get? Did I enjoy it?" he repeats before tugging at his hair with both hands. "That's all you can say?"

I shrug. "Yeah. What did you want me to say?"

"Aren't you in the least bit jealous?" he demands, and I sit up a little straighter.

"Do you want me to be? Do you want me to be angry like you are when I do something to her?" I retort. "Do you want me to get upset and punish you?" I watch as his eyes dilate, and I stand up so we're chest to chest. "I don't feel the need to punish you. I want you to want her. I want you to want the three of us together. I want you to have enjoyed it so that while you're sitting across the dinner table in that house of horrors, all you can think about when her lips wrap around her fork is the way they felt wrapped around your dick."

He blinks at me and shakes off the lust. "I don't know what to do." He almost sounds desperate, and I thread my hands through his hair, pulling his head to the side and biting his neck. He grows pliant under my ministrations, and I lick the bite mark.

"You have to give yourself permission to try, to give a fuck about someone other than us, our team, and Percy and Sadie. You also have to trust that she won't betray you like your mother and every other person you put your trust in as a small child. It took me forever to break down your walls. Don't punish Mac for your past, but if punishing you will somehow make this all better, then you better get down on your knees and show me exactly what she did to you."

I push him down, and he goes without any struggle. Miller gets so stuck in his head that he needs me to take control, make decisions for him, and give him permission not to feel ashamed for enjoying sex. He's come a long way, but sometimes, he still reverts to that broken young man that I met at spy school. It's why he's so good at honey trapping. He doesn't let feeling or emotions get in the way. I never have to worry about him getting emotionally involved with anyone, though I can't help but worry what it does to his psyche. Thankfully he doesn't have to do it often, and this is the first mission in a while. I don't think it will come down to either of them needing to sleep with random strangers if Max and I get the invite we're hoping for.

He reaches up to undo the tie on my sweats. I showered when I got home because I knew he wouldn't be staying to have one with me. I push them down my legs, and since I'm not wearing any underwear, my cock pops out, ready to be lavished with attention. I would love to hear him tell me about what Mac did to him, but he's not going to be able to talk with his mouth full. That can wait for another time.

Miller's hand wraps around my shaft, the callouses on his fingers creating a delicious roughness in his strokes as he leans in and licks the drop of precum from the eye. "Is that what Mac did for you?" I ask him as he runs his tongue around the ridge of the head as he cups one of my balls, rolling it on his palm. My ass flexes, and my toes curl as he slides it slightly into his mouth, hollowing his cheeks and sucking lightly. He's teasing me, and I'm dying to shove it down his throat, but we have this little dance to play first. I let him think he's in control, even if it's for a moment, but I know what he really wants is for me to take all that control out of his hands and skull fuck him. I'll do it, but I love the delightful tease of anticipation, both his and mine.

I groan as he slides me a little deeper, clenching my fists so I don't grab his head—not yet, not until he has me all the way in, my cock in his throat and his nose pressed against my pelvis. I love feeling him swallow around my dick and how he struggles to breathe just for a moment. It's such a rush, seeing him heaving for air, his eyes all foggy with lust and love. God, it feels incredible.

I'm just about to take control when there's a knock on the door and Mac says, "Hey, are you guys ready? We need to get going."

Miller pauses.

"Did I tell you to stop?" I say to him and flex my hips, encouraging him to keep going as I call out, "Come in."

The door opens, and I watch with delight as Mac steps through, stopping suddenly when she sees Miller with my dick in his mouth.

"Oh, fuck. I'm sorry, I thought you said come in," she stammers, but she can't look away, and I don't stop my small thrusts in and out of his mouth.

"You did. I hear that you had my boyfriend's dick in your mouth. He was just showing me exactly what you did, but now that you're here, you can show me yourself. I don't like to be left out." I nod my head at the space on the floor next to Miller and hold my breath. The anticipation is exquisite, and I almost come down Miller's throat, but I grit my teeth as I watch her wrestle with a decision.

My eyes zero in on her lips as she bites them before turning her head to look back the way she came. I think I've pushed her too far, but all she does is put her hand on the door and close it before joining Miller on the floor at my feet.

I want to roar and bang my fists on my chest as I pull out of his mouth and offer it to her. She doesn't fuck around. She wraps her hand around it, feeling so different from Miller's calloused palm. Hers are soft, smooth, and small, but her grip is perfect. I feel my knees shake as she strokes my length before wrapping her lips around the head. Her mouth is as hot and wet as Miller's, but her lips are red and a little fuller than his. They feel incredible, and I give myself a sharp pinch to my thigh, the bite of pain making my impending orgasm slide away again. Fuck, that was close. Seeing the two of them side by side in front of me is a freaking dream come true. I watch as Mac slides my cock out of her mouth and turns her head so she can run her lips down one side, her eyes daring Miller to do the same on the other. Always up for a challenge, his eyes blaze with heat as he leans in. She is exactly what he needs—someone to challenge him, to goad him into action instead of that fucking apathy that always surrounds him. I know he loves me, but I want him to love life as much as I do. I'm hoping Mac will be the ember that sparks his fire.

I moan loudly as the two of them lavish my dick with attention, their mouths meeting at the end of my cock. They tentatively kiss one another before I thrust between their lips again. Fuck, it feels incredible, and my orgasm quickly barrels toward me again. This time, I'm not holding it back.

"Did you swallow my boyfriend's cum, Mac?" I ask, and she pulls away and shakes her head, looking up at me.

"No, he painted my skin with it," she whispers huskily, and I feel my eyebrows jump as I look at my boyfriend who is still working my cock with his mouth.

"You marked her?" I ask, sounding surprised, and when his eyes meet mine, I smile. I can see the truth in his gaze, and the realization that he can't fight it anymore.

"Such a good boy," I praise him, and I see him shudder. Mac's eyes widen, and a shiver runs down her spine. I reach out and stroke her head.

"Don't you think he's a good boy, Mac? I'm going to come in his mouth, and he's not going to swallow it," I say. Miller stays still and lets me fuck his mouth hard. Mac's hand strokes my thigh and fondles my balls before slipping between my ass cheeks. She slides her finger into my asshole, pressing hard against my prostate. I can't hold back any longer, and I groan loudly, the sounds echoing over Miller's quiet pants as I fill his mouth with my cum. When I finish, I pull back, and Mac's finger slips from my ass.

"You're a naughty girl, aren't you?" I stare down at her, and she smirks at me. I love her defiance, and I can't wait to play with her. "Be a good girl and kiss Miller for me now," I order her, and her smirk drops, and she looks at my boyfriend who still has my cum in his mouth. She hesitates, but he grabs her head and yanks her forward, mashing his mouth to hers. I watch as he shares my cum with her and groan as she swallows it down. "Fuck, you are a good, good girl. I can't wait to have some time to play properly."

The two of them aren't paying any attention to me as they make out, their hands running all over each other. The dam finally broken. I pull up my sweats and step away, grabbing a glass of water off my bedside table and filling it in my bathroom before returning. They are sprawled across my carpet, rolling around and fighting for domination. It's such a pretty sight that I feel myself grow hard again, but unfortunately, it's going to have to wait for another time.

I clear my throat, and they stop dead. They both look up at me with a little guilt and no small amount of embarrassment on their faces. I chuckle and hold out the glass of water to them. "We need to get going, otherwise there will be trouble for you two."

That knocks them out of their lust-filled romp, and they separate, an awkward tension between them. I just shake my head with amusement. They are going to have to work it out themselves.

Mac is the first to get up, adjusting her crop top. "I doubt it. I have something on James now."

She takes the glass from me as I offer a hand to Miller. He gets up and adjusts his pants, which are tight across the front, but before I can make a joke, he puts a finger over my lips.

"Don't," he grumbles, pushing his disheveled hair back from his face. I'm kind of jealous the two of them are going home without me now. Oh well, I have a great imagination. I'll keep it occupied with the thought of them until we can do this again.

Mac leaves the room without saying a word, giving us a moment. I gather Miller into my arms and give him a hug and a kiss. "It's your responsibility to make sure she's okay," I instruct him.

"Yeah, yeah," he agrees, kissing me back before pushing me away. "I will."

I follow them out and grab Anders's keys as he puts a couple of stitches in Max's pec. He decided to have his tracker put in his chest.

"Lathan, can you do a deep dive into all of the players? We suspect them, but I want to go back and find their motivation behind this. I also suspect that none of them are faithful to their wives. We know Ted wasn't faithful, because he has a kid with another woman. What else can we find?" Mac asks, and he agrees.

"Sure, I'll see what I can find. I was just searching the cameras to see who put those people in the cells," Lathan replies, sounding annoyed.

"And?" she asks.

"They turned them off. There's a blank space. One moment they are empty, and the next, they have those three people in them. Fuck."

She gives him a kiss on the cheek. "Hey, don't get upset. We know who it possibly was. We'll break this, okay? It will just take a little extra time," she assures him softly, and the tension drains out of his body as she touches his shoulder.

"Yeah, okay," he says as they say their goodbyes to Anders and Dayton. She basically ignores my brother, and I see his jaw clench. Yikes. Just when we got Miller on board, something else happened, but I'm not going to stick my nose in it. Max is a big boy, and they can sort it out between themselves.

"I won't be long," I tell the others as Lathan takes Max's place. Dayton already has a bandage on his neck.

"I'll do yours when you get back, and Dayton can do mine after I finish with Lath," Anders says, and the three of us walk out into the cold night.

CHAPTER 22

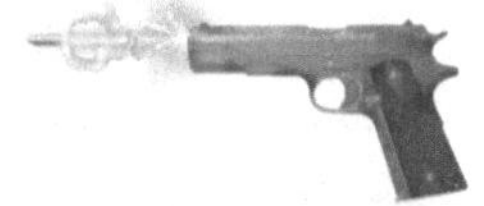

The silence in the car is awkward as fuck, and I want to slap myself for getting involved with whatever that was before I knew where I stand with both of them. The last thing I want to do is come between them, and Miller still seems very on the fence with me. It was hot as fuck having Ryland boss us around, and when he made me kiss Miller and swallow his cum, I almost came right there on the spot. Miller's hands felt amazing all over my body, and he kisses sublimely, with just the right pressure and tongue. When his body weight was on me, and he was grinding against me while we were rolling around, I just about came from that too, but does he actually want me, or was it just the leftover lust from that fucking incredible situation Ryland manipulated us into?

I stare out the window blindly, the dark night rushing past us. Who am I kidding? He didn't manipulate me. I was a willing and eager participant. There's just something about him that is so primal, so dominant, that makes me want to give him everything he asks for.

I am worried, however, about the emotions involved. I can turn those off on a job and not worry about getting attached, but this is different. I am becoming attached to all of these men. I'm worried my feelings are getting in the way of me doing my mission properly, my recent interaction with Max being a prime example.

I'm annoyed with him, and I can't explain why. I know he's only spending time with Stella for the mission, but I can't help the seething jealousy I feel every time I think of them together—of her hands pawing him, of *his* hands pawing at her. My mind is very creative.

When he grabbed me and sat me on his lap, I didn't want to be there. I didn't want him to see how I felt. When he whispered, "I'm sorry," in my ear, though, I couldn't help but sink into him.

He whispered that he was sorry Stella was being so aggressively antagonistic toward me. He said he wants to tell her to shut the fuck up, but for now, he has to hold his tongue. He promised he hasn't done anything but kiss her a couple of times, and that he's managed to use the fact that she wears a purity ring to not go any further. He also said he wishes he could blow her off, but until he gets the invite to the club, he has to keep up the charade.

It really didn't help. I've become incredibly possessive of Maxwell Turner and feel stabby at even that small admission. Has he forgotten who I am? I could easily make the bitch disappear, and no one would know. Just a small cut in her brake line, and the next time she drives her car, it would be all over... or maybe I could make it look like she got a better job offer elsewhere and left town, then I could kill her and dispose of her. It would be ages before anyone noticed, or maybe her parents would care. They seem to be overbearing, or at least the mother is. Ted doesn't seem to give a crap. I was worried for a moment that maybe Max wouldn't actually get an invite to the sex club. What normal father would encourage his daughter's boyfriend to cheat on her? Then again, he has no problem cheating on his wife, so I guess it's not a problem.

"Mac." Ry's soft voice has me jumping, startling me from my thoughts. "We're here," he says, turning around to look at me with a small frown on his face. "Are you okay?" he asks, and I wave a hand before unstrapping my seat belt.

"Yeah, sorry, I was just thinking about some things. Thanks for the lift," I reply as Ryland and Miller lean in and kiss each other. I avert my eyes, feeling like I'm intruding on something, and slide across the seat to climb out of the car, but Ryland's hand shoots out and grabs me, stopping me from going any farther. He and Miller pull away, and there's a sweet smile on their lips. Fuck, I envy these two. Knowing I have someone to come home to every night looks pretty fucking good right about now.

Miller slides out and shuts the door as Ryland turns his attention to me. His hand tightens on my arm, and he drags me forward before sliding his hand behind my head. He slowly brings my head close to his, giving me time to pull away, but I don't. Despite my whirling emotions and my confusion over how I feel, I want to kiss him. I want to feel his lips on mine. I want to know how it feels to be kissed by this man. I turn to look at Miller, but Ryland's hand tightens on the back of my head.

"Eyes on me, princess," he mutters before taking my lips. He doesn't fuck around. There's no tentative-ness. He dominates my mouth. His tongue demands a response from me, not allowing me to give more than my best. The pressure is perfect, and he nips and sucks and teases until I'm panting for more, then he pulls away.

"Good night, sweetheart." He smirks and releases his hold.

I blink owlishly before getting my shit together. "Goodnight," I mutter as I climb out and join Miller for the walk back to the house. Ryland doesn't hang around, and the crunch of the tires on the gravel is almost deafening in the silence of the country air.

Miller and I are quiet as we walk back to the house. I guess neither of us are willing to talk about what happened. I want to, but Miller has been antagonistic toward me whenever we've been alone, and the peace is actually nice. If I bring up what happened, that might change. Alright, fine, yes, I'm a chicken, but feelings and emotional involvement are so new to me, and Miller is probably the one who has the potential to hurt me the most.

I'm about to go in the front door, but he grabs my hand and pulls me around to the tree that leads to his bedroom window. "What are you doing?" I hiss.

"There was a light on in the kitchen. I didn't see James's car, but it might be Martha. She knows the club closes at twelve on a Sunday, so we should technically be home by now."

"But what if she checked our rooms already?" I ask him, and he shakes his head.

"I have a sensor set up in my room to tell me if she goes up the stairs. I haven't had an alert on my phone. I'm guessing she's waiting up for James, or she just got home herself. I could run over and put my hand on her car to feel if it's hot or cold," he explains noncombatively. I quickly nod, and he disappears around the house, hidden by the shadows as I wait patiently for him to return. When he's not acting like an ass, he's an asset to me.

He's breathing slightly heavier when he returns. "The hood of her car was still hot, so it seems like maybe she just returned. We should get upstairs now before she comes to check." He gestures for me to start climbing up the tree. I don't argue with him and start my ascent. I can feel him directly behind me, and it doesn't take me long before I climb through his window. I hold out my hand to steady him as he comes through after me. He slides the window closed then turns to face me. He must have left a lamp on before we left earlier, because his room is dimly lit. He's looking at me with a quizzical expression on his face, but he doesn't seem like he wants to talk.

"Well, okay, um... Bye." I give a half-hearted wave as I back away. The tension between us is off the charts, and I have no idea what to say. I'll probably just mess it up if I do attempt to say something, so I'm going to scurry away like a scared little mouse.

I don't get very far, though, before he lunges at me, tackling me to his bed. A small yelp escapes my mouth, and he quickly shoves his hand over it, and we both look at the door, straining our ears to see if we can hear anything.

"Hopefully she didn't hear that," he says. "I'm going to remove my hand, okay?" He looks down at me, and I can see his gorgeous green eyes a little better now that we're closer to the lamp. They are softer than I've seen them, and he is staring at me like he's never seen me before. He reaches up and brushes a lock of hair off my face, frowning with pursed lips. I can see him thinking, but then it sort of just washes away and his lips curve up in a smirk.

"Do you remember what I said to you last night? After you got home from work?"

"What Ryland does to me, you get to do as well?" I repeat what he said to me when he pinned me against the wall last night. Crap, was that only last night? I feel like it was at least a week ago.

"Exactly." He leans in and presses his lips against mine. Unlike Ryland, who was commanding and sure, he's a little hesitant. He tentatively brushes his lips across mine before pulling away and looking at me closely. I think he might be checking to see if I'm alright, which is a big change, so I take the lead. I thread my fingers through his hair, which has fallen forward to frame his face, and guide his mouth back to mine. I slide my tongue across his lips, asking for entrance.

His whole body melts into mine as his mouth parts, and I slide my tongue along his. This kiss is everything! It's soft and sensual and everything that is right with swapping saliva with someone. It doesn't take long for him to get fully involved. I don't think I've ever made out with someone like this before, just kissing on a bed in the dark like a teenager, and to think it's with the most antagonistic member of Team Basilisk. I can't get enough. There's no removing clothes, just some over the clothes groping and grinding, and I feel like I'm actually making out with my high school boyfriend. It's fun as fuck, but I also know one of us needs to put an end to this. Martha could come up at any moment and check that we're in our beds, and we are so close to breaking this mission wide open.

Miller must come to the same conclusion as me, because he pulls away, resting his forehead against mine. "You should go," he says breathlessly, and I get a thrill from it. I made this man breathless.

"Yeah, okay. I'll see you in the morning?" I ask, and he smiles and nods before placing another quick kiss on my lips. He rolls to the side, adjusting his dick beneath his tight pants.

"Oh, and Kensington?" he calls as I roll off his bed and tiptoe across the room to the stairs. I stop and look back at him. He's off the bed and has stripped off his shirt. All those beautiful tattoos are illuminated in the dull lighting. I just want to throw him back on the bed and trace all of them with my tongue as I discover what they all are. He tosses his shirt to the side and toes off his shoes, knowing exactly what he's doing to me. I bite my lip as his hands go to his buckle, his lips turning up in a smirk. "I can't wait to see what Ry does to you next."

"You know you don't need an excuse to kiss me, Miller," I tell him, and he drops his pants, leaving him in a pair of tight, black boxers that I've become very familiar with.

"I know, but where's the fun in that?" He climbs beneath his sheets.

"Well, I guess it goes both ways then. Whatever Ry does to you, I can do the same thing," I argue, not wanting to leave.

"As you wish, princess." He rolls so his back is to me, the infuriating asshole. He knows exactly what he's doing to me and chuckles as I let out a little groan of frustration.

I move silently down the stairs to my room, where I open the door and step inside. Jessica is snoring like a grizzly bear in hibernation.

I'm not sure what's worse, flirty, playful Miller or distrustful, aggressive Miller, and why the sudden change of heart? Not that I'm really complaining. He is damn delicious, but we are going to have to talk about this one eighty of his. Not tonight though. Tonight, I'm going to enjoy the cease-fire, because tomorrow may see the return of the asshole.

The next couple of days are quiet. I go to school, come home, and do my homework. I don't have to work at the Life Lounge again until Thursday night. The school is abuzz with the gossip of Bishop's body being discovered at the hot springs. Rumors circulate, each one more dramatic than the last, about what happened to him, but no one seems particularly distraught.

I was invited to the movies with the others on Monday night. They wanted to check out the entry to the sex club, but Martha flat-out refused to give permission. Both Miller and I had to stay home, and the guys went on their own. They were able to confirm the elevator inside the movie theater has a card access only basement. They didn't use it because there were too many people around.

Tuesday night, I get a call from Dayton asking if I want to go on a date with him on Wednesday. Holy crap, another date with the delightfully decadent Dayton? Hell yes! I quickly respond that I'd love to, but I need to figure out an excuse for Martha. Work won't cut it because she could ask Matthew, but I tell him I'll figure something out.

On Wednesday afternoon, I get called out of my PE class to see the guidance counselor again. Unfortunately, we aren't running the cross-country track, so I have no excuse not to go see him.

I don't bother changing out of my uniform, since it's my last class of the day, and I grab my things and hurry toward Mr. Marshall's office. When I arrive, I'm surprised to see that not only is he there, but so are Martha and Mr. Turner. Max leans against the wall, his arms crossed as I take a seat next to Martha.

"Is everything okay?" I ask, looking between Martha and the counselor.

"Yes, of course it is. We have some amazing news for you, Mackenzie," Martha gushes as Brock holds up a letter.

"Oh?" I ask. I know where this is going, but I need to show confusion.

"The school received an invitation for you to visit a most prestigious college in upstate New York. MITHOS College has scholarships set aside for underprivileged students, and somehow, you have made it onto the list of possible candidates." Mr. Marshall sounds somewhat bemused. "Apparently your class scores in your previous school were excellent, and they tracked you down when the offer was sent there, and they told them you moved."

"This is so exciting," Martha squeals and gives my hand a squeeze. "I knew you had potential."

"MITHOS College? I've never heard of it before," I say, sounding surprised. I thought they would send an offer to some mainstream school. I guess it's a good reason to send the jet.

"It's a privately funded institution that advocates for education in the underprivileged. Of course, they have their more mainstream admissions as well—how else would they fund scholarships—but they are heavily into advocating for change. A good education is the way to break the poverty cycle." Mr. Marshall hands over the brochure my father created for recruitment. Potential agents are heavily investigated before they are offered a spot. How else is he going to keep a top-secret spy academy top secret? If he invited too many people who said no, then word would spread.

"And they are interested in me?" I sound as skeptical as Brock looks while I look over the brochure.

"And why wouldn't they be, Ms. Walsh? You're an intelligent and resourceful young woman. You would be an asset to their program," Mr. Turner rumbles from his spot on the wall.

"They are sending you a private jet so you can visit and take a tour of the facilities next week," Martha tells me, beaming with pride like she was the one who achieved this. "Oh, if only they had that kind of opportunity when I was young. I would have jumped at a chance to attend a school like that!"

"Yes, but everything worked out for you in the end, Martha. You're running the house you used to live in now, and you're a damn sight kinder than the old dragon lady who was in charge when you, Melissa, Lisa, and June were residents," Brock tells Martha condescendingly. "All four of you made advantageous marriages, and now you are pillars of society."

Martha's eyes narrow ever so slightly as I process what Brock just said.

Holy fuck, it's all I can do to keep my mouth from dropping open. Martha was a foster kid. Not just Martha, but her sister-in-law, and the wives of the pastor and chief of police as well. That seems like too much of a coincidence.

"You lived at Serenity House?" I ask her, and she nods, her jaw tight.

"Yes, I did, then I got into a good college and moved away for a little while to better myself. James and I were high school sweethearts. We had a long-distance relationship all through college as well."

I wonder how often he cheated on her during that time.

"Didn't your foster daddy go to jail for touching one of the kids once you left?" Brock asks, making Martha even more tense. I stay quiet because this is interesting information. "And then he was shanked in jail?"

"I think I heard that," she replies primly.

"So how did you come to run the place?" Max asks quickly before she clams up completely. "You've been so successful with so many children. You are a fine example of what someone can achieve," he adds in a hurry, and it seems to work. She relaxes and preens at his praise.

"Well, James asked me to marry him, and we moved back here. I was working at the hospital. I'm trained as a nurse, you see, but when my foster mother died suddenly, and there was a space open, I knew it was meant to be. I can't have children, and I thought this was God's way of giving me children, so I gave up nursing and have been running the house ever since."

"That's right. You were Dr. Molloy's scrub nurse for a while before he had his medical license revoked for his alcohol problem. I had forgotten that." Brock leans back in his chair and turns to me. "See, you have the chance of becoming so much more than you are now." I can hear the underlining words. Instead of a hooker, I could be a nurse.

"So I can go?" I ask Martha, and she nods.

"Of course, dear. We want to give you every opportunity to improve your lot in life," she replies. "But you should go have a look at that boutique I was telling you about." She lets her gaze drift down to my outfit. Today, I'm wearing cutoff denim shorts, fishnets, combat boots, and another band shirt—some K-pop boy band that has a hundred and one members that I thought was kind of cool. Sort of ironic now. "It would benefit you to be seen fitting in a little better."

"Okay, I promise I will. Matthew said he'd pay me weekly, and Saturday will be my first week, so I'll go on Sunday after church," I assure her, and she looks thrilled. "It says here I need to submit an essay." I point to the brochure. "May I please spend the night in the library writing that? I have to work the rest of the week, so it's my last chance to," I ask her. It's perfect timing. I can sneak out and go on my date with Dayton.

She frowns. "How will you get home? I guess James could pick you up, but I think he will be late at work."

Is he going to be late, or is he visiting a 'friend?'

"My brother would be happy to give her a lift home after. He should probably spend some more time at the library as well. He has some college application essays he needs to write as well."

Martha's eyes light up at the idea of me spending time with Ryland Turner. "Oh yes, that would be wonderful, as long as it's no trouble for him."

"None at all, ma'am. Ms. Walsh has shown she has excellent work ethic, so I'm hoping some of it will rub off on my brother." She preens again like she's responsible for my good work ethic. I've only been staying with her for a week, though it feels like so much longer.

"Yes, her work ethic is excellent. Max has had nothing but wonderful and descriptive things to say about her." Brock leers at me suggestively, looking between me and Max. I feign a confused look and a blush. It's not hard, I only have to think about Max bending me over his desk and the blush appears.

"Well, if that's everything, I have another appointment." Max pushes off the wall and strides to the door.

"I'll get Ryland to meet you at the front of the school. He can give you a lift to the library as well," he tells me, and I quickly agree.

"Thank you."

"We won't wait for you for dinner then." Martha stands up and brushes her dress skirt down. "I'm so proud of you, dear. Now we need to hope Miller and Jessica have the same kind of success."

Max opens the door, allowing us both to leave. We part ways, him going to wherever his meeting is, and Martha and I walking out to the front of the school. It's almost the end of the day, so there is no point in me returning to PE.

"I'm just going to wait here," I tell her, pointing to Ryland's car.

"That's such a nice car. The Turner boys are Summerville royalty. Make sure you are polite to Ryland. We want to stay on his good side. Help him as much as you can. My niece has big plans for him." She narrows her eyes at me. "Remember, getting into a good school is just the first step. Improving your image will go a long way toward helping you succeed in life as well. Boys can come later." I hear the underlying threat.

"It's okay, Martha. I'm not interested in schoolboys at all," I tell her, and she raises an eyebrow.

"Make sure you're not interested in any boys. I won't stand for teen pregnancy, and your reputation is already shaky. It's lucky the school hasn't seen your police record," she says coldly, her demeanor changing in a flash.

"Yes, ma'am." I drop my eyes. "I know exactly what men are after. I plan on taking charge of my own destiny."

The cold glare clears, and she pats my shoulder. "Good girl. Right, I'll be off. I need to stop by the grocery store on the way home. I look forward to reading your essay before you submit it."

Fuck. I feel a moment of panic. I wasn't planning on writing one. I wanted to focus on Dayton. Hopefully Dad has an essay on file or can get one of the analysts to whip one up for me.

"Sure," I tell her, and she hops into her car and heads out of the parking lot just as the bell rings. I won't have long to wait, so I drop my backpack on the ground and lean against the fender of the Maserati. I pull out my phone and send Dad a quick text.

Kenzie: SOS, I need a life essay.

It doesn't take long for him to reply.

Dad: On it! Max already let me know. He figured the foster parents or the guidance counselor might request to read it. You'll have it by the end of the day. Mom says hi and enjoy your date.

I stare at the response in confusion. How do they know I'm going on a date? I can practically feel their smugness oozing through the phone. Ugh!

"What are you doing?" a voice demands, and I look up to find Sophie glaring at me. Lucy and Michelle flank. Jessica has been true to her word all week. She's been eating with us foster kids and is like a completely different person now that she's no longer trying to be friends with Sophie. She's been subjected to Sophie's cattiness, but it's like she grew a backbone overnight and doesn't let any of it faze her. She's witty and has a cunning sense of humor. I've come to really like her.

"Ry and I are doing college essays at the library after school. He's giving me a lift," I tell her, and she squeals and stomps her foot.

"First Miller, now you. What the hell is his interest in you two losers?" she demands as I spy him walking up behind her with Lathan and Miller in tow.

"Well, those two so-called losers aren't nasty spoiled bitches," he replies, glaring at her. "I would rather spend time with both of them than listen to you bitch and complain for another minute."

She whirls around to face him, her mouth dropping open in shock before she raises her finger and pokes him in the chest.

"You watch yourself, Ryland Turner. You may be the governor's son, but my family is important in this town. You don't want to get on the wrong side of them."

Lucy and Michelle look bored, and Michelle rolls her eyes and grabs Sophie's arm. "Settle down, they are just studying. It's not like they are having an orgy. Come on, I'm bored. Let's go shopping. Daddy wants me to have dinner with him tonight, and I want something pretty to wear."

The way she says "Daddy" is kind of creepy, and

I'm not the only one who notices. I see Lathan screw up his nose.

The girls leave, and we hop into Ryland's car, Miller in the passenger seat and Lathan and me in the back. He instantly reaches for my hand, and I feel warm and giggly.

"Was anyone else grossed out by how Michelle talked about her father?" he asks.

"Are we sure she's really his daughter?" I ask him, and he shrugs.

"I didn't dive too deeply. That's what the school records say, but I guess I can look deeper. There's no mention of a mother for either of the girls. Only that Amir and Hinata are the fathers of Michelle and Lucy."

I tell them what I learned about Martha being a foster kid and a former nurse, the foster father going to jail, and the foster mother dying suddenly.

"Well, that certainly shines a new light on things. I'm halfway through my research into all of their back-grounds. I found out that all the men attended the same university in Georgia before moving back to Summerville at the same time. Ted and James's family were already well off. The shipping business has been in their family for generations. Ted took it over as the eldest, and James forged his own path. There doesn't seem to be any resentment because James is a share-holder and gets a share of the profit."

His hand is warm in mine, and I'm slightly distracted by the way his finger is circling my palm. "I haven't gotten to June and Martha yet, but Lisa

Thompson dropped out of college in her second year and worked some low-end jobs as a waitress and a bartender. She even had a job in an adult shop for a little while before marrying David and becoming the quintessential cop's wife."

"And what about Melissa? The pastor's wife?" Miller asks, turning back to look at us. His eyebrows jump when he sees us holding hands, but all he does is smirk. I flip him off with the hand not in Lathan's. I refuse to be teased by him.

"She went to the same college as the guys. She was president of her sorority and graduated with a degree in theology. I did find an interesting thing about her sorority. A couple of the pledges were arrested for solicitation and were kicked out. They claim it was a rush task, but the sorority denied any involvement."

"That is interesting. I can't wait to hear what you find out about Martha and June. We did think someone was involved who had medical training. I had all but ruled them out, but that certainly shines a new light on them." I look around and realize that instead of going to the library, Ryland has taken us back to his place. I guess we're not even going to pretend we're at the library. Hopefully Martha doesn't check, and if she does, I can tell her we went back to his place instead. I'll have an essay in my inbox to show her if she needs proof we worked.

Ryland pulls into the garage, letting the door close slowly behind us. He and Miller get out, but when I try to do the same thing, Lathan holds my hand tighter and doesn't let me go. The other two don't wait, they just go inside, letting the door close behind them and leaving us in the dark garage. The only bit of light is the interior one in the car, but that fades out too.

"I missed you," Lathan murmurs, drawing me closer to him. I don't fight him. I've missed him too. I've grown very attached in a short period of time. I wonder what my therapist would say. She would probably tell me it was bad that I was latching onto this team, and that I was emotionally stunted and making bad choices, but I really don't care. I like how they make me feel valued, respected, and wanted. Being a ghost has been hard, and my alter ego, Princess Kensington, is a bubble head. I can't stand her and would never be friends with someone like that in real life. Sometimes I hate that the world sees me like that, but Mom keeps reassuring me. Reputations can do a one eighty. Look at the woman who is queen in the UK now. She was the hated other woman, and now she is queen.

"I missed you too." I snuggle into his side, and he presses a kiss to the top of my head.

"I just need five minutes with you all to myself before you head off with Dayton. All the others have had their Mac time, and I feel like it's been weeks since I touched you."

"Mac time? You make me sound like a happy meal or something." I giggle, looking up at him. His glasses are slightly askew, and I reach up to straighten them. He smirks.

"Oh, you were a happy meal for me alright." His voice is husky, and I feel a rush of lust as I remember the meal he made of me under the library.

"That was only twenty-four hours ago," I remind him. "You're not completely neglected."

He sighs. "I know, but Lucy keeps pawing at me, and she makes me feel dirty. I just need the goodness that is you."

Oh my lord, this man has mad romance skills. My toes curl at that sentiment as he leans in and kisses me. We make out in the back of the car for a little while, steaming up the windows before the garage door bangs open, and Anders stands there.

He peers through the darkness with a big grin on his face. "Will you two stop acting like teenagers and get in here? Poor Dayton is getting restless. I've had to banish Miller and Ryland to their room because they were both winding him up. I'm worried there's going to be bloodshed."

Lathan and I pull apart. We're both panting, and Lathan's glasses are all fogged up. He takes them off and cleans them on his shirt before giving me one more quick kiss. "Thanks, I needed that."

I smile at him. "Me too. I've never made out in the back of a car before. Thank you for being my first," I tell him, and I see his chest puff up ever so slightly. God, I love this guy.

He climbs out, and I stop. Did I say I love him? I examine my feelings, and sure enough, Lathan has wormed his way inside my chest. I'm not sure if it's love, but it's certainly something.

Nope, not going to think about it. I climb out of the car, taking my bag with me, and follow him inside the house. He and Anders are ahead of me, with Anders ribbing Lathan for our make out session in the car, and I don't pay attention to my surroundings. A hand shoots out, and I'm soon dragged into a dark closet under the stairs. I'm not worried because I can smell both Ryland and Miller as they crowd me between them.

"What are we doing?" I ask as they press my body between theirs, not giving me any leeway.

"Dayton is about to whisk you away on a date. We haven't had a moment of your time today, and Miller tells me you made out on his bed when you got home last night. You rolled around on my floor as well. That's a lot of kisses that you owe me."

"Did it make you hot to hear that he and I made out like teenagers on his bed?" I whisper to him, my voice low and husky. "Did you get hard thinking about the two of us doing that? Did you wish you were sandwiched between us?" I tease him, but he's only pretending to allow me to have the upper hand.

Without a word, he leans in and kisses me, taking my mouth hard and fast. His teeth brand his mark across my lip before he slides his tongue deep, allowing me to hang on for the ride. I feel hands come up around me from behind, lifting my shirt up and over my head, but leaving me tangled in it. Miller lets go of the shirt and then slides his hands over my breasts, dragging my bra cups down and fully exposing me to Ryland—not that he can see anything in the dark closet. He plucks and twists my nipples, and I feel my desire flood my panties.

Ryland pulls back and dips his head, taking one of my nipples into his mouth. He bites and sucks until I squirm between them. Miller's hand slides into my shorts, and he swirls a finger around my clit until I'm on the very edge of an orgasm, my body primed to detonate, and then they both pull away. Leaving me breathless, panting, and needy, they exit the closet without another word.

CHAPTER 24

"What the fuck?" I shriek out as they close the door behind them. I hear the two of them chuckle followed by the sounds of their feet on the stairs above me.

"Mac?" The door opens, and the bright light blinds me. I hold up a hand, not caring that my breasts are still exposed to whoever it is. "What happened?" Dayton looks delightfully confused before his eyes drift in the direction of the upper story. "What kind of game are those fuckers playing now?" he demands, sounding annoyed, but I just grab his shirt and tug him into the closet with me.

"One that makes you lucky," I snap as I wrap my arms around his body and kiss him hard. They worked me up, and they probably thought I would go on my date with Dayton as a hot mess, but I'm not waiting for the date to get what I need.

Dayton doesn't react for a moment, and I start to

pull away, worried I misread this whole thing, but in a flash, he has his shirt over his head and my bra undone. Our naked torsos push together as he takes control of the kiss, kissing me like I'm the very air he needs to breathe.

"Fuck," he curses against my lips. "I swore I would take this slow and woo you like you've never been," he mumbles as I unbuckle his jeans and reach into his pants, wrapping my hand around his cock.

He groans when I stroke my fist up and down his thick length. I'm excited to get my hands on his body, having been denied before.

"Date later, cock now," I tell him, and he doesn't leave me disappointed. He makes quick work of my shorts and tights, sliding them down my body and leaving kisses along the way to unlace my boots. I nudge them off before he moves back up my body, lifting and pinning me against the wall. His mouth takes mine as he lines himself up and slides forward, coating himself in my dripping pussy, primed by the two assholes who left me hanging. Dayton notches himself at my entrance and thrusts hard. Both of us moan loudly, and I watch with wide-eyed delight as I completely unravel this hard to shake man in front of me. His eyes blaze with need in the light of the hall-way, the door behind us still open. His neck muscles are taut with control as his fingers dig into the curves of my ass. He pulls back and slides forward again, and my eyes drift closed as I revel in the sensation, his cock long and thick and filling me perfectly.

There's almost a desperate feeling to our joining. It's like if we don't do it now, it's never going to happen. I wrap my arms around his neck, bringing myself as close to him as I can, melding my body to his as he continues to pound his cock into my pussy. It feels amazing, my pussy pulsing every time he brushes across the perfect spot inside me. Something about our position gives him the perfect angle for it to happen every time. My nipples tighten, and my toes curl up as my orgasm races to completion. I'm not worried about the noises I make here in this house, and the words coming from my mouth are dirty and loud as Dayton's pounding gets even more enthusiastic.

"Yes, God, yes! Your cock feels so good. It fills me perfectly."

One of his hands drifts down, and he flicks a finger over my clit, before tugging on the ring. I'm so close, but I want him there too, so I lean in and whisper in his ear.

"I want you to fill me with your cum. I want to feel it drip down my thighs."

His raspy moan echoes through the small closet, and I feel his other hand brush against my asshole.

"Going to take you here next time. I want to see my cum dripping out of that." He takes my dirty words and doubles down. Who would have thought he had it in him? The pressure of his finger on my clit and asshole, and the filthy as fuck words coming from his mouth are enough to send me flying.

"Fuck yes!" I scream, throwing my head back against the wall, not even wincing at the pain as my pussy clamps down around him, my nerve endings screaming with pleasure as my orgasm explodes. Dayton does his best to thrust through it, but after two thrusts, I feel his hot cum paint my walls. He shudders and groans, trying to keep us both upright in the tiny space.

A sound of surprise has me looking over Dayton's shoulder, and I vaguely remember hearing the garage door open and close, but I was so distracted that I didn't think anything of it.

Dayton's head is against my shoulder, and the two of us are heaving in much needed air after our little fuck fest. Sweat drips off his brow and onto me, and I feel his body tense as he turns to look at the man staring at us in surprise. I like that Dayton gives him a look like he's asking, "What's your problem?"

Max is standing there, briefcase in hand, with his eyebrows raised. "Having a good afternoon?" he asks, sounding slightly annoyed. "I thought you were going on a date."

Dayton flips him off before pulling out of me and allowing my legs to drop to the ground. He pulls his jeans up, which only got as far as his knees, and fastens them before reaching for his shirt. He uses it to clean me before helping me get dressed, not bothering to answer Max's snippy question.

"Sounds like you had a shitty afternoon," Dayton says conversationally, turning to face his friend. It gives me a moment to get my clothes back on, blocking me from Max's intense scrutiny. "How about you pull your head out of your ass and not take your bad mood out on us?"

"Fuck off, D. You've had it easy this mission," Max sneers before storming off down the corridor, and Dayton turns back to face me.

"Sorry, baby, I wasn't thinking. I should have pulled the door closed," he apologizes, bending down to pick up my shoes and tights before grabbing my hand and guiding me out of the closet. I get a little thrill at the endearment from him. I love it, but I try not to show it. "Actually, no, he's right. I should have taken you on that date first." He sounds so disappointed with himself, and I tug against his grip, bringing us both to a stop.

"Stop right there. I very much enjoyed what we just did, and there is nothing to stop you from still taking me on a date where I hope what just happened in the closet occurs again in the back of your car. Don't let his bad mood ruin what was a fucking amazing experience." I get up on my tiptoes and press a kiss against his lips.

"Come on, let's go see what's up his ass." He pulls away, and we walk hand in hand toward the kitchen where we find Max, Anders, and Lathan. Lathan is busy with his deep dive into the women's backgrounds, and Anders and Max both have beers. Max almost drains his in one go.

"What bug is up your ass?" Dayton drops my boots

and stockings by the door, clapping his friend on the shoulder before going to the fridge and pulling out a bottle of wine. He grabs a glass out of the cupboard and pours some in before passing it to me, then he returns the bottle to the fridge and gets himself and Lathan a soda.

"Come sit next to me, sweet thing," Anders calls, winking at me. "You look like you got hit by a hurricane between the garage and here," he jokes, and I self-consciously finger comb my hair before pulling my shit together and flipping him off.

"You look beautiful," Lathan says, absently looking up from his laptop before returning to it. Yup, this guy makes my heart race. I can't believe none of them seem particularly upset that I was fucking Dayton in the closet mere minutes ago. Well, all except Max.

"Those assholes dragged me into the closet, got me worked up, and bailed, leaving me hanging, so Dayton took one for the team," I tease, taking a sip of my wine, and he chuckles.

"He doesn't seem too upset about that. Things appear to be going better with you and Miller as well." Anders points his bottle of beer at me. "I knew the power of a good blow job would solve everything." It's like he's taking credit for Miller's change of heart.

I roll my eyes as Max scoffs angrily, and I'm done. "What the fuck is your problem?" I ask Max, turning to face him.

"You certainly have worked your way through my

team," he says aggressively, and I see Anders and Dayton exchange a worried look.

"Is that a problem for you? They are grown-ass men and have the opportunity to say no if they aren't interested. I don't think I forced them." I think about it for a moment. "Well, okay, maybe Anders was forced, but both Dayton and Lathan were willing participants."

"I was willing and able," Lathan chimes in, glaring at Max. Dayton doesn't even dignify Max's comment with a response.

"Hey, I might have been forced, but I enjoyed every fucking second of it and can't wait to repeat it in our own time." Anders winks at me, trying to soften Max's tirade.

"How about instead of slut shaming Mac, which is fucking below you, you tell us what's really wrong?" Dayton leans forward, resting his elbows on the kitchen table, his gaze steady on his teammate.

"Fuck!" Max shouts, slamming his fist against the table before throwing his chair back and getting up to pace. His movements are so violent that the chair tumbles backward, hitting the floor hard. The guys all jump, seeming surprised that Max is acting like this. I don't know him well enough to discern if this is normal, but I'm guessing by their reactions that it's not.

He goes to his briefcase, pulls out an elaborate envelope, and tosses it onto the table. Anders grabs it before anyone else can, and he pulls out an invitation as well as some candid photos. He studies each one closely, smirking as he looks at me over the top of them before passing them to Dayton.

"What is it?" Lathan asks what I'm dying to know, but I'm pretty sure I can guess.

"Our invitation to a special club night at Primal Release, including a little note blackmailing me. If I say anything or don't attend, they will release images of me fucking a student over my desk at work which, of course, will ruin my dad's career."

"Eww, that club name is gross, but this is what we wanted," I point out as Dayton slides the images over to me, and I hold them out far enough for Lathan to see them while I look. Sure enough, there I am, bent over the desk. You can't actually make out my face, but you can see for sure that it's Max.

Max bends down and picks up the chair. "I know, but this is enough to end my dad's career. We have to get this wrapped up before they use those images to blackmail him. At the moment, they are happy keeping Ry and me on a leash, but that's not going to last."

"Yes, but we knew all that. Your dad is aware of the situation. That's not what's bothering you the most. What is it?" I press.

"Brock, who is the one who gave me those, implied that Mac and Miller will be paid entertainment on Friday night, available for anyone to hire. He was hoping he would get his chance at her." His dark eyes churn with anguish as he looks at me, and I cringe.

"I don't want to, but I'll do what I have to so we can end this mission," I tell him without flinching, though the thought of fucking anyone else now is repulsive. In the short amount of time I've known them, these guys have shown me that I want something else for my life, and that being a ghost agent is no longer satisfying like it used to be.

"Easy enough. You and Ry hire them for exclusive use for the night. Offer them an amount they can't refuse. Percy will approve the expense," Lathan replies like he isn't worried in the least.

"That's not all. Damn it, Max, what's bothering you? You said you wanted to pursue whatever this is we have with Kensington. Are you changing your mind? We said all in or all out. Miller was the only one holding out, and he's on board now. Have you changed your mind?"

I'm unable to stop my flinch at Dayton's words. I guess they had a conversation when I wasn't around, I would have liked to be included, but at least I know why Miller has suddenly changed his tune. "So glad you all had a conversation that didn't include me," I say sarcastically, crossing my arms defensively. "It might have been nice to ask what I want."

I mean, I'm very interested in exploring my relationship with this team. Despite my earlier reluctance, I've come to the realization that I'm tired of being alone and using my body to trap the bad guys. I want to use it for my own pleasure. I'm not ready to give up the spy game, but I'm very ready to be a part of a team.

Knowing they'll always have my back in a tight situation is so reassuring. I haven't had any moments of panic during this mission, and it was a common occurrence when I was on my own. Thinking on the fly became my modus operandi, and it's exhausting. The fact that I want to bang all their brains out is just a bonus, but it is nice to be included in conversations.

CHAPTER 25

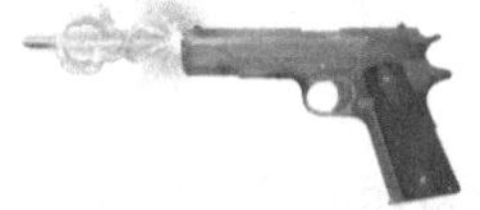

I watch as guilt floods three out of the four faces in front of me. Max is still too pissy to care about what I want. "Mac. I, ah… Shit." Lathan runs his hands through his hair before taking his glasses off and cleaning them on his shirt—his go-to fidget move.

"Don't be too hard on us. It was a moot point if we didn't get the whole team on board. We've come too far, and it was either all or nothing. Our team wasn't willing to put up with another problem child like Bishop, no matter what your dad insisted," Dayton says calmly, and I don't take offense.

"Okay, I guess I can understand that, but it would have been nice to be included in the conversation once you came to a decision," I argue.

"We were waiting on a decision from Miller. I guess he decided but didn't bother to inform us, if his behavior in the cupboard is anything to go by." Lathan sounds excited, and I can't help but smile at him. So adorable!

"I think we should all hold off on making any decision until this mission is complete," Max announces, crossing his arms and glaring at us. I guess the other guys are shocked, if the looks on their faces are anything to go by.

"What the fuck, man?" Anders demands loudly.

"I think everyone is getting their feelings mixed up with the mission, and I worry that when it's over, we're going to realize we made a mistake." He looks directly at me when he says this, and I have a feeling he means me specifically. I feel like I've been stabbed in the heart. The hurt is so acute, I'm kind of speechless.

"You're a fucking asshole." It's Lathan who explodes, and I feel my mouth drop open as he whirls on his teammate. "Just because you're feeling left out and are annoyed at having to pander to Stella, that doesn't mean you get to take it out on us, especially not Mac."

"He's right, man. We've all had to do things we're not happy about for a mission, so what's so different this time? What's making it worse?" Dayton asks calmly as Anders puts his hand on Lathan's arm and drags him back into his seat.

I'm still speechless and have no clue what to say to any of this. Maybe I made a mistake. It's my first chance at a little bit of something for me, and I latched onto it like a bloodsucking leech without thinking it through clearly. Have I made a massive mistake? I kind of just want to leave and go back to Serenity house and wallow in my misery.

"What the fuck is going on down here?" Miller and Ryland both appear in the kitchen doorway. They are wearing sweats and look rumpled and flushed, and I guess the two of them were relieving their own frustration, and we interrupted them.

"Ask your fucking brother," Lathan snaps, shaking off Anders's hand and picking up his laptop. He grabs my hand and drags me out of the kitchen. "We'll be in my room when you finish getting Max to pull his head out of his ass," Lathan tells Dayton, who nods absently, still focused on his friend and teammate.

I allow Lathan to drag me out of the room. I don't want to be involved in the conversation. I don't want to have my heart stomped on repeatedly as they discuss the "situation." Just when I thought I found something for myself, it gets snatched out of reach.

We head up the stairs and down a corridor. I don't pay attention to my surroundings, my mind a whirling ball of self-loathing. He pushes a door open, and we enter a dark room. There must be shutters over the windows, because not a single drop of light gets in. He goes over and switches a lamp on next to his bed, placing his laptop on the desk against the wall.

I'm standing in the entrance, not really sure what to do with myself. He sighs and returns to my side, closing the door behind us before dragging me over to his bed. He gently pushes me, and I fall back against the mattress. It's soft below me, and I don't hesitate to crawl up and make myself comfortable, curling up in a ball. Even on my worst missions, I have never felt this kind of hurt or self-loathing.

He hesitates for a moment, but I seriously need some Lathan love, so I hold out a hand, and that's all it takes. He toes off his shoes, crawls up the bed, and wraps his arms around me. I bury my head in his chest, and I can't stop the sob that comes from my mouth as tears spill onto my cheeks.

"Shh, it's okay." He presses a kiss to the top of my head and rubs soothing circles on my back. "Ignore Max. To be honest, I think he feels guilty, like he's cheating on you with Stella, and it's making him grumpy. I know he tried to talk to you about it last night and you shut him down."

"I can't help it," I stammer through my tears. "I get so freaking jealous every time I see them together. I don't know what's wrong with me, and I didn't know how to explain it to him. We've only just met. I shouldn't feel this way."

"Oh, sweetie, it's because it's the first time you have ever had feelings for anyone. It has to be confusing and messing with your head."

"More than just Max," I tell him, worried he doesn't understand that I mean all of them, but he chuckles and kisses me again before pulling back so he can look at my face.

"I know, baby. We all do, so don't worry about us being jealous. We're okay sharing amongst ourselves.

We always knew it would be the best solution for us as a team, but no one has ever fit as well as you do. For you to suddenly be bombarded with all these emotions when you kept them cut off before has to be terrifying."

Holy crap, how is this man so freaking intuitive? He perfectly described my state of mind with only a few words.

"You're so confident in everything you do. You excel as a ghost operative, but let's face it, it's not a career that lends itself to any kind of emotional involvement. You have to be cold and unfeeling to do it." I start to argue, but he puts a finger against my lips. "I'm not trying to make you feel bad, it's just what it is. You couldn't do your job effectively if you let emotions get involved, but now that you're working with us, you've allowed your heart to feel probably for the first time, apart from your family and fellow ghosts. Am I right?"

I nod, but I don't say anything.

"Well, Max is the same. You know he's dominant, and that he likes to be in control all the time, but you make him feel out of control. He hates being dictated to, and the ring manipulating him is pushing all his buttons. It was bound to blow up. Your attitude isn't helping. I think, deep down, he understands that your feelings are new to you, but he has daddy energy. He just wants to make it better for you, and he hates that it's his behavior that is causing it." He chuckles and shakes his head. "I know I'm probably not explaining this well, but try to forgive him. He doesn't mean what he says, it's just his way of trying to regain control."

I take a moment to think about what Lathan just said. It makes sense. As much as I haven't allowed my emotions to be involved before I met Max, all of them are probably the same way. There has to be a level of detachment to be a successful agent. I'm not giving them enough leeway, and they are all in the same boat. None of us expected to have feelings involved when Dad first told us we were going to be working together. Hell, it's only been a little over a week, and I never knew feelings could develop so quickly.

I sigh and rest my head against his chest, snuggling in like a kitten. "Okay, you might be right, but I don't want to talk about it anymore. There is some serious lack of snuggling in my life, and right now, all I want to do is feel your arms around me, breathe in your scent, and enjoy being here with you. Is that okay?"

His arms tighten as he pulls my body closer so he's wrapped around me. "We will need to talk about it, but for now, I am fully on board with snuggling. I've been dreaming about it." A smile stretches across my face at his confession, and I fall a little harder for this man.

I must fall asleep, because the next thing I know, a hand is shaking me awake. "Mac, we need to go." I raise my head and blink at Miller. He's looking down at us with a gentle smile. Lathan's body is wrapped around mine, and his leg is thrown over me like he's holding me in place. His eyes are closed, and he looks younger than he is.

"It's ten. You missed dinner and your date with Dayton, but he insisted we let you sleep. If we don't go soon, though, Martha will blow up our phones."

I wipe a hand across my mouth, worried that I was drooling in my sleep—the wet patch on Lathan's shirt makes me suspicious. I cringe when my hand comes away wet, but Miller just snickers.

"Come on. As much as I want to leave you, we have to go." He pulls at my hand, and I untangle myself from Lathan, who cracks an eye open.

"Love you, Mac," he mutters sleepily, and I freeze, my brain stroking at his words.

"Don't overthink it." Miller tugs at my arm, and I look at him with panic in my eyes. "He's half asleep."

I allow him to pull me out of bed. "So you think he doesn't mean it?" I ask, unable to hide the disappointment in my voice, and Miller chuckles.

"Oh, I don't doubt he means it. I just doubt he meant to tell you yet. Lathan is a romantic at heart, and I'm pretty sure he fell the moment you opened those gorgeous eyes in the hospital room, despite looking like a domestic abuse victim."

His words dampen my disappointment and fill me with hope until I think about the last part. "Ha, you're the reason I looked like that," I argue, and he grins like he succeeded in whatever he was trying to achieve.

He drags me downstairs. The house is quiet, and the rest of the guys are missing. "Where is everyone?" I ask him as he takes me into the kitchen where my shoes and tights are. My backpack is there as well. I think I must have dropped it in the closet, so someone must have retrieved it for me.

"Anders and Dayton took Max to poke around the shipping yard. He needed to work off some of his frustration because he was being a real asshole." It's Ryland who answers. He's leaning against the doorframe leading to the conservatory. He says it casually, but I can tell he's worried about his brother.

"Oh, okay. Well, hopefully they find something." I don't worry that they are doing something without me. In the past, I probably would have felt either guilty or annoyed that they hadn't asked, but I can see the benefit of having a team to spread the jobs across. I don't need to be involved in everything.

"Are you okay?" he asks me as Miller opens the fridge and pokes around for a moment. He pulls out a covered container of something. I turn my back and pull my fishnets on, followed by my boots as I think about my response.

"Yeah, I am. Lathan helped a lot," I tell him, and he smiles gently. "You all have to remember that this is new for me—feelings are new to me. I learned very early on to compartmentalize, and I'm good at it, but I haven't seemed to be able to distance myself from this team. You all wormed your way in, and I'm not sure I can get you back out." I'm being brutally honest, and I know he recognizes that. "I'm going to fuck up, and quite frankly, I'm jealous as fuck when I see him and her together. I know rationally that he is doing it for the mission, but emotionally, I'm a mess. I just want to put a bullet between her eyes and toss her into a shallow grave for predators to nibble on."

Ryland blinks, and I think he's kind of lost for words, but Miller snorts with amusement as he slides a steaming bowl of food in front of me. It's in a to-go container with disposable cutlery.

"We saved you some dinner. You can eat it on the drive," he tells me, going to the fridge and grabbing a can of soda, placing it in front of me before picking up my backpack. The food smells familiar, and when I look down, I find a bowl of mac and cheese staring back at me.

"Come on, we can talk in the car." Miller waits for me to get up and grab my food before he leads the way to the garage entrance. I can feel Ryland following behind us.

"He called Sadie and begged for the recipe, told her you were having a bad day and wanted to make you feel better. I could hear her scream of excitement from across the room," he whispers behind me. I blink, looking down at my food again, before reaching for the fork to take a bite. The familiar flavors of my mom's mac and cheese hit my taste buds, and I burst into tears. Miller spins around with a look of panic on his face as Ryland wraps an arm around my waist and pulls my back against his chest.

"What? Did I do it wrong?"

"You made me mac and cheese? You called my mom?" I blabber, and his panic melts as he glares at his boyfriend.

"I was hungry and craving mac and cheese. It's not a big deal," he argues, trying to make less of a deal of it than it is, but I shake my head.

"It is. It's the nicest thing anyone has ever done for me," I tell him. I shuffle forward, the bowl held against my chest like it's treasure, dragging Ryland with me. I can hear him chuckle under his breath, but I ignore him and lean my head against Miller's chest. "Thank you."

"It was nothing," he mutters, but his arms come up, embracing both me and Ryland, and I lean into the three-way hug, feeling all sorts of emotions that I won't look at too carefully. They are too close to the ones I felt for Lathan earlier, and I'm not ready for that.

"Come on." Miller gently extracts me before helping me into the back seat of the car. "Make sure you eat that before it gets cold. Ry can get rid of the trash for us when he drops us off," he instructs me, placing my backpack on the floor near my feet before going around to the passenger seat. I just gape at him, completely blown away by this new version of Miller.

"Sexy, isn't it?" Ry mutters to me before closing the door and climbing into the driver's seat.

"Hell yes," I reply, scooping up a bite of my food and squirming on the spot as the familiar and comforting taste explodes across my taste buds. It is glorious, and I won't tell him this, but it tastes even better than my mom's because he made it for me. Kind and loving Miller is hot as fuck.

CHAPTER 26

The guys' search of the shipyard turned up nothing of interest. They said there are plenty of empty containers, but nothing that points to them trafficking people in. They placed a few cameras around the yard, and a team of analysts back at the Lighthouse will be watching around the clock for any suspicious movements.

Lathan's deep dive into the women's backgrounds was a little more interesting. The old lady who used to run Serenity House prior to Martha died in a car accident. Her brakes failed. Upkeep on the car wasn't the best, and it was lucky she didn't have any foster kids in it when it happened. She was originally rescued by EMTs and brought to the hospital where they managed to get her into stable condition, but later, she had a heart attack exacerbated by her injuries. It was deemed an accident, and the case was quickly closed.

Lathan dug a little deeper, however, and learned

that the brake lines had small slices in them. Also, there wasn't anything wrong with her heart that would have caused a heart attack. There was an overabundance of adrenaline in her system, and the coroner blamed the accident, but there were also large traces of epinephrine in her system. The coroner ruled that as nonsuspicious, because it was used to try and resuscitate her. This is the same coroner who also covered up Bishop's and the other girl's deaths. If that's not suspicious, I don't know what is. Martha was also one of the nurses treating her.

Brock's mention of the foster father going to jail was a red flag, and Lathan looked into the case. He was charged with almost fifty counts of sexually abusing a minor over the time they ran the house. The foster mother swore she never knew anything about it on the stand, and I guess a lack of foster homes allowed her to keep running the place.

Over the course of the next few days, Dayton made some calls to some of the former foster kids, and they said she knew all about it and threatened them all to keep their mouths shut. Four former kids had committed suicide during their stay at the house.

"Are we assuming that the four women who are now prominent members of Summerville society were four of the children who were abused?" I ask Anders quietly as we set up the bar for Thursday night.

"I don't think it would be much of a stretch to assume that," he replies, leaning against the bar as I cut up a lime.

"God, that's awful. I feel a little sorry for Martha now. She can't have kids, and she married a serial philanderer. What does she have? I wouldn't blame her if she was the one who killed her former foster mother. Hell, I've taken care of the same kind of scumbags in my job—coworkers or partners who looked the other way while their friends, lover, or colleagues abused people or did horrible things," I point out, and Anders nods.

"Yeah, I guess she's just trying to make the best of a bad situation. We wondered why she reported her foster kids missing if her husband has ties to the trafficking ring, but I bet it's because it reminds her of what she went through, then maybe it's her way of trying to make better choices. She can't kill the ones responsible, but she can make sure they pay."

"What I don't understand is how or why her husband let her do that." I stop cutting and look at him. "Surely that draws attention to their actions."

"Yes, but no. What if he let her report it to appease her, but expected the police chief to bury it? One of the other deputies took her report, and it was in the system, so when the police chief tried to hide it, it was too late. It had already appeared on our radar." Anders pushes off the bar as Miller and Keith both return from storage with straws, peanuts, napkins, and spare bottles of alcohol. We can't continue our conversation, but we have even more information to go on now.

"It's ladies' night," Keith croons. "My favorite night of the week. All the desperate and dateless are out and looking to get liquored up. Watch out, boys, you'll get your pick of prime pussy tonight. No one goes home lonely."

He places his bottles on the bar and rubs his hands together as the music switches on, making it difficult to talk quietly. Once the doors open, we are slammed. I have no idea why we are so busy. The dinner crowd is loud and obnoxious, but when they all finally depart, the club crowd pours in like we're the last club in the state, and the only one to provide alcohol. Thankfully there are more staff members on tonight—ones I haven't met before—because we would have been screwed without them. Matthew even opens up the upstairs bar, and the club is packed to capacity.

I barely get time to breathe, but it's getting close to one in the morning when Matthew stops me, my tray piled high with empties. "Let Carla do that. I need you up in one of the cages," he tells me.

"What?" I ask him, sounding confused.

"Just go up and see Anders, he'll tell you what to do. I need Cindy down here. There's a friend who would like to see her." Matthew nods at the end of the bar where a big, burly guy is waiting impatiently, tapping his finger on the bar, the beer in front of him barely touched.

"Oh, okay, sure," I reply, leaving the tray of glasses near the washer. He takes over stacking them into the dishwasher for me. He has been working the bottom bar with Keith and another man named Larry. Anders and Miller moved to the upstairs bar.

Apart from Cindy, there are five other girls on tonight in addition to Meri, Sam, Carla, and me. All of them have that hollow-eyed, slightly damaged goods look to them, but they seem happy enough to be working the club.

I use the staircase and dodge patrons as I make my way up to the top level. I cringe at the sound of bass when I get up there. The music is louder, it's hotter, and the air is ripe with the scent of sweat and sex. Dancing is most definitely not the only thing happening on the dance floor, but that isn't my problem. The bar runs along the back of the club, and on either end, there are ladders leading up to the cages that have dancers inside them. The dancers are basically wearing a G-string and pasties, and they are writhing in time to the dance music. Between them is the DJ booth, and I can see the DJ waving his hands in time to the music. I didn't even realize we had one the last two nights I worked. Nobody introduced us, and I thought it was some prerecorded tracks that were playing. Some super spy I am.

"Hey, which one is Cindy?" I ask Anders, waving to the girls in the cages. "Apparently I need to swap with her."

"You do?" He sounds surprised. "Well, okay then. It's the redhead on that end. There is a spare dance outfit in the staff room at the end of the bar." He nods in the opposite direction, past Miller and the ladder leading up to the cage.

"Can't I just dance in this?" I ask him, waving at the tiny uniform, and he shakes his head.

"No. I'm guessing this is a test. He probably wants to see if you will cooperate or argue about wearing one of those outfits."

I wrinkle my nose and sigh. "You're probably right. Okay."

I leave him and head to the office, closing the door behind me. I'm surprised the music is considerably lower. It must be somewhat soundproof in here. There are a couple of office desks with papers strewn on them, as well as a cupboard area. I'm assuming the costume is in one of those, so I move over to it and pull open one of the doors. I blink in surprise when I don't find a dance costume, but a pile of various little baggies of drugs—or I'm assuming that's what they are. I reach in, and there are at least thirty little bags of pills similar to the ones Matthew left for me on Sunday night. I tucked them away under the dresser drawers with my gun and laptop. I didn't want Martha to find them if she went snooping in our room. There's also the same number of small bags filled with white powder, and lots of rolled joints. Suddenly, the door slams open, and Meri appears on the other side.

"Oh!" She looks shocked to see me as she closes it behind her. "Did Matthew ask you to sell some of those too?" she asks me, nodding at the drugs before coming over and loading a few of each item into her apron pocket.

I shake my head. "No, I was looking for a dance

costume. Anders told me the spare ones are kept in here."

Her confusion clears, and she smiles, pointing to the next cupboard. "That one, but here, have one of these. Matthew lets the dancers take a pill. It makes it more fun to be exposed to everyone in the cage." She shoves another one of those baggies at me, and I look down at it.

"I'm not sure," I hedge, and her smile drops. She gets serious, and I'm instantly on alert.

"Trust me, it makes things easier. Even if you don't take them tonight, I'm going to recommend you keep them on hand for tomorrow. The private parties are much easier with a drug fog going on. Matthew insists on it. He says he wants the girls nice and relaxed and approachable, but we do make great money."

That's ominous. I don't want to take one tomorrow either. I'd rather keep a clear head, but it sounds like I may not have a choice. I'll have to warn Miller and the others.

"Okay, I'll hang onto them for tomorrow," I promise her as I open the other door and pull out a brand-new, sparkly purple thong. Well, it's not quite a thong, but it only covers half my butt cheeks. I look around for a top but can't find one.

Meri giggles at my confused expression and points to two sparkly star stickers. "They go over your nipples. He's not allowed to have nudity with the license here, but that will be different tomorrow, hence the X. It makes everything we have to do easier."

I blink at the purple star stickers and cringe. I'm not overly endowed, but I have decent-sized breasts and could have used a little support while dancing. Whoever came up with this outfit was definitely a man.

"Ugh, my boobs are going to hurt," I grumble as I take off my top and reach in to place the stars over my nipples. Meri leans against the cupboard and watches.

"Yeah, it's why I don't like to dance in the cages. Cindy and Ginger have small titties, and they hardly move, so it doesn't make a difference to them. Just shake your ass and run your hands over your body without moving too much. That's what I do. Matthew doesn't care as long as it's sexy." She pushes off the cupboard and gives me a wave as I remove my hot pants. "Have fun, I'll see you at the end of the night."

"You think I'll be up there for the rest of the night?" I ask her, and she nods.

"Ah, yeah. Cindy has something else she needs to do. A few clients are here to see her because they can't make it tomorrow night."

My eyes just about bug out of my head at that, but I manage to frown and look confused instead. "Clients?" I ask her, and she bites her lip, looking a little worried.

"Ah, um, massage clients. You know?" She winks, and I shake my head.

"They have massage rooms in here?" I didn't see any when we were poking around after our shift the other night, and Anders never said anything, but now that I think about it, we didn't poke around on this level because we assumed the club was underground. It is, but I guess we were pretty lax in our search.

"Yeah, there are a couple of rooms on this level. It's a special service for VIP clients. I'm sure you'll hear more about it tomorrow."

"I don't know how to massage." I continue to pretend to be clueless, even though I know it's not a massage the clients are after.

She winks. "It's pretty easy to pick up. Great tips too. Oh, lose the boots. You can go barefoot in the cage." She doesn't wait around for me to reply, rushing to the door and giving me a wave before disappearing.

None of us realized Matthew had whores working out of this club too. No wonder he asked me to blow Anders on the first day. Hell, Anders hasn't said anything either, so I'm assuming he doesn't know. That would have been something to tell the team for sure. The rooms must have been where Meri and Sam took Ted and James the other night. I assumed they ducked into one of the bathrooms. Hopefully I can get a look at one when we close up this evening, but with so many staff members working, it might be a little tricky.

I can't stall anymore. I remove my underwear—there's no way I can leave them on under the costume—and pull up the purple thong thing. Then, I sit down and unlace my combat boots, putting them and my socks with my uniform. I stand and stare at myself in the mirror on the inside of the cabinet door. I'm practically naked, but the bruises have mostly faded from my body. I do look a little pale and worn, the dark hair I have for this mission making my eyes pop. The circles under them, though, just make me look tired. After this mission, I'm going to take a long vacation, maybe on a tropical beach someplace where I can get some sun and relax. I pull out the ponytail holder and shake out my hair, and it falls sexily around my body. It's not much, but it helps me feel less exposed. I can't put it off anymore, I have to go out there. Matthew will get annoyed the longer Cindy's "friend" has to wait.

I pull the door open and step out behind the bar. Both Anders and Miller turn to look at me, and Miller's mouth drops open in surprise as he catches sight of what I'm wearing—or really, what I'm not wearing. Anders nods his approval but keeps serving the person in front of him. Miller's eyes run the length of my body, and I see the approval in his gaze before he curls his lip up, and I brace myself for whatever he's about to say.

CHAPTER 27

"What the fuck, Mac?" He grabs my arm, a flash of possessiveness in his tone. It kind of gives me a thrill but also annoys the fuck out of me. Hell, I'm as bipolar as him.

"Dude, get your hands off me. Matthew made me. Stop being an idiot, people are looking," I hiss, and he seems to get his shit together and drops his hand, looking around. Sure enough, people on the other side of the bar are watching our performance. He loses the sneer and grins affably before slapping me on the ass. "Have fun," he calls, and the crowd at the bar cheers. I glare at him with a promise of payback in my eyes, and he winks. Asshole.

As I climb the ladder to swap spots with Cindy, I see him pull out his phone and send a text message. I'm guessing I'll probably get an audience of at least Ryland and Lathan very shortly. Who knows if they will tell Max and Dayton too, or if Max is with Stella again?

I wave to get Cindy's attention. She comes over to the edge of the cage and leans in so I can talk to her. "Matthew says a friend is waiting for you at the bar," I tell her, and she nods. Her eyes are foggy with drugs, and she smiles.

"Cool, have fun," she tells me as we trade places. The cage doesn't move, since it's bolted firmly down. I was worried it was going to swing, which would make dancing tricky, but that's not the case.

I get into place and look out over the sea of writhing bodies. I'm almost certain we are packed beyond capacity, because there's barely an inch of room to move on the dance floor. I take a deep breath and tune in to the music. I've spent time at dance clubs in Europe during missions, so it's not that hard to start moving in time to the beat. I don't recognize the song, but then I don't listen to this style of music very often.

I let my body move to the rhythm, closing my eyes as the music washes over me. I take Meri's advice and don't move around too much. My damn breasts are swaying in time to the music as I run my hands over my body. When I feel eyes on me, I open mine, and sure enough, there are a bunch of guys watching my boobs like they are a hypnotist's pocket watch. Internally, I roll my eyes but slide my hands down over my breasts before turning around and slut dropping. I stick my ass out and shake it in time to the music. I think I almost gave them a heart attack as they whoop and holler their approval. I stand back up and grab hold of the cage bars, swinging my hips back and forth as I scan the rest of the crowd. I catch sight of Cindy tugging a man toward the opposite side of the club. She opens a door, and the two of them disappear behind it. Now I know what I have to check out once the club closes. Maybe one of the guys can cause a distraction so I can take a peek.

Unlike before when I was running drinks, time seems to drag while I'm on display in the cage. I'm not wearing a watch, so I have no clue what the time is, and the crowd on the dance floor isn't thinning. At one stage, I do notice Lathan and Ryland take up a spot at the end of the bar. Both of them stare at me with lust in their eyes before talking with each other. Neither of them stare at me too obviously, but I have no doubt they are here because Miller messaged them. Who would have thought that wearing not much more than nipple pasties and a thong would bring out his possessive side? Hell, he saw my tits with less on them last week.

The night has to be close to being over when Max and Dayton finally make an appearance. They join Lathan and Ry at the end of the bar, and for the first time in a long time, Max doesn't have Stella glued to his side in public. I wonder where she is. How did he extract himself from her tight hold? My jealous mind runs all sorts of scenarios through my head. Maybe they were together earlier, and it's only because it's so late that she isn't with him. It is a school day tomorrow, after all, and they both have to work.

Fuck, I need to stop obsessing about it. I don't look at him, even though I can feel him trying to catch my eye. I ignore all of them as the music suddenly lowers in level and the DJ yells out, "Last call," to everyone. I sigh with relief, knowing I can get down and get dressed very soon, but it's still probably a good half an hour before the music stops and security starts to push the still sizeable crowd downstairs.

I heave a sigh of relief and climb down the ladder. Anders passes me a bottle of water when I reach the floor before handing one to the other girl who climbs down the other ladder. She's a small thing with bleach blonde pixie cut hair. She gives him a kiss on the cheek and slaps his ass enthusiastically, and I see red. I want to pick up the paring knife and stab it into her throat.

A body blocks my view of them laughing and flirting. Sure, I know Anders is like that. I've seen him work the bar, and it never bothered me before. I have no idea what has just come over me. "Hey, settle, tiger. He's just being friendly with the staff." Miller reaches out and puts a finger under my chin, lifting it so I will look at him and not at Anders and the other dancer—Ginger, I think.

"Fuck, what's wrong with me?" I ask him, my voice slightly breathless from both dancing and my anger.

He chuckles. "Jealousy is a curse, and it really doesn't belong in our career," he teases.

I scoff at him. "Hello, pot. Meet kettle." I point from him to me, and he shrugs.

"I'm not denying it. Believe me, it's a constant work in progress." His gaze moves to something behind me, and I find him looking at his boyfriend, who is eyeing both of us like we're a snack he wants to devour. Whatever this is between the three of us is going to come to its forgone conclusion soon, and I have a feeling it's going to be explosive.

"Come on, we need to clean up," he says before slapping my ass. I yelp in surprise, but he just chuckles and moves quickly out of my reach.

"You will keep, Miller. Just when you think you're safe, I'll pounce," I threaten him as security approaches the bar to clear out the last of the stragglers. The rest of Team Basilisk leaves without acknowledging us.

"Sure thing, Mac," he says, humoring me as he wipes the bar just as Matthew arrives from downstairs.

"How did it go?" he asks, approaching me with a raised eyebrow.

"Yeah, it was fine. I'm tired, but it was fun," I tell him, and he nods, looking pleased.

"Can you help Anders and Miller clean up here? Then he will run the two of you home."

"Sure thing, I'll just get changed," I tell him as I turn around to do just that, but he grabs hold of me, his hand tight on my arm.

"I didn't tell you to get changed. Do it in that. I'm

sure Anders and Miller will like the view," he demands, and I look down at the floor.

"Can I put my boots on? The floor is sticky," I ask timidly, even though I want to throat punch him for touching me.

"Sure, why not? Need to keep you in prime condition." He releases my arm and turns his attention to Miller and Anders, who have been watching the conversation. "No touching. I saw the Turner boys' interest in her tonight. She's going to make me bank tomorrow night," he warns the two men.

"Yeah, Max is really keen on getting to know her," Anders replies suggestively.

"You tell your roommate to come and see me as soon as he gets to the private party tomorrow. I'm sure we can work out some kind of deal." Matthew is practically gleeful.

"You'll enjoy looking after Max Turner for me, won't you, Mac?" he asks, staring at me like he's waiting for me to refuse. "He will be very handy to have in my pocket."

"He's my teacher at school," I argue half-heartedly. I can't seem too eager.

"And that's stopped you in the past, has it?" Matthew raises an eyebrow. "Brock said he heard some interesting noises coming from Max Turner's office when you were in there for tutoring."

I blush and look away from him, not meeting any of their eyes. "I don't know what you're talking about," I deny lamely.

"Sure. I bet if you're good to him tomorrow, you won't have any problems passing history." He walks away, the discussion obviously over. "I'll see you all tomorrow. Meet us here, and we will take you to the private party," he instructs. "Don't be late or even think about not attending. I have that video, and I can make both your lives hell." He stops and looks back at Miller and me. "Understand?" he asks, and we both nod.

"Don't worry, boss, I've got you. I'll make sure they are there," Anders assures him, and both Miller and I glare at him, almost in sync.

Matthew just chuckles. "You're not doing yourself any favors, Anders. Not sure Mac will help you relax anymore."

Anders shrugs. "Not like I'm short on pussy working here, and I'm pretty certain hers will be flogged out by the time Max is done with her. He's not known to be gentle."

Matthew laughs a deep belly laugh. "Well, that is interesting to learn. I may have to charge a fee for any damage. You break it, you buy it kind of policy. Alright, see you all later." He waves a hand and disappears down the steps.

"I call dibs on putting a bullet in his brain," Miller mutters quietly so that only I can hear.

"Be my guest," I murmur and go to find my boots, feeling slightly queasy at the knowledge they've been doing this a long time. This town is going to suffer when we finish with all the arrests. They are going to be down a few prominent business owners as well as a pastor, school guidance counselor, and chief of police —not to mention whoever else we discover using the sex club tomorrow. It's not a big deal if they have consensual partners, but prostitution is illegal in Georgia, and I have no doubt people at the end of all this will be charged.

When I return, the guys are out on the dance floor, collecting empties from the various tables scattered around the perimeter. I look around to make sure we're alone before saying, "Did you know there are sex rooms here?" I ask Anders, going over to the door I saw Cindy enter. I lost track of time and didn't see her come out, but I'm assuming she did. Still, I carefully open the door and sigh with relief when no one is in there.

"Holy crap! I had no idea." Anders appears behind me and looks over my shoulder. This room has a bed in it with rumpled sheets, and it smells like sex. "The extra staff that were on today only work Thursday nights. For some reason, it's one of the biggest nights of the week. I've never noticed them coming and going like they did tonight. All five of them took a turn in the cage before swapping out. I wonder if they all had clients."

I go to the other room, and it's in the same condition. I screw up my nose. "Well, I hope they changed the sheets between clients, because there are only two rooms."

"Are we supposed to clean these too?" Miller asks, and Anders shrugs.

"I have no idea. I didn't even know they were here."

"Let's leave them for now. Matthew isn't an idiot. He would have said something if he wanted us to clean them," I suggest, and the other two agree with me. I just close the door and grab a few glasses off a table when one of the other staff members appears. She's towing a man by the hand, and they are giggling to one another.

"Oh, hey!" She stops and looks surprised to see the three of us. "Um, we're just going to..." She trails off and looks at the sex rooms.

"Have fun," I tell her and turn my back on them. The guys continue to clean up while they go into the rooms. We continue to clean, but soon enough, loud sex sounds start to ring out.

"Fuck, I guess those rooms aren't soundproof," Miller grumbles, and I giggle at what we're hearing.

"They don't need to be when the music is playing, I guess." Anders smirks.

We keep cleaning, Miller and I focusing on the tables and empties while Anders concentrates on the bar. I'm just wiping down the last of the tables when the noise gets louder, and I roll my eyes.

"She's totally faking that," I say to the guys as the girl shrieks and begs and pleads. I return to the sink to rinse out my cloth.

"Sounds like she's having a good time to me." Anders chuckles, and I roll my eyes.

"Please, nobody sounds like that during sex."

"I don't know, I'm pretty sure I heard those kinds of sounds coming from the closet under the stairs yesterday, and I'm certain it wasn't a house elf." Miller bursts out laughing at Anders's cheeky words, and I just stare at him in amazement. I don't think I've ever seen him laugh before. It's stunning.

"I don't sound like that." I shake off my daze and glare at Anders.

"Sure, Dobby. I'll make sure to record you next time. I almost came in my pants from the sounds," Anders says, losing the laughter as his eyes heat with something else.

"Are you almost done?" Keith appears at the top of the stairs, smirking when he hears the noises coming from the sex room.

"Yeah, we are. Mac just needs to grab her clothes," Anders tells him, waving me away as Keith's eyes latch onto my mostly naked body.

A piercing whistle comes from his mouth as he saunters closer to get a better look.

"Well, I wish I tended bar up here tonight. Look at those titties. I bet you two had a hard-on the whole time." He winks at Miller, who glares sullenly at him, but of course Anders puts on his sleazy persona.

"My man..." He holds out his hand for Keith to slap it. "I can't wait to get home to rub one out. My cock has been pressing against my zipper the whole time."

Keith laughs it up. "Dude, why didn't you take her for a spin in there?" He nods at the sex rooms, and Anders feigns a frown and a groan.

"Matthew says she's off-limits until after the party. He has plans for her."

Keith purses his lips. "What a shame. Maybe next week. Matthew normally doesn't care. They even usually give us freebies if you sneak them drinks while we're working."

This man is disgusting. I feel my fists clench, the need to reach out and strangle him fierce, but Miller steps between us, blocking my view of him. "Go put some clothes on. Martha will kill us if you come home like that," he snaps at me, and I feel my fury seep away. Fuck, that was close. Can't blow the case because some asshole is making sleazy comments. *Come on, Kenz, get your head in the game. Business as usual.*

I head into the office and pull my uniform on over what I'm wearing. I don't bother taking anything off because I just want to go home. I'm done with the club tonight, and I need to be in a better head space to deal with everything that's going to happen tomorrow night.

"What about her?" I hear Anders ask Keith as I come out of the office, and Miller and I make our way downstairs.

"Don't worry about it. She'll clean up those rooms when she's done. It's always the job of the girl who finishes last," I hear Keith answer behind us. He and Anders are following us down the stairs.

"Are you coming?" Anders asks him as we enter the staff area to grab our things.

"Nah, man, I'm going to wait for Shelby. She will usually suck my cock if I help her change the sheets."

"Can Keith have an unfortunate car accident on his way home from work tonight?" I ask Miller, and I hear him huff out a sound.

"From your mouth to God's ears," he mutters as we both grab our bags and wait for Anders to join us. When he does and is alone, and he looks pained.

"Fuck, I hate that man," he mutters under his breath so any cameras don't pick it up.

The three of us leave and walk to his car. "God, I'm tired," I grouse as I climb into the back seat. "I can't believe we have to go to school in two hours," I say to Miller when I read the dashboard clock, and it says it's four in the morning.

"I'm not going. When Ry picks me up in the morning, I'm going to go spend the day napping at his place. We need to be on the ball for tonight," he tells me, and Anders nods.

"You should do the same. Max will cover for you."

"But what about the rest of the foster kids? They might say something to Martha. Or Sophie? She will definitely say something to her mom, who will say something to Martha if we all aren't there," I point out.

"Nah, Sophie isn't going to be there. I heard her tell Ry that she and Stella were going to Savannah today for shopping with their mother. She wanted Ry and Max to go with them, but Max told them he couldn't miss work and that he didn't want Ry to miss school."

"Well, okay then. I guess I could spend the day resting," I agree and close my eyes for the rest of the trip home. I must have fallen asleep, because Anders wakes me as Miller gets out of the car.

"Sleep well, baby," he tells me as I lean forward and give him a quick kiss on the lips. He blinks slightly—shocked, I think—before grabbing me and kissing me back. I smile as I get out of the car, and Miller rolls his eyes.

"Come on, it's cold and we still need to get into the house. I'm not sure Martha knew we would be working this late on a Thursday."

"No, I thought we'd be done by twelve too. I'm exhausted." I drag ass as I follow him down the driveway. My feet are sore, and it's all I can do to put one in front of the other. Thank God we don't have to climb the tree tonight, because I'm not sure I would be able to manage it.

CHAPTER 28

We make it inside and upstairs without incident. I wave goodbye to Miller, but he tugs me into the stairway leading up to his room, pushing me up against the wall like he did the last time.

"Ugh." I lean my head against the wall. "What is it? I'm too tired for your games tonight," I whisper, and he grins, the bare bulb light making eerie shadows on his face.

"Don't be like that. I just thought I'd help you get changed." He reaches for the hem of my crop top and peels it over my head. I raise my arms to make it easier for him, then I blink with surprise as he stares at my nipple pasties.

"Fuck, I've wanted to do this all night," he mutters as he uses a nail to lift one of the stickers before peeling it back. I wince as the glue pulls my skin, but he quickly replaces it with his mouth, soothing the sting with his tongue. Holy fuck. I groan and thread my fingers through his hair as the pull of his mouth makes my core clench.

He pulls back and smirks before repeating the action on the other side. When he moves away, the tiredness is gone, and it's replaced with a hunger that only Miller can tame. I reach for his belt, but he stops me, placing his hand on mine before removing it.

"Sleep well," he says before leaning in and giving me a kiss. He turns and heads upstairs, rolling the stickers up in his hand.

"What the fuck?" I hiss and hear a quiet chuckle as the door to his room opens and closes behind him. "You'll pay for that," I say to the empty staircase before holding my shirt over my naked breasts and hurrying to my room. Once again, Jessica is snoring like a bear when I go in and strip off the bottom half of my uniform and dance outfit and replace it with a fresh pair of undies and a soft T-shirt. My nipples are tight, and my panties don't stay fresh for long as my pussy aches with the need Miller created. What a fucking asshole. He will pay for this. I'm not sure how, but I will have him begging at my feet sometime soon.

I huff and roll over on my side as the sky outside lightens ever so slightly. Fuck, morning is coming. I am definitely taking them up on their offer to nap at the Turners' today. I need to be fully functional tonight, and that isn't going to happen without a little more sleep.

It feels like I only just fell asleep when Jessica shakes me awake.

"No, Mom, I don't want to get up," I mutter and push the hand away.

Jessica snorts before giving me a harder shove. "Get up. Martha is losing her shit downstairs. Neither you nor Miller got up on time. She says she will stop you from working at the Life Lounge if you don't get your ass down there in five minutes."

"Fuck!" I bolt upright in bed and peer blearily at the girl, and she chuckles.

"Man, you look like shit. Did you even take your eye makeup off?"

I look down at my white pillowcase, and sure enough, there are black smudges on it.

"No," I groan. "I was too tired. We got home just after four," I tell her, climbing out of bed and searching for something to wear in my dresser. I find underwear, a pair of leggings, and another band shirt and quickly pull them on.

"Wow, you must be tired," she says as she watches me.

"You have no idea. I'm blowing off school and napping at Ry's place today," I tell her, and her mouth drops open in surprise.

"Sophie won't be happy if you all aren't at school," she warns me, and I shrug.

"Apparently she's not going to be there. She has a shopping trip to Savannah planned with her mom and sister." Her worried frown clears, and she nods. "Well good, that means Michelle and Lucy won't be there either. Today will actually be pleasant. I'll make sure to tell the others not to say anything in front of Martha."

"Thank you. I have to work a private party tonight, and I don't want to fall asleep during it. I need the money. I'm doing a college tour next week, and it might just be the chance I need."

She smiles, but her eyes dim a little. "I haven't gotten any offers yet, but I keep hoping. I can't believe Martha won't let me get a job where you're working either."

"Yeah, I don't blame her. It's more than I thought it would be," I tell her, hoping she can read between the lines. "You should see if the Mug Shot diner is hiring. I'm sure you'll earn good tips there, and the hours aren't as unreasonable as the club ones, except on Saturday night."

"Yeah, that's a good idea. I didn't before because Sophie insisted it was demeaning, but at this stage, I'll take whatever I can get."

I forgot to speak to my dad about these kids in that house. I will do that at some stage today, when I've had a little more sleep.

"I'll cross my fingers for you," I tell her. "I just need

to wash my face, and then I'll be down there. Can you tell Martha I'm coming?"

"I will," she says as frantic footsteps are heard on the floor above us. She giggles. "I guess Ty woke Miller."

We exit the room and see Ty appearing from Miller's stairway, rubbing his cheek. "Fuck, he got me."

"He hit you?" I ask, sounding shocked, and he grimaces.

"Yeah. James found out the hard way when Miller first came to stay. He tried to wake him the first morning and ended up with a black eye, so we try to avoid it if possible, and he mostly sets his alarm, but Martha insisted he was going to oversleep. Will beat me in a round of rock-paper-scissors so it was my turn." Both of them have pitying looks on their faces, and I feel myself mirroring them. I wonder what happened in his past that causes him to wake with violence if disturbed.

We hear Martha shouting, and they hurry downstairs as I go into the bathroom to wash my face. When I'm done, I emerge at the same time as Miller, and the both of us hurry downstairs with our backpacks.

"About time," Martha grumbles as we tear through the kitchen just as the others are walking out the back door. "I'll be talking to Matthew about your hours. Don't plan on working next Thursday. I won't have it disturbing your education," she calls after us.

We make our way down the driveway in no time

and stop at the end to wait for the bus. "Hey, Miller, do you think Ry could talk to the owners of the Mug Shot Cafe about Jessica getting a job? I'm sure someone told me their families are friends." He looks surprised but nods.

"Ah, yeah. Sure, I guess." Before he can say anything else, the bus pulls up, and everyone gets on except me and Miller.

"Aren't you coming?" Cassie asks, looking between us.

"Nah, we're blowing school off today and hanging out at Ryland's place," I tell her. Sally gives me a dirty look, but Stephanie just smiles.

"Have fun then," she says as they all get on and the bus drives away.

"Phew, that was easier than I thought," I say to Miller as Ry's car pulls up, the dust from the bus swirling higher, and we climb into the back seat.

"How's everyone feeling this morning?" he asks cheerfully, and in unison, Miller and I flip him off.

"How is it that you've had as much sleep as us and you are wide awake?" I ask him as he pulls away from the bus stop.

"He's a cyborg, always disgustingly happy in the mornings," Miller grumbles.

Lathan stares at the two of us with wide eyes.

"Hell, neither of you are morning people. Are you as violent as Miller in the morning?" he asks with a smile, and Miller flips him off too.

"I'll have you know I am a perfectly pleasant

morning person with the required eight hours of sleep," I say primly, and Lathan and Ry chuckle.

"I will have to see it to believe it," Lathan replies.

I poke Miller in the side, and he jumps. He leaned his head against the window and his eyes drifted closed.

"Tell them. Haven't I been pleasant every other morning?" I insist, and he waves a hand and grumbles, "Less talk, more sleep."

I gape at him in shock, and Ry and Lathan laugh again.

"Yeah, ask him again in a few hours, and you might get a more coherent reply," Ry says affectionately as he concentrates on the road.

"Are you going to school?" I ask them. "Neither of you got much sleep last night either."

"Actually, we were asleep when Miller sent us the text saying you were in the cage. It was my brother's bellow of annoyance that woke us up, and he insisted we go down and keep an eye on you. So yeah, we'll go for the morning at least."

"Why was Max pissed off?" I ask, feeling even more tired at that.

"Because he can't control what happens to you, and it's messing with his head. His protective instincts are in overdrive, and all he can do is wait around for you to take care of yourself, which he knows you can do, but it's messing with his core character." All signs of laughter are gone as Ry explains this to me. "Have patience with him."

I grimace and decide I need to be honest with everyone if I'm going to expect the same in return. "Don't worry, I kind of get it. I have not so positive feelings about him spending time with Stella, and it's a new experience. Jealousy isn't something I've ever dealt with before."

"We know, it's an adjustment for all of us. None of us expected for this to go the way it has," Ry replies.

"Not that we're complaining," Lathan adds, but I wave him off.

"I know. It's fine."

The rest of the trip is quiet as they take us back to the Turner mansion. Neither Ry nor Lathan get out. They just drop us off, and I follow Miller into the house. He drops his bag in the kitchen, and I add mine to it before he leads the way upstairs. He pushes through a door and drags his shirt and jeans off before climbing under the blankets. I stand awkwardly in the doorway. I can smell that this is Ry's room. It has the same fragrance as the cologne he wears, and a shiver of want runs down my back. I'm not sure if I should join Miller or go down to Lathan's room. I look at his closed bedroom door and decide I'm probably safer going down there when Miller calls out to me.

"God, I can hear you overthinking from here, and I'm trying to sleep. Ditch the clothes and get your ass in here," he mumbles from under the covers. It takes me a moment to comprehend what he's saying, and obviously that's a moment too long.

He huffs and throws the sheets back, swinging his

legs off the bed and stomping over to me. He grabs my hand and drags me back to the opposite side of the bed, where he strips off my leggings, pulls my shirt off, and undoes my bra. He turns back to a dresser and removes a shirt before tugging it over my head. He does most of this with his eyes barely cracked open. He then points at the bed, ordering, "Get in," before going back around to the other side, climbing in, and pulling the covers over himself.

I'm speechless and so shocked that I obey him, climbing into really nice thread count sheets and pulling the down comforter over myself. I'm facing Miller, my eyes on his back, when he huffs again.

"God, do you ever stop thinking?" Miller grouches, and I feel him move closer, and then his foot touches mine. "Go to sleep. You can worry about what this is when we wake up. I'm tired, and you're keeping me awake. We both need to be on the ball for tonight."

He reaches out and grabs a remote, and the sound of rain comes out of speakers somewhere. I feel my body start to relax, and my eyes grow heavy. He's right, I'm exhausted, and I think my brain is failing to comprehend what just happened. I'll take his advice and worry about it once I have a few more hours of sleep.

I'm not sure how long I've been asleep, but it's the murmured voices next to me that have me waking from the dead sleep I was in. It's then I notice the heavy weight on my stomach as well as the dipped mattress in front of me. I hold my breath as I try to work out who it is. Finally, my brain catches up, and I recognize Ry's and Miller's voices. Ry is in front of me, and Miller is behind me, and they seem to be arguing about something.

I don't pay too much attention because I'm trying to figure out how I'm pinned to the bed. I turn my head a little and open my eyes and find Miller pressed against my side. I'm on my back, and he has an arm and a leg wrapped around my body like I'm his favorite teddy bear, and he needs me to get a good night's sleep. His hair is messy, and he has a soft look on his face as he talks to his boyfriend.

He breaks off as I reach up and push a lock of hair behind one of his ears. "You snore like a bear." He looks down at me and wrinkles his nose. "A very loud, smelly bear."

My mouth drops open, and I'm fucking mortified. Did I fart in my sleep? Oh my god!

"Gosh, you're an asshole. You just can't help yourself." Ry pushes him, and he falls back onto the bed, removing his arm and leg from my body. "He's lying. You were so cute, and there were a few snuffles, but definitely kitten snuffles, and absolutely no farts," he reassures me.

"You're my next favorite after Lathan," I tell him, rubbing a hand over my sleepy eyes as I try to work out what time it is or even why he's here.

I sit upright and look around, a wave of panic rushing over my body. "Fuck, is it home time? Martha thinks we're coming home on the bus. It's Friday night. She has the night off, and we have to do everything." I start scrambling to push the blankets off, but somehow, I've become completely entangled in them.

Ry reaches out and stops my frantic struggle. "Hey, whoa, relax. It's only lunchtime. I came back to check on the two of you. I brought some food," he explains, and I feel my panic recede as I flop back on the bed.

"Oh, cool. Okay, thanks," I say as his eyes fix on the shirt I'm wearing.

"How did you end up in one of my shirts?" he asks, sounding slightly amused and possessive.

"Fuck, don't overthink it. It's what was close, and she didn't have anything comfortable," Miller mutters, and both Ry and I look at him skeptically.

"Weren't you wearing a baggy band shirt this morning?" he points out, and as I nod, Miller flips him off. Ry smirks, and his phone starts to ring. The smirk gets wider when he sees who it is and answers it.

"Hey, Percy, what's going on?" he answers, and a small squeak leaves my mouth. I grab the blankets and yank them up over me as he turns the call into Face-Time. I feel him climb onto the bed and sandwich me between them.

"Hey, boys, how are you?" I hear my dad ask, but

before either of them can answer, I hear another voice, and my stomach sinks.

"Oh, Ry and Miller! Both my boys! I am so lucky today." My mother sounds delighted.

"Hi, Sadie. How are you?" Ry replies, but it's Miller's words that have me melting.

"Marhaban ya 'umu qalb," he says to my mom in Arabic. *Hello, mother of my heart.*

Her reply has tears welling in my eyes, and I have to smother the sob that escapes. *"Mrhbaan ya fataa aldhahabi."* *Hello, my golden boy.* Fuck, I had no idea. No wonder he was so hostile to me.

Obviously I wasn't quiet enough, though, or I moved too much, because the next words have me wincing.

"Is there someone else in your bed under the blankets? I can see something moving," she asks.

"Would you believe we got a puppy?" Ry asks.

"Well, I would say you're probably smothering it," I hear my dad say, and I know we've been busted. I take a deep breath and push the blankets back to see my parents smirking at me on Ry's phone screen.

"Hello, parentals," I say dryly, and Dad chuckles while my mom squeals and claps her hands together.

"I knew it! I knew my girl wouldn't be able to keep her hands off all that gorgeous male flesh." Both Dad and I cringe, and Miller and Ry shuffle uncomfortably.

"Miller and Mac spent the day napping before the private party tonight," Ry explains. "They finished at the club at about four this morning."

My mom's delight disappears at the reminder of what tonight has in store for us, but Dad nods his approval. "Good thinking. Did you all input the trackers I sent?"

"Yeah, Anders did them Sunday night. We won't be able to remove the stitches for a few days, but we used the excuse that we got new tattoos. Nobody has questioned it," Miller tells my dad.

"Good, and Lathan and Dayton will be monitoring everything that goes on through your earpieces, and both Ry and Max will have cameras in buttons on their shirts so we can record everything you see."

I wince, and Dad sees it. "What's wrong?" he asks, and I sigh.

"Look, I understand why it needs to be recorded, but can you have one of the techs or someone else watch it? If we have to do what I think we have to, I don't want to know you're on the other end of that camera."

My dad blanches, and my mom smothers a giggle. "Fuck no. Of course I have someone else watching the footage. Neither of us need those kinds of scars."

"Thank God," I hear Miller mutter under his breath, and I feel my body relax.

"Be careful tonight, and be ready for anything."

"We will, Dad, but I think tonight is a way to lure Ry and Max in. Miller and I are the convenient bait. I'll be interested to see if any of the victims from the cells are forced to entertain the patrons."

"We'll debrief on Wednesday when I see you, but

let me know when you get home tomorrow morning, please," he orders us, and we sign off with I love yous from me and my parents.

"Well, that was awkward," I comment as Ry tosses his phone onto the bedside table and rolls so he's facing me.

"Yes, but not as awkward as it would have been if I'd been doing this." He leans in and kisses me.

I kiss him back until I'm breathless, and when he pulls away, I chase after his mouth, but he stops me. A finger on my chin has me turning my head, and when my eyes meet Miller's, I don't get a chance to say anything before his mouth is on mine too.

Holy crap. They kiss completely differently, but both have the capacity to make my toes curl and my core throb with need. I'm completely lost in my need for him when he, too, pulls away, and I mewl with distress.

"Mac," Ry calls, and I reluctantly turn to look at him. "You know there's a good chance that we're all going to have to fuck tonight, right?"

I nod my head. "Yes, of course. It's not a problem for me," I assure him, but then I feel a stab of anxiety. "Is it a problem for the two of you?" I ask, looking between them, but they both shake their heads.

"No, of course not." Ryland is talking for both of them. "But neither of us want our first time with you to be in front of a bunch of cameras or perving assholes."

Oh my lord. That was not what I was expecting.

"Oh yeah, no, of course," I answer awkwardly and want to fucking slap myself. *Way to go, Kenz. Smooth, real smooth.* "So what did you have in mind?"

Ry smirks and looks at Miller. "How about we just show her?"

CHAPTER 29

R y strips off his shirt and crawls over me until he straddles my body, trapping me in place. "Kiss her," he orders Miller, who is quick to comply. He leans in and takes my mouth with his. Like most of our interactions, it's violent and demanding, his tongue lashing mine before he bites down on my lip, and I grunt in shock. Miller's mouth gets torn away from mine as I reach up and dab at the drop of blood he drew.

"Gentle, we need to build her up to your brand of loving. Lose the pants," Ry cautions him, and Miller growls but climbs off the bed and removes his boxers, his hand stroking over his long length. I can't tear my eyes away from his cock or the silver bars lining it. Fuck, I didn't remember how big it was, or that it was pierced.

"Pretty, isn't it?" Ry smirks at me as he pats the bed, inviting Miller back up on it. "Why don't you get a little closer so Kensington can get a better look?" he tells Miller, using my real name. I have a feeling he's trying to separate what's happening now with what's going to happen later—real life as opposed to work.

Miller does as ordered and shuffles up toward my head. Ry reaches out and pushes against my cheek, encouraging me to take Miller's cock in my mouth. I reach up and replace his hand with mine before licking the tip.

"That's right, baby, get it nice and wet for me," Ry says as he crawls down my body, taking my underwear with him. He parts my legs and settles between them, staring at my pussy, and groans. "I have wanted to get my mouth on this since I saw you that first day when I picked Miller up. Fuck, you were standing there in that skirt that barely covered your ass and my mouth watered. I wanted to offer you a lift as well, but this asshole and Bishop wanted to test you." He points at his boyfriend who rolls his eyes and leans down, gently extracting himself from my mouth and peeling my shirt off my body.

He's quick to retake his place though. One of his hands threads through my hair, encouraging me to continue. It's my turn to smirk at him, but I do as he asks. I'm fascinated with his piercings, and I tug on them with my teeth, causing him to groan.

"Miller likes a bit of pain," Ry says as he licks a finger and runs it lightly over my clit, teasing me. My breath hitches, but I keep my attention on Miller's cock. It's not enough to distract me yet.

Ryland removes his finger, replacing it with his tongue. He draws circles around my clit, barely brushing over it, before flattening it and licking from my entrance to my clit. I moan around Miller's dick. Ry gives me no mercy, and he licks and sucks and uses two fingers to bring me to the brink of an orgasm before slowing down and retreating. He does this twice, and I end up groaning in disappointment after the second time. Poor Miller is being teased as well. I'm super enthusiastic while Ry's mouth is on me, trying to give Miller as much pleasure as I'm feeling, but when Ry pulls away, I lose focus.

After the second time, Miller grumbles, "Dude, stop teasing us."

Ry sits up, chuckling, before climbing over my body. He's still wearing pants, so Miller reaches out and undoes them, helping Ry remove them. The entire time, he thrusts lazily in and out of my mouth. I mean, that's talented. The guy has mad concentration skills. I watch as they kiss each other, running their hands all over their bodies with an ease born of familiarity.

God, they are gorgeous, and I get so distracted watching them, I forget about Miller's dick in my mouth.

"Can you distract her again? She gets lazy when she's overthinking things," Miller says, pushing his partner at me, and Ry grins.

"Gladly," he says as he lines his dick up with my entrance and slides in. I knew it was girthy, since I've had my mouth around it, but my pussy is tight from all his teasing, and it takes him a couple of thrusts before he's fully seated.

We moan in unison. "Oh yeah, keep doing that," Miller encourages his boyfriend. "I want to fuck her throat, so get to work keeping her mind off what I'm doing."

Ry pulls back and thrusts again, and my pussy flutters around it. Ry rolls his hips, circling his cock, his pelvis brushing across my clit with every stroke. He reaches up and collars my neck with his large hand. I close my eyes and relax my throat, and Miller slides deeper and holds there for a moment before pulling out.

"Oh yeah, she likes that. You should feel her pulse," Ry says to Miller. "You really like the two of us working your body. I wonder what other kinds of things she likes. Would you like Miller and I to take both your holes?" he asks, and I can't reply, but he smirks when my pussy walls flutter even harder.

"I know. What if I fucked Miller while he fucked you?" Ry hits on one of my biggest fantasies, and I just about come on the spot. "Oh yeah, that's the one. Grab the lube, baby. We're about to make Kenzie's fantasies come true."

Miller pulls out of my mouth and climbs off the bed, looking around in the bedside drawer before pulling out a bottle of lube. He tosses the bottle to Ry, who pulls out of me. I moan at the loss, the disappointment real, but there's a giddy excitement in my stomach at the thought of what we're about to do. I watch as they make out in front of me for a bit, my hands grabbing the sheets so I don't start grabbing either of them. Eventually, they pull apart, and Ry shuffles out of the way and moves Miller into his spot.

I watch with wide eyes as he leans down and licks Miller's cock from root to tip once, twice, as Miller holds onto his head, before pulling back and spitting on it. It's dirty and raw, and I am so here for it. Ry reaches for the lube while Miller runs his cock through the mess Ry made of my pussy. It's weeping with the loss of him. Miller looks up, his eyes locking with mine, and wraps his hand around my throat, squeezing as he slides his dick deep with one thrust. My eyes roll back in my head. The pressure from both his hand and his dick is out of this world.

"Look at our good girl, taking your dick like that. Her pussy is so nice and tight, isn't it, babe?" Ry grabs Miller's chin and turns his head so he can kiss him while he lubes up his cock. His hand drops away from his chin, and Miller lazily thrusts in and out a couple of times before he grunts, and his eyes widen slightly. "Such a good boy," Ry coos as I watch him work his hand back and forth. Although I can't see over Miller, I know Ry is prepping his ass for his cock.

"Miller doesn't like it gentle, so brace yourself, Mac, so you don't end up bashing your head against the wall," Ry warns as he pushes on Miller's back, encouraging him to lower. When he gets close enough, I lean up and take his mouth with mine. He jolts with surprise and then moans into my mouth as Ry works himself into his ass. His mouth slips from mine, and I feel him suck and then bite my neck. When he pulls away, his eyes are closed, and his neck muscles are taut as Ry whispers words of praise to us. I've never seen them look more perfect together. I feel a slight pang of jealousy and worry that I'm always going to be on the outside.

Ry sees right through me though. "Be a good boy and look after our girl, babe. Make sure she doesn't hurt herself," Ry says, and Miller opens his eyes, a blissful haze making him blink a few times. He reaches for a pillow and shoves it behind my head. Satisfied with what he's done, he leans in and suckles on one of my nipples, and I gasp when he nips it before moving to the other one.

"Ready?" Ry asks, and Miller nods, not taking his attention away from my breasts. "Good, because I'm about to make the two of you feel so good. I love that I can control both your orgasms." Ry pulls out slightly before thrusting hard, causing Miller to do the same. "I'm like the conductor, and you are my orchestra. Now let me hear the beautiful sounds of your plea-sure," Ry croons as he works himself in and out of Miller, his pace punishing. Miller's helpless to do anything but hang on for the ride, his thrusts into me an echo of Ry's.

I'm not sure how long it takes to build, but before long, both of us are panting and pleading with Ry, and he wraps a hand around Miller, sliding it down where we are joined, and starts flicking my clit. Miller's hand, which has been loosely on my throat this whole time, starts to tighten, and he leans in and bites my nipple hard. It's enough to send me flying into outer space, my orgasm sending pulses of pleasure throughout my body. I clamp down on Miller's dick like a vise, and he groans loudly.

"Fuck," he mutters, and I feel his dick throb inside me, his own orgasm triggered by mine. It only takes Ryland two more thrusts, and he pulls out. I watch over Miller's shoulder as he paints his back with his cum, marking him just like Miller marked me. His eyes meet mine, and when he winks, some of my doubts flow away. There will be plenty of time to talk about what this is. It's so freaking hot, I feel a second, smaller orgasm flow through my body, and Miller's eyes widen with shock before a small, dirty smirk stretches across his lips.

"I think you're going to fit in just perfectly, you filthy girl."

The three of us must fall asleep again, because a knock on the door has me waking a little while later, hot and smothered. Lathan sticks his head in.

"Hey, Miller and Mac need to go home. School's done," he says, smiling at us fondly.

Miller groans, but I feel freaking refreshed. It's

amazing what a little sleep and a couple of orgasms can do for a girl. I slap his naked ass.

"Come on," I tell him as I roll over Ryland, giving him a quick kiss on the way. He's lying there, all happy and smug, with his arms behind his head.

Miller's still grumbling, but Lathan and Ry watch my naked form as I scramble around for the clothes Miller discarded earlier this morning. I'm not embarrassed, everyone's seen me naked now.

"I'll see you tonight?" I ask Ry, and he nods before sitting up, grabbing my hand, and dragging me toward him.

"Yes, you will. Be careful. I won't be able to talk normally to you tonight," he warns me, and I nod my head.

"Don't worry about me," I tell him as he kisses me again.

"Actually, Max wanted to talk to you as well, so while you wait for grumpy bum there, why don't you see him? He just walked in," Lathan suggests as Ry rolls over to get Miller moving.

"Yeah, okay. Let's go." I head out of the bedroom, but as Lathan walks away, I grab him and pin him up against the wall, then kiss him. "I missed you," I tell him breathlessly when I pull away. I don't want him to feel left out or forgotten.

He looks adorably shocked, and a cute grin crosses his lips as he becomes coherent again.

"I missed you too. You look like you had a good day. I wondered why Ry hadn't returned, but I guess it was too tempting to walk away." There isn't an ounce of jealousy in his tone and I give him a quick hug in thanks as we start back down the stairs.

"Yeah, I feel great. I'm ready for whatever tonight will bring," I tell him as we walk into the kitchen. Max, Dayton, and Anders are there.

"Ah, good. I want to talk about tonight." Max is leaning against the sink, and he narrows his eyes, looking at me closely.

"Someone looks like they did a little more than sleep." Anders chuckles, and I frown.

"What do you mean?"

"You have the biggest hickey on your neck," Dayton says, pointing to a spot on his neck.

"What?" I freak out and hurry to a bathroom close to the stairs. Sure enough, there's a fucking hickey on the right side of my neck. "For fuck's sake!" I vaguely remember Miller sucking on it while we were fucking. No wonder he looked so freaking smug. That's going to be difficult to cover up with the limited amount of makeup I have, and I doubt Matthew will be amused.

"We'll have to stop by the drugstore on the way home. I need something heavy duty for that," I tell them when I return to the kitchen. Lathan is sitting down with Dayton and Anders, and he has his laptop in front of him.

"Sit down," Max says, nodding to a chair grimly. "Tonight, I'm going to have to say and do things that are probably different from what you're used to."

"Yeah, that's okay. I'm prepared," I reassure him, but he grimaces.

"You know I'm dominant, and I like to take control, but it's also about giving my partner what they need. I'm pretty sure this club is more on the extreme end of that. I may have to do things we are both uncomfortable with, so if I hit you or demean you, please know that I don't mean any of it." I can see how sick he feels about this, and I stand up and wrap my arms around his waist, resting my head on his chest.

His entire body shudders under my touch, and I can feel the tension seep out of him as he brings his arms up to hold me. "I promise I'll be fine. I've endured worse from people I fucking hate, so I can deal with anything you'll do to me because I don't hate you, and I know you don't hate me." That's as far as I'm willing to go with him about my feelings. Max's and my relationship is complicated. I've spent less time with him than any of the others because of the situation, but we were the first to fuck. It's kind of backwards and messed up, and I wish we had more time to talk about this and sort through our feelings, but now is not the time.

"Come on, let's go." Miller barrels into the room and picks up his backpack that's lying on the table with mine. He stops when he sees Max and I hugging. "God, you're not being all dramatic, are you? We all know you're dominant and like to boss people around. Mac will be fine. Now come on. Martha will kill us if we're not home for a couple of hours before we go to work."

After giving Max a big squeeze, I pull away and turn to glare at Miller. "What the fuck is this?" I ask him, pointing at the mark on my neck before going around to Dayton and Anders and giving them both hugs. I just kind of feel like we all need it before tonight, and I feel the tension drain out of them when I do. I'm sure it will return, but for now at least, they aren't all so worried.

He smirks, and Ry, who came in behind him, rolls his eyes. "He likes to mark his belongings." He lifts his shirt, and I see a hickey on his chest that I hadn't noticed before when I rolled over it.

"You're such a fucking child," Max grumbles good-naturedly.

"The timing kind of sucks. I'm not sure Matthew will be happy seeing that since he's trying to sell me to Max. We need to stop at the drugstore so I can cover it. Let's go." I grab my bag and wave goodbye, but before I can hurry to the car, Lathan swears violently.

"Fuck!"

"What's wrong?" Max asks, instantly on alert as he pushes off the sink and goes to look over Lathan's shoulder.

"The cells have three more people in them. There are six now." I can practically feel the tension rise in the room again as we all gather around to look at the screen.

Like the other three, I can't make out features from

the cameras, but we can see they are drugged and have catheters as well.

"There's a blank spot on the cameras again when they brought them in," he tells us.

"I very much doubt they brought them through the club this time," I point out, "It must have happened sometime last night. It was packed, and Matthew was there all night."

"No, they must have used one of the other entrances," Dayton says as Lathan's fingers fly across the keyboard. "I doubt it was the library one. It would have been too tricky to get them through the library, down the elevator, and then through the two storage rooms."

"And I doubt it was the ranger's cabin either. They would have had to get them all the way out there first and then over the bed and into the tunnels. That's a lot of work." Anders rubs his chin thoughtfully.

"And the ones in the cinema would be out, unless they used the loading dock. That's a possibility," Ry says. "We should have stuck one of our cameras at each of the entrances."

Lathan looks up and grins smugly. "I did when we went on Monday, but it shows no sign of being used."

"So that leaves where?" Miller asks, and I think about the map and what Ben told me.

"Ted and June Standish are supposed to have an entrance in their house. Have you been there with Stella?" I turn to Max, not sure I really want to hear the answer.

He shakes his head, and I feel a wave of relief. "No, I only ever dropped Stella off, I never went inside despite her begging me to. Thankfully she still lives with her parents, so it would have been awkward as fuck, but she did mention a basement. She was thinking of asking to convert it into an apartment.

I wrinkle my nose at that thought, but I really have no leg to stand on. I still live with my parents too. "So they could have used that one?"

"It would be a safe bet," he confirms, and because their place is surrounded by landscaped gardens, nobody could see anything from the street.

"If I gave you a camera, do you think the next time you went, you could slip it close to the basement entrance?" Lathan asks.

"Yeah, I guess. She's been trying to get me to come inside from the start."

A wave of irrational jealousy washes over me, followed by a desire for deadly violence. I suck in a deep breath and let it out again in the hopes it will help my turbulent thoughts settle. It doesn't work, and now I need to get out of here. I don't even bother with goodbyes, I just turn around and head out of the kitchen. I can't worry about them and their feelings. I need to focus on me tonight.

Thankfully, only Ry and Miller follow me, because I'm not ready to discuss what just happened, and they don't force me to. We don't talk on the drive, the three of us getting into the right head space for tonight's part of the mission. It's a major step and should show us who all the players are. If they are parading the captured teens around, then we know the auction has to be soon, and some of the potential buyers will be in the room.

Lathan will hack the system and make note of everyone who attends, though I remember the girls saying most of them wear masks, so that may be a problem. I'm hoping they take them off if they use one of the rooms, and he can get their faces then.

Ry delivers us to the back door this time, and Martha's frown turns into a smile and a wave when she sees him.

"The power of a family name. Imagine if she knew who you really were," Miller mutters as we say goodbye to Ry and make our way inside. "She would wet her pants."

CHAPTER 30

Miller and I help make dinner and eat quickly before getting ready for the night.

"I wish you weren't staying out all night, but Matthew says it was a wonderful opportunity for you both," Martha fusses as we pull our jackets on over our uniforms and prepare to leave. Anders is picking us up in his truck, and we said we'd wait down at the end of the driveway.

"I'm looking forward to saving more money for college, but if I can get a scholarship, this will help with living expenses," I gush, and Miller grunts his agreement.

"What about you, Miller? Have you gotten any offers yet?" she asks lightly, and he shakes his head.

"No, I was planning on looking for an apprenticeship. Maybe something working with cars. I'd like to own my own business one day."

She claps her hands joyfully. "How wonderful, but

maybe some business night classes would be a good idea as well. You need to know all the ins and outs of keeping a business afloat," she suggests, and he seems to consider the idea.

I keep switching back and forth on my opinion of Martha. Although her background with her former foster parents is suspicious, and her nursing degree made me think she might be involved, she encourages us to make plans for our futures. God, she's really messing with my head.

"Okay, I'm off too." James comes in, his car keys in his hands. "I'll be home late. We have a big game planned," he tells Martha, brushing a kiss across her cheek.

"Poker is the devil's game. You know that, dear." She purses her lips disapprovingly, and he chuckles.

"A man has to have a vice, dear, otherwise other temptations might become appealing," he counters, and I don't think I was supposed to see it, but she rolls her eyes.

Huh. Okay, maybe she isn't as oblivious as I thought. The three of us walk out with a wave, and as we part to go in opposite directions—James to his car, and us to walk down the driveway—he winks. "See you later."

Miller and I don't say anything to him, but as we get out of hearing range, I say, "I don't think he meant that in a general way."

"No, I don't either," he agrees.

It's not long before his car drives by slowly so he

doesn't kick up too much dust in our faces. Anders's truck is waiting down at the end of the road for us, and he smiles grimly as we get in.

"Ready?" he asks, looking between us, and we both nod.

"Let's do this," Miller replies from the passenger seat, but he reaches for my hand. I lean forward and grab his, and he gives it a squeeze.

We've kept up our facade at Serenity House. We didn't want to risk anyone catching us being overly friendly to one another. There would be questions, and there are already enough of those after my supposed orgy with the three guys at the party and then me skipping school today. Cassie tried to pin me down all evening to grill me, but I made it impossible for her. Sally just glared at me the whole time. Jessica laughed and muttered to me under her breath that Sally has a crush on Miller and not to take it too personally. Dinner was fun. Thankfully, none of them brought up the fact that he and I skipped school. There is mad loyalty amongst the kids in that house.

When I spoke to Dad earlier, I forgot to ask him to find them somewhere safe to go, because I really don't think Serenity House will survive the coming conclusion, whatever it is, so I pull out my phone and send him a message, asking him to do something. It doesn't take him long to reply.

Dad: On it!

Anders pulls into the parking lot of the Life Lounge, and before the three of us climb out, he hands us ear comms. These are so little, there is no way anyone will see them unless they get up close and personal with my ear. I slip mine in, and the three of us climb out. The lights on the sign are off, and the doors are shut with a note saying it's closed for a private party. There are a few cars in the lot, but I'm assuming it's the rest of the staff who are working.

When we enter via the side door, I'm surprised to see how many people are in the staff room. Matthew, Keith, Sam, Meri, and Carla are there, but so are Ginger, Cindy, and Shelby, whom I met last night, as well as two other girls whose names I don't know. In addition to them, there are two males and another three females whom I don't recognize. They are all wearing very little, and I can tell by the slightly manic tension in the room that the drugs are already flowing. The lines of coke on the table are an obvious giveaway as well.

"Good, you're here. I thought you might have bailed. That would have been very bad," Matthew says, looking at Miller and me. Anders leaves us and does one of those manly handshakes with Keith while he glances around the room. All of the women are wearing bottoms, exactly like the ones I had on in the cage last night, except they're gold lamé and nothing else. I watch as Meri and Sam paint gold shimmer dust onto everyone's bodies, giggling and laughing. The two males are wearing gold boxers as well.

"Put these on," Matthew demands, throwing us both a pair of underwear. "And then get the girls to paint you up. Oh, and take these. I want you nice and relaxed. You two are going to be our live sex act tonight." He hands us both some pills with that announcement.

"Live sex act?" I stammer, and a sleazy grin stretches across his lips while Miller glares defiantly.

"Yes. Don't be coy, Mac. We all know you aren't afraid of being watched, and don't look like that, boy. She apparently has grade A pussy. Be happy I didn't make Nathaniel over there fuck your ass, or then again, you'd like that, wouldn't you? Maybe we'll do that after the two of you finish. Now hurry up, we need to get moving." Both of us glance over at the boy he pointed at. Nathaniel gives us a finger wave and blows a kiss to Miller, who glares, and I elbow him.

Miller and I shove our bags into a locker and strip, pulling on the underwear. Miller looks fucking phenomenal, and I'm hoping we get to take them home. Hell, maybe I need a pair of sparkly hot pants for all my guys. I can just see them all lined up in front of me, their bodies oiled up and glistening, catering to my every need. I bite my lip at the thought, and Miller chuckles under his breath.

"Keep whatever you are thinking in your mind tonight. Focus on that, and not what's going on around us," he whispers, his eyes bright with lust as he looks at me.

"Not the first time I've fucked in front of people, and I very much doubt it will be the last," I whisper back, winking before turning to find Meri right behind me, makeup brush in hand. Sam's next to her, and they get to work covering our bodies with the gold dust.

"It's edible," she tells me, and I can tell by her eyes that she's already partaken in the drugs. "Have fun with it." She winks, excited for the night. Maybe she doesn't realize the depraved things that go on down there. My eyes rake over her naked body, and she has no scars, so obviously she hasn't been cut or hung up.

My eyes flick across all the other people present, and none of them show signs of that kind of abuse. Hmm, that doesn't bode well for the captives. I really hope they don't use them for that kind of entertainment, because then I won't be leaving tonight without killing a few people.

"Take those, it makes everything easier," Carla slurs as she approaches us, her body shaking ever so slightly. "Then have a line of coke too. Before you know it, your mind will be someplace else," she says dreamily before stumbling away again.

Sam shakes her head. "I don't know why Matthew keeps forcing her to be here. She doesn't like it, and she's usually too traumatized for days afterward to work at the Life Lounge."

Carla's frame is borderline emaciated, and she looks like she would break in half with a partially decent thrust. I guess Matthew must have something over her too.

"She's not wrong though, everything will be better with those," Meri says as Anders brings over a bottle of water.

"Matthew says to take them. He's watching," he says coldly, passing the bottle over. I look up, and sure enough, he is watching from across the room. He gives me an encouraging nod, so I pop the pill into my mouth and take a swallow of water before handing it to Miller so he can do the same.

"Do a line of coke too." Meri finishes dusting me and drags me over to the little coffee table where she shoves me down. Sam does the same with Miller. He and I exchange a look before picking up the straws and snorting the lines waiting for us.

Fuck, it burns. It's been a long time since I've had to snort coke for a mission. My eyes water as the chemicals burn the inside of my nose, and I can taste it in the back of my throat.

I wipe my hand across my nose, hoping there isn't residue, and watch as Miller's jaw clenches and he shakes his head.

"God," he rasps, and when he turns to look at me, I watch, mesmerized, as his pupils dilate, the black irises taking up all the beautiful green until there's only a sliver left around the edges.

"Let's go," Matthew barks, and Keith and Anders approach us, both holding up blindfolds.

"Sorry, boss's orders," Keith tells us, not sounding sorry at all while they tie the blindfolds around our eyes and grab our arms, guiding us. The rest of the group chatters loudly ahead of us as we walk down the corridor that leads to the storage area. I roll my eyes behind the blindfold. Matthew must believe we're idiots if he thinks we don't know where we're going. Though I guess he doesn't know, and the drugs are probably enough to befuddle us. The coke is already kicking into my system, and I feel a buzz of energy run over my skin.

It must take two trips in the elevator, because the sounds of voices die out as they head down to the basement. I'm guessing it's the four of us remaining, but I'm not sure if there is anyone else. Soon enough, we're moving again, and it's apparent we're in an elevator. We step out, and I can hear the voices again, but they are farther ahead of us, like they didn't wait and are already in the tunnels, because it echoes back to us.

"Where are we going?" I finally ask, thinking it's something I probably should have demanded already.

I hear Anders chuckle darkly. "And here I thought you were going to be a good girl and not ask any questions." His hand brushes lightly against my breast as he maneuvers me around something, and I can't help the moan that escapes my lips.

"Damn, the drugs are kicking in. I can't wait to see you fuck her," Keith says. I guess he's talking to Miller. "I saw that metal in your junk when you stripped. I bet you'll destroy her pussy. Can you make it hurt? I do like to hear them cry and beg for mercy."

Anders's hand tightens on my arm as he answers my original question. "The club is in a secret location, and your loyalty needs to be tested first."

"And yours doesn't need to be?" I ask him, and he chuckles again.

"Matthew said I'm as good as dead if I say anything. He also said that he would revoke Max's membership and release video footage of him fucking you in his school office to ruin his dad's reputation, so yeah, I plan on being very loyal. No skanky bitch is going to ruin my friend's life, no matter how big a hard-on he has for her."

"I hear Governor Turner's sons are big pervs. Funny how he was offered a membership to the club back in the day and denied it. I bet his wife was a frigid bitch." Keith chuckles, and this time, I can almost feel the violence surrounding Anders.

"Don't talk about their mom that way. She was a fucking saint—kind, loyal, and loving—exactly what anyone would want in a wife and mother. She died of cancer when the boys were young, and you should have a little bit of fucking respect," Anders snaps at Keith.

"Whoa, sorry, man. I didn't know." Keith doesn't sound very apologetic, and I bet it's taking all of Miller's control not to deck him.

We walk quietly for a little while. We must pass the cells at one stage, but nobody says anything, which is weird. It would be more suspicious for Anders not to ask about them, so I wonder why he didn't. Maybe they are empty.

We finally stop, and a door opens before we are led in, and the blindfolds are removed. Everyone else is there, and the drugs are buzzing through my system. I should feel more concerned than I am, but I feel nice and relaxed and happy. Fucking ecstasy. My tolerance used to be good against most drugs, but it's been a while since I worked on my resistance.

"Alright, get out there and make me some money." Matthew is a cliché bad guy as he rubs his hands together gleefully before turning his attention to me and Miller.

"You two, follow me."

CHAPTER 31

Anders doesn't even look at us as he walks away with Keith. Matthew follows after them, leading us down a long, dimly lit hallway with doors are evenly spaced on either side all the way down. Each door has a light above it, I guess to show if it's occupied or not. Ry and Dayton told us about the layout. These are all sex rooms, as well as a hospital room, which worries me.

When we get to the door at the end of the corridor, it opens into a luxurious, large space that's also dimly lit with wall sconces and table lamps. There are sumptuous couches and seating areas all focused around various sex apparatuses—a St. Andrew's cross, numerous spanking benches, a set of stocks, and a stage with a stripper pole—but it's the large cage Matthew leads us over to. It's double the size of the one I was dancing in last night, and it has a bench seat in it as well as arm and leg restraints.

"Get in." He opens the door and gestures for me and Miller to hop in. We do as he says, and he closes the door and then goes over to the wall. The cage lifts into the air, until it's hanging about four feet off the ground. We are literally a centerpiece in the middle of the room. He flips another switch, and a couple of spotlights light up the cage.

"You two better perform, or I will make your life very unpleasant. I have some business to deal with before I will let anyone touch you. I'm hoping you both are going to make me some very good money tonight."

Before he can say anything else, a woman walks toward us, and my eyes meet hers through the bars. It's all I can do to hide my shiver when I see the dark look in her gaze. I know before she even opens her mouth that this woman is evil.

"Matthew, I hear that blood play will not be allowed this evening. Explain," she demands waspishly, and I see Matthew roll his eyes before turning to face her.

"Lucinda, darling!" he cries joyfully and gives her air kisses. She just wrinkles her nose but accepts them. "I have the governor's sons on the hook. I just need to reel them both in. I'm worried your little blood sports might be pushing them too far, and until I have them firmly ensconced within the society, I'd rather not risk them balking at your idea of fun."

She huffs and turns her attention to the two of us in the cage. Her eyes widen, and a look of interest crosses her face. "It looks like you have some new entertainment. They are delightful. Give them to me for the night to make up for my disappointment." She loses the haughty attitude and pouts at Matthew like a spoiled child.

He tuts. "I'm sorry, but these two are my bait for my whales. You'll have to find someone else to play with. Brock will be here, why don't you find him? He does enjoy your attention."

She fake gags. "Ugh, that slug. Fine, I guess I can take my frustration out on him, but then I want a turn with these two once your whales are finished. I'm assuming they won't have exclusive rights all night."

Matthew shrugs. "I can't tell you that. I haven't discussed the arrangements with them yet." He looks up as the doors open from the foyer and people start to pour in. I'd been paying so much attention to the conversation in front of me that I wasn't watching the rest of the room. The rest of the staff is scattered artfully around the space. Nathaniel, the guy who winked at Miller, is strapped into the stocks and is being railed by the tiny pixie girl, Shelby, who's wearing a strap-on. In front of him is the other guy whose name I don't know, and he's ramming his cock down Nathaniel's throat. Lust beats at my body, and I can't stop the moan that slips from my lips at the sight. God, I wish that was Miller, Ry, and me.

"Get to it." Matthew points at us before walking away, greeting masked people as they make their way farther into the room. Lucinda rolls her eyes and walks over to watch Cindy twirling around the stripper pole. She leans in and asks her something, and I watch her blanch slightly before she nods. They walk off toward the back room together. I feel a pang of anxiety, but there's nothing I can do for now.

My eyes drift back to the stocks as I feel Miller's hands slide up to grab my hips, hauling my body back against his chest. I let my head fall onto his shoulder as he leans in and kisses my neck. He caresses my breasts gently as he rubs his hard cock against my ass. "Do you wish that was us?" he asks quietly enough that the masked couple who stopped to look at us can't hear.

"You know if you decide to stay with us, I'm sure we can arrange some special fun. Max has a sex dungeon in our house, or he will if we ever get time to furnish it. We have a huge basement. Your parents think we're going to turn it into a game room, and we will for half of it, but the other half is now behind a secret wall. We had a separate arrangement with the contractor who built it, and that's going to be our playroom. I'm sure Max would be happy to get some stocks for it."

My pussy drips, his words and the ecstasy making my panties grow damp when I think about having fun with them. I am so down for that. The man in front of us pushes his hand through the bars to stroke my body. Miller growls and whirls me around so I'm out of reach. The man frowns, but the woman laughs out loud. I don't recognize either of them, and I lose track of them as Miller pushes me back until he sits me on the seat in the middle of the cage. He stretches out one arm, attaching one of the restraints before doing the same to my other, then he steps back and looks at me, my arms spread wide for his enjoyment.

"Fuck, you look pretty," he mutters, adjusting his hard length, which is pushing against his sparkly shorts. He bends down and slides my panties off, leaving me completely naked. I should feel self-conscious because more and more people are gathering around the cage to watch, but the coke and ecstasy are riding my system hard, and I have no fucks left to give. I clench my thighs together, trying to relieve some of the ache in my core.

"Nope, I want to see your pussy dripping with need," Miller mutters. I don't think he wants the crowd to hear us. Even though we're performing in front of them, what he's saying is just for us. I could kiss him for it. He pushes on my thighs, forcing my legs open before reaching for a cuff and wrapping it around my ankle, then he does the same to my other one. He steps back and looks at me. I'm sitting spread-eagle for everyone to see. Although I feel eyes all around us, my focus is completely on the man in front of me. He gets down on his knees like a slave before a queen, and runs his tongue up my folds, stopping at my clit and sucking it into his mouth.

I shudder with the sensation and throw my head back. "God," I cry out, my inhibitions at an all-time low thanks to the drugs in my system. I totally get why

Meri and Sam recommended we take some. I'm not sure I could have done this without them. I thought I was just going to be sold to Max, not put on display for everyone.

Miller makes a meal of my pussy, and I squirm and cry and plead for him to give me what I need. He uses his tongue and fingers to drive my pleasure higher and higher, but just when I think I'm going to come, he pulls away. I don't know how long he tortures me, it feels like it goes on indefinitely, but when tears flow down my face, and I'm hoarse from begging and pleading, he pulls away and stands up, kicking off his own shorts and approaching me. He kisses me, and I can taste myself on his mouth, but I don't care. I just wish I could get my hands on him.

"Holy fuck, look at the hardware in that. That has to hurt!" I hear a male voice shout, but I already know what it feels like, and I can't fucking wait.

"Shut up, David. I want to see that." I recognize the second voice. Fucking Brock Marshall. I guess Lucinda hasn't gotten her talons in him yet.

Miller pulls away, stroking his cock with one hand, and I hear another voice say, "Boys didn't look like that when I was younger." It's female, and I don't recognize it, but I hear others giggle with agreement.

Miller lines up and smoothly pushes into me. Thank God for all his prep work, because he isn't small or patient. I groan wantonly as he fills me.

I'm about to beg for more when a loud, pompous voice calls out, "What the fuck? We paid for these two exclusively tonight. That means they are our entertainment, nobody else's."

My eyes snap open and find Max's crystal blue gaze blazing with fury. Beside him is Ry, whose matching blue eyes are fixed on where Miller's cock is deep in my pussy. Both wear tailored suits and look mouth-wateringly delicious.

"Of course. I'll get them out of there for you now." Matthew is behind them, smirking with unfettered glee. He comes over to the cage and lowers it to the ground. Miller grabs for one of the bars so he doesn't fall over with the movement. As soon as the cage hits the ground, Max yanks the door open and steps in.

"Unstrap her," he commands Miller, who hurries to do as he commands, rubbing my arms and legs to help with the blood flow.

"You are my brother's plaything tonight," Max approaches us and pushes Miller away. "Go with him. I'll take care of her." I can hear the underlying care, but anyone else would hear a threat. Miller plays his part and hesitates, and Max backhands him. My mouth drops open in shock, and I slap a hand over my mouth, but it's not quick enough to smother my surprised gasp. Max's hand shoots out and wraps around my throat, cutting off my air.

Fuck, I know he said he'd have to do things that he wouldn't normally do, but I wasn't expecting this. I don't think he pulled his punch either.

Miller grabs his cheek and glares at Max.

"Fuck, big brother. You know I don't like my meat

tenderized. Keep your hands to yourself," Ry jokes, playing the spoiled playboy, but there's no denying the steel behind his words.

I hear whispers in the crowd surrounding the cage.

"Are those the Turner boys?"

"Wow, I never would have pegged them as deviants."

"Looks like the older boy has a temper."

"I would gladly let him boss me around if he would put his hands around my throat."

"Wonder what their dad's constituents would say if they could see them now."

"Come on, I want to lick your cock and find out what my brother's plaything tastes like." Ry smirks at Max as he drags Miller out of the cage and in the direction of the playrooms.

"On your knees." The icy voice has my gaze returning to the man who still has his hands wrapped around my throat. He eases his grip slightly, slipping his hand down to my shoulder and pushing.

I don't fight him. The drugs are still rolling through my system, and I am a sweaty, needy mess. I will obey anything he says if it gets me what I want. He runs a hand over my sweat dampened hair, pushing it back off my face.

"Well, I must say, having you at my feet with tears staining your face is so much more satisfying than I expected," he growls loudly for everyone to hear, playing the consummate showman. I have no doubt the dominant stuff is real. My eyes are at crotch level, and I can see his dick is hard behind his suit pants.

"Eyes on me," he snaps, and I look up at him. He reaches into his pocket and pulls something out, stepping behind me. I feel him wrap something around my neck before he fastens a buckle in the back. When he steps in front of me again, he's holding something in his hand. He gives it a little tug, and I feel it on my neck. Holy crap, he put a collar on me. My rational mind tells me I should be horrified, but my slutty, drug-induced happy mind is preening with joy. My pussy gushes, and if I wasn't spacey, I'd be mortified that I can feel my desire leaking down the inside of my thigh. If he waits too long, it's going to drip onto the floor of the cage.

"Come." He reaches for my elbow and hauls me to my feet before moving out of the cage, taking me with him. He strides, leash in hand, across the room, with me trailing obediently behind him until he gets to a free section of the bar that has a reserved sign on it. Anders comes over and removes the sign, and Max pats the bar top. "Up," he commands, and I just blink at him stupidly.

"Huh?"

He tuts. "Oh, and I did have high hopes for you. I'll try again. Hop up on the bar," he says slowly, and I look at it, not quite sure how to get up there. He sighs and puts his hands on my waist, boosting me up there and manhandling me until he has me stretched out along the length. My drug-addled brain is slow to catch up, and when it does, Anders has placed a shot of tequila between my breasts, then he taps my chin so I will take a piece of lime in my mouth. I'm just wondering where the salt is going to go when he holds the shaker over my damp, swollen clit and sprinkles it. I brace myself for the pain, but it doesn't actually hurt. I guess it's not a raw, open wound.

Max and Anders are chatting benignly. "Ry couldn't wait to get his hands on that foster kid. He said they've been dancing around since he enrolled at school. He wants to own his ass tonight."

"Hopefully he won't be so fucking grumpy anymore." They are completely ignoring me. People come and go at the bar, and I feel the urge to squirm. I feel like I have fire ants under my skin, but I instinctively know if I knock over his shot, I will be punished. I have my eyes locked on a spot on the ceiling above me, because even moving my head will cause the shot between my breasts to wobble.

I feel a hand brush over my forehead, pushing my hair back off my face. "Such a good girl," he croons. "Get me a bourbon, will you, Anders? Neat."

"Ah, Max, I just wanted to give my condolences on the loss of your friend. Such a tragic thing, drowning. I hope his family finds peace now that they know what happened to him." I recognize Father Sweeny's voice, but of course I can't move.

"Thank you. It was a tragedy, and we're still in shock. Tonight will help take our minds off it," Max replies.

"Well, I'm not surprised. That looks like a delightful way to drink tequila. Maybe once you're done with her, we can all have a turn."

Fucking hell, the men of this town are nasty. I'm almost certain they are all going to come to a sticky end, and not the fun kind—the kind that's red and gray and splattered over something.

I hear Max rumble his answer. "I very much doubt I'll be done with her for a while. If tonight goes well, I plan to negotiate exclusive rights to this one and the one my brother likes."

"Oh, I thought you two were hot and heavy with the Standish girls," Father Sweeny remarks, and Max scoffs.

"Stella and Sophie will be perfect politicians' wives, but I doubt their tastes are the same as mine and Ry's."

"No, you're probably right. It's why this place is so popular. Thank goodness none of our wives know about it."

I smother the snort of laughter that wants to escape and concentrate on staying very still. The lime between my lips is making my mouth pucker with the sourness, and it's slightly numb. Men are fucking clueless. I would bet every last dollar of both my grandparents' fortunes that they know all about this place and are relieved their husbands' needs are being addressed by someone else.

Anders passes Max his bourbon, and he throws it back. "Yes, and that's how I plan to keep it. I may be looking into buying some property soon. Of course, I won't be able to keep either of them in my father's home, but somewhere close by would be convenient. Let me know if anyone in the congregation has a small apartment on the market."

"Of course. Us men need to stick together," Father Sweeny replies, and I feel Max stand up from his bar stool.

"Now, if you'll excuse me, I think I've wasted enough time. I want to play with my purchase."

CHAPTER 32

MAX

With that comment, I lean over and lick a path over her clit, claiming the salt. I smirk as she jolts with surprise, and the tequila flows down her body like a waterfall. I use my tongue to drink it all up, trying to catch every single drop of the spicy liquid, then I lean forward and snatch the lime with my mouth, sucking it before spitting it to the side and taking Mac's mouth with mine. I plunder its depths in a punishing kiss, and she returns the kiss with the same kind of fervor, her tight body squirming on the countertop. Our kiss is tangy, salty, and tart from the things I just consumed, and I can't help my smile as she moans and mewls into my mouth, lifting her hands to reach for me. I pull away and slap one of them. She yelps and snatches them away, pouting adorably.

"Ah, Max, looks like you're having a good time. Would you like a line of coke? On the house, of course," Matthew says behind us, and a wave of irritation washes over me. This man is fucking annoying. Why can't he fuck off and bug other people? I turn around and chuckle like a good old boy.

"Why not? It's been a while since I've let loose. Would you mind if my man here had one too?" I accept the coke and ask for Anders to join me, keeping up my spoiled playboy persona. Ry will have to be the only one of us who is sober. "Line them up on here." I point to the smooth expanse of Mac's skin, just above her clit.

I gesture to my friend, who reaches over and wipes down her body with a paper towel, making it dry enough so the coke doesn't stick to her. I watch impatiently as Matthew's drug girl arranges two lines across her pubic mound. When she's done, she hands Anders and I each a small straw with a smile. Without messing around, we lean in and snort the white powder.

The chemical burn makes my eyes water, and I can see Anders is struggling with the same thing. I shake my head to clear it.

"Thanks, Matthew, your hospitality is very generous. Line up another on the bar for my pet, will you?" I ask and hold out a hand for her. She struggles to sit up, so I help her by placing my hand on her elbow and supporting her. She slides to the ground, and I can see she's slightly disoriented, so I keep my hand on her until she gets her bearings. She blinks a couple of times before looking up at me. Fuck, I could come in my pants from that look alone. This woman is making me come undone.

I turn my attention from her to the club owner, and he's frowning at me. I raise a questioning eyebrow.

"Are you sure that's a good idea? She already had a line, and she's rolling on Molly."

"She is?" I look back at Mac, and when I peer closer at her eyes, I see that her pupils are just about swallowing her pretty irises.

"Yeah, I'm surprised she managed to stay still for so long, to be honest," Anders chimes in, looking at Mac closely, and she smiles.

"I'm a good girl," she slurs slightly.

Fuck my life! "Yes, you most definitely are." I run a hand over her head again, stroking her hair gently, and she preens.

"Maybe a little baggy to take to our room. Ry might like some," I say to Matthew, who smiles indulgently.

"Of course, I'll have one brought to your room."

"Hey, boss." A man wearing a security earpiece approaches. He leans in to whisper, but he gets an A for effort, because we hear everything he says. "There's a glitch on cameras one, five, and eleven. They aren't working tonight. Should I call someone in?"

"God, you're a fucking idiot, Jonesy. What do you think a service tech would say if they saw all this?

There's no one in eleven tonight, and five is Max's. I'm sure he won't hurt either of his charges." Matthew smiles at me. "The cameras are for our staff's safety, of course," he explains.

"Oh, of course I won't hurt them," I agree quickly, knowing Lathan has worked his magic. He was keeping an eye out for which room we entered and was going to mess with some of the cameras so we didn't have to perform the whole time we were in there.

"And Lucinda was seen heading into one." The guard grimaces, and I see panic flash in Matthew's eyes.

"With whom?"

"Cindy," the guard replies, and Matthew stiffens like a board.

"Fuck, I'm going to have to go deal with this. If you'll excuse me, have fun, and I hope to talk to you later." The two of them hurry away, and I can see Mac frown slightly as she watches them. I wonder what has her concerned. I guess I'll ask her later when we're not being watched.

"We'll see you later." I wave to Anders and take Mac's arm, leading her away. Father Sweeny is still at the bar, eyeing Mac like she's a piece of meat he can't wait to get his teeth into, and it's making me twitchy and aggravated. Brock Marshall is standing next to him.

"Come, pet." I tug on Mac's leash, and she takes my cues perfectly, following slightly behind me like a good and obedient girl. I reach down and adjust myself, my dick aching behind the zipper of my suit pants.

I parade Mac through the club, allowing everyone to see my possession, but also giving us both time to determine if any of the prisoners from the cells are here. As I look around, making note of familiar and unfamiliar mask-covered faces, I don't actually see anyone who doesn't want to be here. Even all the staff members seem happy being touched, fondled, and more. The members are making very good use of the facilities, and the ones who aren't engaged in sex acts are either standing around and watching, or drinking and chatting. I see James and Ted Standish in one corner with a couple of girls I'm sure I saw in the Life Lounge wearing the same uniform as Mac. Both girls are making out with one another, while Ted's face is buried in one's pussy and James finger bangs the other. Mac sees them and shudders ever so slightly, but she doesn't pause in following me.

I give up and head in the direction of the back rooms. When we get to number five, I enter without knocking, tugging Mac in behind me. As soon as the door is closed, I drop the leash, whirl around, and pull her into my arms.

"God, are you okay?" I ask her and feel her nod against my chest. Her body is warm and soft under my hands as I rub circles against her back. I love how pliant she feels in my arms. I'm pretty sure the drugs are riding her hard now. I was surprised when Matthew said she was on Molly.

Sounds of pleasure have me raising my head and looking at the couple on the bed. Ry is railing Miller. "What the hell, man?" I ask him.

Ry looks up and grimaces at me.

"Fuck, it wasn't planned, but he's high on Molly, and you know what that's like." My brother doesn't miss a beat, and I avert my eyes. I love him, but I have no interest in watching him fuck his boyfriend.

Mac whimpers, and her own body starts to squirm as she listens to Miller plead and beg for Ry to fuck him harder. I turn her around to face them, and she moans as she catches sight of what they are doing. I grin against her hair and decide I can make use of this unfortunate timing. I lean in and place kisses along her neck as I slip my hand down to play with her clit. I slide my finger through her folds, her pussy is soaked, and I use the lubrication to rub circles on her clit, driving her to a quick and furious orgasm. Her knees buckle, and she cries out. I wrap my arms around her before she falls to the ground.

"Please, Max, I need you. It hurts," she begs, running her hands all over her own body, pinching her nipples and rubbing her clit again.

Looking around the room, I spy an interesting couch. It has a huge back, perfect for lying a body across. I tug her over to it, positioning it so she can still watch Ry and Miller, before pushing her over the top. She goes willingly, putting her in a perfect position, her head down and her ass up in the air for me. I kick her legs apart as she begs for me to stop the pain.

I crouch down and lean in, running my tongue through her folds. I swore if I was going to do anything tonight, I would finally get to taste her. My eyes roll back as the coke kicks in, and I feel fucking invincible. Mac tastes like every fantasy come true. I bury my face in her pussy to try and lick up every precious drop. The first orgasm is quick and dirty, and I'm feeling pretty fucking good with myself when I remember something Matthew said to me. I stand up and go over to the cupboard, pulling it open. There are closed packages of brand-new sex toys for the members' pleasure. I pick up a small butt plug and a bottle of lube and return to the fainting couch. I crack open the package and pull the rubber toy out, coating it generously with lube. Returning to her, I rub some extra lube around her asshole, using my finger to push some into her. She tenses for a moment but slowly relaxes, and her words become jumbled as she begs for more. I feel a smile stretch across my lips. I love how responsive she is. I just wish she was in her right mind and coherent.

Once the plug is in, I finger fuck her into another quick orgasm before pulling away and stripping my clothes off. Her eyes are still glued to the two on the bed, but I want her attention on me, so I move in front of her and feed her my cock. She instantly responds, taking it deep into her mouth, gagging a little at how forceful I am. I stroke her hair and tell her she's a good girl, and she relaxes her throat, taking me deeper.

She's the perfect little submissive, and I look forward to having more time to explore this side of her. I slowly fuck her mouth for a few moments, and she lavishes my cock with attention, but I watch as her hands creep back to her pussy. The orgasm only gave her momentary relief with the Molly rolling through her system.

"Hands off, that's my pussy to play with." I lean over and slap her ass, and she yelps around my cock but practically purrs when I rub the sting away. I see her relax even further. Good to know. I pull out and return to the other side. Reaching down, I roll her over so she's facing me before kissing her. She responds eagerly, her tongue meeting mine stroke for stroke, and when I pull out and bite it, she moans wantonly.

I stand up and rub my cock through her folds. Her eyes roll, and she lets her head drop back. All the blood is going to run to her head in this position. I wrap my hand around her throat as I slowly slide my cock into her pussy, tightening my grip. Her eyes widen before they roll and drift closed, her groan louder than the noises Miller is making as I work myself into her. It takes a bit of work with the plug in her ass.

"Please fuck me, fuck me hard," she begs, and I don't wait any longer, I plunge into her hard, wrapping my other hand around her throat as well as I pound into her. It only takes a couple of strokes, and her pussy clamps down hard, her body convulsing as she flies into her first orgasm. It takes all my willpower and looking at Ry and Miller to stop my own orgasm from exploding through my body. I ride her through the first one before driving her into another, dropping my hands from her throat to pluck her nipples and clit. I'm not gentle, but it makes no difference to Mac. She's flying high, and she begs for more.

Her second orgasm washes over her, and she floods where we're joined with her desire. Still, she begs and pleads for more, so I pull out and flip her over again. Her body is pliant and loose, and she's mostly mindless at this stage. I press against the plug in her butt before gently removing it and replacing it with my cock. I push in a little, and she shouts out loud. I pause, worried I've gone too far, but when I focus on her words, she's pleading and begging me to fuck her ass. That's enough permission for me, and I slowly push forward. I'm not small, and it's tight. I don't want to hurt her, but eventually, I'm balls deep. Just like her pussy, her ass grips my cock like a glove, and I feel my toes curl with my impending orgasm. I clench my cheeks and breathe, but she continues to squirm. I slap her ass cheeks, and she squeals and flinches, her ass tightening around me even harder. A moan rips free as I rub a hand over her plump cheek, my red palm print a blazing slash across her pale skin.

"Max, please," she sobs, and I finally give in.

Holding her hips hard enough to leave fingerprints, I destroy her body in the most delicious way. It only takes a couple of strokes, and she screams loudly. If anyone is listening, there is no doubt about what's going on in here. Her orgasm batters her body, and she becomes limp. I manhandle her, pulling her up against my chest. She is sweaty, and her skin slips against mine, but it gives me a tighter angle, and I fuck her for a couple more strokes before I empty my load into her, praising her and whispering words of encouragement the whole time.

If I didn't know before, I certainly know now that this girl is mine and my team's, and she is fucking perfect for all of us.

CHAPTER 33

The club night is a complete disappointment. We spend most of the night lounging in their hired room, fucking over and over again until Miller and I come down from our highs. I'm exhausted, and Max and Ry do a good job with our aftercare, bringing us water and snacks provided for the members. They completely monopolize us, much to the disgust of the rest of the patrons and Matthew's glee. He made bank off Miller and I, and ensured Max and Ry were well and truly on the hook. Anders drives us both home afterward, where we proceed to spend the day in bed. Martha looked at us with worried eyes and fussed slightly when we got up the following evening, but we had to go to work again, so we didn't have to listen to her berate us over and over again.

The rest of the weekend flies by. Matthew doesn't come into the club on Saturday night, and its business as usual. Miller loses his shit at one of Keith's suggestive remarks, though, and Anders has to separate them. Keith keeps his mouth shut after that. Carla doesn't come in all weekend, but Meri and Sam are present physically, even if their minds are altered chemically.

We're in the middle of French class on Monday, with Stella being her normal, bitchy self, when someone's phone alarm blares through the room.

"Whoever that is, turn it off now," she calls, glaring at all of us. Lathan winces and pulls his phone out of his pocket. He looks at the screen and blanches before he stands up.

"I have to go, it's an emergency." He picks up his bag and bolts out of the classroom. Ry stands up and shakes his head. "Sorry, Ms. Standish, but he must have forgotten I'm his ride." With that, he leaves too. Miller and I exchange a glance, but there is no reason for either of us to leave, so we stay put.

"Why, I never!" Stella huffs, staring at the closed door.

"It might have to do with their dead friend," Lucy says helpfully, which seems to appease Stella slightly.

The two of us have to endure the rest of the class, but the minute the bell rings, we're both out of there. Miller pulls his phone out and checks his messages, but before I can leave the room, Stella calls my name.

"Ms. Walsh, a moment please." Fuck, I don't have time for her games, but I also can't kill her in broad daylight—shame—so I tell Miller to go on without me, I'll catch up.

"Do you want me to wait?" Jessica is by the door, and she's looking between me and Stella with worry in her eyes.

"Ms. Walsh is a big girl. She doesn't need you to hold her hand." Stella dismisses Jessica with a wave of her hand. She looks at me, and I give her a small nod. Fuck, I eat bad guys for breakfast, and Stella is less than nothing.

Jessica closes the door behind her, and it's just me and Stella. She doesn't say anything, just looks down her nose at me. "What do you want, Ms. Standish? I'm going to be late for history."

"Don't think I don't know where you were on Friday night," she hisses, her eyes blazing with anger.

Huh, I was not expecting that. I knew the men were being idiots, thinking their significant others didn't know about the sex club.

"Oh? You mean that I was working a private party for Matthew?" I say, acting confused. I'm not admitting to anything.

"That you were whoring yourself out to any man who had enough money to pay for you," she sneers at me, and I smile, not rising to the bait.

"No, you're wrong." I shake my head, and her face flushes red with anger.

"You weren't whoring yourself out? What would you call it?"

"Oh no, I was most definitely whoring myself out, but it wasn't to *any* man who could pay for me. One man paid for the pleasure of having me all to himself for the night, and if you weren't such a frigid bitch" —I nod to the purity ring on her finger— "then maybe he wouldn't need to hire whores."

With that mic drop, I leave the room. I hear her scream as I walk down the corridor and smile. She only wants to stir up trouble, and I desperately want to know what was on Lathan's phone that made him bolt out of the room, so I don't have time for her drama.

When I catch up to Miller, he's standing out front of Max's history classroom, the two of them deep in conversation. I join them.

"What did Stella want?" Max asks, and I grimace.

"Just to tell me she knows what I did on Friday night. Don't worry about it, I handled it," I tell him. He can deal with it later if she decides to bring it up with him.

My little gift to him, which I will have a giggle about later.

"What was wrong with Lathan?" I ask, and Miller shows me his messages.

Lathan: Auction has gone online. Countdown clock puts it for Friday evening. There are now ten captives in the cells, and each of them are on the website with a couple of remaining spaces saying, "Coming soon."

"Well, okay, we can finally wrap this up. Is it an in-person auction?" I ask, and Miller shakes his head.

"No, all bids are done anonymously. We will have to let it happen and then intercept the delivery. It should be easy enough. We'll just watch all the entrances. Your dad will send a few more agents to help if we need it."

"Yeah, okay, good. I just have to get through Wednesday night, and I'll be back first thing Thursday. Can you guys coordinate with Dad? We will want some agents stationed at the shipping yard as well in case they get past us."

"Yeah, that won't be a problem. I think it won't hurt to have them here sooner rather than later. There aren't enough of us to put a tail on each of the key players, and that's what we need now," Max says, and I agree with his assessment. He's right. For now, the seven of us have to keep our covers, so having a few extra agents in town is smart. The last thing we want to do is allow any of them to slip through our fingers.

"After Friday night, I'm beginning to suspect the sex club and the auctions are two separate entities. Were there any records in the sex club of previous auctions and where the trafficked teenagers may be?"

"No, but we didn't get a lot of time to look over them," Max answers.

"But Lathan said all of the USBs were named. Would they have known the names of the trafficked teens or even cared about them? I doubt they would have taken the time to learn them," I point out, but Miller shakes his head.

"We do know a few of them, the kids who used to live at Serenity house. If we can get back into the club, then we can at least search for their names amongst the USBs. That will give us a definite yay or nay to there being any record of them."

"One of us will go tonight," Max agrees. "If there aren't any, then we are going to have to search the houses of the people involved and hope we can find something between now and the night of the auction. All of this will be a waste if we don't find out where all the other victims have gone."

"Agreed. Miller and I will search Serenity House. I'm sure we'll get a chance to over the next couple of days." I smirk and arch an eyebrow. "I'm pretty sure you aren't going to have problems getting into Ted and June's house now. I bet by this afternoon, Stella will relinquish her purity ring and will be ready to bang your brains out. You're welcome," I tell him, patting him on the arm. He frowns with confusion, and I turn and walk into the classroom, leaving him wondering exactly what I meant.

We're all on edge the following day, and it doesn't get any better. They discover that there are no records of any sold teenagers in the club, it's all blackmail material on the members, so they plan on doing a little breaking and entering while I'm gone.

On Wednesday morning, I get up early. I pack my

bag with a change of clothes and meet Martha down-stairs. She drives me to the small, private airport just outside of Summerville. It's basically deserted when I arrive, but there is a small private jet, with MITHOS College written on the side, waiting.

I climb out, and Martha rolls down the window. "Have fun, and be safe. I'm certain this is just a small step on the path to the rest of your life," she tells me and waves goodbye before driving away. I look around. There's a small hangar about a hundred meters from where the plane is parked, but there is no one around. It's actually slightly creepy, and I feel like I'm being watched, so I quickly hurry up the stairs of the plane.

"Ms. Watson, nice of you to join us today." My dad's personal pilot is waiting with a grin on his face.

"Hey Brenton, good to see you." I give him a hug, and he steps back and looks at me. Brenton is older, probably in his forties, and he's been Dad's pilot for at least ten years. I've flown with him often.

"That's certainly a different look than what I'm used to." He chuckles as he takes in my new outfit, which Martha supervised me while buying on Sunday after church. I was kind of hoping she had forgotten, but she hadn't. I'm wearing a pastel green pencil skirt, with a matching top and a white cardigan over it. I have white heels on as well, and my black hair is tied back in a bun at the nape of my neck.

"Yeah, isn't it adorable?" I say sarcastically as I step around him, allowing him to pull the cabin door closed.

"Holy fuck, who went and made you a Stepford wife?" The voice behind me has me smiling and striking a pose.

"You like?" I ask my cousin Katie. She's reclined in one of the chairs, wide-eyed with shock.

She lifts her phone and snaps a shot before her fingers fly across the screen. "I'm sending that to Keely and JB. They'll think it's hilarious. Oh, and our parents and granddad and King Yusaf... They won't believe their eyes."

"Yeah, yeah, laugh it up." I throw myself into a chair and strap in, placing my backpack off to the side. I feel the plane start to taxi back to the runway. "I wasn't expecting you to be here," I tell her as the plane speeds up before lifting into the air. My stomach lurches, and my ears pop, but I swallow a couple of times, and it doesn't take long for it to equalize.

"Yeah, I know, but I didn't trust anyone else to bring you an outfit and all the necessities." She smiles, pointing at a pile of things sitting on one of the other sumptuous chairs.

"Awesome. Once the plane reaches cruising altitude, I'll get changed."

"There's an outfit in there for lunch. We're meeting with the crew before going to the opening tonight." I groan, wrinkling my nose, and she grimaces. "I know, but you know how it helps sell our covers. We also have a room at the Plaza for the night so we can get changed for the gala there."

"Fine," I agree, and we're quiet for a little while

before I take a deep breath and blurt out, "While I have you here, there's something I want to talk to you about."

She was looking out the window, but she turns to face me. "Oh?" She sounds wary.

"I'm thinking of giving up my ghost status and joining Team Basilisk." I let the words rush out before I can stop and think. If I do, I might not say them.

She heaves out a sigh. "Damn it, Kensington, I owe Dad a thousand pounds now. I thought you'd at least hold out until six weeks after the mission was over." She pulls out her phone and tries to send another message, but I snatch it out of her hands.

"What do you mean?" I demand, and she looks at me with knowing eyes.

"Babe, we knew this was a limited career option, and I knew after that awful one you finished prior to this that you were almost ready to throw in the towel. Why do you think you were suddenly assigned a team assessment you had never had to do before?" she asks. "We all knew it was just a matter of you coming to the realization yourself. I'm almost certain your mother has been praying daily for your birth control to fail and for you to become pregnant since you joined your new team, so you'd give up spying altogether."

I shudder at the suggestion and shake my head violently. "I'm afraid she's going to be waiting a very long time. I am not cut out to be a parent."

"Amen, sister." She holds her hand up for a high five. Our mothers are really going to be so disappointed in the girls they produced. We giggle, but her eyes turn serious.

"Are you happy?" she asks, and I don't even have to think about it.

"Yes. It's new, and who knows if any of it will work out once the mission is over, but it has made me realize that I'm ready for something for me. I'm ready to attempt to have feelings and to put my heart on the line, and if it gets kicked to the curb, I know I'm strong enough to pick it back up and try again."

She reaches forward and gives my hand a squeeze. "I'm happy for you. Now, before we play dress-up, there is something else I need to talk to you about." She's serious again, and I brace myself for what she's about to tell me.

CHAPTER 34

The two hour flight passes in no time, and after a heavy conversation with my cousin, I'm ready to have a few drinks and blow off some steam. Princess Kensington Watson is ready to party.

I stare at myself in the mirror, happy with the way my wig looks. You can't even tell it's not my real hair, and unless I get into a hair pulling, nail scratching fight, then everything should be fine. Hell, it might be fine even if we do, because the glue Katie used to stick it on was powerful shit. Luckily we have some remover for tomorrow afternoon when I return to Georgia.

I have on a pair of designer jeans that haven't even hit the shop floor yet thanks to our connections with the designer. She loves having us wear her clothes. It's good publicity, so she sends us free things. The long-sleeved top is designer too. New York is a little cooler than Georgia, and it's later in the year. The leaves are turning, and the days are getting shorter. I have a cashmere designer coat over all of it and a pair of funky black ankle boots with cute buckles to set it all off.

"Darling, you look amazing," Katie says in the posh accent she uses in her Lady Katherine Watson persona. Like me, she also changed, but instead of jeans, she's wearing a pair of designer leggings tucked into a fabulous pair of knee-high boots, with a long-sleeved, off the shoulder designer top in green and a long, knee-length, camel-colored knitted cardigan.

We carry our things off the plane, waving to Ben and climbing into the waiting limo. We drive from the private air strip on MITHOS grounds and into Manhattan, stopping at the Plaza to drop off our things. We then catch a taxi to a trendy little cafe in Soho to catch up with our "friends."

Air kisses and fake compliments are exchanged, the only one I genuinely feel happy to see is my cousin Kamel. He and I have a love-hate relationship—mostly love unless he did something to piss off my grandfather and he's in trouble, which happens quite often. Usually it involves women and him being indiscreet, then he gets annoyed and calls me the golden child.

"*Kan jidiy yas'al eanka. mataa satati lilziyarati?*" he says to me in Arabic. *Grandfather was asking about you. When are you coming to visit?*

"*Qrybaan,*" I reply. *Soon.*

He nods approvingly. "*Jid, sawf yuzil baed aldaght eani.*" He grimaces, and I roll my eyes. *Good, it will take some pressure off me.*

I guess he did something again that is going to get him yelled at, and guessing by the very young blond-haired, blue-eyed beauty attached to his arm like a leech, I'm assuming she has something to do with it.

Lunch goes for hours, and it's almost five when we arrive back at the hotel. I'm freaking exhausted, but we can't stop now. We eat a quick meal delivered to us by room service before getting ready. The dress Katie provided for me is a long, emerald, sleeveless sheath that hugs my body from neck to ankle. It shimmers and sparkles in the light as I slip on a pair of four-inch silver heels and some matching platinum diamond and emerald earrings. The neckline doesn't allow for a necklace, so I slip a diamond and emerald tennis bracelet onto my wrist and a matching ring on my middle finger.

I had my full range of makeup to work with, and I look nothing like the emo goth teen from Summerville, Georgia. You could hold a photo of each covers side by side and still not tell it's the same person. I removed my long-term contacts, so my eyes are their normal deep blue color, and my wig is my natural shade of golden blonde.

"Are you ready?" Katie asks, holding a black clutch in her hand. Her siren red dress is short and sexy, and she paired it with black, sky-high heels.

"Yup, let's do this. I'm looking forward to seeing Mom and Dad." It's a short ride to the Met from the Plaza in the limo. We could have walked it if we weren't wearing heels. Lights flash as I take the proffered hand and carefully climb out of the vehicle, holding my skirt so the large split in it doesn't expose everything to the photographers.

I look up and blink with surprise when, instead of the driver, I find my dad standing there. "Hi." He grins before leaning in and kissing my cheek.

"Dad!" I give him a hug, and we move out of the way, letting Uncle T step up and do the same thing for his daughter. She's just as surprised as I am, and the two men chuckle with delight that they managed to surprise us.

"Come on, your mothers are waiting inside," Dad tell us, gesturing for us to make our way up the red carpet. Photographers catcall, trying to get our attention, and Katie and I, ever the pros stop, once or twice and strike a pose so they can get their glamor shot for whatever gossip magazine they work for.

We're halfway to the door when another limo pulls up behind us and the cameras turn their focus to it. I turn to look, and out steps a man who looks familiar, but I don't know why.

"Oh, hold up, Kenz. It's Jeff, and I want to introduce you." Dad pulls me to a stop, and the two of us wait while Governor Turner is bombarded by the press, but movement behind him has me focusing on the man getting out next.

Holy hotness, Batman. It's Max, and he's wearing a fucking tux and looks delicious. I fan myself with my own clutch as Katie sidles up to me and whispers in my ear.

"Would you get a look at the deliciousness that just stepped onto the red carpet?"

"Back off, bitch, he's mine," I hiss at her, and she blinks with surprise.

"What?"

Dad chuckles, and I blush because he overheard everything.

"That is one of Kenz's new teammates," he tells her quietly, and her eyes widen.

"Holy hell, no wonder you're considering joining their team. Hell, if I had someone on my team who looked like that, I would be giving my mother exactly what she wants and letting him knock me up—or at least practicing very hard." She winks as Governor Turner and his eldest son walk toward us.

The governor looks pleased to see my father, and they exchange handshakes and back slaps. Max's eyes rake over my body, somewhat disbelievingly.

"Do you remember my son, Max?" Governor Turner says to my dad, keeping up the act in front of everyone who knows nothing about our real identities.

"Of course. Good to see you again." Dad holds out his hand, and Max shakes it, smiling affably.

"Good to see you too, sir," he says before Dad turns to me.

"Have you two met my daughter, Kensington?" he asks, and Jeff smiles.

"A very long time ago. I doubt she would remember."

I say a polite, "Hello," before returning my attention to the man who rocked my world only a few nights ago. "It's a pleasure to meet you," I tell him, holding out my hand for him to take. He does, and he bows his head over it, placing a kiss on the back.

"Oh, I assure you, the pleasure is all mine, Princess Kensington," he purrs, and I start to melt into the sidewalk, so I steel my spine.

"Kenzie, please."

"Come on, let's go," Katie says impatiently, and Max holds out his arm.

"May I escort you?" he asks.

I smile and take his arm as cameras flash all around us, guaranteeing that Max and I will be having a sudden, torrid affair tomorrow. I'm not sure how that's going to go back in Summerville, but surely they have a plan.

"What are you doing here?" I ask quietly, still smiling as we enter the Metropolitan Museum of Art, where the fundraising gala for my mom's project is being held.

"The boys didn't like the idea of you going off to New York on your own."

I roll my eyes at the ridiculousness of that notion, but before I can say anything, I hear, "Kensington Watson, if the wind were to change, your face would be stuck like that." It's my mom's prim voice that scolds me, and it's all I can do to stop myself from repeating it. "I'm sure the handsome man on your arm doesn't want to see you making such ridiculous faces."

I sigh, and Max chuckles as my mother saunters up

to us, taking me into her arms and kissing me on both cheeks. "Ah, my baby, you look so beautiful when you're not making such silly faces." When she's finished with me, she turns to Max, smoothing over the lapels of his tux.

"Oh, my handsome boy. Don't the two of you look so beautiful together? You would have such beautiful babies for me to snuggle," she says, raising her eyebrows and looking between us. I stiffen, but Max just laughs and drops my arm before sweeping my mother into a low dip and kissing her on each cheek.

"Sadie, my love, when are you going to leave your wicked husband and run away with me?"

My mother giggles and blushes like a schoolgirl as he sets her back on her feet again. "Oh hush, you big lug." She slaps at him. "Save all that charm for my girl." She turns to look at the rest of our group, her eyes zeroing in on Max's dad. "Jeff, don't you think our children look like they are made for one another?" He smiles and nods, humoring her while continuing his quiet conversation with Dad and Uncle T. I wonder if he's filling the governor in on what we discovered, or if he and Max debriefed earlier.

"Enough business," my mom scolds them as Aunt Felicity joins us, giving me a kiss on the cheek.

"You girls look beautiful tonight," she says.

I thank her as my mom claps her hands. "Come. Eat, drink, and spend some money on a good cause. There is plenty of time for us to talk later. Kenzie, I see your cousin Kamel is here. Who is the girl on his arm?"

She frowns, pursing her lips. "Hmm, I think I'll go say hello." She wanders off, and I spy my cousin with his latest love both holding glasses of champagne.

"Well, that's not going to go well. Come on, let's save the idiot from my mother." I grab Max by the hand and follow after my mother, who seems to be on a mission. We don't need to let family drama ruin a fundraiser for an important cause.

The night is long but successful, and my mother raises a nice chunk of change for her cause.

Max tells me he has a room at the Plaza too, and he invites me to come back for a drink. We share a car back to the hotel, leaving our parents to make their way back to their own homes. Mom gave me a suggestive wink that she didn't try to hide, and I heard Max smother a chuckle.

Katie and I part ways with a big hug. "Girl, I completely get it now," she whispers before we pull away. "If your whole team is like him, no wonder you're done being a ghost."

Max leads me back to his room. I remove my jewelry and makeup, ready for a repeat of the other night, but instead, he unzips me, leaving me in just my underwear, before helping me into his huge bed. He undresses, leaving on his boxers, and climbs in behind me, pulling me into his arms. He releases a huge sigh as his body relaxes once I'm tucked neatly into his side. "I just want to hold you. I feel like we've done this backwards, and we have some catching up to do."

I smile and wiggle my ass back into him. I am all for that, but I can't help teasing him a little.

He groans, and his hand grips my hip. "Stay still, wicked wench. I have time in the morning to give you what you need, now sleep. Who knows what the next few days are going to bring us."

I groan as he nuzzles my hair out of the way and runs his tongue over the mark he left on my neck, matching the one Miller left. Thank fuck for good makeup, or Princess Kensington would have looked like a cheap, two-dollar hooker in the press—not that they won't speculate about my and Max's relationship and decide we are having a torrid affair.

He places a couple of kisses on my neck, stroking his hand over my hair in a soothing manner, and I feel my eyes start to get heavy as I become putty in his hands. God, the things this man can do to me are nothing short of amazing. With a smile of genuine happiness, I feel myself drift off to sleep.

CHAPTER 35

ax did not deny me when we woke up the following day. We spent a leisurely morning exploring each other's bodies and getting to know one another better while enjoying breakfast.

"What about hobbies? Do you have any?" he asks over scrambled eggs, bacon, and toast.

"Does target shooting count?" I ask him, having to think really hard about what I enjoy.

He chuckles. "No, it doesn't."

"To be honest, I've never really had the time to develop any. I like reading and watching movies when I'm not on assignment, but most of the time, I'm carefully cultivating my Princess Kensington cover, so I don't have time for hobbies."

He takes a sip of his coffee, keeping his eyes on mine. "Well, if you decide to join our team, we'll have to work on rectifying that."

I contemplate what he just said, and what he

seems to be offering. "And is that what you want? Is that what all of you want?" I inquire carefully, and he is very quick to nod. I can tell that he wants to get up and take me into his arms, but he's being patient, not wanting to scare me off.

"Yes, Kenzie. We would very much like it if you would join our team. I know things are going to be different than what you're used to, and it might take a while to work out all the kinks, but the six of us are in agreement. We want you in every capacity, as a valuable member of our team and family."

"And would I live with you or continue living in my parents' home?" I ask, wanting to know exactly where we stand.

His eyebrows jump in surprise at the question, but he answers without hesitation. "There is a room with your name on it, but we didn't want you to think we were rushing you or anything."

I nod, appreciating their restraint. "I think we should test the waters and give this a trial run, with full involvement. There's no point if we discover we all hate living with each other." I am secretly freaking thrilled about the prospect of moving into their house, but I'm trying to be cool.

He smiles widely and nods. "I think that's an excellent idea. Our house is finished but mostly unfurnished. You'll be able to have a say in how we decorate it." I wiggle in my chair with excitement, but his frown stops me. "You know, after last night, the tabloids are going to insinuate we're a couple," he says slowly, and I nod, shrugging.

"Yeah, it's par for the course for me," I say, unperturbed. I'm regularly linked to a man if all I do is say hello to them.

"I'd like it, and the guys have agreed to us making it look like we're more serious as opposed to just a fling. Then it won't matter if you're seen in public with any of us."

"Unless I'm caught kissing your brother or one of your friends. The headlines would be scandalous," I joke, and he rolls his eyes. "No, I think that would be a good idea."

He finally stands and comes around to my side of the table, picking me up and taking my seat before dragging me into his lap. I snuggle into his arms and rest my head on his chest.

"This is nice," I tell him as he presses a kiss to the top of my head. "Last night was my first sleepover," I admit to him.

"Really?" He sounds surprised, and I shrug.

"Yeah. I've never been in a real relationship, ever, and staying the night was never on the cards once I killed someone," I tease.

"Well, this will be every morning once we finish this mission," he assures me, giving me a tight squeeze.

"I want to learn to play the drums, and maybe take some cooking lessons," I blurt out, and he turns me so he can see my face.

"What?" He sounds confused, and I pat his cheek.

"Keep up with the conversation. We've moved on, and I'm telling you the kind of hobbies I'm interested in."

His confusion clears, and he smirks. "The drums? Yeah, I can see that." The smirk grows. "Miller plays the drums."

My head flops back against his arm, and I roll my eyes. "Of course he does."

"I'm sure he would teach you. I'm sure he would give you plenty of incentive to get his instructions right."

"I'm listening," I say, and he chuckles.

"What time is your plane leaving?" he asks, changing the subject and not elaborating on said incentives. It's okay, I can be patient.

"Two, so I arrive back in Summerville at about four. Martha said she would pick me up from the airport. Do you want to catch the flight with me? We can tell her you were at the gala and the college dean offered you use of the plane. It isn't a lie."

He shakes his head. "I'm sorry. Dad has a fundraising dinner tonight, and he wants me to go since I'm in town. I won't head back to Summerville until after. Dad's letting me use his jet. It's how I got here so quickly. It was the trade-off for sending it down for me yesterday."

I feel a wave of disappointment. "Bummer, but okay. I guess I'll see you tomorrow in class."

He groans. "I can't wait for this mission to be over.

I'm done teaching. Have I told you how horrible it is?"

I run my hand through his short hair. "Poor baby. I bet I can make your day a little more fun. How about I pop in and see you at lunchtime, and we can play in your chair for real?"

I feel him grow hard underneath me. The robes we wear are doing nothing to hide it.

"It's a deal." He stands up, carrying me bridal style, and walks back to bed. "I still have two more hours to monopolize your time, and I'm going to make the most of it. I'm going to have to go back to sharing you with others when we return."

He tosses me on the bed, and I point between us. "If this thing works, then we are going to need little one-on-one getaways regularly, so that you all get a little extra attention."

I see his approval in his eyes as he strips off his robe. Words fail me as he crawls up the bed and takes my mouth with his, and I fall back, allowing him to worship me for a little longer.

The plane ride is uneventful and quiet without Katie. I use the small bathroom on the plane to remove my wig and change back into my Mac persona —heavy on the eyeliner, and I cover the two big hickeys on my neck—then I sit back and close my eyes until we land. I'm still trying to catch up on my sleep, and I know the next few days are going to be eventful.

Max and I called the team earlier, and Lathan said that bidding started on the auction, but there were still three empty places. We hypothesized that maybe they are for me and Miller, which is what we were planning. Once we are taken, it will simply be a matter of tracking our chips to wherever they are planning to take us.

Arrests will be made all around, and this end of the trafficking ring will be shut down—or that's the plan. It seems too easy, so things are bound to go wrong.

When the plane lands, I wave to Ben and leave, clutching my backpack. He quickly turns the plane around and taxis out to the runway before I can even walk all the way to the hangar. The sky is overcast, and Martha's car isn't here, so I decide to wait over there until she arrives in case it rains.

The MITHOS plane launches into the air, and I slide the hangar door open, peering around for some-where to wait. A clash of thunder has me jumping out of my skin, and a little squeal escapes my mouth. Some freaking spy I am, scared of a little thunder. The sky opens up, and I pull the hangar door closed behind me. It's empty, except for an old work van and some tools on one side. There's a desk chair next to the tool bench, and I decide that's as good a place as any to wait.

I grab my seat, dropping my bag at my feet. The rain is incredibly heavy and loud on the roof of this tin shed. I pull my phone out of my pocket to see if there are any missed messages from Martha telling me she's going to be late, but there's nothing. That's strange. I'll give her ten minutes, and if she doesn't arrive, I'll call one of the guys to come and get me.

I spin around a couple of times on the chair, kicking my legs back and forth, bored out of my mind. There aren't any games on my phone, and I am really regretting that right now. I stand up and fiddle with the tools on the bench, picking them up before putting them down again. I lift a wrench. It has good weight, and I bet it would make a great weapon. I'm just about to put it back when I catch movement out of the corner of my eye. I spin around, wrench in hand, and lash out, but it's too late. Blinding pain radiates through my skull, and I drop to the ground.

My head throbs, and my mouth feels like ass as I try to remember what happened. I was on the plane coming home, and then Martha wasn't there. The hangar! Someone was in the hangar, but because of the rain, I hadn't heard them. Fuck, Dad may as well revoke my MITHOS clearance. I'm a terrible spy. I try to open my eyes, but they aren't cooperating yet—same with my body. It just feels like one, big, throbbing open wound. What the hell happened?

I listen to figure out if I'm still in the hangar or not, and that's when I hear shouting.

"Did you see the papers? He was photographed with that fucking princess last night." There's no denying the screeching tones of Stella Standish.

"Stella, pull yourself together. We have all that blackmail material, and we will bring him to heel as soon as he returns to Summerville." That's her mother, June.

"And what about that whore? What are we doing about her?" she asks, and I know she's talking about me.

"We just listed her on the website, and there are already bids in the six figures for her. Not all of our clients want virgins, some of them want whores who are happy to do anything."

"I don't care, as long as she is no longer here. God, I hope she ends up with someone who wants to fuck her with a knife or something."

"We just have to get rid of that boy so Sophie can have Ryland. Thanks to your father's disgusting club, we have all the blackmail material we need. At least they are useful for something."

"When is she going to wake up? I want to be here to see the look in her eyes when she realizes where she is and that despite her efforts, she's never going to be any better than a used up, dirty whore."

"Stella, your jealousy really isn't attractive." That's Martha's voice, and I hear a male chuckle.

"Are you sure she has to go? She and the boy were really popular the other night. I've already had requests for them in the future." That's Matthews voice.

"No, they have to go. They bother my nieces, and the girls can't see the usefulness of their future husbands having available whores on the side. I'm sure that will change, but at the moment, they have tunnel vision." I crack my eyes open, and Martha is staring at me through the glass door on one of the cells. "Ah, Mackenzie, you're awake."

I struggle to sit up. There's no IV in my arm, so I haven't been drugged like the other prisoners, but I'm groggy from the hit on the head. I wonder who it was and if I managed to get them with the tool I'd been holding.

"Where am I?" I croak, feigning ignorance, and she smiles. There is no sign of warmth in her eyes anymore. I can't stop the shudder from running down my spine, because I know I'm looking into the eyes of a psychopath.

"Just in a holding cell until your new owner transfers the fund into our account. Then, we will know where we have to send you," Martha explains, looking at the watch on her hand.

"New owner?" I ask. "But I work for Matthew." I point to the man in question, and he shrugs.

"Sorry, kid. We could have made plenty of money

together, but she's the boss, and she says you have to go."

"Boss?"

"Yeah, Martha and June here single-handedly run a human trafficking operation that has made them very wealthy women," he tells me.

"There it is." Stella steps up into my line of sight and presses herself close to the glass, a smug, satisfied grin spreading across her face. "The realization that she is literally fucked. God, it's worth it. I wonder if she's going to cry."

I sob just to make the last moments of her life a little happier, because if I get out of here, I'm going to snap her neck. Deep down, I'm satisfied as fuck, because Stella has a welt across her cheek with a couple of butterfly bandages on it. I bet she's the one who knocked me out, but I clocked her first.

"I have to go. I have business dealings with Amir and Hinata at the club tonight. I'll deliver the boy to you when he finishes his shift. Keith will bring him down." Matthew departs, leaving me with the three Standish women.

"Very well, I have to be going too. It will be dinner soon, and my kids will be waiting for me," Martha says.

"What are you going to tell them about this?" June points at me through the glass, and Martha shrugs.

"That Mac decided to stay in New York, and they offered for her to start classes early."

"You," I rasp out. "You are responsible for your

missing foster kids. But why?" I ask, because this is what I really want to know.

She steps closer to the glass and leans her shoulder against it. "Why? Because I like money, and why should anyone else have a decent foster home to live in? I certainly didn't. That filthy old man violated us regularly, and that nasty old bitch would just turn a blind eye. After the first time it happened to me, I swore I would get even, and I did. Watching her gasp for air with her hand against her chest as the life slowly drained out of her was one of the happiest days of my life, right up there with realizing there was a market for forgotten children, and I had perfect access to them."

"You're an animal!" I cry out.

"No, I am what happens when the prey becomes the predator. Don't you forget that. I was planning on leaving you be, and just let Matthew use you for as long as he wanted, but then you caught Maxwell Turner's eye. I had no idea he was a predator himself, but my Stella wants him, so you have to go. If he becomes a problem later, we can either ruin his career or get rid of him. I will do anything to keep my nieces happy, which is why Miller will be joining you this evening. I sold you as a two for one special. At least you will have each other as company."

She pushes off the glass, and without a backward glance, walks down the tunnels, followed by her sister-in-law and niece.

I quickly look around the cell, but there's no point

in me trying to escape until they transport us to our final departure point in the US, so I sit on the bed and look into the other cells. The lights are out in all of them, but I can make out a figure in nine out of the ten cells, leaving only one of them empty. I wonder if they will put Miller in there, or if there will be another delivery tonight. I'm guessing it's still Thursday, because the auction wasn't wrapping up until Friday.

For now, I have to sit back and wait and hope that when the guys discover I'm missing, they stick to the plan.

CHAPTER 36

MILLER

When Ry drops me off after school, I head upstairs to my bedroom to wait for Mac to get home. Martha was picking her up from the airport at four, and then she was going to come straight home. I look at my watch, and it's only four thirty now, so they'll probably be a little longer. I head downstairs to see who has dinner duties tonight, that way I'll know when they arrive home.

I shake my head in wonder as I make my way down the stairs. I have no idea how it happened, but Kensington has wormed her way under my skin. Max messaged us after they parted with a photo of what she looked like at the gala last night, as well as one he took of her asleep in his bed. I'm not sure which one was more beautiful, but both were so completely different from any other way I've seen her—minus black hair and heavy eyeliner.

He informed us that he had a discussion with her about joining our team, and to our immense pleasure, she agreed to a trial run, including moving into our new house. Ry was all twitterpated when he heard the news and started shopping for a bed. Dayton was able to put a stop to it by suggesting she might like to choose her own. He calmed down after that, but when we parted, he was busy trying to find the perfect welcome to the team present. I suggested a custom-made handgun, but he shot my idea down.

When I get downstairs, I find Jessica and Sally in the kitchen, and they seem to be having a heated argument. It stops as soon as they see me, but as I move to the kitchen, I hear Sally take a breath.

"Are you gay?" she asks me, and I almost burst out laughing—not because it's funny, but because I'm being interrogated by a teenager. Once this mission is over, no more roles in high school. I feel like I'm in that old eighties show *21 Jump Street*.

"Um, not that it's any of your business, but I'm bi," I answer her.

"So you fuck both boys and girls?" she asks bluntly, and I look to Jessica for some help, but she just shrugs.

"Yes," I reply honestly.

"So you really had a threesome with Mac?" Ah, I see where this is going now.

"Well, technically it was a foursome," I say,

confirming the supposed rumors, and her mouth drops open in shock while Jessica snickers.

"I warned you not to ask."

"So all three of you fucked the same girl?" I actually get the feeling Sally isn't being judgmental, she's just curious.

"Yes. If you google Pornhub, I'm sure you can find an orgy to watch if you're really interested in what goes where."

"Are you a top or bottom?" she asks, and it's my turn for my mouth to drop open. She's fifteen. Do normal fifteen-year-olds know that kind of thing? Or is this a foster kid thing? Before I can answer, James arrives home. He has Will and Ty with him. He picked them up from a basketball game they had after school.

"Hey, kiddos, how's things?" he says cheerfully as he helps himself to a beer out of the fridge. You'd think things would be awkward between us because of Friday night, but he's going about his business like his mask made him completely unrecognizable.

"Phew, you smell," Sally tells the two boys. "You better go have showers before Martha gets home." They take her advice and leave the kitchen.

"She isn't here?" James asks.

"No, she went to pick Mac up from the airstrip. The private jet was bringing her back today," Sally tells him, sounding envious. "I wonder what she had to do to get an invite from that school." She sounds skeptical, but before I can answer, Jessica does.

"Has anyone ever told you that you shouldn't

judge someone by how they look? Mac is probably one of the smartest kids in our year." She then nods at me. "Miller's probably not far behind her either."

James looks at me, surprise in his eyes. "Good for you, kid. Martha said you'd like to go into something mechanical. I have an in with the local garage. I can ask if they are taking on any apprentices if you want," James offers, and it's all I can do to keep my face neutral. It's actually really nice of him, and not what I expected. "Well, I guess maybe the plane was late. How about we order some pizza? Then she won't be frantic about dinner when she gets home." James pulls out his phone and slides it across the table to Jessica. "Use the app, and I'll run upstairs and get changed. Suits are professional and all but really not comfortable."

He follows the boys out of the kitchen, going to his bedroom to change. Jessica and Sally argue over which pizza to order when I get a text.

I pull out my phone, and there's a message from Ry asking if Mac is home yet.

I reply, telling him not yet, and we text back and forth for a little while. It's only once the pizza gets delivered and everyone else joins us that I start to worry.

"Where's Martha and Mac?" Cassie asks, frowning as everyone grabs a plate and a piece of pizza.

I'm just about to send her a message when headlights appear, coming down the driveway, so I put my phone away and eat my pizza. We won't have a lot of time to get ready for work before Anders picks us up. There's a buzz of excitement, making my veins feel fizzy. I'm excited to see our new team member—our possible girlfriend. God, I feel like a sap. I'm giddy like Ryland gets, and I kind of want to punch myself in the junk.

When Martha walks in alone, though, my blood runs cold.

"Where's Mac?" Jessica asks, looking over Martha's shoulder.

"Oh, good, you got pizza. That's wonderful. Good job, dear." She presses a kiss to James's head, and because I'm watching closely, I see him flinch.

"Jessica asked a question, Martha. Where's Mac?" he asks carefully, and it's in that instant I realize this man doesn't have a clue where she is. He has nothing to do with her disappearance. Were we wrong about all of this?

Martha takes off her cardigan and hangs it on a hook before facing us with a huge smile. "I'm sorry I'm so late. Mac called me this afternoon to tell me they offered her early admission, and she was starting this week. There seemed to be no point in returning to Summerville. Jessica, dear, could you pack up Mac's things? We will ship them to her."

That little speech is what has me shifting my theory from James to Martha. Was she the kingpin all along, and we didn't realize it? Or did she really receive a call from someone pretending to be Mac, and she is now in the wind? Fuck, I need to speak to the guys, and Lathan needs to track her.

It's all I can do not to jump to my feet and bolt out the door as the rest of the kids express their excitement for Mac.

"Really? Well, that is a surprise." James's eyes are narrowed on his wife, and his tone has a suspicious lilt to it.

"Aren't you excited for her, Miller?" Martha is looking at me with a quizzical tilt to her head, but her eyes are cold.

I force a grunt. "Yeah, sure, whatever. It just means I'm going to have to work harder tonight. I better go." I grab my jacket off the hook and leave, waving a hand so I don't seem completely rude. I get about twenty yards away from the house and turn back to look, and I see Martha there, watching from the front room. I keep walking until she can't see me anymore, then I cut through the bushes, running at full speed in the direction I know our bike is. Anders isn't actually picking me up for another hour, and this news can't wait, nor do I want to tell them over the phone that the plan has been executed.

I tear off the tarp and toss the spare helmet to the side. Thankfully Mac left the keys in the ignition, so I throw my leg over it and crank it to life. It roars loudly before settling down to a gentle idle. I don't fuck around. I put the helmet on and engage the gear, throttling hard. The tires spin on the gravel, kicking a whole heap up behind me. I'm careful on the dirt road, but the minute I hit the asphalt, I open up the throttle, speeding as fast as I can for the governor's mansion where the guys should be. My heart pounds, and my mind whirls as I run through all the possible scenarios. Logically, I know this is what we wanted, and Mac is a talented and skilled agent, but emotionally, that girl was in my bed and is working her way into my heart, and these feelings have me in a panic. It's residual trauma from my childhood, but it still manages to creep up on me at inopportune times.

I don't pay any attention to the change of speed limit as I get into the more built-up areas. My urgency is far more important than possibly being stopped by the police. I bring the bike to an abrupt halt around the back of the mansion, putting the kickstand down as I remove my helmet and run up the back path to the rear door.

Ry is there, holding it open with a look of concern on his face.

"Hey, what's wrong?" he asks as I push past him and find everyone but Max chilling in the kitchen, remnants of dinner still on the table.

"Hey, you're early. Did you get sick of waiting?" Anders jokes as he washes some dishes.

"Where's Mac?" Lathan looks beyond me, frowning, but only Ry appears behind me.

"She's gone," I announce, and they all stop what they are doing.

"Gone? What do you mean, gone?" Dayton asks

quietly, and I run a hand through my hair, pushing it back off my face.

"Martha returned without her."

Lathan jumps into action, leaving the kitchen to grab his laptop, as the other three curse up a storm.

"Get Max on the phone," Dayton instructs a pale Ry. He nods and pulls his phone out of his pocket, quickly dialing his brother and putting him on FaceTime.

Max answers, and we hear a lot of background sounds. "Ry, I'll be home in a few hours. This couldn't wait?"

"Mac's gone," Ry tells him flatly.

"What do you mean, she's gone? I saw her to the plane myself," Max growls, and we hear him move somewhere quieter.

"Martha came home without her," I reply as Lathan returns, flipping open the computer and bringing up the auction page. Instead of a still photo, like there is of all the other auction items, there is a live video of Mac. We can see her pacing back and forth across her cell. I lean in and point to her face where there's a trail of blood down one side. "She's injured."

"But we know where she is, so that's a start," Anders says calmly.

"What did Martha say exactly?" Dayton asks me.

"She told us that Mac called her and explained she had been offered early admission and decided to not waste time and take it. She said Mac asked for her belongings to be sent and that we should be happy for her."

"So do we think someone impersonating Mac called and told her this, or do we think Martha is involved?" Ry asks, pacing back and forth across the kitchen, chewing on one of his nails. When he passes me again, I grab him, pull his finger from his mouth, and wrap my arms around him. I need the comfort as much as he does.

"My gut tells me she's involved, but I don't think James is. He seemed as surprised as the rest of us."

"Okay, well, let's not panic, this is what we hoped would happen. Mac is where she needs to be. We have agents bidding on all the lots. Percy let me know when I had a meeting with him before Dad's party. It's easier for us to control the whole deal if we are the buyers—not that they know that. They are all being bid for with bulletproof aliases. Is Mac's tracker online, Lathan?" Max asks, and Lathan nods.

"Yes, it's showing her in the cells at the moment."

"Good, so we just wait until bidding finishes tomorrow and they make their move. Go about your day like nothing is wrong. We don't want to make anyone suspicious when we are this close." Max looks at me when he says that.

"Oh fuck," Lathan mutters and looks up at me. "Mac is being sold as a two for one deal. There is a video of the two of you in the cage from Friday night. You are part of the deal."

"Good." I feel a rush of relief. "At least we'll be together. The two of us will be fine."

"So that means they need to get their hands on him sometime soon," Anders points out. "It will probably happen tonight."

"The last spot is filled too, but the cells still don't have the right number, so I guess they will get another delivery tonight."

"We'll stay alert, and I'll be home in a little while. For now, the only thing we can do for her is not blow her cover. I have no doubt she will be fine. Don't think about the beautiful, funny, loving girl we've gotten to know. Think about Phantom, who very nearly kicked all of your asses on her own."

Max hangs up, and Ry gives me another squeeze. "Please be careful," he whispers, because we both know this will be the last time we see each other until the end of the mission. "And take care of our girl."

He looks frantic, and I give him a big kiss, taking charge for once. I grip his chin and angle his mouth so I can kiss him fully. When he pulls away, he's dazed, and I feel a little smug.

"I won't have to. She has this shit," I assure him, positive I'm telling the truth.

CHAPTER 37

DAYTON

The next twenty-four hours are frantic. Max returns home and suggests we get some rest, but I'm pretty sure none of us do. When I hear Anders's truck pulling up early Friday morning, I hurry downstairs to see if he has any news. I find Lathan fast asleep with his head on the kitchen table, his screen showing the cell that Mac is in, but now it's not just Mac. Miller is there as well. He's unconscious, and she is sitting on the floor with his head in her lap. I can see her stroking his hair and whispering words to him, but there is no sound.

Anders walks in looking dejected and tosses his keys on the table. "He's gone," he mutters as he pulls a beer out of the fridge, popping the top and downing half of it.

Ry bursts in and looks around, and his shoulders

sink when he finds Miller missing. "They took him?" he asks flatly, and Anders nods.

"Yeah. I was distracted after work. Matthew needed me for something, and in that time, he disappeared. Keith told me he got a lift home with a female friend."

Ry scoffs, but Lathan waves him over so he can see his boyfriend on the screen. "He's hurt," he says, looking at our teammates.

"Yeah, same as Mac. He'll be alright." I try to reassure him, but I doubt it works.

"There was another delivery too. Just after midnight, they brought another girl in. She was kicking and screaming. She was a real fighter. I could see her and Mac talking once they were left alone, but of course I can't hear what was said." Lathan sounds exhausted.

"Okay, it's business as usual. The auction finishes at ten tonight, and payment is required within the hour. The merchandise will be shipped as soon as funds appear in the correct account. We need to be ready to move. Agents are watching the ports and trailing our suspects."

"We just need to wait for Mac's and Miller's trackers to move. This will be fine. Be suited up and ready to go tonight by ten—full combat gear, vests, and helmets," Max orders us.

"I'm not going to school today," Ry argues, but Max shakes his head.

"You have to, or it will seem suspicious if you

don't. You also need to ask where Mac and Miller are. You've been seen with both of them, so of course you're going to notice they are missing."

Ry looks pained, but he doesn't argue. None of us head back to bed, so I make us some breakfast. Nobody is particularly hungry, but we need to keep up our strength, so we pick at the food. My friends are unusually quiet and subdued as we all get ready for our day. Anders and I are going to keep an eye on the video feed. If anything goes wrong, we will extract Mac and Miller while the others stick to their covers. I already advised Kevin I wouldn't be in for the next few days.

Max, Lathan, and Ry head off to school as I make a pot of coffee and take the first watch. Anders is going to grab a few hours of sleep, while I keep an eye on the video feed. Tonight can't come quickly enough for me. I can't wait to see the back of this town.

LATHAN

The day drags. There are a lot of questions regarding Miller's and Mac's disappearance, and by the end of the day, the rumor is he knocked her up and they ran off together.

At lunch, Jessica is overheard denying the rumors.

"Mac was offered early entry to college and took it, and Miller worked late last night, so Martha gave him permission to stay in bed."

I wonder how long it will take the house to realize that two more of the teens who live there have gone missing. Hopefully it's the last time, and Percy will find suitable places for the rest of them.

Stella is practically gleeful in French. She keeps looking at Mac's and Miller's empty seats and giggling, but the woman does have a huge bruise blooming on her cheek, so maybe she has a slight concussion. Somehow, I have a feeling that Mac is responsible for the damage, and I can't help but feel pleased.

When we get home, Dayton and Anders report that Miller woke midmorning, and that he was okay. I dug through the footage last night when we realized she'd been taken, and once again, there was a blank spot on the film, so we still don't know for sure who is responsible. The only good part is that both Mac and Miller must know by now—unless they were caught by surprise.

I obsessively watch the auction page. The bids are creeping up, but the ones for Mac and Miller are the most furious. Eventually, it gets to an amount that leaves only three bidders. Usually, I'm happy being stuck behind a screen, but this feels like somewhat of a nightmare. I have the same training and skills as the rest of the team, but I prefer to be behind the scenes. I lack the confidence that's needed when bullets are flying, but I'm still an asset with my other skills. It took me a long time to feel like I was an equal part of this team—not that any of them made me feel that way. I was considered an equal by them from the start, but my upbringing wasn't the easiest. My foster homes weren't nightmares like Miller's, but at best, my foster parents were indifferent. They were happy that I had an interest in technology, and they didn't have to entertain me. It wasn't until Percy approached me personally and invited me to the academy that I felt seen. This team is everything to me, and Mac has quickly found a place in my heart. I love being around her, and I love that she sees me and doesn't feel like she needs to change me. She likes me for me, nerdy traits and all, and that's what I love best about her. She is going to bring fireworks when she does finally move into our house. It's going to be a blast to watch her butt heads with all of our strong personalities. I'm going to make sure I have plenty of popcorn.

Ry and I arrive home before Max. The four of us hang around in the kitchen, at a loss for something to do while we wait for the final bids. Max walks in about half an hour later.

"I just got invited to a poker night with the 'boys.'" He makes quote marks with his fingers. "Brock told me it was nonnegotiable if I didn't want to ruin my father's career."

"Fuck. What time?" Anders asks, and Max grimaces.

"Ten."

"What the hell is going on?" Ry explodes. "Are they not moving the teens tonight?"

Max rakes a hand through his hair. "I have no idea, but you four will be okay without me. I need to stay on their good side just in case. You have all the backup you need. They are on high alert tonight."

"I don't like this," Dayton says, "but we can't do anything about it now. Keep us updated, and we'll do the same for you."

MAX

It's late when I arrive at Ted Standish's place. When I pull into the driveway, there are a couple of cars as well as a big removal truck. I snap a photo of it and send it to the guys. "Be ready," I tell them.

Putting my phone in my pocket, I press the doorbell. Stella answers and beams at me. "Max, honey, come in," she calls, and I frown.

"Oh, hi. I thought I was playing poker with your dad tonight," I say, giving her a kiss on the cheek. She tries to turn her head, but I'm ready for it and shift my trajectory, so it stays on her cheek.

"Yes, you are. Mom, Aunt Martha, and I were just heading out," she tells me, showing me into a room off the side of the hall. It's like a men's drawing room, and there's a large poker table with Brock, Ted, James, Chief Thompson, and Father Sweeny sitting around it.

"Ah, Max, good of you to join us. Grab a seat." Ted waves me over, and I take the last remaining seat. Matthew isn't here, and neither is Isaac Palmer.

"Thanks for the invite, Ted." I shake hands with him before taking a seat. Stella skips over and kisses me.

"We're off, Daddy. Have fun, and don't lose too much money. You know how Mommy gets mad." Stella is slightly manic this evening, and I feel a ball of worry build in my chest. She leans around me, and this time, I can't dodge the kiss she presses to my lips. She tries to slip her tongue in, but I hold my lips firm. She pulls back and frowns.

"Soon you won't be able to think of anyone but me," she murmurs, stroking a hand down my chest and brushing her hand over my cock. "Remember, my daddy knows all about your dirty proclivities. You might want to keep me happy if you don't want those getting to the press. Imagine if they knew Governor Turner's son was into schoolgirls. If you want a schoolgirl that badly, I have a costume I can wear, and I can be a very bad little schoolgirl. Forget about that whore. She's never coming back."

She pulls away, and I see the manic glint in her eye. "Bye, have fun." She waves and hurries out of the room.

Brock huffs out a sigh of relief. "Fuck, your daughter is crazier than a sack full of cats."

Ted gets up and goes over to the window and peers out. "Let's wait five minutes, and then they will be gone," he tells the rest of us, and I feel confused. Everyone else discards the hand they were holding and moves out of the den, farther into the house.

"Come on, Turner. You can help us, and we'll be done quicker. This is what it means to be a part of this town." Father Sweeny gestures for me to follow them.

We arrive at an elevator. "This leads to the basement. We have something we need to break up and load into that truck, which then needs to be taken to the shipping yard, okay?" Chief Thompson explains.

"We have a very small window to get it done in, because the ship needs to pull out at exactly midnight," Ted tells me.

"Help us, and we'll cut you in, or my niece's threats will seem like child's play," James tells me threateningly.

"Yeah, sure. It's fine, okay? I'll help. No need for threats. What are we moving?" I ask as the door opens and all of us squeeze in. The doors close, and I feel it move, taking us down. When the door opens, we all step out. The basement is filled with huge vases, or maybe pots for the garden. Anyway, they are definitely big enough to hide a person in. My heart races, and I feel my adrenaline kick in as I look at how many there are—ten, one for each human. This is it.

"How are we going to move them?" I ask. "They look heavy."

Ted disappears behind them and reappears with a dolly in each hand. "Work together and be careful. We can't break them. My buyers would be really upset, and they are not people you want to anger."

I'm confused. I didn't think the bidding finished for another twenty minutes or so, but I guess he knows the kind of people he's dealing with and wants to be prepared. We all work together without much talking, but there is a lot of grunting and groaning. None of them are particularly fit or athletic, and they really are heavy, but eventually, we get them into the truck.

"Alright, James and I will ride up front, and you guys sit back here and make sure none of those vases tip over," Ted orders before closing the truck doors, plunging us into darkness.

"Ugh, I hate riding in the back. I get nauseous," Brock grumbles, and a light switches on. Chief Thompson has his phone in his hand, and the three of them settle against the side walls, sliding down and getting comfortable.

"Aren't we supposed to hold them?" I ask, and Father Sweeny scoffs,

"They never move. Ted and James are overly cautious."

Shrugging, I join them and pull out my own phone. I look over, but nobody is paying attention, so I snap a quick shot of the pots and send it to Dayton. I tell him we're on the move, and in a moment, I get a confused face emoji.

DAYTON

Lathan says Mac hasn't moved.
Where are you going?

MAX

To the shipyard.

DAYTON

Agents are on your six.

I sit back and wait, knowing this is all about to end.

The truck eventually slows down, and through the side, I hear Ted speak to someone. The truck starts moving again, but slower this time, until it finally stops completely.

"We're here, thank fuck." Brock jumps up and rushes toward the door just as it opens.

"Okay, we need to get those moved into this container," Ted explains when I jump down.

This time, he has a forklift, and we watch as the operator moves it to the truck and lifts out the first vase. Chief Thompson and Father Sweeny stay inside the truck and slide each vase close to the edge so the forklift can pick it up. I look around the shipyard. No one is in sight, and I can't make out any of our agents either. I hear my phone ring, but I can't look at it because just at that moment, the forklift driver hits a pothole, which jolts the whole machine. The pot wobbles precariously, and Ted shouts for someone to steady it, but nobody is fast enough.

Just as it tumbles to the ground, the area explodes with shouts of, "Freeze," "Police," and "Don't move." I watch in horror as the pot crashes to the ground, praying that neither Miller nor Mac is in it. My horror becomes more acute when I look at the mess on the ground, and instead of seeing a comatose body, I see a bunch of white bricks. The agents quickly round up all of the men I'm with as I step forward and pick one of them up.

"Agent Turner?" One of the other MITHOS agents holds out a knife and quickly cuts a hole in the pack. I dig out some white powder, and my stomach sinks. This isn't a human trafficking ring. This is an everyday drug trafficking operation. We got it all wrong.

CHAPTER 38

ANDERS

"Mac hasn't moved, so I don't know what Max is doing. Do you think it's a trap?" Lathan asks. Our eyes have been on the tracking program since Max sent us the message telling us he was on the move. The large Asian vases certainly looked big enough for trafficking people in.

"Fuck, he's not answering!" Ry shouts as he tries to call his brother again. He's in a panic, worried his brother is going to get hurt or worse, end up dead.

"The auction just finished," Lathan announces quietly. We all gather around and peer over his shoulder as he flicks between two screens—the one with the video feed, as well as the one with the auction. Each lot has a "closed" graphic over the top, and underneath, it says payment is pending. One by one, we watch as the red letters turn green and change to payment approved.

That's when things start to happen on the screen. We were worried that they would turn the footage off, but they must be in such a hurry that they didn't this time. Matthew and Isaac appear, both pushing wheelchairs. I guess it's the easiest way for them to move the comatose patients. Then, my mouth drops open as five women, all dressed in black, also appear on the screen. Martha moves from cell to cell, removing the catheters from the seven unconscious victims. One by one, Matthew and Isaac lift them into a wheelchair, and they are wheeled down a tunnel we didn't notice. It's hidden right at the back of the cells, and none of us went that way.

They take the first five before they return to take the next batch.

"Where do you think that leads to?" Ry asks, biting his lip.

"We'll know as soon as Mac and Miller get moved."

Dayton's phone beeps, and he looks at the message. I hope it's Max, but I can tell by his face it's not.

"The private airfield. Our agent following Martha Standish followed them to the private airport. They disappeared into the hangar. There must be an entrance in there, because when he peeked through a window, it was empty again. There is a large private jet waiting on the runway. He snapped photos of the men who are waiting with them."

Dayton passes me his phone, and I hold it so Ry and Lathan can see too. It shows the darkened airfield with the waiting planes. In front of one of them are Hinata and Amir.

"Well, that tells us how." I hand Dayton his phone. Ry tries Max again, and this time, he gets through.

"It's not them!" he shouts at the same time Max shouts something. Ry switches him to speaker.

"Fuck, we were wrong. These were just drugs. A huge haul, but no people," he rushes out breathlessly.

"We know," Ry replies. "Get to the private strip on the outskirts of town. We're leaving now."

We all jump into motion, Lathan bringing his laptop. We are loaded with gear and ready to take down all those women. Shit, I wasn't expecting that at all. This is certainly going to be an interesting arrest.

We jump into a blacked-out SUV, which is standard MITHOS issue. It's bulletproof and reinforced, and I drive like a bat out of hell, hoping we can get there in time.

"They are moving Mac and Miller at gun point," Lathan announces, still watching the video feed on his computer. Ry swears as I grip the steering wheel tighter.

"Drive faster," Dayton orders, and I push the SUV to its limit.

MILLER

"Left the best for last." Matthew chuckles, waving his gun at both Mac and me. He's not the only one. Isaac also has a gun, and unfortunately, so does Stella.

"Let's move," she demands and steps back, leaving enough room for us to get out of the cell. We're both feeling pretty awful. Mac has vomited twice, and I can't get my eyes to focus. Both of us were hit pretty hard, and I think we both have concussions.

"Do you know how to use that thing?" Mac asks her dryly. "I'm pretty sure your mom just sold us to someone. How unhappy do you think they will be if we are killed before they can get their merchandise?"

"Shut your whore mouth. They care if you're alive, they don't care if you can ever walk again. It's your pussy, mouth, and ass they need to function. They don't care about your knee, and that's where I'll put the first bullet. Then, I'll put one in pretty boy here." She jabs her gun into my side, and I have to control my flinch. Her finger is hovering very close to the trigger.

"Such a shame we didn't get a chance to play with that one," Isaac says to Matthew, and Stella screws up her nose.

"Keep your homo kinks to yourself. Get the last one," she orders. Neither June nor Martha have returned, so they must be supervising wherever they've taken the others.

I'm not worried, I know they will be tracking us. I'm just curious where we are being taken.

Isaac and Matthew exchange an annoyed glance but does as she orders. A girl steps out of the last cell, and she also looks like she may have been hit a few times. She has short red hair and is tall, with a willowy body. She spits at Stella, who pistol-whips her.

"Hey, hey." Matthew stops her when she pulls her hand back to do it again, while Isaac keeps his weapon trained on us. Mac and I could take them, we're not even bound, but we want to get to the end first. "I know this is your first time, and it may seem like she doesn't care, but your mom will be pissed if you damage the merchandise."

Stella wipes the spit off her face and glares at the girl. "I hope you get fucked with a knife." She waves the gun. "Move."

We make our way down a tunnel none of us had noticed before, and it's quite a distance. Finally, we get to an elevator shaft, and Isaac swipes a card over the reader, opening the doors.

"In," Matthew demands pleasantly. "I do like payday," he says cheerfully.

The elevator rises, and when it opens, I realize we're in an airplane hangar. Mac groans. She's been quiet since the girl was hit. Biding her time, I would guess.

"Fuck, of course. I am such an idiot," she mutters, and I raise an eyebrow at her in question, but she just shakes her head slightly and mouths, "Later."

They lead us out onto the runway. A large, private jet is waiting, and at the bottom of the steps are Michelle's and Lucy's fathers, who are talking with Martha, June, Lisa, and Melissa. All the wheelchairs are lined up in a row as someone drives the luggage conveyor over. There are a couple of security guards lazily walking the perimeter of the plane, but they don't look too concerned.

A sound has us all looking up, and another plane lands on the runway, using the full length before turning around and taxiing back to us.

"Ah, excellent." Martha smiles and turns to look at the redhead with us. "That's your buyer. Right on time." I feel Mac stiffen next to me and sigh heavily.

They finish hooking up the conveyor, and Melissa and Lisa break off, leading the first of the wheelchairs to it. Two men help them load the first one, and we watch as the victim and Melissa disappear inside the plane, then Lisa takes a turn.

It seems like a well-organized process, and Martha leaves them to it as she turns to look at the three of us. She frowns when she sees the redhead's nose bleeding. "What the fuck happened?" she growls, and Stella shrugs petulantly.

"She walked into a wall."

"Keep your fucking hands to yourself, or I will cut one off," Martha says quietly to her niece, who blanches and nods quickly.

"Yes, ma'am."

Martha turns her back on us as the final plane comes to a stop just beyond the larger one. Martha gestures for the redhead to follow her, and Isaac nudges her in the side. She responds slowly. The hit must have dazed her, and she stumbles slightly. Isaac reaches out to steady her, and all hell breaks loose.

"Freeze, police. You're surrounded." The words are shouted, and for a split second, nobody moves, but then guns start to fire, and bullets zing around us.

KENSINGTON

I watch as Miller tackles Matthew to the ground, wrestling the weapon from him before he can even get a shot off. Stella gapes and starts to wave the one in her hand. I kick out and knock the gun from her hand. She shouts with surprise before I punch her in the nose. I hear the crack of cartilage, and the blood splatter makes my heart go pitter-patter. She wobbles back and forth, looking stunned, so I pull my fist back and hit her again. This time, she goes down like a heap of shit. As much as I want to see her brain matter scattered all over the runway, I want to see her suffer in a maximum security prison more. There's always time for brain matter later.

I look around. It was all over so quickly, I feel slightly disappointed. All the bad guys have been subdued and are being cuffed, including Amir and Hinata.

"Mac!" Miller shouts, and I turn to him, hearing the worry in his voice. "They are getting away." He points at the other plane, and I see it start to taxi down the runway. Martha and Isaac are running next to it, begging for them to wait. Miller starts to take off after it, but I grab his arm and shake my head.

"We won't catch it," I tell him, feeling somewhat guilty. "And they are not stopping for those two." I point as the little plane picks up speed and leaves Martha and Isaac in its wake. The two of them are still running, but they change direction and head for the bushes. A car with flashing lights quickly gives chase as the rest of our guys reach us.

"You look like you've been having fun." Anders laughs, looking down at Stella who's groaning on the ground. Max pulls out a pair of handcuffs, turns her over, and puts them on her.

"I bet when you thought of being handcuff by him, that wasn't what you had in mind," I quip to her, but it isn't fun when she can't really retort.

Ry throws himself at Miller and me, hugging us hard, but Miller shakes him off.

"We need to get a fighter jet in the air to track that plane," he says, sounding frantic, and I sigh. If I'm going to fully embrace this new life, I can't start it with lies.

"Miller, let it go," I tell him, and he turns to look at me.

"What?" He sounds confused, and I can tell the others are too.

"We still haven't found the records for the rest of the trafficked kids. That's one we can track," I explain.

"How can we track that one?" Lathan asks gently. "None of them had trackers."

"Actually, she did, because that was my cousin, Katie." I drop the bombshell, and they explode into sound, except for Max.

"Come on. Let's get this all sorted out, and I'm sure Mac will explain everything when we are done," Max says.

He slaps Miller on the back, and Ry grabs Miller's hand, tugging him to get him moving. The seven of us walk back to the rest of the agents. They load all our suspects into transport trucks just as five ambulances pull up with their sirens blaring.

"If you don't mind, the name is Watson, Kensington Watson," I say in a posh British accent, and the tension between us breaks. We're going to be okay. I just hope and pray Katie will be too.

AFTERWORD

Hi! I know you probably turned the page and went WTF Lexie. But if I didn't end it there it was going to blow out big time. They got a HEA for now. I know there are some things I did not show you. But be patient with me. There will be a small novella giving you all those answers which will allow me to segue into Katie's book. But first I have two more series I want to wrap up which was always this year's plan. You just got this one earlier than I had scheduled. I do hope you enjoyed it. I struggled in the beginning. I couldn't find all my story notes from book 1 and well it took me a little while to get into the swing. I'm fairly pleased with the way it turned out. If you did enjoy it, it would be super awesome if you could leave a review wherever you bought it, because I'd love to hear what you thought of the story.

In the mean time why don't you check out one of my other series. You can find everything you need to know here.

www.lexiewinston.com

Acknowledgments

To my cover designer Natasha, of Dazed Designs. The cover is beautiful just like you.

Thank you to both Jess at Elemental Editing. My book is pretty and readable thanks to you.

My ever reliable and faithful beta readers, Kerry and Tegan... You da bomb xxx

And lastly to you guys the readers. I love what I do, and probably would do it regardless if anyone read them or not, but you guys make it that much sweeter so thank you.

Until next time, happy reading

Lexie

TRY SOMETHING ELSE FROM LEXIE

ICE ME OUT

Secret baby, hockey/college reverse harem

Miriam

"Jorja, honey, you have exactly thirty seconds to get your cute butt down here so I can do your hair, or you are going to school with a bird's nest on your head," I call up the stairs to my wayward daughter.

"Coming, Mama," my daughter's high-pitched voice calls back, so I head to the kitchen with my fingers crossed, hoping she doesn't get distracted by something on the way.

Pouring coffee into a travel mug, I add sugar and milk before taking a sip of the sweet, rich brew, causing my tastebuds to sing. Hopefully my tired and travel weary body will start to function more normally.

I lean against the counter and survey my kitchen. The cupboard and counters are shabby, and the wooden floorboards need to be stripped and resealed, not to mention the stove needs to be replaced, but I can't help but marvel that it's mine. My kitchen! My house. It was left to me by my eccentric great-aunt— the same woman who took me in when my own family sent me packing. I loved her like a mother, and she had certainly been better to me than my own flesh and blood.

They felt shamed by their seventeen-year-old daughter's accidental pregnancy, too Catholic for an abortion and too social climbing for a pregnant teen. I was sent to live with Aunt Jocelyn in London so I wouldn't embarrass them. They didn't even give me a chance to tell the father of his impending fatherhood, and they haven't talked to me since except to say I was not welcome back in my family home. In fact, I was cut off from everyone. My grandparents and friends all seemed to forget I exist.

When the will was read after Aunt Jocelyn's untimely car accident, I was shocked to discover that while she bequeathed most of her vast fortune to her immediate family, she left me her house in my own hometown and a large sum of money in which to reno-vate it and take care of ourselves. I was like the grand-daughter she never had, and she was thrilled to call me that. Her only son hadn't cared. In fact, he'd been happy for me, but he warned me it had been empty longer than I had been alive, so not to expect too much.

After living in London for the last six years, I bid them farewell with many tears and hugs and returned to the States with my five-year-old daughter in tow, both excited and nervous for the next stage of my journey.

We only arrived a few days ago, and while the house was partly furnished and livable, it really was in desperate need of some work, but that would all have to wait. Now that Jorja was in school full time, I was going to college. I finished high school in the UK, while Jocelyn watched Jorja for me. When I decided to come home, I applied to college in my hometown and was accepted.

Today is both of our first days, and I can't say I'm not excited.

The sound of little feet on the staircase has me cringing as I wait for her to slip in her rush, the rickety staircase another priority on the long to-do list, but she apparently manages to navigate them with ease. She comes in carrying her *Paw Patrol* backpack and throws it up on the counter before climbing onto the stool sitting next to it.

She's small for her age. I had a difficult pregnancy and was bedridden for the last three months, and she arrived at only thirty weeks. Each and every day was a struggle, seeing her in the NICU fighting for her life, but she must have a lot of her father in her, because she didn't give up. Eventually, I was able to bring her home. She was a sickly baby, always catching everything that was going around. Some days I just wanted to cry, and that was with the support of Aunt Jocelyn. Thankfully she got better, and apart from slow growth, everything else about her is perfect.

"Mama, can you give me two braids today?" Jorja holds out her brush and a couple of pretty hair bands to go on the ends. She recently lost both of her front teeth and lisps all her words at the moment, but I try my hardest not to smile because it upsets her.

"Of course, princess." I take the bows and brush and untangle her long, unruly black curls, which she does not get from me. I have white blonde, dead straight hair and brown eyes, but Jorja is the spitting image of her father with her bright, Caribbean blue eyes. I always feel a pang of longing when I look into them, wondering if he still lives in town and succeeded in his dreams, or if he ever thought about me after I was shipped away.

My parents confiscated my phone and had someone scrub my social media accounts so I practically didn't exist, and I didn't know any other way to contact him. I begged them just after I arrived to tell him where I was, but they told me he had moved on, that he was dating someone and that he hadn't asked to see me at all. I tried to contact his sister, who I thought had been my best friend, but I got no response, so I gave up. I had a new life growing inside me, and by then, I was so sick that I didn't have the energy to worry about anything else except getting her to full term.

"Mama? Are you going to do it or not? I don't want to be late for my first day." She shakes me out of my memories, and I smile at her.

"Sorry, baby. Let's tame the wild beast, and then we need to get moving." I start to gently brush her knots, and I make a note to grab some detangling spray when I go to the store. Thankfully, Jocelyn left me enough money so I could afford to live and go to college without needing to get a job, so I don't need to worry about money for groceries or bills, and there is a car in the garage.

Seamus, Jocelyn's son and my mom's cousin, sent a mechanic out to make sure it was running. Imagine my surprise when we opened the shed on the back of the house and discovered a mint condition Chevy Impala sitting under a dust cloth. It needed a service and some new tires after sitting for so long, but when he got it started, the thing purred like a beast, and the guy promptly offered me a decent sum of money for the thing. I turned him down of course. Being a huge *Supernatural* fan, I was excited to drive the same car as Dean.

I quickly work Jorja's unruly curls into some semblance of neat braids. Hair is not my forte. If she wanted a ponytail, then I was her girl, but I had spent many nights watching YouTube videos to keep my little girl happy. I'm not great, but I try, and that has to count for something, right?

"Okay, done. What do you want for lunch?" I ask her, and she spins around on her stool.

"Mama, they give us lunch at school," she says, her eyes wide with excitement.

I screw up my nose. "Oh, baby, that's not necessarily a good thing," I protest, but she shakes her head.

"No, Mama. I want to eat at school, please." She tries to flutter her eyelashes in a way she saw on TV, but she just looks constipated. Again, I hide my smile.

"Okay, you can today, but if you don't like it, we can make it tomorrow. Deal?"

"Deal." She looks pleased as she holds her hand out for us to shake on it. We do, and then I lift her down from the high seat and pass Jorja her backpack.

"Okay, munchkin, let's rock and roll. I need to drop you off at school then hurry to my first class." I pick up my phone from the counter and check the time. Yup, we need to get moving. I grab my keys and my backpack, which has my books and laptop, and follow her out the door that leads to the attached carport. She opens the back door and climbs in, and I strap her into her child seat before jumping in myself.

"Okay, baby, don't fail us now." I pat the car's steering wheel and cross my fingers, turning the key over in the ignition. Thankfully the engine roars to life, and Jorja cheers as I breathe out a sigh of relief. Although it runs like a dream, she has been temperamental when starting, and I haven't had time to get the mechanic to look at it, but today we are good to go.

Shifting it into gear, I slowly back out of the drive. Despite having learned to drive here in the US, I got used to driving in the UK, so I'm cautious of driving on the opposite side of both the car and road, but I manage to get us onto the street and to Jorja's school without horns beeping at us or being flipped off, so I call that a win.

I pull the car into a spot and then help Jorja out of the car. All around us, moms are parking with their BMWs and Mercedes. My Impala looks a little out of place, but I don't care. Seamus paved the way for Jorja to come to this private school and is paying for it. He and his husband adore us both, and they said that if they can't look after us in person, then they will from afar.

I thought Jorja might be nervous for her first day at a new school, but she practically drags me up the path and through the door. We had a tour a couple of days ago, so we know exactly where to go, and she beelines to her class despite all the other children milling about. My daughter most definitely has single-minded determination, and not much stops her.

When we get to the classroom, her teacher, an older matronly woman named Mrs. Brady, greets us with a warm smile. "Good morning, Jorja and Miriam. How are you today?"

"I'm great, thanks, Mrs. Brady," Jorja replies, looking around the classroom with excited eyes.

Behind Mrs. Brady's voluminous skirts, I see a little dark-haired girl peek around. Mrs. Brady sees where I'm looking and steps to the side. A little girl, slightly taller than Jorja, with dark hair and a tearstained face, is standing there.

Mrs. Brady takes her by the hand. "Jorja, this is Lola."

"Hi, I'm Jorja." My vivacious five-year-old skips over and gives the girl a hug before she can get out a word. "We're going to be best friends," she declares.

"Oh, honey, go easy there," I say, trying to temper the rabid beast, but Lola's eyes widen with interest.

"But, Mama, Lola and I have to be best friends. She likes *Paw Patrol* too." She points at the girl's backpack, which matches hers. I am almost certain ninety-nine percent of the class is going to be into *Paw Patrol*, but before I can point that out, Lola giggles.

"You talk funny."

Mrs. Brady frowns and is about to say something, but my confident daughter just shrugs.

"That's because I'm from London. That's all the way across the ocean. We came in a big plane to get here, and Uncle Seamus paid for us to have the good seats so we didn't have to slum it with the oi polloi." Jorja mangles the last bit, but Mrs. Brady snorts with smothered laughter, and Lola doesn't care either way. Her lips round in a big O.

"You know what? I have a map. Why don't we get you two settled, and then I can show you both on the map where London is and where Storm View is?" Mrs. Brady takes one in each hand and leads them away.

All around the room, parents kiss their children goodbye, but all I get is a quick wave over the shoulder. "Bye, Mom," Jorja calls before they disappear into the crowd.

Well, fuck. I guess it's my turn to go and make friends. With a small lump in my throat, I hurry back to the Impala and make my way across town to the university campus. I won't deny that a few tears trickle down my cheeks as I take a moment to be sad in the car before I get moving. Jorja is starting a year after she's supposed to. Being sick so often meant I couldn't start her schooling when she was supposed to, and this will be the first time we've been apart for a whole day since she's been born. I guess it's long overdue, but it's extremely hard when it's been her and me against the world for what feels like forever.

Apart from Aunt Jocelyn, Seamus, and his husband, Darcy, I didn't really have friends in London. I devoted all my time to Jorja, and this next step is fucking nerve-racking, but I suck it up and turn the key. Hell, at seventeen, I was kicked out of my house and moved across the world, and just before my eighteenth birthday, I gave birth, so college is going to be a breeze.

The campus is on the opposite side of town, and I have to drive through my old neighborhood to get to it. Thankfully I don't have to drive past my parents' house, because I'm not ready to face any of that yet. I have no doubt that I'm not going to be able to avoid them forever, but for as long as possible works for me.

My father's family is wealthy, and my parents and my dad's parents live in mansions next door to each other. I used to be very close with my grandparents, but I guess they must have been just as ashamed of me as my parents were, because not once did they reach out to me.

Aunt Jocelyn was my mom's aunt and the black sheep of that side of the family. She had been disinherited by her father for being a little too wild. Aunt Jocelyn married three times—once to a woman—and had outlived them all. People would whisper about the fact that she was now a very wealthy woman due to being widowed three times, and maybe she had something to do with it, but each of her loves died from a tragic accident or natural causes. After the third time, she swore off marriage and had many lovers. She said life was too short to be tied down and live within society's confines. At sixty-five, she was still going strong when she was taken from us.

When I grow up, I want to be just like Aunt Jocelyn, not worrying about how people look at me. I just want to love and be loved and screw society and its ass-backward rules. It's my life goal to be as happy as she was.

I drive through town in a daze, and before I know it, I'm pulling into the student parking lot on campus. After hopping out and locking the door, I hurry across campus to my first class.

I took a virtual tour online because I hadn't had a chance to come in person, so the building I need isn't too hard to find. I pass plenty of other students gathering around or hurrying between buildings—thankfully no one I recognize from when I attended high school six years ago. Most of them wouldn't be freshmen like I am, although my first class of the day is mixed, so I cross my fingers, hoping I won't run into anyone I know.

My marketing class is half full, and I quickly take a seat at the back of the classroom. I'm so nervous. I haven't studied since I graduated high school when Jorja was two. I worked in Seamus and Darcy's flower shop while raising Jorja. I loved it and decided I wanted to do something similar. The two men offered to finance a store here in town for me, but I decided that I needed to take some business classes before I accepted their blind trust in me. I wouldn't want to let them down by not being able to manage the business side as well as the creative one. They agreed, but Seamus said he would keep an eye out for a suitable building for us.

All the classes I'm taking are business based. I have marketing, accounting, and business law this semester.

I'm so distracted with taking out my laptop and notebook that I don't notice anyone approaching my corner of the classroom until they slip into a seat in the row in front of me. He has his hoodie pulled up and slumps down in his chair like he doesn't want to be noticed, so I leave him be. As nice as it would be to make some adult friends, I'm not going to force myself on someone who looks like they want to avoid contact. Every time someone walks into the classroom, I see him stiffen until they take a seat elsewhere. His body relaxes minutely until the next person gazes around the classroom for a seat. It's an interesting few minutes until a teacher finally walks in, closing the door behind them.

The woman looks to be in her early fifties. She's dressed in smart work attire, and her heels click on the parquet flooring as she smiles at the class.

"Good morning, I'm Sarah Carlyle." There are a few gasps amongst the crowd, but I have no idea why. "Your original lecturer was in an unfortunate accident over the summer, and the dean has asked me to fill in for him as a favor. For those of you who don't know me, I am the CEO of the Carlyle Agency. We are one of the biggest marketing firms in the US, and this semester, we will be covering everything, including how to brand your business, social media marketing, and consumer behavior. This was a last-minute thing, so while I read through the curriculum, I want you to talk to the person closest to you about famous brands and which ones have marketing that resonates with you. Make some notes on why, what attracts you to their brand, and why you think it appeals to you. I'll give you half an hour, and then we're going to discuss them."

The class is silent for a moment.

"Well, get to it." She gestures for us to get moving.

The only person close to me is hoodie boy, so I lean forward and tap his shoulder. "Hi, can we work together?"

WANT MORE? GET IT HERE